Saef glanced across the training pad at Lars, the Thors-world cadet who had forced this duel. Shorter and probably twenty-percent heavier than Saef, all muscle, sinew, and bone.

He immediately found the mountaintop of calm that old Devlin had named "the Deep Man," and fear could gain no purchase in him. His vision broadened, his shoulders relaxing, and he saw Lars step onto the training pad.

Saef drew his sword and knife, using both for the first time in a duel. It was a counterintuitive move, where most non-heavyworlders would want both hands free to wield a sword grown suddenly heavy in the increased gravity.

As he felt the familiar press of ramping gravity squeezing every fiber of his body, Saef remained in the pool of calm as his stocky heavyworld opponent stepped nearer, sword in hand.

"Regain what you may, dog!" Lars snarled at him, in a wrathful approximation of the formal words.

Either truly angry . . . or frightened . . .

Since Saef had never given a true reason for offense, he bet on fear, but either emotion held benefits over a calm, calculating opponent.

Saef lifted his sword smoothly up and held it pointing directly into Lars's eyes. He heard the murmur of the onlookers, likely surprised that he managed the increased gravity so well, but Saef knew he could only manage this rocklike hold for a short time.

"I had no quarrel with you," Saef said, looking down the blade into his opponent's wide eyes. "But for the honor of my family I do this." He lowered the blade to low guard and advanced.

BAEN BOOKS by
MICHAEL MERSAULT

The Deep Man
The Silent Hand (forthcoming)

To purchase these titles in e-book form,
please go to www.baen.com.

THE DEEP MAN

MICHAEL MERSAULT

THE DEEP MAN

This is a work of fiction. All the characters and events portrayed in this book are fictional, and any resemblance to real people or incidents is purely coincidental.

Copyright © 2022 by Michael Mersault

All rights reserved, including the right to reproduce this book or portions thereof in any form.

A Baen Books Original

Baen Publishing Enterprises
P.O. Box 1403
Riverdale, NY 10471
www.baen.com

ISBN: 978-1-9821-9246-4

Cover art by Kurt Miller

First printing, January 2022
First mass market printing, February 2023

Distributed by Simon & Schuster
1230 Avenue of the Americas
New York, NY 10020

Library of Congress Control Number: 2021044263

Printed in the United States of America

10 9 8 7 6 5 4 3 2 1

Scrawled within my soul's dark night,

Warmed by only Lilo's light.

THE
DEEP
MAN

Chapter 1

"The dichotomy of the successful modern human is witnessed in the rebuilding of instinct into a tool of more than mere animal survival...."

—Devlin Sinclair-Maru, *Integrity Mirror*

CABOT SINCLAIR-MARU FROWNED AS HE WALKED beside the Family's current House Combatives instructor, his cousin Eldridge. Although they both appeared of a similar age, Cabot had lived many decades before Eldridge's birth, and he found Eldridge's enthusiasm anything but infectious. It seemed puppylike, annoying, and inappropriate for this early hour of the morning. Still, they strode together from the Family's ancient manor house, Lykeios, toward their goal, a short distance away: the circular stone building they called the "equestrian center," though all Family knew it to be the training annex.

"Yes, it's a small class, I admit, Cabot," Eldridge said. "But it's not just against his peers that I'm measuring. Trust me."

1

Cabot's frown deepened, his gray eyes surveying the dawning horizon without favor. "Child prodigies don't interest me. The Family needs more friends in the Emperor's circle, not more gifted troublemakers."

They reached the reinforced doors of the training annex, and the House Intelligence, Hermes, obligingly opened the way before them. Eldridge paused in the stone entrance, impulsively grabbing Cabot by the arm. "Trust me—" he began, then broke off as Cabot stared down at the offending hand gripping his sleeve. Eldridge pulled his hand away and began again, "Trust me, Cabot, this kid is like nothing I've seen in the family. He takes to House doctrine as natural as . . . as . . . I don't know what. He quotes *Integrity Mirror* at us about everything, and we've got to force limitations on his high-gee time. He'd be stunted for life if we didn't lock him out. As it is, we probably allowed him too much—"

"Fascinating," Cabot interrupted in an un-fascinated tone of voice. "I'm here, Eldridge. Let's see this prodigy of yours."

"Right," Eldridge said, shrugging. "Trust me—"

"You said that already."

Eldridge closed his mouth and led the way down the old stone hall. Together they began descending the six-hundred-year-old steps that had felt the tread of nearly every Family member since Lykeios Manor had been founded. As they made their way together into the subterranean depths Eldridge found the courage to say, "You will eat your words, Cabot."

They felt the tingle of graviton flux before they entered the observation area, so it was no surprise to see the small class of Sinclair-Maru youngsters floating past on their way to the distant ceiling. The training room formed a sort of wide tube, much taller than it was wide, with a variety of obstacles at both poles. Unlike most of the great families, the founders of the Sinclair-Maru, Mia Maru and Devlin Sinclair, had decreed that House Combatives training would take place under a wide range of gravitational conditions. At astronomical expense they had installed the gravity generator (pure Shaper tech, of course), back when Family fortunes ran high, and it had served the Family for centuries without fail.

Cabot's implanted electronics package, buried in the base of his skull, received constant information from the house Net, and data streamed constantly across his optic nerve in glowing characters and icons. Like all Sinclair-Maru adults, and most Vested Citizens of the Imperium, Cabot's use of the implanted User Interface had become second nature.

Just now that UI superimposed a glowing identity icon for each student as they soared past the observation window. Eldridge unnecessarily nodded toward one boy who floated past. The identifier said, SAEF SINCLAIR-MARU.

Cabot eyed this "Saef" with a critical eye. There was nothing so remarkable to see, unless it was the telltale marks of extended heavy-gravity work. The boy wore the same tight black training suit that all Family students used, the common short training sword and training pistol affixed to his belt. Among the students flitting by, Saef seemed about average in age—ten standard years, Cabot knew—but he seemed perhaps a whisker more muscled and stockier than his peers and he wore an earnest expression on his face as he moved through the exercise.

Since the children would not receive their own enormously expensive, implanted Shaper electronics until they obtained full growth, each wore HUD—heads-up display—lenses along with the secret training tool of the Sinclair-Maru: the scaram fear generator. This tool, developed centuries before by Devlin Sinclair as the cornerstone of his warrior philosophy, shaped the minds and reactions of generations of Sinclair-Maru fighters.

Saef Sinclair-Maru soared to the ceiling with the staggered cluster of his classmates, moved through the elaborate obstacles mounted there, then kicked off, bound for the floor but at an oblique vector.

"Too fast, show-off," Cabot muttered aloud. "He's going to pile in, or bounce."

Just as Cabot uttered those words, Saef managed to rotate in flight, and struck the observation window, leaving a streak of shoe tread as he executed a neat trick of braking and redirection. He completed his transit, skidding into the floor beside an instructor and grabbing a padded stanchion to check his momentum.

The other students glided to the floor in a more direct and leisurely way, and Eldridge shot a measuring glance at Cabot before turning back to the view of the training ground.

Hermes automatically directed good audio to the observation booth, so the sound of eight children's labored breathing came clearly to their ears.

The instructor, clothed identically to his students, and armed with nearly identical training weapons, glanced at each of his students, allowing the House UI to display their vital signs through his optic nerve as a visual overlay. Speaking to the House Intelligence, he said, "Hermes, restore gravity, please."

"Very well, my lord," Hermes' disembodied voice replied. "Caution: Gravity is returning to one-point-zero gees."

Cabot and Eldridge felt the fringe of the gravity shift, even within the observation booth, and the high tube of the training room rained bits of hair and dust now brought to earth by their sudden weight.

"I will begin activating scaram units now," the instructor said. "Compose yourselves."

Cabot and Eldridge observed clenched looks on most students' faces, and they both recalled their own days learning the terror that was the self-imposed birthright of the Sinclair-Maru.

"Sarah," the instructor said, "you are ready for level three now."

The young girl seemed to pale, but she nodded firmly. "Yes, my lord."

From the observation booth, Cabot switched through his UI screens to an instructor view. Since he was already here, he might as well gauge the vitals and brain activity of the latest crop.

The young girl seemed to sway as the scaram ramped up, her heart rate and respiration leaping, her brain frantically firing in the deepest regions of primal fear. *Fire, darkness, glowing eyes and drowning depths*; the scaram touched the ancient terrors at the core of the human mind. A level-three power setting seemed quite intense for a child of her age, and Cabot watched his UI overlay as her terror mounted and spread through greater portions of her system. Her heart roared along with the staccato gasp of her breath.

Then Cabot watched the transformation as she

found the Deep Man, feeling an answering glow in his own mind from his thousands of trials under the scaram.

Her brain activity calmed, her heart rate abruptly slowed, and one shuddering breath brought stillness to her quivering limbs. She stood, apparently calm, as the scaram pulsed away into her brain, screaming terror that she now ignored.

"Are you well, Sarah?" the instructor asked.

"Y-yes, my lord," she replied after a moment. Cabot observed her control of the Deep Man beginning to slip as she lost focus, but she averted disaster, staying afloat in a sea of fear, regaining control. The instructor moved on to the next student, setting his scaram low, at level one. The next two students received level-two scaram settings, but the third, a young boy, crumpled, vomiting and weeping under the lash of the scaram. The instructor stood impassively by for agonizing moments before triggering his UI to shut down the boy's scaram.

The boy lay supine, gasping, and the instructor moved on to the next student as a small dumb-mech scuttled over and began sucking up the vomit.

Cabot turned his disinterested gaze from the fallen student and observed the next handle a level-one setting, but he noted as he eyed her vitals on his UI, she merely gritted it out through sheer willpower, pale, sweating, barely capable of speech.

The next student accepted a level-two scaram setting, and the next battled his way to mastery over terrors of a level three.

Then young Saef stood before the instructor. Cabot actually grunted in surprise as the instructor said,

"Saef, you will receive a level-six setting." Eldridge shot a knowing, triumphant glance at Cabot.

Saef said, "Yes, my lord."

Cabot studied Saef's brain activity and vital signs very closely as the scaram ramped to a level so high it approached that of the masters. The boy's swirl of firing synapses responded to the scaram's assault, but nothing seemed quite right in what he saw. The heart rate and respiration barely quivered upward before stabilizing. For a child of ten standard years, the terror unearthed by the scaram at a level six should have been debilitating, and yet Saef's face remained merely determined under the mental assault.

"Saef," the instructor said, "are you well?"

After one deep breath, Saef said, "All . . . all fear is the fear of the unknown, my lord. Because we cannot know the unknown, we must know fear. This is the path to the Deep Man."

In the observation booth Cabot grunted again, lip pursing. "He's quoting *Integrity Mirror*? Under a level-six scaram ride?"

Eldridge nodded, "He often quotes old Devlin."

Out on the floor the instructor chided, "A simple 'yes' will suffice, Saef."

"Yes, my lord."

Cabot continued frowning and looked over at Eldridge. Quoting from old books with the scaram flaying his brain? "Are you certain he hasn't hacked his HUD? Pretending to quote while he's reading it? Under a level six that would be impressive enough—"

"No," Eldridge interrupted, smiling thinly. "He has actually hacked the scaram itself."

Cabot's expression deepened into irritation. "Hacked

the scaram? Then why, pray, are you wasting my time with—"

"Cheater!" a voice yelled out across the training room, causing Cabot to turn, his impatience visible in every move of his body.

A tall young teen stepped into sight at the edge of the training space. His startling yell overset several of the students who lost their focus, losing their grip on the Deep Man, the crushing fear of the scaram pouring into their minds with staggering force.

As the instructor hastened to shut down the scaram units on the impacted students, in the observation booth Cabot said, "I grant you, a young scrub hacking the scaram is interesting in its way, but I am far from—"

"Shh," Eldridge interrupted. "I sort of arranged this." Cabot's lips thinned as he glared at Eldridge, but he turned back to the drama in the training area.

"Saef's cheating," the teen loudly declared. Cabot noted the teen's name highlighted in his UI: Richard Sinclair-Maru . . . Saef's older brother. "He's hacked the scaram!" Richard pointed at Saef, a triumphant smile on his lips.

"That's a very serious charge," the instructor said, and Cabot observed that the instructor must have expected the outburst. He rolled far too easily with the shocking interruption to have been surprised.

The next words came from Saef, and for the first time Cabot's frown disappeared as he became genuinely interested in what was occurring. Though somewhat unsteady, these words were well learned by every Vested Citizen in the Imperium, feared by most.

"B-by your dishonor, my honor is taken," Saef stammered. "I will have my due."

Cabot watched the smile fall from Richard's lips, apparently surprised by his brother's formal challenge to a duel. After just a moment Richard replied. "Well, uh, regain what you may, I will meet you." The formal rejoinder came from Richard's mouth, but Cabot was surprised to see what looked like fear in Richard's expression. Fear of what?

As the respondent, under Imperial law binding all Vested Citizens, Richard now held the right to choose the place where they would duel. Within this code, "place" not only meant the physical location, but also the gravity level, which could be set to the standard of any Imperial territory, from the asteroid cities with near-zero gravity, to the crushing gravity of Thorsworld or Ericson Two.

Cabot naturally assumed Richard would choose to duel in standard gravity. Thrashing his little brother shouldn't offer much challenge to Richard, he thought. No matter how prodigious the child prodigy, there's an immense gulf of development between a child of ten and a youth of fourteen.

"Here, now, one-point-five gees," Richard declared, hustling out of his jacket and shirt, revealing a well-formed but very slender torso and thin arms. He donned a provided training suit, matching his little brother, and snatched up his sword. Since he still lacked six years until his full majority, he too carried a training sword.

He joined Saef on the smooth expanse at the center of the training ground, the high ceiling soaring up the inverse training ground mirrored high above them.

Saef, looking stocky and diminutive beside his brother, drew his sword and stood waiting.

Cabot scanned Saef's vital signs on his UI, pausing at the indication of Saef's brain activity. It certainly appeared that the scaram chewed at the boy's psyche even now, though possibly at a much lower setting. That made little sense... No one would willingly duel while riding the scaram's assault.

Eldridge's words interrupted Cabot's reverie. "Someone has been sneaking in more low-gee time, it appears," Eldridge murmured, and Cabot could see what he meant. Richard seemed unusually thin and willowy compared to the usual Sinclair-Maru mold. That, along with his blond hair, contrasted sharply with the stocky, dark-haired Saef.

The instructor spoke: "Hermes, please increase gravity to one-point-five."

"Very well, my lord," the House Intelligence intoned. "Caution: Gravity level increasing."

Cabot felt the ripple of the increase, and saw the shift in both boys as their bodies became heavier and heavier, their swords dipping in their hands.

Saef responded first, lifting his sword steadily to high guard. Cabot recognized the smooth motion of extensive high-gravity training on Saef's part, but he saw the sword wobble in Richard's hands. Those long arms, and Richard's apparent affection for low gravity, were not helpful when everything suddenly became fifty percent heavier.

Saef began to move, circling to his right, moving slowly but forcing Richard to rotate. Both of their steps seemed ploddish in the heavy gravity. Richard sent out a feeler, making a slow, halfhearted feint, and Saef attacked immediately. His sword cracked down, knocking Richard's training blade off center, and he lunged, no hint of slowness in his attack.

Cabot saw Saef's sword point score below Richard's collarbone, saw Saef lower his sword as he began to speak the formal "first blood" statement, saw Richard's enraged face as he swung.

In the heavy gravity, foolishly caught off guard, it was nearly a miracle that Saef managed to raise his sword at all, but Richard's blow, aided by the heavy gravity, struck through Saef's guard.

Cabot dispassionately observed Saef's vital signs spike as Richard's training sword cracked across Saef's temple and jaw. Brain activity exploded as clear signs of high-powered scaram waves rippled through Saef's synapses.

"I thought you said he hacked the scaram," Cabot said, continuing to watch as Richard struck twice more, dropping Saef in an insensible heap.

Eldridge took his eyes off the training ground to shoot a self-satisfied smirk at Cabot. "He did hack it. He's been riding a level-two setting the whole time, then took six more points on top of it."

Cabot held only the blandest interest in what was occurring out on the training ground, his attention fixated upon the data flowing from Saef's system to Cabot's own UI implant. "You're suggesting this child just fought his first duel while riding eight levels of the scaram?" He had to admit the data flowing from the convulsing boy matched this interpretation.

The instructor stopped the duel, killed Saef's scaram, and returned the gravity to standard. Richard walked stiffly from the training ground, snatching up his clothes and ignoring everyone around him.

"Yes," Eldridge said. "Since he unearthed the scaram hack he's been riding a level one or two almost all the time . . . while he's studying, training . . . even while he's peeing."

Cabot nodded, his lips pursed as he mused. "And you just set him up for this beating?"

"That I did," Eldridge said. "You ready to eat some of your words, Cabot?"

Cabot looked back at Saef's nearly unconscious form as the instructor and a House mech treated his injuries. He nodded again. "A few. I will dine upon a few of my words." He tapped his chin in contemplation. "You're right, this child is somewhat intriguing to me—but so is the brother."

"Richard?" Eldridge asked, surprised. "Why him? He shorts his high-grav time, and probably sleeps in low-gee when he can, and he can barely reach the Deep Man at a level two on the scaram. His sword work is weak, just a moderate hand at the range, and he all but scorns Family doctrine."

"Scorns Family doctrine?" Cabot snorted. "He becomes more interesting to me by the moment. What's driving him? What's the attraction to low-grav? Why the sibling rivalry?"

It was Eldridge's turn to frown. "Richard'll harp about changing the Family image if you give him a chance. Skimps high-gee to retain his height, I think. He seems to believe we're getting lumped with the heavyworlders, so height would help, I guess. In political circles, I mean."

"Interesting," Cabot said.

"One brother's like old Devlin all over, quoting from *Integrity Mirror* all the time, while the other brother can't get far enough from Devlin's ways."

"Thus the sibling rivalry?"

"Maybe, Cabot. Or maybe it's something else alto-gether."

Cabot shrugged. "No matter. Angle the young one for command school, and fix his scaram hack before he permanently scars himself."

"Very well," Eldridge replied. "And Richard?"

Cabot thought for a moment, referencing his UI with a flick of his eyes. "I see your uncle Grimsby is the new head of our Trade delegation. Get Richard apprenticed in Trade, in the next year or two, if possible."

Eldridge nodded. If Cabot wanted it, then it would happen. Cabot turned to leave.

"That's it?" Eldridge demanded, staring at Cabot's retreating form.

"Well," Cabot said over his shoulder, "I'll want to see the younger one sometime."

"Okay, when?" Eldridge asked, somewhat mollified, bringing up his UI scheduler as he hurried after Cabot.

Cabot paused with his foot on the first ascending step. "Schedule something here in . . . hmm, twenty years. In the summer, if you please."

Eldridge abruptly halted. "Twenty years?" he choked out.

"If you please," Cabot repeated. "And Eldridge? Please make a note to inform me if either of those two dies before then. Can you do that?"

Chapter 2

"Elevation in social class must promote the Honor Standard. Deviations from the Honor Standard must result in lethal duels. In this way Peers will themselves prune the tree of nobility...."

—*Legacy Mandate* by Emperor Yung I

AS THE DIRECT REPRESENTATIVE OF EMPEROR YUNG V on Battersea, Winter Yung generally amused herself in whatever way her jaded tastes permitted. She'd found, over many years of service to her great uncle, the recently deceased Emperor Yung IV (may he rest in peace... just as soon as she laid hold of his assassins), that her appetites usually produced more good intel than all the cloak-and-dagger methods at her disposal.

On this blighted day, unfortunately, her armored skimcar represented an almost-direct extension of the new Emperor's will, wending its way over hills and through picturesque forests of the vast old Sinclair-Maru Family holdings. Her rarefied tastes did not steer her course, as they usually did. Corporal Standish steered the course, and the secretive family manor of the Sinclair-Maru drew rapidly nearer.

It felt like a voyage into history, and Winter Yung loathed history.

She sighed, crossing her elegantly clad legs and easing her platinum queue against the skimcar's luxurious cushions. The small fortune of microelectronics crammed within her skull afforded a dynamic view, even when only boring fields and blue skies filled the panorama. A glowing path of ever-diminishing klicks stretched out before her, indicating the range and path to her destination, while a glance above displayed the status of the IMS *Fury*, her light destroyer escort, vigilant and invisible above the blue sky.

Though she lacked the characteristic "Yung" almond eyes, now known as "Imperial eyes," her nondescript brown orbs concealed more than just a ruthless mind. Beyond her status as Imperial consul to Battersea, Winter ranked near the top of her Imperial Uncle's intelligence service. That role granted her the latest in implanted Shaper tech, to provide godlike insights into the world around her. Her enhanced optic nerve projected a shifting User Interface constantly across her vision, not entirely unlike the UI most Vested Citizens of the Imperium enjoyed. Most such citizens, though, would find themselves baffled by the complexity of Winter Yung's UI, and horrified by the sheer intrusive power of her specialized systems.

It had taken Winter nearly ten nauseating years to master the suite of tools that an agent of her status was now provided, tools lodged in implanted hardware within her brain. At times Winter had thought she might truly lose her mind before she conquered the barrage of overlays, data streams, and glowing reticles flickering constantly across her vision. In rare quiet moments, Winter sometimes thought she really *had* lost her mind back then. It would certainly explain a few things.

With the Imperium still reeling from the assassination, and the Ericson Cluster worlds forming a rebellion, Winter knew this trip's importance, but nearly everything about the Sinclair-Maru family bored her to death. She had attended command school with Bess Sinclair-Maru—gods, it seemed a century ago! Winter frowned, furrowing her porcelain brow. *Has it really been nearly eighty standard years?*

Even then, when the Family still enjoyed the last flickers of their fading glory, the Sinclair-Maru bunch shared a certain odd reserve that left Winter clammy. Passion, emotion, heat; these characteristics appealed to Winter, and they often made her intelligence work so much easier to accomplish. But Bess and her legendary Family never seemed to realize that their antiquated addiction to the honor standard, which served the Family so well in wartime, became a positive liability during the centuries of peace. While the rest of the major Families of the Imperium plunged into court politics during the Pax Imperium of 5677 that Mia Maru and Devlin Sinclair helped secure, the Sinclair-Maru failed to change with the times.

When a Family's loyalty to the Emperor became boringly consistent, appointments, contracts, lands, and other concessions flowed to other families who formed and betrayed various coalitions, backstabbed the occasional ally, and otherwise manipulated Imperial favor. The Sinclair-Maru never seemed to comprehend this.

The great Family, forged by Mia and Devlin in a time of blood and fire, withered in the shadows of a five-hundred-year peace, like some ancient, loyal watchdog. But that peace was gone now, and the loyal watchdog might have some use at last, withered and boring though it was.

Mostly boring, Winter amended to herself. This young man, Saef Sinclair-Maru, intrigued Winter for reasons not particularly germane to her mission. That he had fought seven recorded duels was not all that remarkable. Young Vested Citizens often dueled because it was fashionable. They generally clashed swords until someone obtained a cut severe enough to settle any question of honor, and hopefully leave a heroic-looking scar. For a few days those fights would populate the Nets and feed gossip.

No, the way in which Saef Sinclair-Maru deliberately (and very unfashionably) killed all seven opponents, this intrigued Winter Yung. It argued a great passion or—a tingle of pleasure flickered in Winter—a blood-thirstiness that was quite unlike Saef's stolid family.

Winter briefly considered pulling up the vidstream collection from Saef's Imperial Command College tests, but a glance at her augmented vision showed Lykeios, the old Sinclair-Maru family manor, drawing near. She required all her focus to capture any details on this foray. Imperial Security had recently begun wondering about the offensive and defensive capabilities Lykeios might have squirreled away. With blood flowing once again, every major Family fell under fresh scrutiny. This trip could serve as a rare opportunity to *politely* penetrate the twice-damned security, and it mustn't be squandered.

Winter's unlined face remained serene, but her pupils snapped open, like the twin muzzles of a weapon turret. As the skimcar descended from the forested hill, she took in everything.

The broad valley of the Lykeios Manor stretched before her sight, joined by a live, top-down view from the *Fury* perched directly above in the planet's magnetic field. Reticles of glowing red and green generated by her analytics hardware overlaid her view, highlighting each notable feature and estimating capabilities on the fly.

A hilltop stand of trees pinged as a probable sensor array, while the large structure adjoining the manor house issued a nominal graviton signature, indicating an advanced House Combatives training area. Grain silos at the periphery of the manor park just happened to provide interlocking fields of fire—if they contained heavy weapons instead of grain, as she guessed they might. Winter's expressions remained placid as they came through the low, thick curtain wall, but her eyes jigged from feature to feature.

The manor itself was constructed by Devlin Sinclair and his wife, Mia Maru, after most of their respective forebears were gunned down in the uprising of 5677. Together they founded the new Sinclair-Maru line at a bloody turn in history, and the construction of the Family seat displayed this in myriad ways.

Alerts flashed in Winter's vision as her advanced Shaper hardware detected the barely visible pattern of emitters concealed around the circumference of the manor yard. Analytics estimated a sixty-five percent likelihood that huge energy-shield generators existed here, and Winter nearly jerked in surprise.

Two generations of the Sinclair-Maru family *aged* without access to the prohibitively expensive Shaper rejuv treatments, yet some half-billion credits' worth of Shaper shield technology lay at the heart of this ancient stone manor.

Winter could scarcely believe that in the centuries of peace since Mia and Devlin built the place, no one had sold the shield generators in exchange for youth. Now that war came roaring back, a little paranoia made sense, but it was a hell of a wait for a payoff.

Her gaze swept the grounds one last time as Corporal Standish pulled up to the entry. Her UI didn't sing out, but Winter noted the two circular planters that undoubtedly housed pop-up emplacements to cover the gates. Also, she figured, a battery of heavy dampers must hide somewhere, completing the manor's main defenses.

Her skimcar stopped and Winter stepped out, snapping her sword to her waist. "Wait here," she commanded the corporal, stepping away before he could reply.

A man wearing the livery of a Sinclair-Maru servitor bowed his head respectfully. "Welcome to Lykeios, Consul," he said. "You were not expected."

It was the nearest to a rebuke Winter would likely hear. "Unavoidable, I fear," she said.

The servitor's eyes flickered, and Winter's analytics snapped onto the telltales, informing her that he communicated via implanted UI with someone. Another surprise.

It was only then that Winter noticed the black wristband of a Vested Citizen on the servitor's arm. The usual symbol of full citizenship, a sword, was impractical for those engaged in certain manual labor tasks, but most manual labor fell to inexpensive demi-cit laborers or dumb-mechs, not Vested Citizens.

Servitors with skull implants instead of inexpensive HUD lenses? Vested Citizens instead of demi-cits for the grunt work? Yet, the Sinclair-Maru family lacked the funds for any significant Shaper tech these days. Bizarre . . . or was it?

Since only Vested Citizens could be held to full accountability on oaths and contracts, any demi-cit worker represented a potential security breach, immune to any harsh penalties for oath-breaking.

"If you would accompany me, Consul," the servitor said, leading the way through the broad, thick door into the manor house.

Winter noted the immense breadth of the stone walls, the positive air pressure, and the defensible entryway. Her UI chirped as it discovered shielded Nets frequencies. With a neural flick she directed it to ignore them. The House Intelligence might detect any signal hack, and take it personally.

"Consul Winter Yung," a low feminine voice greeted.

Winter rotated to see an older, thicker, browner version of her old classmate, Bess Sinclair-Maru. Older and thicker, yes, but not as greatly touched by the decades as Winter might have guessed. There had been some old rejuv action at work, probably way back in Bess's teens.

Winter's analytics highlighted elongated earlobes, thickened wrist bones, and corded neck muscles: all indications of extensive high-grav training. A second flag provided the useful fact that Bess had fought only two known duels in her 102 years as an adult Vested Citizen, won both, killed neither of her opponents.

"Dame Sinclair-Maru," Winter replied, hearing the contrast between her own youthful contralto and the drab notes from Bess. "It's been some decades, but no time to chat about our school year, I fear."

"The uprising. The Ericson Cluster," Bess stated, her expression so unreadable that Winter's analytics uttered no hints of deeper emotion.

"Yes, in part." Winter gauged the stolid figure before her, the somber, uniform-like attire. "Do you speak for the Family, Bess?"

Bess nodded, slowly. "Let's step into the study, if you don't mind, Consul. Refreshment?" Bess led the way to another imposing door that silently opened as they approached.

"Nothing for me, thank you."

The room they entered exuded premillennial charm, with bare wooden beams, actual pulp-fiber books in a shelf, and a fire on the hearth that Winter's UI assured her was genuine burning wood. Winter loathed the entire room on sight.

Her UI highlighted a well-worn long rifle over the hearth, scrolled out range and damage estimates across her vision, then flashed a couple of historical images that really caught her attention. The historical images showed the well-known figure of Mia Maru standing beside her husband, Devlin Sinclair, an identical rifle cradled in her arms. In that famous image they stood in the smoldering rubble of Imperial City, both smudged with dirt and maybe blood, Devlin holding a sword loosely in hand.

That day's action, defending Emperor Yung III, created all the dwindling wealth and power that surrounded Winter Yung now.

"Is that *the* rifle?" Winter asked.

Bess glanced up at its place above the mantel. "The very one."

Winter nodded, pursing her lips as she strode slowly to a deeply inset window overlooking the immaculate old grounds. She turned back to find Bess gazing levelly into her eyes.

"The very rifle," Winter said. "Long ago your ancestors defended the Emperor with that rifle."

The door to the study opened to admit a nondescript man of average height and build. Winter's UI went to work trying to match his face to known figures.

"Cabot Sinclair-Maru," he said by way of introduction, and Winter's UI immediately brought up a two-hundred-year-old image of Cabot Sinclair-Maru. He was of the older generation, back when their family resources had been much greater. He looked younger than Bess, without even a touch of gray in his dark hair . . . exactly as he appeared two centuries before.

Good, Winter thought, clear memories of faded glory should help.

"Pleased," Winter said. "We were just speaking of this reliable old weapon that protected the Emperor long ago."

Bess kept her gaze riveted on Winter's face, and Winter's analytics flickered telltales of probable suppressed anger. "The weapon *is* reliable and old," Bess said quietly. "But, perhaps it has been neglected."

Cabot said nothing, glancing from woman to woman before stepping to a refreshment dispenser and preparing a drink.

"Surely now," Winter replied in her most refined contralto, "it rests in honor upon the wall, and that wall upon vast lands gifted by the Emperor. That hardly seems neglect."

Bess's eyes flashed, and Winter's UI unnecessarily tagged it for anger and indignation. With difficulty, it seemed, Bess controlled her wrath. "Even the most reliable weapon needs a little ... care, from time to time, Consul, if it's to be ready for service someday."

Now Winter felt her own anger flare. *This backwater family owns a few pages of history, and they think the Emperor indebted to them?*

Cabot finished preparing his drink and turned. "Perhaps we can speak plainly."

Winter turned her focus from Bess to the blank slate of Cabot, where nothing at all was revealed. After a moment Winter said, "Assure complete privacy. No record. And I will share the Emperor's mind."

Bess barely glanced at Cabot before looking vaguely upward. "Hermes?" Bess inquired.

"Yes, my lady?" the House Intelligence of Lykeios responded, audibly for Winter's benefit.

"Seal this room, please. Stop all monitoring until further notice."

Winter's UI instantly went crazy, flashing alerts, as all bands and frequencies fell suddenly silent. Winter suppressed an involuntary start; she hadn't been separated from the Imperial Nets for years, except for those brief spells in transition during inter-system travel. She sent a terse plain text message on her quantum-entangled communicator: ALL WELL. FWD TO IMS FURY.

It wouldn't do for *Fury* to panic at her sudden disconnection, and begin raining down Marines from above.

QE comm technology was known to many within the Imperium, though not at the scale that Winter operated. Nothing could stop or block a QE message, nor could it be intercepted, but messages could pass only between two mated comm units. The almost unbelievable fact that Winter carried a miniature QE comm in her skull was a matter of highest Imperial secrecy.

"We are secure," Cabot said, sipping from his glass. He turned and stood looking out a window. "Please tell us how our family may assist the Emperor."

Winter looked from Bess to the profile of Cabot.

Was he consciously evading her analytics? Did he have some hint of her "mind-reading" capabilities?

She turned back to Bess. "What I am about to share is a matter that must never be discussed again in the detail and breadth I offer." Winter eased gracefully into a seat and Bess hesitated a moment before sitting across from her. Cabot swirled his drink, sipping as he continued to gaze out the window.

Winter flashed an irritated glance at Cabot but continued, her attention focused back upon Bess. "After centuries of talk, the Imperium faces three challenges at once."

"The assassination of the Emperor, the Ericson Cluster uprising, and...?" Cabot said without turning.

Winter really began to dislike Cabot Sinclair-Maru. "Yes," she replied. "But the rebellion may be tied to a larger issue, something that the Imperial counselors keep ignoring, something that we must uncover."

"We?" Cabot said.

Winter ignored him. "We may have a rebellion within a rebellion; something that goes to the top, impacting even the delivery of Shaper tech."

Winter's analytics read shock and disbelief on Bess's face.

"Fleet," Cabot said, surprising Winter again.

"Yes."

"But you must represent a faction, eh, Consul?" Cabot said, turning to look at her, finally. "So what's amiss in Fleet politics that's split the inner council into warring parties? Why stoop to this old Family, so far from all the court games?"

Winter felt the smooth planes of her face flash into jagged lines of anger, but she immediately reassumed the mask. She did not allow anyone inside the circles of her manipulation, too close to the truth to be twisted to her purposes. *Damn it! Where has this man been for the last two hundred years?*

She only said, "There are always divisions, you know that. But I *do* speak for the Emperor on this matter." Winter's analytics flagged hints of respectful acceptance in Bess's face. Good. But Cabot remained an unreadable slate.

Winter looked from Cabot to Bess. "Fleet is run by admirals, commodores, and captains who have risen from the testing of command school and years of duty. They come from diverse clusters of the Myriad Worlds, but what group dominates the command structure?"

"As you just said," Bess offered with confusion, "the command of Fleet is scattered among officers from many worlds. No one world or cluster dominates."

Cabot hissed a breath, and for the first time Winter's analytics found a purchase on his expressions: dawning awareness, shock. "Heavyworlders."

"Yes," Winter said, feeling suddenly, perversely attracted to Cabot as much as she had hated him a moment before. "Kush, Thorsworld, Ericson Two, Kabah, Al Sakeen, and the rest of the heavyworlds; they supply disproportionate numbers of Fleet officers, and always have. A majority of the Admiralty Board are heavyworlders, so you can see that if they were to join together..."

"Aside from heavy gravity, though, the heavyworlds have nothing in common. Not heritage, ethnicity, religion...nothing," Bess said.

"Ill usage," Cabot said. "They all feel shat upon."

"So eloquently said," Winter murmured. "Possibly correct, though."

"Possibly? Nothing creates solidarity like shared suffering. Before the first Shaper armada, heavyworld child mortality stood over fifty percent. You fool yourself if you think they forgot that."

"You preach to the converted," Winter said.

"Very well," Bess said, "let's accept this theory. Now, how can the Sinclair-Maru assist the Emperor?"

"We need someone loyal in the command structure, someone who can perform some odd tasks for us—soon."

"We weren't the first Family you approached on this," Cabot stated.

Damn him! "No," Winter said without expression.

"How many before you came to this loyal old hound?"

Winter internally jumped at Cabot's words, so closely mirroring her own uncomplimentary imagery. "You are the third," Winter said, truthfully. She saw Bess flush with anger at this, but Cabot only nodded.

"The other two declined?" Cabot asked.

"No," Winter said. "They died."

"Died how?" Bess inquired, her voice schooled

into an even tone, but Winter's analytics yelped about anger, suspicion, and resentment.

"One duel. One mysterious hit."

"And all this happened in the weeks since the Ericson uprising?" Cabot asked.

"Yes."

"Interesting."

"Perhaps you haven't noticed," Bess said in a voice dripping with resentment. "Our Family hasn't anyone in Fleet command anymore. The toadies and heavy-worlders seem to fill the command ranks, while our candidates are always frozen out."

Winter had time for one puzzled grimace before Cabot said, "Saef. He must have done well on the Fleet command test."

"I take it you hadn't heard, then?"

"We've heard nothing from Saef," Bess said. "Regardless, his command experience in Battersea's System Guard was commended, but that's never created much excitement in Fleet."

Winter looked from Bess to Cabot. *They really don't know. Why hasn't Saef contacted them?*

"Well," Winter said, smiling, "it's a pleasure to be the bearer of even more good news."

They both stared at Winter, their faces blank in that odd, unpleasant Sinclair-Maru way.

"As you have divined, your Saef performed . . . amazingly well on the command test. He achieved the highest command score on the record . . . by a far margin."

"He has always tested well," Cabot said in a mild voice, while Bess patiently awaited the implications.

"That's a . . . substantial understatement in this case," Winter said. "The previous record stood for nearly two centuries. Your Saef outperformed the previous record holder by a factor of three."

The only reaction observed in her audience was a slight rising of Bess's eyebrows, and a curl of Cabot's lip that spoke of impatience.

"As the new record holder, Saef's System Guard time will be credited as seniority in Fleet. He is eligible for captaincy, and an automatic cruise."

Finally, Winter obtained a small reward as Bess leaned back, taking a deep breath.

"The question is," Winter continued, "does Saef possess the additional qualities the Emperor requires?"

"That's not the question at all," Cabot said. "The question is, can the Family afford the outlay for a Fleet command position on such short notice?"

Bess ignored Cabot entirely, her gaze fixed upon Winter. "You undoubtedly sifted his file, and you're here. It appears he must hold the qualities the Emperor requires."

"He's still a bit of a puzzle in some ways," Winter said, feeling a warm stirring, as her appetites and her duty aligned for the first time of the day. "His physical scores ranked near the top. No surprise. It's a rare candidate who formerly served as a ground warfare instructor. His other scores are unremarkable." She paused, feeling a tingle of pleasure. "And then there is this bloodthirsty streak..."

"The duels?" Bess said. "No, we have a very complete brain scan record and psyche work-up since childhood. He's not bloodthirsty at all."

"Oh? Really?" Winter's fires banked somewhat.

"Saef adheres very closely to the *Legacy Mandate*... very closely," Cabot said.

Winter felt the remaining spark extinguish, and she tried to suppress the disdainful twist of her lips. "He's ... *'pruning the tree of nobility'* is he?"

"According to the words of your revered ancestor, yes."

"Well ... that's reassuring," Winter said, overwhelmed with that clammy Sinclair-Maru feeling, and wanting very much to leave. "Let's get to business, then. Can your Family provide the necessary outlay for a light frigate captaincy?"

Winter did not need advanced analytic systems to detect the pure avarice in Bess's eyes. "Yes, a half-million credits ... with a few Imperial concessions."

Cabot said nothing and his expression was unreadable by any means.

"What concessions?" Winter asked flatly. "For our purposes there can be no visible strings to the Emperor."

"This will be quite invisible," Bess said. "Leak us the top five Trade items requested by the incoming Shaper armada. We'll reposition our inventories and get 'lucky' as we sometime have before."

Winter mused momentarily. "I will leak you two of the top five items, three in the top ten, and you will have a fully equipped Saef Sinclair-Maru in Imperial City within ten days. I have a personal QE comm unit in my skimcar for him. He will receive his instructions and make his reports through that, as needed."

"Agreed," Bess said without looking toward Cabot.

Winter nodded, checking off various points in her mind. She thought of one lingering curiosity. "You must be very pleased with this young man, Saef. But tell me, how did he so surpass all records of the command test?"

"Refresh my memory," Cabot said, unable to tap into the Nets with the room sealed to all signals. "What sort of test is it precisely, again?"

"The command test measures a subject's ability to command a warship. It's a simulator, complete with a normal bridge complement. As the test progresses, challenges increase and bridge officers are removed, one by one, leaving the subject to manage ship resources through command UI, solo. About half the candidates surpass the first phase, operating the simulated warship alone, with no bridge officers." Winter paused, and her audience of two sat silently, without expression. *Like conversing with rocks!*

"The second phase simply increases the stress, step by step. Failing systems, hazards, attacks . . . that sort of thing. Only three subjects have ever managed to continue beyond the eight-hour mark before their simulated ship failed or they collapsed under the stress. The previous record holder lasted nearly twelve hours. Your Saef endured for nearly *thirty* hours." Winter paused, looking for some reaction, but after a moment she sighed and continued. "At the end he was delirious, kept speaking of the path to the Deep Man. That's not a term from command school curriculum. How'd he pull this off?"

Neither Bess nor Cabot answered for a moment, and Winter's analytics flagged concealment and distrust on Bess's face, but Cabot's expression remained merely contemplative.

Just as the prolonged silence became uncomfortable Cabot answered, "We provide an advanced implant and UI to all Family members. Saef mastered a complex UI when he was very young."

"He's still very young," Winter said.

"Thirty isn't that young in this Family, Consul," Bess said.

Winter frowned. Was that a rebuke because the Sinclair-Maru could no longer afford the extended youth of Shaper rejuv? Or did she refer to the famed, but secretive, training system of the Sinclair-Maru?

Winter said, "His earlier simulator scores were all high, but nothing like this, and what about this 'Deep Man' business? Does that mean anything to you?"

Bess glanced at Cabot, and Cabot pursed his lips before speaking. "Saef is very accomplished under pressure, as you see. And recall his meritorious service in the System Guard. He commanded several gunboats. But I'm afraid I must remain silent beyond that. The *Legacy Mandate* forbids discussion of House Combatives between Families."

Winter shook her head. "You're saying that House Combatives—dueling skills, really—have some great connection to commanding an interstellar warship?"

"That *was* the original intent by your honored ancestor, you may recall," Cabot said.

Winter despised everything about her "honored ancestor," Emperor Yung the First, except that he made her youth, her longevity, and her lavish lifestyle possible, but she especially loathed his damned book of preachy maxims: the *Legacy Mandate*.

Winter stifled a sneer and rose to her feet. "Very well. You'll get your list of Shaper requests, and you get Saef to Imperial City. He needs to be on a shuttle off this rock within two days to make our schedule." She nodded to Cabot. "I hope your vaunted House Combatives are up to the task. I want him to survive long enough to get where we need him."

Cabot tossed back the remainder of his amber-hued beverage and said, "It seems likely we may already be too late on that score."

Bess and Winter simply stared at him, but Cabot just nodded to himself and looked at his empty glass. "It's been, what? Two days? Two days since the test, and we haven't heard from Saef. That seems surprising, considering."

Bess fumbled a touch panel, hailing the House Intelligence back into the room. "Yes, my lady?" the voice of Hermes inquired.

"Locate Saef Sinclair-Maru, please," Bess said.

"Searching for Saef Sinclair-Maru. A moment, my lady."

Winter felt her own connection to the Imperial Nets rush back into her skull as the House Intelligence unsealed the room. She immediately set her own Nets search in place, but before she could do little more than initiate, Hermes returned.

"My lady, Saef is listed as unavailable. Last location was his lodging at command school, Port City. Status was normal."

"He's not sending? He's not on any public Nets?"

"No, my lady," Hermes replied. "I do detect a potentially useful connection."

Winter nodded in appreciation. These old House Intelligences accumulated so much Family pattern data over the centuries that they could be enormously useful, nearly prescient, but very expensive to develop.

"Proceed," Bess said.

"Claude Carstairs also listed command school as his location twelve hours ago. He cancelled appointments today, with an 'affair of honor' as his stated purpose."

"Saef's dueling this Carstairs character?" Winter asked as her UI supplied an image of a somewhat vacuous-looking but handsome young man.

"No," Bess said. "Claude is a childhood friend, likely serving as his second."

"What do you wish to wager that Saef's opponent is a heavyworlder?" Cabot said without expression. He set his empty glass down. "Would you care to dine with us, Consul? We should hear shortly if Saef survives, I would think. Or will that warship loitering above us become anxious?"

Winter nearly grimaced, wondering if Cabot shared his awareness of her orbital escort as an olive branch, or as some sort of threat. "I haven't time to linger, sadly." She fired a salvo of messages through her UI to her Port City agents. "We will just have to place our faith in the famous skill of your House, and hope for the best."

Damn! They moved faster than I had thought! If Saef dies, this entire tedious day has been for nothing!

Chapter 3

"Both fear and anger lean forward into
every approaching moment of conflict.
This produces imbalance...."

—Devlin Sinclair-Maru, *Integrity Mirror*

CLAUDE CARSTAIRS CRITICALLY EXAMINED HIS
appearance in the reflection from the skimcar window.
He touched one blond lock of hair, adjusted the
golden tassel of his cloak. *Thank god cloaks are back
in fashion again!*

"Rest easy, Claude," Saef Sinclair-Maru said. "You're
beautiful."

Claude continued to twist his head about, looking
for any flaw. "Damned kind of you to say, Saef, but
honestly, you wouldn't know. Fashion escapes you.
Always has."

Saef shrugged and crossed one tall boot over the
other, turning his gray eyes to the view outside. Just
before a duel every detail of life seemed significant.

He felt an odd satisfaction, enjoying a rare moment with his UI entirely silenced. Natural vision seemed all too vivid as the skimcar wove through the maze of Port City.

Once, Saef knew, the Family possessed vast offices and warehouses here in the largest city of Battersea. Before his time, they were long gone. But perhaps, perhaps he could do as old Devlin once had, and somehow pull victory out of the ashes. It was a hopeful thought, yet Saef felt the plague of misgivings rising up even now.

"I say, Saef," Claude said with rare tones of thoughtfulness. "You know I would *never* interfere in a matter of honor, never, ever... but, I must say it would be... er... grand if this fellow you're fighting survived the duel."

"I think it would be rather nice if *I* survive the duel, Claude."

"Oh, of course! Goes without saying. That would be good, too. But my cousin, you see, on m'mother's side, she has a bit of business with this Lars fellow's family."

"How enterprising of her."

"Yes," Claude agreed, nodding vigorously. "Yes, and profitable, too!"

"And you want me to... what? Throw the duel somehow?"

Claude's eyes started wide. "No!" he almost shouted, looking about the skimcar as if lurking listeners might somehow be concealed about the bare cushions. "Gods, no. Saef... Hah! The things you say. Hah. Throw the fight? No, no, no. Just let him live, you see. My cousin'll watch it on some vidstream—this duel is sure to be all over the Nets, you know—and I'll tell her that I *persuaded* you to spare the damned scrub. It'll do me no end of good with the Family."

"Claude, no one but other heavyworlders have beat a Thorsworld native in a high-gee duel. Not for a century or so."

"Well, if you lose, Saef, you needn't fret about my cousin. It's if you win that has her worried, you see."

Saef laughed despite himself, shaking his head. "Why do I endure you, Claude?"

Claude smiled, "Because we've been friends forever. Because I advise you on fashion, which clearly *no one* else does, and because I attract beautiful women into your orbit who would otherwise flee from your scowling, unfashionable self."

"Surely I don't scowl," Saef said.

Claude mused a moment before saying, "Except for right this moment, it sure ain't a smile."

Saef's smile faded. "We all have our burdens, I suppose."

"Yes, very true, Saef," Claude said, forcibly struck by the comment. "Burdens. I've got a ton of 'em! Aside from you and your scowl, and my cursed cousin and her business, there's that party tomorrow. What am I possibly going to wear? While you . . . !"

"Me? Yes?"

"You! You haven't a single worry."

"Really, Claude? This duel, perhaps?"

"No, no. Not a single worry, Saef. You look just fine, I assure you. And you will *never* have a moment of distress again. I'm frankly envious, I must say."

"I really don't see what you—"

"Uniforms!" Claude declared.

"Pardon?"

"Uniforms, Saef. Go to a party, uniform. Funeral; uniform. Luncheon. Uniform." Claude clapped his hands together. "All of your problems have disappeared. Poof."

"Claude, I really don't see—"

"And a damn fine idea it was, too. Passing that Fleet test. Smashing! Never would have expected such sense from you. Uniforms for life. And the Fleet officer's get-up is devilishly handsome, I tell you straight away, devilishly handsome."

"Well, thank you, Claude, I'm glad to have redeemed myself in your sight." The Fleet test: a mighty success that warmed Saef's bones, but an unfamiliar tension teased him, even beyond the unease of his approaching duel. And then the Family...

"I had despaired, but all's well now."

"If I don't get killed here in a moment, yes."

"There's that, too," Claude said, nodding seriously. "I've been thinking about that, Saef."

"Oh, really?"

"Yes, yes. If this Lars fellow does get a lucky slash in and puts you down, I was wondering something..."

"I'm a-sweat to hear it," Saef said.

"Since this will be all over the Nets, what do you think would look better, since you're my best friend and all: just a look of grim sadness? Or do you think honest-to-gods tears are in order here?"

"I think rending your clothes in grief sounds about right."

Claude's eyes nearly started out of his head. "Are you completely mad? Have you even looked at this shirt? And think what an ass I would look on the Nets! No, no, I think grim sadness, Saef. Maybe a single, solitary tear down my cheek." Claude trailed a finger down his cheek and looked sorrowfully into the distance.

"Since I'm your best friend," Saef said.

"Since you *are* my best friend."

"Your destination, sirs," the skimcar's modest Intelligence chimed in.

Saef and Claude entered the old demi-cit athletic club together, Claude's slender, elegant figure beside Saef's more robust form. The place stood empty except for a clutch of Vested Citizens standing on the far side of the graviton training pad.

"Ah, there's that Lars chap and his second, right there, Saef. I'll go make sure we're ready." Claude walked across the training pad, his cloak billowing dramatically around him.

Saef took off his jacket, folded and placed it on a nearby cushion that looked moderately clean. His pistol belt joined it. He stretched his shoulders and shook out his hands. Only a couple of days prior he had collapsed, nearly catatonic, after the grinding, thirty-hour ordeal of the command test, and he could still feel its lingering effects. Part of Saef's mind wondered what the Family thought of his success. Would they *finally* acknowledge Saef's efforts in some meaningful way? Or would they find some fault even now? Would they even back his new command opportunity? His thoughts returned to the moment, and the possibility of impending death.

Saef glanced across the training pad at Lars, the Thorsworld cadet who had forced this duel. Shorter and probably twenty percent heavier than Saef, all muscle, sinew, and bone.

Lars had all but spit in Saef's face to force this duel, but why? They both attended the Imperial command college, but had barely known each other.

Saef shrugged to himself and continued scanning the other figures in the crusty old athletic center. Six people stood around Lars, while Claude and his counterpart stood to one side, chatting and gesturing about. At the periphery of the room, seated in the shadows, a lone figure sat, and something about him looked vaguely familiar. Aside from the hair color, the man could be one of the Sinclair-Maru cousins.

Saef turned away, drawing his short sword and long knife. Each blade came from the Family auto-fab, but despite the claims of some purists, a Sinclair-Maru blade held qualities superior to any handmade blade. The Family utilized elaborate (and secret) programming to produce wonders in metallurgy, layering diverse alloys in a complex bonding that provided lightweight strength and a razor edge.

He re-sheathed the blades and paced out onto the training pad. With a neural gesture he activated the scaram fear generator implanted with his House UI electronics. The familiar jolt of primal terror driving ice into his guts brought him back to a thousand training cycles. The instinctive narrowing of his vision, increased heart rate, and shortness of breath barely began before disappearing.

Saef immediately found the mountaintop of calm that old Devlin had named "the Deep Man," and fear could gain no purchase in him. His vision broadened, his shoulders relaxing, and he saw Lars step onto the training pad.

Saef redrew his sword and knife, using both for the

first time in a duel. It was a counterintuitive move, where most non-heavyworlders would want both hands free to wield a sword grown suddenly heavy in the increased gravity.

As he felt the familiar press of ramping gravity squeezing every fiber of his body, Saef disengaged the scaram. He remained in the pool of calm as his stocky heavyworld opponent stepped nearer, sword in hand.

"Regain what you may, dog!" Lars snarled at him, in a wrathful approximation of the formal words.

Either truly angry . . . or frightened . . .

Since Saef had never given a true reason for offense, he bet on fear, but either emotion held benefits over a calm, calculating opponent.

Saef lifted his sword smoothly up and held it pointing directly into Lars's eyes. He heard the murmur of the onlookers, likely surprised that he managed the increased gravity so well, but Saef knew he could only manage this rocklike hold for a short time.

"I had no quarrel with you," Saef said, looking down the blade into his opponent's wide eyes. "But for the honor of my family I do this." He lowered the blade to low guard and advanced, working hard to lift his feet naturally.

Fear. Saef saw it written in his foe's eyes, in the rigid face masked with anger, in the sword lashing too early, trying to keep Saef at bay.

Constricting vision, poor muscle control, repetitive thought loops: these were the enemies defeating Lars before Saef ever touched him.

Saef rationally knew that Lars could quite easily best him, just by maneuvering defensively for a time, allowing the heavy gravity to wear down Saef's non-heavyworld muscles. But instead, Saef took hold of his own route to victory, plotting his path in three distinct moves.

Saef advanced, thrusting low with the knife in his left hand, clashing against his opponent's sword, and again, though slightly nearer. Lars frantically parried a second time, his eyes locked on the wicked blade stabbing toward his belly, ignoring all avenues to counterattack. Saef advanced and jabbed the knife in another identical thrust, Lars's sword leaping to parry. He didn't see Saef's straight sword-thrust from the deceptive right hand until far too late. It pierced Lars through, just beneath his collarbone.

Saef jerked his sword free but did not step back. For only the second time in his life he began to utter the "first blood" statement, sparing his opponent's life. "First blood. My honor is—"

Terror radiated from Lars's eyes. He made a guttural sound, one hand at his wounded chest, slashing recklessly at Saef. Saef barely stopped the blade, and continued the motion, feeling the razor edge of his Family sword pass through flesh and click against bone.

Lars crumpled to the ground, his light fading, his vitality an expanding pool fanning out behind him.

Someone shouted for restored gravity, the crushing pressure eased, and Claude appeared at his side.

"Oh, well done! I daresay, well done!" Claude chortled, hustling Saef to the side while a medico went to work on Lars, attempting to save a life that was surely gone. "My cousin can't say a cursed thing now. Good thinking, offering first blood like that. Now I'm off the hook."

Saef wiped the thin line of blood from his blade, feeling a heaviness beyond gravity.

"That!" Claude exclaimed. "That right there. That's the scowl, Saef. Millions of beautiful women will see your mug on the Nets tonight and say, 'My god, would you look at that appalling scowl! But wait. Who's that devilishly handsome fellow there beside the scowler? He's nearly perfect.' And you will be gone from their minds. Poof. Gone."

Saef belted his pistol in place, slid into his jacket, and moved toward the door.

"You're still scowling, Saef. It's going to stick like that, old fellow."

"He was terrified, Claude," Saef said. "I offered him his life, but he was too frightened to take it. Frightened of what?"

"That's a quizzer. Daresay it is. But no sense asking him now, eh?"

Saef nodded as he awaked his implant, bringing up his House UI. A flood of glowing alerts spun across his vision, most notably a priority call pending from Cabot Sinclair-Maru. Saef grunted in surprise, placed his earpiece, and triggered the call.

Without preamble Cabot began talking. "It appears you survived. Is he dead?"

Saef swallowed his surprise at the unprecedented call. "Y-yes, it appears that way."

"Very well," Cabot said.

"Who's that?" Claude asked, standing to one side.

Saef ignored Claude as Cabot continued. "Get back to Lykeios by tonight. Consider yourself a target. Take every precaution, and do not return to your lodging. There may be an ambush awaiting even at your current location. Get in motion."

"I . . . yes, Cabot." Saef scanned around the room

again as Cabot clicked off, this time with a more critical focus.

"What's afoot then, Saef?" Claude asked.

"I'm not sure," Saef answered, used to a lifetime of peremptory commands from his Family betters. "Let's find a back door."

"A back door? Really? To some sort of alley? In these boots? You have noticed my boots, haven't you? I think not! Sure to be filthy."

Some of the figures around Lars's prostrate form did seem rather intently focused upon Saef, he thought.

He pulled up his new Fleet Command overlay on his UI, queried for location, and flicked through the blueprints, each flashing across his vision in glowing trails.

"This way," Saef said, turning on his heel without looking back.

Grumbling, Claude followed.

Only a score of steps brought them to a small passage and a side door. The manual entrance readily yielded to Saef's Fleet authorization, but before Saef opened the door, he thought again of Cabot's warning.

Take every precaution . . .

Saef hesitated a moment before drawing his pistol, moving smoothly out the door, onto the side street. Directly ahead, he saw an older skimcar waiting, a man and woman seated within, windows open.

They noticed Saef at almost the same moment, their expressions reflecting recognition, but also relief. Saef kept his pistol low at his side.

"Commander Sinclair-Maru? Imperial Security," the woman said. "We can't be seen with you, but there's a hired skimcar for you and your companion just around the corner on your right."

A legitimate Imperial validation code flashed into Saef's UI, verified by his Fleet overlay.

Without a word, Saef nodded and set out for the skimcar, holstering his pistol, his gaze flashing from the unimpressive heights of this old section of Port City, scanning blank windows, to the scant passing traffic.

"Saef, gods!" Claude demanded. "What the devil was that about?"

"Not entirely sure, Claude. I'm heading straight to Lykeios. You're welcome to come with, if you like."

"You, old fellow, have lost your wits," Claude declared, struggling to keep up with Saef's pace. "Lost 'em! Don't you remember there's a party tonight? You, in your uniform—uniform!—you will be the toast of the town."

Saef shook his head. "Something's wrong, Claude. Not sure what, but I've got to get home."

"Something's wrong? Something's wrong?" Claude repeated, outraged. "Clearly. You are going to sit about with all your hangdog relatives instead of going to a party with me and dozens of open-minded women... in your uniform! Yes, something is clearly wrong."

The skimcar, a standard livery job, to Saef's eyes, idled just ahead, and Saef strode straight to it, his eyes scanning.

"Amazing. Just amazing," Claude declared. "Why do you even fight all these duels? When the very best part of dueling is the party, and you always miss 'em!"

Saef shook his head and climbed into the skimcar. "I'm a slow learner. Be patient, Claude."

"Slow learner?"

"Lykeios Manor, if you please," Saef said to the skimcar.

"You're not just leaving me in the street here,

Saef!" Claude hollered as the skimcar's door closed. "Saef? Damn it!"

The skimcar purred away, and Saef waved a farewell as Claude yelled after him, "You're just leaving me in the street! I'm your best friend, you—you...!"

Claude stood watching in disbelief as the car disappeared in the distance before he noticed a demicit bystander staring curiously at him. "I'm his best friend," Claude said by way of explanation, swirling his cloak angrily out behind him. "What a burden!"

Chapter 4

"All intelligent species in existence are merely so many strains of bacteria infecting the Body Galactic. Humanity must strive to be the most antibiotic-resistant vermin imaginable...."

—*Legacy Mandate* by Emperor Yung I

THERE IS NOTHING THAT CREATES GREATER FOCUS in an intelligent species than the prospect of utter and immediate extinction. Thus humanity's first encounter with an intelligent starfaring alien species, the "Slaggers" as they came to be known, resulted in vast changes to human society.

The slaughter of the entire populations from a few planets in 5202 rang through the surviving worlds, galvanized human ferocity, and left an indelible mark on nearly every aspect of the human Imperium.

The brilliant military leader of the Li Dynasty, Admiral Yung, led humanity's forces to victory over the Slaggers, but he didn't stop there. He overthrew the effete Emperor, Khan Li, established the House system, wrote the *Legacy Mandate*, and created massive reforms of the Vested Citizens and demi-cit processes.

He incidentally flogged the Imperial Fleet into a state intended to drive tactical and technical innovation. This, conjoined with the social reforms that opened merit pathways to full citizenship, poured streams of heavyworlders into Fleet positions. No longer were heavyworlders the abject gutter of the social ladder. They elected to promote to Vested Citizenship at higher rates than their lighter-world compatriots, they provided superior performance in Fleet ships that were (in that era) subject to constant high-gravity conditions, and they could no longer be blithely dishonored without risk of a dueling blade through the vitals.

For a few short years the heavyworld citizens shot toward total dominance in Fleet. Then the second nonhuman intelligence entered the scene of humanity's affairs, and with this new contact came the artificial gravity technology that ended the heavyworld path to domination.

The second alien encounter for the Imperium arrived in heart-stopping suddenness, the memory of the Slaggers and wholesale slaughter all too fresh in mankind's memory. The first Shaper armada simply appeared in Core system, in vessels so vast they could contain the entire Imperial Fleet. Peaceful intentions were easily discerned. If they had desired war, no one doubted the outcome.

As soon as rudimentary communication was established between the Emperor and the Shapers, trade began. The technology flowing from the Shapers stood so far above human capabilities that many technologies provided were thought theoretically impossible, and these "magical" treasures swiftly became the most desirable human possessions in the galaxy. Artificial gravity generators created one great ripple within the Imperium, but a new interstellar drive system restructured the Imperium overnight. Powerful implantable computers, radiation and kinetic shield generators, and universal fabrication machines continued the shock wave.

But perhaps the single greatest impact upon humanity came from the Shaper longevity advancements. These treatments and the related rejuv technology pushed human vitality and youth to new heights. Instead of a century of health, those with the necessary financial resources might expect four centuries or more of youth. As scientists of the Imperium optimized Shaper longevity technologies, the effectiveness gradually increased.

The reborn Imperium under Yung I rippled with the ramifications of Shaper advancements. That ripple continued for centuries as Shaper tech flowed out to the fringes of the Imperium's Myriad Worlds and trickled down to the lower strata of the social ladder. Of course humanity attempted to reverse engineer the technological wonders bestowed upon them, and occasionally succeeded. Still, it took nearly three centuries to discover that the Shaper interstellar drive held the key to nearly everything the Shapers provided.

The Shaper's N-drive thrust starships into some realm or dimension that defied all theories, all measurement, all comprehension. It came to be known as "N-space," for obvious reasons. A starship actuated the N-drive, transitioning into N-space for a brief subjective and objective period of time, and emerged from N-space light-years distant. It was magic...very, very expensive magic.

Shaper fuel cells swiftly became the most valuable commodity in known space, and N-space transitions gobbled up Shaper fuel with heartbreaking rapidity. Still, it beat years or decades of constant acceleration, which was the only other alternative with humanity's own stutter-drive technology.

Over time, humanity's engineers discovered some interesting effects during those brief N-space transitions. In the midst of a transition, light and time behaved differently, for starters. Then they realized that many Shaper mechanisms, such as crystal computers, suddenly and dramatically increased their performance, producing output and calculations at ten times or one thousand times greater efficiency and speed. This led to several key epiphanies.

First, it became clear that the Shapers' immense ships were not merely *transporters* of trade goods, they were vast interstellar factories. They constructed their amazing devices and gathered mysterious energies during unimaginable interstellar voyages, because these capabilities could only be touched within the envelope of N-space.

Even with this knowledge, humanity could not curb its dependence upon the Shapers. True, most starships now carried fab systems to quickly manufacture advanced tech items during their all-too-brief transitions through N-space, but true N-space "factories" remained far out of reach.

The N-drive transitioned starships through the corridor of N-space, invisible light-years sailed by in minutes, and the starship popped back out at the desired location in ridiculously short periods of time. A trip of ten light-years might take fifteen minutes instead of a decade. This meant that very little production could take place inside that envelope of N-space minutes.

Aside from the vast expense of N-space transition, there was yet another catch. Any destination fed to the N-drive system must be fully ray-mapped. This meant humanity's N-drive-equipped vessels could only visit star systems that they had already visited and mapped. Meaning that at the start of Emperor Yung V's reign, Imperium vessels could travel just scores of N-space minutes from one edge to the other edge of known space. And, of course, each such transition consumed Shaper fuel cells available only from the Shapers themselves.

The end result was that ninety-seven percent of Shaper tech flowed only from the Shapers, despite humanity's best efforts.

For the Yung Dynasty, the bright side continued to be that the Shapers dealt only with Imperial representatives, so all Shaper tech flowed through Imperial hands, while every Fleet and private starship utilized every moment of N-space to create Shaper-type tech as efficiently as possible. All in all, it was a good system . . . for the Yung Dynasty at least.

On a quantum-entangled communicator, the Shapers sent lists of desired raw materials from wherever they happened to be to the Emperor, and the Emperor, in turn, dealt out nuggets from the Shapers' shopping list as Imperial favors to his favored subjects. Each time, before the Shaper armada arrived in Core system, the Emperor held millions of tons stocked up and waiting. Every seven or eight Core years the Shaper armada appeared, and vast containers hauled by Fleet vessels flowed from the lockers of Core Alpha, the vast orbital platform above Imperial City, out to the visitors. In turn, cases and cases of shield generators, fab machines, implantables, N-drives, and various formulations of nanotech returned from the armada, filling those same lockers in Core Alpha.

Those lucky Houses who directly supplied the Shapers' needs obtained the first cut of the Shaper inventory—after the Imperial slice, of course. The less-fortunate Houses either found themselves tightening the belt and waiting another seven years for the next armada, or working out arrangements with those Houses currently basking in the glow of Imperial favor.

New Shaper shipments flowed outward from Coreworld, mostly on House Trade vessels. On every human world, access to Shaper tech represented the only *real* wealth, and the value of any commodity became established by its relationship to Shaper trade demands.

Sometimes the Shaper armada appeared, demanding some commodity in addition to their pre-transmitted list. Families had risen to significance when the Shapers abruptly requested ten thousand tons of some unexpected material that the House just happened to possess. One arriving armada added the bizarre items of wood products and a particular strain of yeast—both desired in vast quantities—and the only House to possess inventories of these products profited greatly.

Through the centuries, the established Houses attempted to predict and cover any likely Shaper demand, eventually forming a loose guild called, simply, Trade.

Trade formed a powerful network with a constantly shifting hierarchy that shared or hoarded information, analyzed Shaper commodity trends, and, most important, worked together to amass vast quantities of every imaginable product ready to supply each incoming armada.

In the rare instances when some items on the Shapers' shopping list could not be provided before their departure, the economy of the Imperium quaked. Less trade meant less Shaper tech to receive, and that meant even higher prices. Every soul in the Imperium immediately knew that the already exorbitant *necessities* provided by the Shapers became that much harder to obtain. With another near-decade to wait for the next armada, crazed levels of acquisition overset markets, and fortunes in real property shifted from party to party, House to House.

It was in everyone's best interest that the Shapers obtained all the trade goods they desired and, more important, that they left as much of their invaluable tech behind as possible.

Thus, with the QE comm link to the Shapers in Imperial hands, the Emperor cemented control of the most valuable pipeline in human history. At random times between armadas, the QE comm dribbled out lines of text describing the Shaper shopping list. Those humble lines of text became golden morsels, doled out to various Houses and coalitions.

Among the thousands of parties jockeying for Imperial favor, the Sinclair-Maru family possessed a history and natural resources that should have equaled nearly any House in the Imperium. Aside from land and sea holdings on the planet of Battersea, producing plant and mineral abundance, the Sinclair-Maru family also held an extensive claim in the rich asteroid belt of the Battersea system.

Hawksgaard, a Sinclair-Maru base and processing center in the asteroid belt, had once been the most elaborate (and profitable) such facility in the Imperium, but centuries of decline in the Family fortunes appeared quite visibly there now.

After so many years on a slow downward glide, the Sinclair-Maru Family leaders took the extraordinary step of placing one of the "younger" generation in the House executor seat. Cabot Sinclair-Maru and those of his generation—all of whom enjoyed the benefit of full Shaper rejuv from the years of their more affluent youth—stepped down from leadership, relegated to counselors.

"Young Bess," the Family leaders figured, would view their plight from a more modern perspective, and since her un-regenerated days of life drew rapidly toward a close, she might enjoy the wonderfully sharpening effect of impending death itself to figure a way out of their fix.

She instituted many immediate reforms, trimming back some House efforts, while expanding other areas. She invested heavily in updating Hawksgaard to more modern standards, expanding the bio-med research labs, and optimistically securing more warehouse space in Core Alpha. She also outfitted the House Trade delegation to a more modern, lavish style. In Trade, she knew, appearance mattered nearly as much as substance, and the Sinclair-Maru suffered from a challenging has-been image.

With the next Shaper armada expected within

two years, the Sinclair-Maru Trade delegation finally seemed to make headway, the Hawksgaard facility finally began clearing a profit once again, and in the midst of this Bess called an immediate and mysterious Family meeting.

Most of the family leaders assumed it must involve the recent Ericson Cluster uprising, and in a way it did.

Chapter 5

"Allow bravado only for balance attacks. For the kill, subtlety and the silent hand are your allies."

—Devlin Sinclair-Maru, *Integrity Mirror*

WHEN SAEF STEPPED THROUGH THE DOORS OF Lykeios Manor some hours after Winter Yung had departed, Hermes informed him that he was expected immediately in the central comm room, but no Family member arose to greet him. As always, Saef felt a mixture of emotion upon returning to Lykeios. Each year the small signs of decline leaped out, and he labored as hard as anyone to restore the Family, yet few of his betters seemed to regard him as anything more than a quaint member of the younger generation.

Saef had neither dined nor washed since his duel with Lars, and he spent his entire skimcar trip from Port City obsessively sifting through Fleet crew information via his UI. Since Cabot would share nothing about this mysterious summons over the comm channel, he tried to channel his tension over his impending command opportunity to good use. Now, aside from the impression of familial disdain, Saef felt rather tired and irritable.

He removed his jacket and placed it upon the hook that Hermes helpfully extended to him.

"Thank you," Saef said. "No time to dine?"

"I am afraid not, Commander. I will send something down to central comm shortly, if you wish."

"If you please," Saef said. As he began walking, a notice pinged into his UI. Hermes had sealed Lykeios, shutting down all signal access, sparing only the internal Family Nets. Something serious indeed roused the Family.

Central comm lay in the depths beneath Lykeios manor, illustrating the war footing of the Imperium during the manor's construction over five hundred years before. It served as a secret and secure location for the technological core of Lykeios, with the Family's precious few QE communicators beside Hermes' crystal stacks and all the other more conventional communication and control systems.

Since it was the Family's holy of holies, Saef felt little surprise in seeing a gathering of Family leaders behind the massive doors of central comm, but he was surprised to see the tall, fair figure of his brother, Richard, seated beside Grimsby, the Family Trade leader. Saef felt far more surprise in seeing a youthful stranger standing casually beside the seat occupied by Bess. Strangers were never permitted in central comm or most other secure areas of Lykeios. The stranger compounded the peculiarity by leaning against a parapet wall, idly munching a bright red fruit. Saef observed that the stranger—a young woman—wore a sword, but her thin face, blue eyes, and short blond hair gave him no other clues to her identity. His UI displayed no further clues.

Saef barely paused in his assessment of the stranger, sweeping the rest of the small gathering with one level look and a curt nod. He stepped over to the refreshment dispenser and Hermes had a whiskey waiting.

"Saef," Bess greeted. "This meeting regards you, in part. We've heard of your success in the command test."

Saef sipped his whiskey and nodded again. Apparently not everyone had heard about the command test, because Richard and Grimsby looked sharply up at him, and Anthea Sinclair-Maru, head of Family security, raised her eyebrows in surprise. Cabot and Eldridge just waited without expression, and the holo projection of Kai Sinclair-Maru from his office way out in Hawksgaard remained unchanged. The transmission traveled the great distance out to his location at mere light speed, creating lengthy delays. Two other Family leaders were present only in text form via QE comm. The glowing characters flowed down two walls as Hermes transmitted every word spoken to their locations on distant worlds, reaching them instantaneously.

"Of course," Bess continued, "this is a chance we have sought for many years, so we must act wisely."

The central comm chamber lay in two rectangles beneath a high, arched ceiling, one rectangle within the other. The sunken inner rectangle held the large conference table and twenty-two comfortable seats, surrounded by tall parapet walls containing comm screens, holo projectors, and manual input banks. Stairs rose through the parapet walls to the second, larger rectangle surrounding the sunken recess of the conference area. Posh furnishings contrasted with defense stations, shield generators, and tactical computers filling the outer rectangle.

To Saef the chamber had always seemed an oppressive reminder of the Family's overriding caution.

"What exactly is the situation here?" Grimsby asked in a gruff tone. Several eyes turned toward Saef, but he sipped from his whiskey, settling into a chair pushed far back from the conference table, letting the alcohol warm his tired core. He had suffered enough snubs through the years that he rarely spoke before the Family leadership except when commanded to.

"Saef's success," Bess said, "earns a Fleet captaincy."

An appreciative murmur rose around the table, but Grimsby frowned and Richard audibly sighed, looking upward.

Eldridge alone visibly demonstrated much enthusiasm. "Why, Saef, that's fabulous! After all these years, finally back in a Fleet command position. Well done indeed."

"Wait a moment," Grimsby growled. "A captaincy? Captain of what? We don't have the cash to cover the outlay for a captain of much."

Anthea spoke, her face nearly expressionless but her tone reproving. "Grimsby, you must jest. After all this time, finally in Fleet. And just in time for war. Sinclair-Maru, a command position, and war have been the second most profitable combination in Family history."

"If my brother can finally figure out who to fight, and who to befriend," Richard interjected with a snort.

Saef saw the flash in Richard's eyes, but beyond

Richard, on the far side of the table, he saw the strange young woman pause in her chewing and stare at Richard with a narrowing gaze.

"You refer to his duel today?" Bess inquired in a mild tone, though Eldridge's and Anthea's eyes flashed at Richard's interjection.

"Of course," Richard answered, adjusting his sleeve, avoiding the eyes of his elders. Thirty-four was considered a bit young to blurt out opinions in a House leadership meeting.

"What duel?" Eldridge and Anthea asked at the same moment, and even Grimsby turned a puzzled look in Richard's direction.

Bess waved a hand, and one holo filled with the ratty interior of the demi-cit athletic school. Saef swallowed a gulp of whiskey and felt it burning down his throat. He suddenly found himself wishing he had fought his duel in more visually appealing surroundings.

As Saef watched his own figure on the holo lifting his sword and pointing it at Lars, he was suddenly distracted by another holo where the image of cousin Kai shifted position, smiling brightly and nodding. He must have just received the bit about the Fleet captaincy.

Saef's gaze drifted back to his own figure blocking the last, desperate strike of the Thorsworld native, ending the fight in one quick motion.

"Well done, well done," Eldridge said. "In heavy grav, no less."

Richard made an explosive noise that may have been a stifled laugh. "Since when have the Sinclair-Maru become so ostentatious?"

Saef swallowed his last gulp of whiskey and looked

very pointedly at Richard's fashionable, colorful clothing, then up to his eyes. "When indeed, Richard?"

"I saw no ostentation," Eldridge said. "That opening challenge was a classic balance attack. Perhaps you recall those, Richard?"

"Let's move on, please," Bess commanded. "The duel today has meaning for only one reason that I will share with you in a moment." She swiped a hand and the holo disappeared.

She placed both hands upon the tabletop and looked at everyone for a still moment. "A Fleet captaincy in wartime is too golden an opportunity for us to miss. I have already agreed to a half-million credit outlay."

"What?" Richard spluttered. "In Trade we could—" Grimsby covered Richard's hand with his own, and Richard fell silent, shaking his head.

"A half-million credits?" Grimsby barked. "With even a quarter-million we could obtain the full list from the previous armada for analysis."

"We've heard that more than once," Anthea snapped. "And we've spent millions on Trade without ever reaching the first tier."

"And we've brought millions back into the Family," Grimsby argued.

"Perhaps breaking even?" Eldridge said.

"What?" Grimsby bit out. "What are you implying?"

They argued like this for some moments, and Saef watched each snarled phrase appearing in glowing text upon the wall, as Hermes dutifully transcribed every heated word. After a moment Saef found the blue eyes of the young woman fixed on him from far across the table. It appeared she had yet another red fruit that she steadily consumed as their eyes locked.

How many of those does she have? Saef wondered. *Stashed in the pockets of her cloak? A cloak...? Maybe Claude was right and cloaks really are making a comeback....*

"What sort of ship will you command, Saef?" Anthea asked, jarring Saef from his idle pondering.

"They haven't said as yet, ma'am," Saef said.

"Probably a tug," Grimsby said.

"We've been told it will be a light frigate," Bess said.

All the voices murmured at once, but Grimsby's cut through: "Told by whom?"

Bess flicked barely a look at Grimsby. "Because of the sort of opportunity we now have, I will spare no effort of energy on obtaining success. That means a cash outlay for crew bonuses, N-space fab patterns, and all the rest."

"One disaster, Bess, one bad damned moment, and the entire investment's gone," Grimsby said.

Bess sighed, looking down at her hands resting on the table. "Listen, we all know the Family is dying. We are dying a slow death." She held up her hand, darkened and beginning to wrinkle with age. "No one knows this better than I."

Grimsby looked away uncomfortably. "Bess, we are all aging, too, but with that kind of investment in Trade, we could—"

Bess cut him off. "I have news for Trade, too. Perhaps I should have started with that and avoided all the...pointless discussion."

Grimsby and Richard shared a look and turned back to Bess.

"Just today I obtained several items from the List... the incoming List."

Grimsby's gloomy expression disappeared. "How...
how did you—?"

"But we must discuss one last issue of pressing
importance to the Family. And this brings us back to
today's duel," Bess said, turning from the stammering
Grimsby. "We received information that today's duel
was an arranged event to eliminate Saef."

Only Cabot and the strange young woman seemed
unfazed by this intelligence. Of course Kai, minutes
behind the conversation in Hawksgaard's asteroid
fastness, still frowned over the earlier bickering. And
the two leaders attending via QE comm could very
well be in matching comas for all their input.

"Apparently we have a rival of some sort who resents
this captaincy going to our Family." All eyes locked
on Bess. "The intel I received suggests that they are
heavyworlders, and they may attempt to eliminate Saef
by any means necessary."

"This Lars fellow's family, perhaps?" Grimsby offered
but Bess shook her head.

"Bigger than that."

"This is unheard of! Are they mad?" Eldridge
demanded.

"No," Anthea answered, staring levelly into the
invisible distance. "It's not unheard of... just old-
fashioned. We haven't faced this sort of threat in
many, many years."

"That's why I want security increased at every level,
every Family holding, every Net," Bess said. "Paranoia
is fashionable once again."

Richard grimaced at the comment, but he was far
too caught up with the idea of a true List from the

incoming Shaper armada to express any more negativity than that.

"Okay," Bess said, slapping the table lightly with both hands. "Two opportunities and an apparent enemy developing all at once. We will pursue all three as best we can. I believe it to be the only sensible course. Last word on this, anyone?"

"You're right," Cabot said, speaking for the first time. "This rebellion is our chance. We push now and succeed, or we watch while our people fade and die all around us."

Cabot looked around the room. As the eldest, and the former Family leader, he carried great weight. He nodded, and both QE comm feeds chirped at almost the same moment, spelling out the word AGREED on both screens.

"Very well," Bess said. "Hermes, push the Shaper List to Grimsby and Richard, please. And if you will all excuse us, I would like to discuss some details of the captaincy with Saef."

Everyone nodded and stood, moving toward the door, except the strange young woman, Saef, and Bess. The huge doors slid shut with finality.

"Saef, come nearer for an old woman, please. There's more to tell, and I'm afraid you're even more likely to be killed than I said." Bess smiled. "Would you like your dinner now?"

Chapter 6

"Every decision, every action or inaction,
every breath you take must serve the purpose
of attaining your ultimate goal...."

—Devlin Sinclair-Maru, *Integrity Mirror*

SAEF EYED THE STRANGE YOUNG WOMAN AS SHE
perched on the arm of a chair near Bess, one booted
leg swinging, but he did as Bess requested, taking a
seat near the two women.

"I'll eat later, m'lady. Hermes was going to send
something down..."

"Yes," Bess said. "Hermes has been pestering me
about it, but I wanted to wait. You don't contribute
enough when your mouth *isn't* full."

Saef shrugged. "Politicking isn't one of my strengths."

"As a Fleet captain, that must evolve, Saef."

He felt the unwavering focus of the strange young
woman's eyes upon him, and it felt oddly disconcerting. "Fortunately, there's a war," she said. "Less talk,
more action."

Saef finally looked up at the young woman. "I don't believe we've met," he said.

She smiled broadly, but the smile did not reach her eyes. Saef noted an almost feral, cat-like aspect to her slender face. Her teeth looked sharp and white as she said, "Oh, but we did!"

Saef regarded her fixed smile for a moment before looking back to Bess, who said, "This is Inga Maru."

Inga Maru.

Saef pursed his lips, thinking back fifteen years or so. Eldridge had brought Saef and several of his cousin classmates into a squalid section of Port City. He remembered the decay of condemned buildings, and wondered why any demi-cit would remain in such horrible straits, when modern, mod-housing stood available.

Then Saef recalled his shock when he saw the man greeting them, dressed in tattered clothes...a cheap old sword at his waist. This impoverished man was a Vested Citizen, clinging stubbornly to his citizen status rather than demoting and accepting the Imperial stipend and housing all demi-cits were entitled to.

And Saef remembered the man's three children, staring at him and his cousins, the strong, well-fed Sinclair-Maru. The oldest of the three children, he now recalled, was a starved-looking young girl with disordered blond hair and startling blue eyes. She had been holding something...What was it? A doll? A pet? He couldn't place it now, but he still felt the shock when he heard their surname: Maru. The poor blighted scrubs were distant relatives, bearing half the Family name, descendants of Mia Sinclair-Maru's brother. He also remembered the heartache he felt for their plight.

"I remember," Saef said, looking at her again. "We took you to the spaceport."

"Yes," Bess interjected, while Inga just smiled in her disconcerting way. "To Hawksgaard. She worked for me there these many years, and now she'll be working with you."

"Working *with* me," Saef said slowly, frowning.

"Yes. She's Fleet rated, and she'll serve as cox'n or mid in your new command."

Saef looked again at Inga sitting on the arm of the chair, her leg swinging, her cloak gathered about her. "She's old for a mid, and young for a cox'n."

"You'll make it work," Bess said.

"M'lady," Saef said, feeling his brow lower, "I have trained hard for this my whole life. Perhaps it would be better if I followed my own training in Fleet matters."

Inga continued to smile, unmoved, and Bess stared at him for a moment. "Hermes, seal the room, please," Bess said without taking her gaze off Saef.

"Yes, my lady," Hermes said. "This room is now sealed, and I am withdrawing." In his UI, Saef saw his connection to the Family Net disappear as Hermes killed all the signals to the room.

"Okay," Bess said. "The other part of the equation, now. I have agreed to enlist you as an intelligence resource for Imperial security."

Saef merely stared at her.

"In addition to your duties as a Fleet captain, you will be investigating a possible faction of heavyworlders in Fleet. You will be reporting your findings to . . . a highly placed Imperial operative via QE."

"Perhaps, m'lady," Saef said in a low voice, "you should have consulted with me on this matter first."

"Why? I obtained items from the List, and a shot at bringing a little Imperial favor back to the Family. What could you have to say about it?"

"I'm not well suited for this cloak-and-dagger nonsense—"

"Of course you're not, Saef. That's what Inga's for."

Saef glowered at Bess, then up at Inga, who just continued to smile. "And she *is* suited for it?"

"Trust me to know my tools well," Bess said. "I don't simply want you to succeed, Saef. I'm not just betting your life on this, I'm betting my life, too."

Saef gazed critically at Inga. "I would not wish to contradict you, m'lady, but surely vanity's not a job requirement for a spy. She's too thin to have spent the high-grav time for any kind of strength."

"Trust me. There are strengths you cannot see," Bess said. "But enough about that. She's got a Fleet rating. I want her with you all the time, so make it work."

Saef nodded his head stiffly, resigned. "As you wish, my lady."

"Very good. You'll be out of here tomorrow, on your way to Imperial City. I've had your effects gathered from command school and they'll be here by morning."

"Tomorrow, then," Saef said, beginning to rise.

"Wait," Bess said. She reverently lifted a small box of carved wood, placing it on the table between them. "This is for you."

Saef glanced curiously at both women before sliding the box nearer and opening the delicate lid. Within lay a flattened gray oval, about the size of his hand. It took Saef a moment to realize that he beheld a piece of legendary Shaper technology. His next thought was of the million credits or so that it represented.

"Old Devlin's shield generator," Saef said in a low voice, looking up to the fixed gaze from Bess.

"Yes."

"I can scarcely believe it is still in the Family."

"There are a few old treasures remaining even still. You will use this always. Like old Devlin said, 'the silent hand,' eh?"

Saef nodded. "It is a great honor, m'lady. But with this sold, you might afford rejuv."

Her eyes flashed suddenly. "I will not live and grow young while my siblings and cousins—our children—all wither and die!" She stared hard at Saef. "And neither will you. We both live or die on this one turn of the cards. You will be as hard to kill as I can contrive."

Saef nodded, feeling a sudden warmth. It might represent nothing more than pragmatism on the part of Bess, but it was by far the most personal and generous token the Family had ever bestowed upon Saef. "I understand. I will take it, then."

"Yes. Use it always," Bess said, calming. "It sips power from the standard Shaper cell very slowly. And once Hermes stops suppressing this signal, it will link with your UI."

Saef stood to his feet and inclined his head to Bess, then turned to Inga. "Mistress Maru, tomorrow we become shipmates, it appears."

Inga stopped swinging her leg and stood to her full height. She stood taller than she first appeared, and she looked Saef nearly eye-to-eye. "Yes, Commander," she said, her smile gone, her face still and serious. "We'll get on famously, you'll see."

"Perhaps," Saef said. "There is this whole chain of command, taking orders bit that we will need to explore. It's a funny old tradition in Fleet, and they're damnably stuck on the notion."

Inga's mouth quirked back to her smile. She mystified Saef by winking at him, producing another red fruit from somewhere, and settling back on the arm of the chair.

"Saef," Bess said, "only the three of us in this room will ever fully know Inga's role in your efforts. I will not inform the Imperials, and I suggest you follow suit. She'll serve as a cox'n with a degree of invisibility, I believe, and follow orders in that role rather admirably."

Saef felt far from certain in this, but nodded. "Very well, m'lady."

Bess stared appraisingly at him. "Trust me, Saef. I have raised her like family. Like Family. You know what that means."

Saef hesitated only a moment before nodding again, although he wasn't sure that he *did* know what it meant.

Chapter 7

"In deep waters, a calm surface may hide treacherous currents that lie beneath...."

—*Legacy Mandate* by Emperor Yung I

TWENTY HOURS LATER, INGA AND SAEF STROLLED through the airlock onto the quarterdeck of the *Goose*, a ten-thousand-ton inter-system freighter filled with Sinclair-Maru agricultural products. The days of starships wearing the Family crest were long gone, but the *Goose* operated under a long-term Sinclair-Maru lease, so it still provided safe, anonymous transport to Coreworld and its capital, Imperial City.

It struck Saef, as he stepped onto the Spartan companionway, he probably carried as much sheer credit value on his personal luggage as the ship's entire cargo was worth. With an Imperial QE comm, a kinetic body shield, and a crate of exotic fab materials, he should feel like a wealthy new Fleet captain, not the cash-strapped provincial that he knew himself to be.

The heavy sense of mounting responsibility threatened to choke him, and Saef fought down the weight, finding the Deep Man even as he made his way into the ship.

Saef's UI chirped as the *Goose* granted him user access to their internal Net, and with that access came a glowing wireframe overlaying his vision. It was no Fleet-level interface, but at least it allowed Saef to see the layout of the ship superimposed upon his natural sight.

A greeting from the captain followed, chirping his UI with a friendly message, and visual routing to their humble staterooms.

Inga paced quietly alongside, her head turning as she sized up every detail. She held a food bar in one hand, munching, and in the other she grasped the leash of her dumb-mech that scampered along behind carrying their substantial luggage. She wore her cloak like a perpetual uniform, always concealing her slender form beneath its dark fabric, one arm or the other emerging when called upon.

So far Saef really knew very little about her, his first crewmember.

Except that she must have the metabolism of a weasel, he thought to himself.

It was rare to see her without something edible in hand, at least in the brief time that he had known her.

They had departed Lykeios in the old family execu-jet, clambering from the manor's airfield, slowly toward orbit via the jet's mag-drives (figuratively sneering at so-called "escape velocity" along their leisurely way).

The *Goose* had done the rest, dropping down the well into a lower orbit to fetch the two passengers and their varied cargo.

Now, Saef knew from his System Guard service, it

would take a day or two of flight-lane jockeying on both ends of a quick N-space transition. That would bring them near Coreworld, to the massive orbital platform, Core Alpha, fixed at the top of the tether-way above Imperial City.

That is where everything changed, where the first of the Sinclair-Maru Family for many long years would receive a starship captaincy in Fleet. Even aside from the potential bounties of war, a starship captain possessed regular access to N-space during required transitions, and access to N-space, properly managed, equaled wealth.

"What do you think of *Goose* so far, Commander?" Inga asked as they approached the staterooms, situated in a short, dim corridor adjoining a tiny galley.

Saef actually thought the *Goose* an outmoded, colorless slug of a ship, but after a moment's hesitation he said, "For a freighter, it seems to have some rather nice features." He knew the godlike listening powers available to a starship captain, and formed his words with this in mind.

Inga stopped beside their doors, the dumb-mech clattering to a halt on its six legs and easing to the deck right beside her. She gave Saef one of her wide-eyed, expressionless looks for a bare moment, and an encrypted text message chirped into Saef's UI. Inga's bright smile flashed, and she turned to her door.

Saef read the message: AND YOU THOUGHT YOU HAD NO SKILL IN POLITICKING!

Saef found himself amused and somewhat impressed. It took a rare talent for someone to compose a message solely within her UI, with no visible muscle movements—not even her eyes—in less than two seconds.

"I look forward to a more technical opinion at some point, Commander," she said, opening the stateroom and herding the dumb-mech within. She snatched Saef's travel case from the pile of luggage on the mech's back, and set it at his feet.

"How long were you on Hawksgaard?" Saef inquired, thinking about how many vessels she had likely surveyed in her life.

Her smiled revealed the tips of her pointed white teeth. "It seemed like a thousand years, Commander." Her door closed.

Saef sighed, thinking that she could stand to learn how to properly answer a question.

Another text message chirped into Saef's vision: I'LL BE BORED TO TEARS, it read. HAVE ANY WORK FOR ME?

Work?

Saef thought about that as he hefted his travel case and stepped into his own small stateroom. He did have that stack of Fleet ratings seeking berths. Sorting them into some sort of order that he could sift for potential crew was a task that he didn't much welcome.

It was a moment's effort to pipe this crew file through *Goose*'s private Net to Inga's implant. He included the personal note: LOOKING FOR CREW. SORT INTO SOME SORT OF ORDER, IF YOU LIKE.

Inga's response was near instantaneous: WONDERFUL!

Saef had no idea if that represented a genuine sentiment or merely sarcasm. He shrugged to himself. The weight of his cares already piled so high, what was one more concern?

After getting situated in the small stateroom, Saef

began his own work, sifting through his much smaller digital field of potential bridge officers, even as he moved in the practiced steps of his shipboard exercise routine. The names and personnel briefs floated before his eyes in a stream of data, as a rivulet of sweat poured off his body. He wondered again if he was truly ready for the challenge before him. So many questions, so many unknowns...

For the first time in his life he found himself regarding heavyworld officers with anything other than a mild degree of respect. Their names, their blunt features leaped out to him as the information flickered across his vision. Every one of them now represented a potential enemy, and a potential source of intel so desperately sought by Imperial Security.

Though only about two percent of the Imperium's population, heavyworlders comprised nearly a fifth of Fleet officers, and more than half of all Imperial Marines. To exclude all heavyworld officers from whatever command they gave him would send a startlingly obvious flare into the firmaments of Fleet.

Also, it seemed likely that his cursed "spy" job might be doomed from the start if he didn't have some heavyworlders aboard to observe.

Saef's work, both physical and mental, paused as he received an incoming voice call: Claude Carstairs.

Saef thought for a moment before accepting the call.

"Disaster averted!" Claude announced in place of a greeting.

"What?" Saef asked.

"And you didn't say a word," Claude continued unchecked. "Just like the time when I thought body paint was all the rig. You said nothing. Nothing!

Remember, old fellow? And I made cursed cake of myself."

"What did I say nothing about this time, Claude? There are so many things I don't say that I don't quite recall."

"The kilt."

"Beg pardon?"

"My fabulous kilt. It was going to be my...my—damn! There's a word for it...My own signature contribution to fashion. What's that word?"

"I really have no idea, Claude."

"Well...one of those. But my poor legs," Claude mourned. "They really don't pull it off. Look rather paltry dangling about down below, if you can credit it. You always said I should muck about more in the high-grav, like you."

"That's true," Saef agreed.

"I say!" Claude exclaimed. "The kilt! It would be perfect for you. You've got the legs for it, and the way you go slashing about with your beastly little sword, no one would dare laugh at you."

"I don't think so, Claude."

"Oh, but you must. Think of the immortality a fashion leader enjoys. Think of that frumpy, boorish family image you have hanging about your neck like a...a...a rhinoceros!"

"Albatross, I think, is the word you're looking for, Claude."

"What? Daresay you're right. About your neck!" Claude declared. "Frumpy, bellicose, backward, boring—"

"I get your point, Claude."

"—old-fashioned, almost bestial. Poof! Gone...With your *new* look...the new Sinclair-Maru look."

"Uniforms, Claude, remember? I'm set for life."

"Oh yes," Claude said in a dejected tone. "That's right. And I take it you're not coming to my party?"

"Uh . . . no," Saef said. "I've got to head to Imperial City for my commissioning."

"Right away? Off to duty and glory and a damned fine uniform, eh?"

As Claude spoke, Saef felt a slight shiver in the deck beneath his feet. Artificial gravity concealed their acceleration beautifully, but the initial engine burn transferred through the deck in these old "tin-can" spacers. The *Goose* was leaving Battersea orbit.

"Well, yes," Saef said. "Hopefully glory, and yes, very soon."

"Ah, Imperial City!" Claude said. "I haven't been there for years. As I remember, the parties there are *scandalous*. Scandalous! Delightful place. I shall visit you."

Saef almost laughed. "Remember, Claude, I'll hopefully be off on Fleet business most of the time."

"Of course, of course. Dashing about, saving people, blasting things. Such fun! And when you return, you'll find me waiting. And I'll be dressed amazingly."

"But not in a kilt."

"Gods no! I haven't the legs for it, I tell you."

Saef smiled. "I look forward to it. Send a message ahead and I'll clean a piece of floor for you."

"Not likely. I've seen your quarters—Oh! I almost forgot to tell you. Today, some poor sod moving into your old quarters at command school had some sort of remote explode his face. Boom!"

Saef felt the smile slide from his own face. "How strange."

"Strange?" Claude demanded. "Downright uncivil, I say. Good thing it wasn't *your* face that exploded, eh? Scowl and all, it'd be a waste."

"I agree," Saef said. "I am rather attached to it."

"Daresay. A uniform—even a Fleet uniform— wouldn't look at all right without it."

"I really couldn't agree more, Claude." Saef shook his head, thinking. "I really must be going, my friend."

"Oh very well, old fellow," Claude said. "Keep the kilt in mind, will you? Just marinate on immortality."

"Mortality will certainly be on my mind." Saef ended the call.

After a moment of contemplation he resumed his exercise, but he did not return to his staff work. Instead, he contemplated the unpleasant subtleties of assassination; another weight upon his shoulders.

Chapter 8

"A leader is merely the one at the front of
the column, leading the way into excellence,
or decadence ... or mediocrity."

—*Legacy Mandate* by Emperor Yung I

WHEN THE ALIEN SLAGGERS ATTACKED HUMANITY
back in 5196, the standard method of inter-system
warfare was well established. The fleet of then-Emperor Khan Li numbered ninety vessels capable of
interstellar travel, each equipped with a stack of fast
nuclear missiles, a beam weapon or two (for close-range desperation), and sand cannon to create crude
defensive screens of flying silica "teeth."

When battle was joined in those early years, nukes
were launched, sand cannon spewed, and ships accelerated under crushing g-forces, squeezing the human
crews to unconsciousness, as elementary autopilots
attempted to escape from the other side's nukes.

By the time humanity finally crushed the Slaggers

(after less than a century of warfare), costly antimissile missiles were standard equipment, along with more refined defensive beam weapons, but otherwise space battle remained the same game of high speeds, huge nuclear barrages, and crushing acceleration.

When the Shapers arrived, all that swiftly changed.

Artificial gravity meant that incapacitating acceleration was a thing of the past, while dampers suppressed nukes and other high-explosive reactions at a survivable distance. Shield generators deflected kinetic projectiles, micro-asteroids and most radiation with equal facility.

Instead of long range, launch-and-run combat, the new *theory* leaned toward "close-range" slug matches, with weapons raking opposing ships until heat sinks and shield generators failed. Then boarding penetrators packed with Marines could be employed, or the opposing ship could simply be shredded where it lay. Since starships became the largest repositories of Shaper tech outside direct Imperial oversight, they were not lightly wasted.

Although the "new" theories of space battle remained largely untested in actual combat, simulation models drove Fleet toward larger and larger warships, mounting ever more firepower to overwhelm any theoretical enemy's shields. Centuries before, in the war against the Slaggers, a large vessel simply meant a bigger target that was harder to accelerate. The largest missile carriers in those days enclosed ten thousand imperial tons, while current Fleet battleships averaged over one hundred thousand tons, and a few new ships rose to nearly five hundred thousand tons.

The standing view held that hulls were cheap. It was all the Shaper tech that came so dear. Fleet relied entirely upon the Shapers for N-drives, shield generators, and artificial gravity generators, along with Shaper fuel to power them all. Dampers, crystal computer stacks, and smart alloy had all fallen to human reverse engineering efforts through the years. Of course, all Fleet officers—or nearly all—carried Shaper implantables in their skulls, too, illustrating exactly who enabled Fleet growth and development.

The fact that the Shapers had apparently not heard of planned obsolescence represented a tremendous boon. Most Shaper hardware functioned for centuries, but consumables, such as power cells, nanotech, and rejuv elements disappeared into the pool of humanity, and the population of 139 worlds hungered for more and more Shaper handiwork.

In the midst of this crescendo of demand, the Ericson Cluster staged a sudden uprising, seized dozens of Fleet warships, and crushed a few more in the frenzied combat of the first few days. The Tyra system fell a day later, with little resistance, its vast orbital platform and tether nearly a duplicate of Core Alpha.

The Emperor, it was said, was apoplectic, and as a result the Fleet Admiralty Board expressed fury and outrage, and generally tried to act busy.

The physical result of their busy-ness involved dispatching powerful task forces to systems deemed "at risk" by the intelligence types. One such system was Skold.

Skold possessed a useful, friendly star, a lush, populated planet, a rich asteroid belt, and a very advanced orbital processing station. Its system defenses amounted to little more than a nuisance by modern standards: two intrasystem cutters, four QE sensor posts, and two old defense platforms.

In the view of Task Force Commodore Thiel, Skold's defenses provided a small selection of methods to die heroically, and little else. Fortunately, the Fleet task force he commanded entered the Skold system with a much more substantive mix of tools. He stood on the bridge of his flagship, the seventy-five-thousand-ton *Titan*, a reinforced heavy cruiser mounting a vast array of modern weapons, and as he turned his head left and right, his command UI panned, displaying the glowing icons of his other flotilla members. My *command*, he proudly thought.

As if on cue, his UI indicated each of the vessels powering their shield generators up, the standard Fleet procedure upon transitioning through to a target system.

The two destroyers, *Ramses* and *Medusa*, represented his most powerful assets, like scalpels for a field surgeon. Though both vessels had served Fleet for over a century, Commodore Thiel well knew the weight of weaponry they both mounted, but more than that, he knew both captains very well.

Captain Susan Roush was one of the only Fleet officers to cross swords with the rebels in this weeks-old war, so technically the only officer in his task force with any *real* combat experience. Her previous ship, scorched and hulled, lay at the Strand orbital yard for refit . . . or salvage. Thiel considered himself fortunate to get Captain Roush in a good ship and his task force.

Thiel's own combat experience, serving as a Fleet officer for more than forty years, amounted to trading shots with a pirate on one occasion, and with a smuggler on another.

Captain Roush, on the other hand, had managed to extricate her ship from the ambush at Ericson Two on the first day of the rebellion, and every officer in Fleet had watched and rewatched the vidstream of her running battle to escape. That after-action vidstream graphically displayed the only actual combat between modern warships ever recorded, and every Fleet officer had watched the eight-hour drama with a dry mouth. Most truthful officers admitted that several moments of the vidstream, such as Captain Roush's terse command to "vent deck three to vac before we fucking explode!" haunted their dreams.

Of course all Fleet officers took part in very realistic simulations as a key part of regular training, but this gritty vidstream surpassed anything they ever simulated or imagined. The undercurrent of fear recorded in every voice, the shrill curses, even the short, desperate cries of pain as Roush's Marines got shredded—these created a stark, unfamiliar palette coloring this fresh canvas of war. Here, the new white stars of Roush's desperate antimatter charges, the ruby flickers of enemy beam weapons cascading across her failing shields, and her regular orders, should have seemed familiar territory from countless simulations. It wasn't.

Commodore Thiel felt nothing but respect for Captain Susan Roush, even before watching the Ericson battle vidstream. He had known her for many years, and he knew her to be a very capable, efficient, and frugal officer, making every effort to keep expenditures to a minimum, just like the Admiralty demanded. She apparently needed her captain's efficiency bonus just as much as he needed his commodore's efficiency bonus.

Hopefully, Thiel thought, his need for such unpleasant economizing might soon be over . . . if only the rebels chose to attack the Skold system soon. . . .

His bounty on even one captured vessel could be in the millions, if he was so blessed as to encounter a sufficiently substantial enemy. He began to calculate what the commodore's percentage would be on, say, a thirty-thousand-ton destroyer, even as he observed the last three vessels of his task force power up their shields and begin closing ranks.

Transitioning to and from N-space required considerable "sea room," with very little mass allowed near any vessel entering or exiting the N-space envelope. Scientists, after centuries of study, still did not know if this was some sort of Shaper safeguard, or if it demonstrated some real quality of N-space physics. The end result meant making all transitions some distance from any planetary gravity well, and spreading formations far apart during transitions. Fortunately "far apart" meant only fractions of a light-second between ships.

His last three ships were not as impressive as the *Ramses* and *Medusa*, with two old light frigates and an equally aged expedition force carrier. The carrier, *Bulldog*, possessed few qualities Commodore Thiel valued in any imagined battle. Its Marines *could* prove useful, but its atmosphere-capable fighters, launch ships, and tiny shield generators seemed almost pathetic anachronisms in modern warfare. Its large supply of missiles and drones added some capability to his force, but they also represented one more ship he would need to divide any bounty with. If he had to share loot, he wanted to share with a ship that would actually contribute to the lightning victories he dreamed of.

The two small frigates, *Knight* and *Daimyo*, were much better equipped for a modern battle, in Thiel's opinion, but they were both tiny by modern standards; just four thousand and five thousand tons respectively.

He knew the frigate, *Daimyo*, intimately well. He had served aboard her as a young mid nearly fifty years before. His initials would still be carved on her inner-hull access panel to this day if the nosy ship Intelligence hadn't ratted him out almost as soon as he had finished carving.

Though composed of older ships (none but the *Titan* constructed of smart alloy), Commodore Thiel still knew he commanded a powerful force. Out of the 1,800 commissioned Fleet vessels currently serving the Imperium, *Titan* ranked as the 190th most powerful vessel. The rebellion only possessed a handful of ships more powerful, and combined with his other ships, Commodore Thiel felt more than comfortable meeting nearly any individual rebel ship, and crushing them.

"Sensor returns are beginning to log, Commodore," the ensign at sensors announced.

Thiel could have set his command UI to show sensor returns, and nearly every other input or output of the ship, but over the many years of his command experience, he found all the constant flashes, ripples, alerts, and updates behind his eyelids to be quite unnecessary...and a cause of migraines, honestly. That's what bridge officers were for. His own UI provided the most basic overlay for his task force members, then as he turned his gaze across the bridge, the overlay of the officer names and dispositions scrolled past his eyes. Beyond them, Thiel set his command UI to simply display status colors in individual departments. The only exception to this being the detailed readout on his private pantry. Trying to keep those sly devils from siphoning off any more of his expensive liquor stores seemed an impossible task. No matter how long he kept a clerk, or a cox'n or a personal chef, they all seemed to be eventually drawn like magnets to his liquor. The ship Intelligence *should* be bright enough to figure out warranted versus unwarranted access to the liquor, but on new vessels, the ship Intelligences often lacked the rich dataset of human observations to develop much horse sense. *Titan*'s Intelligence was as thick as a whale sandwich, Thiel thought.

"Put sensor returns on the holo, Ensign," Thiel commanded.

"Aye, returns on the holo, sir."

Upon entering the Skold system, all passive sensors placed everything where it belonged without adding objects of concern. The four QE sensor posts all apparently functioned, the defense platforms orbiting Skold Three without distress. Now the active sensors began receiving return waves from those blasted into the system the moment they transitioned in-system. Of course most active sensors faced the limiting factor of the speed of light, and those sensors not so limited were, unfortunately, not very useful either.

The active sensor image resolving on *Titan*'s holo tank struck Commodore Thiel like a blow. He stared at the holo for a long, frozen moment, peripherally hearing startled gasps from his bridge crew.

The holo revealed a number of new shapes that had apparently materialized in the Skold system in the last thirty minutes or so.

Commodore Thiel couldn't be sure what ships he faced, since Shaper shield generators could inhibit many active sensor waves just as they inhibited most other forms of radiation, but some of the ships appeared to be sizeable.

Eight ships. Eight probable enemy ships.

Thiel finally spoke. "Transmit to task force: eight enemy ships sighted. Prepare to engage," Thiel ordered, his voice sounding more solid than he felt. What ships did he face? Surely the rebels wouldn't send any great force to a system so poorly defended...would they?

"Sensors, give me optical soundings on those targets, now."

"Aye, sir," the ensign replied with a quavering voice.

Thiel turned to his left, his UI focused on *Medusa* and highlighted. "*Medusa*, accelerate at twenty gees, deviate on this heading"—he touched his command panel—"in three hundred seconds. Engage the enemy on your own initiative."

Thiel heard Captain Susan Roush reply with a terse affirmative, her ship already torching ahead of the squadron, but he was turning to the pathetic old *Bulldog*, his UI locking onto its icon. "*Bulldog*, deploy drones and first missile salvo, accelerate at six gees. Link up with Skold orbital defenses and hold."

Bulldog affirmed, and Thiel observed the small swarm of missiles floating slowly out from the aged carrier. Its four drones rocketed ahead toward the enemy as Thiel ordered *Knight* and *Daimyo* into an intercept path that mirrored *Medusa*. Together the two small frigates might form the opposite force in a pincer attack...depending on what the enemy was doing.

He would keep *Ramses* on station with *Titan*.

With his orders set, his squadron in motion, and

sensor data tricking in, Thiel began to feel his heart rate just starting to settle back down. He had at least thirty minutes before any ship closed sufficiently for action.

"Very well." Commodore Thiel had initially received a nasty start, finding eight enemies suddenly materialized before his eyes. It had not felt at all as he had often imagined; his avarice for financial bounty an hour before now felt childish. For a long moment he felt only the steady thump of his heart and an undercurrent of unease.

Thiel's UI chirped with a private message from Captain Roush. Her ship still accelerated hard, but she was less than a light-second ahead of *Titan* thus far. He accepted the message, his unease growing.

COMMODORE, Roush's message said, I AM SURE YOU HAVE REALIZED THE ENEMY ANTICIPATED THE MOMENT OF OUR ARRIVAL, SO THEY MUST SURELY KNOW OUR STRENGTH. I AM UNEASY. THAT IS ALL. ROUSH, OUT.

Ice poured into Commodore's Thiel's veins, his heart rate soaring back up. Calm, calm... If he had not been so overset with his initial surprise and panic, he would have—should have—realized that whatever force the rebels sent to Skold it would be enough... more than enough for them.

He tried to get a grip on his rattled nerves, to think clearly.

"To squadron: belay acceleration. Begin calculation for N-space transition to Core." As he said the words, Thiel knew he may have just doomed his entire military career. The Admiralty Board might view this as cowardice. One could never be sure.

All thoughts of the Admiralty Board disappeared a moment later, to be replaced by more immediate, pointed concerns.

"Sir!" the sensor ensign almost screamed. "New sensor contact at one-one-four right azimuth, one-two-zero positive, range is...is three hundred thousand klicks and closing!"

The ice around his heart deepened. What could he do? What was it? What first?

"It's...it's big, sir."

The ever-calm voice of *Titan*'s Intelligence chimed in, "New contact at one-one-four is a Dreadnought-class battleship, Commodore."

Dreadnought! It had transitioned from N-space almost on top of them, about as close as the drive would permit. How had it managed that timing?

"Commodore?" the XO called with a pinched voice.

Three hundred thousand klicks? Close. He had no room. An ambush.

"Commodore?"

Thiel ignored the XO and stared at the holo. "To squadron: disperse and transition if possible."

"Commodore?" The XO stood at Thiel's side now, her face white, frightened. Thiel looked at her, then through her.

"To *Ramses*," he said, and he felt surprised that his voice sounded so calm, "emergency acceleration. Break away if you can."

"Commodore!" the XO quavered. "Shouldn't we calculate our transition? We can still get away."

"Launches!" Sensors yelled out. "Inbound missiles."

"Weps," Thiel commanded, continuing to ignore his XO, "bring that salvo *Bulldog* laid down, and drop a dozen antimatter mines in our wake. Detonate when we're clear. Point defenses go to work."

"Commodore," the XO grabbed his sleeve, "we might still get clear. Shall we calculate a transition?"

Thiel looked down at her hand distractedly, shaking loose. As he stared at her he said, "Sensors? Range to the Dreadnought?"

"Two hundred twenty thousand klicks, sir," the sensor ensign replied.

"See?" Thiel said. "There's no running for us. We can't transition with that great hulk here so close. He may even have enough mass in missiles to block us."

As if on cue, they felt the steady thumping of the dampers begin, working away on inbound missiles, suppressing their explosive reactions. One missile reached them and careened off *Titan's* kinetic shields, spinning away into the blackness. The XO staggered back, pale, her head shaking in disbelief.

"This Dreadnought is the *Zeus*?" Thiel asked, but he already knew the answer.

"Yes, Commodore," the ship Intelligence responded.

Only six Dreadnought-class vessels had emerged from the mighty Imperial shipyards, and the rebels possessed only one.

How sadly appropriate, Thiel thought. *Zeus* destroys the *Titan*.

Ramses still torched away at a shallow angle, trying to run for a transition point, while the two frigates, *Knight* and *Daimyo*, along with the carrier, *Bulldog*, all had plenty of room to transition. Thiel felt especially glad that *Bulldog* could make it away. The two thousand Marines wedged aboard embodied pure helplessness in a fight such as this.

In *Titan*'s wake the antimatter mines detonated beautifully about halfway between the approaching *Zeus* and *Titan*. Mines employed advanced stealth materials, and in all the rocketry their launch might not have been detected by *Zeus*. Thiel hoped it was a surprise as the dozen expanding white spheres shimmered into small glowing suns, greedily consuming all missiles streaming toward them. *Zeus* disappeared behind the curtains of cascading energy.

"Weps," Thiel commanded, "target on their last known position. Fire everything as we come about. Nav, bring us broadside."

Like all modern warships, *Titan* was constructed to make optimal use of Shaper shield generator technology. Gone were the days of spherical, ovoid, or any distributed "pod-type" hulls. Any new warship hulls must enable coverage using as few shield generators as possible, and enable Fleet captains to angle their ships so enemies faced plenty of armament without offering much target surface in return. This initially resulted in hulls that resembled flattened chocolate bars and, more recently, in wedge-shaped hulls. Aside from the practicalities, most Fleet officers found the newer wedge shapes to be much more appealing to the eye.

The wedge shape of *Titan* rotated in place, continuing to move away from the shrinking globes of scorching antimatter at the same .05 C velocity it held since entering the system. When its armored broadside faced directly into its wake, *Titan* finally unleashed its fury.

Thiel felt the slight jolt even through the artificial gravity and smart alloy hull, and heard the staccato chatter faintly resonating.

Two patterns of missiles fishtailed "below" the plane of fire and raced off, back toward the ever-shrinking glow of the antimatter mines, while the four gauss cannon fired three scorching salvos per second. *Titan*'s beam weapons optimally locked and focused at a very precise point in space, but the gunnery logic estimated the range of their opponent, still invisible behind the antimatter explosions. They fired, stabbing back through the murk.

As the beam batteries charged for another shot, the *Zeus* appeared. It came through, torch first, dumping velocity hard, its point defenses flickering through the blackness, trying to chew up everything that *Titan* threw at it.

Titan's beam weapons reached out again, splashing, diffused across *Zeus*'s hull, and gauss fire careened off in brilliant fireworks, all largely quenched by powerful shields.

Titan's Intelligence clarified and magnified the optical feed, filling the holo with their massive foe. Despite the fact that outgoing torches of missiles provided the only frame of reference for scale, *Zeus* looked enormous to Thiel's eyes. Perhaps it was only because he knew *Zeus* outmassed and outgunned *Titan* by a factor of three, making it the most powerful vessel in rebel hands.

Thiel numbly observed *Titan*'s continuous barrage streaming into *Zeus*, knowing that the destructive power *Zeus* shrugged off could blacken an entire planet.

Zeus's torch disappeared and she rotated, slowly bringing more of its batteries to bear on *Titan*, but as the rotation began Thiel saw the stab of *Titan*'s beam weapons streak out again, and instead of splashing harmlessly across *Zeus*'s shields, a glowing white ring appeared on her smart-alloy hull, a barely visible puff of misty ejecta spewing forth.

"A hit!" Weps yelled out. "We got through."

Thiel clenched his fist. *Please let their shields fall, and I can still pull something out of this.*

"Focus fire!" he shouted, but *Zeus* continued to rotate away, and with nearly a half light-second of range, any chance to probe that weak spot disappeared. Now *Titan* faced the squat, armored flank of *Zeus* where the shield strength overlapped. They also faced the brunt of offensive weapons now lining up on them.

"Show me a track on *Zeus*," Thiel commanded, feeling a strange detachment as fear slowly drained out of him.

The holo displayed a visual path relative to *Titan*. Unless *Zeus* engaged her engines again, she would continue to overtake *Titan*, passing a relative stone's throw "above" *Titan*, undoubtedly on a steady rotation to keep the armored broadside bearing as they traversed.

"Optical view, please," Thiel said in a calm voice that he hardly recognized.

Zeus completed her rotation as *Titan*'s rippling fire continued to careen off her shields.

"Nav, give me ten gees now," Thiel said. Maybe it would help displacing a little, since *Titan* had not maneuvered at all thus far.

Thiel couldn't feel any sensation of movement as the *Titan* accelerated, but he also couldn't feel the torrent of fire *Zeus* suddenly unleashed. It rained upon them visibly and invisibly. Beam weapons washed over *Titan*'s shields, heating the hull almost red hot, and projectiles of various kinds began to arrive seconds later, skipping from their shields like fat multicolored sparks.

In this spell of unreal stillness, Thiel suddenly

asked, "What's the damage assessment for our hit on *Zeus*?" Maybe they had managed to strike a drive component, and he could maneuver away even now.

"Damage assessment based upon a probable weapon penetration of sixteen meters on deck four," *Titan's* Intelligence said, "indicates a likely destruction of heat-sink banks ten through twenty."

No miraculous escape after all.

As the incoming fire seemed to surround them, Thiel asked, "How're our heat sinks holding up?"

"Not good, Commodore," the XO said, her composure hanging by a thread. "We won't last four hundred seconds before shield generators begin to fail."

Thiel thought for a moment, his eyes fixed on the optical field of their enemy, flicking in the exchange of destructive energies. In the back of his awareness he noticed the UI alert of his private liquor stores being pilfered once again; his cox'n likely on a desperate mission to die drunk.

"Where's that salvo *Bulldog* left for us?" he asked.

"Th-they're inbound, silent, at one-two-zero left azimuth, two-zero negative, range about two-hundred thousand, velocity is—"

"I see," Thiel interrupted, looking at the holo where *Titan's* Intelligence helpfully added the track for the cluster of nukes. "Bring them in and—"

A hollow clang rang through *Titan* and a momentary change in air pressure caused Thiel's ears to pop. His heartbeat surged as he gulped to clear his ears.

"Damage?"

"Penetrator damage, deck one galley and food storage," the ship Intelligence immediately reported. "One crew fatality."

"Okay, okay," Thiel said, thinking furiously. "Bring the *Bulldog's* salvo in, spread and daisy chain just outside *Zeus's* damper range."

"Al-alright—I mean, yes sir," Weps stammered. "What's the range of their dampers?"

The ship Intelligence said nothing, so Thiel answered. "Say a third greater range than our own. Should be a safe margin."

Another loud bang resonated through the ship. Before Thiel could ask, the ship Intelligence said, "Missile impact. Dampened, and failed to penetrate flank armor."

"Commodore!" the XO yelled. "All dry-side heat sinks are at redline!"

"Thank you, XO," Thiel said.

Another dampened missile bulled through their shields, impacting without penetrating the thick smart-alloy flank armor. The *Zeus* coasted rapidly nearer.

"Sir," the sensor officer said, "*Zeus* is rotating its broadside away."

Thiel heard the relieved tone of voice and the exhales from around the bridge as much of the enemy's weaponry began to turn from them, but Thiel gripped a sterling moment of clarity and yelled, "Nav! Keep us dry side to dry side. Do it! Full emergency acceleration."

Titan's torch exploded into life, launching them into massive acceleration, having much greater distance to cover than *Zeus*, but their broadside bombardment did not relent as they looped relative to the galactic plane, nearly keeping pace with *Zeus*.

"Weps," Thiel ordered, "get *Bulldog's* nukes on her dry side before we come over. She'll keep rotating to hide that flank from us, and we can't possibly keep up long."

"Yes sir. Twenty seconds out."

"Continuous launch our entire battery! Forget patterns, just target everything on their dry side and launch!"

"Commodore! Heat sinks are failing!" the XO yelled, and another loud bang rattled their bones.

"Missile penetration on deck two. Damped. Sealed. Two crew fatalities."

The golden glow of thirty tiny new fifty-megaton stars cut sharp black shadows across *Zeus* and *Titan* as the salvo of nukes left behind by the decrepit old *Bulldog* finally got into the action. Though by old measurement standards each nuke yielded only about fifty megatons of explosive force, the big benefit at this moment arose from sheer thermal energy.

Zeus continued to corkscrew to keep its wounded flank from *Titan's* Olympian broadsides, and rotated right into the mounting shower of infrared radiation from old *Bulldog's* nukes.

Titan's entire missile arsenal leaped from the racks and launchers, tracing the shrinking distance to *Zeus* in a stream of fishtailing arcs, curving to impact the targeted flank of *Zeus*.

"Shield failure!" the XO screamed. "Generator one and two—" Her voice could not compete with the staccato ring of hull penetrations and the wave of heat that washed over the bridge crew.

"Penetrator damage on decks one, two and three," the ship Intelligence calmly tolled. "Beam weapon damage of—"

"Keep firing everything on *Zeus*, damn it!" Thiel

shouted over the top of startled oaths, cries, and the ship's frank monologue.

"—thirty-one crew fatalities," the ship Intelligence finished reporting.

Another crash resounded and Thiel felt a muffled explosion, but he watched the optical display as *Titan*'s outgoing fire suddenly scored two clean hits on the behemoth target, the white glowing pits in the enemy hull touching Thiel like precious gifts. Streams of *Titan*'s missiles began impacting now, too, their explosive charges damped but their kinetic energy unabated.

Nukes, antimissile missiles, sod busters, chase missiles—these all began smashing into the vast hull of *Zeus*, or fell to the flickering point defenses striving to kill every incoming projectile.

Thiel saw one of *Titan*'s energy-weapon batteries burn a clean hole amidships and a dozen missiles strike home, but felt an answering shock through the deck beneath his feet.

"Nav, cease acceleration," Thiel ordered, hearing the ship Intelligence detailing twenty new impacts in the background of his thinking.

"Weps, keep firing as *Zeus* rotates."

Thiel smelled smoke and ozone.

"Sir, three ships inbound and closing!" Sensors yelled.

Thiel watched the optical feed as *Zeus* rolled its crumpled side away from them. *Titan*'s remaining weapons peppered the broad expanse revealed to them, and Thiel's heart fell as he saw each hit flash upon strong shields.

He didn't hesitate. "XO, transmit our surrender. Weps, cease firing and redirect all outbound missiles."

Both bridge officers affirmed, and Thiel sat back on his command seat, his hands beginning to shake. At least he had clawed *Zeus* well above his weight.

"Commodore," the ship Intelligence said in a tone that sounded strangely solicitous, "I'm afraid your private pantry was struck by enemy fire. Your liquor was destroyed. One crew fatality."

Thiel's cox'n at least—drunk, then dead—achieved his goals.

From her position over a million klicks from *Titan*, Captain Susan Roush captured the entire battle and the resulting surrender as she ran all out, the final Fleet vessel left standing yet again.

She could have made her transition at any time in the last thousand seconds or so, but she had sent a salvo of nukes back toward *Zeus*, and she wanted to record the battle for Fleet Intel if she could.

She only contemplated for a moment before redirecting her nukes toward her two pursuers angling to cut off her transition.

She knew Thiel had experienced tremendous luck in his battle with *Zeus*, and she pondered the outcome had *Medusa* remained to fight beside *Titan* as the other eight rebel vessels streamed in on them.

As persuasive as it seemed, she felt reasonably sure that all the ships in the Fleet task force couldn't have beat *Zeus*, or only just beat her. *Zeus* would have destroyed *Bulldog* and the frigates in seconds, overwhelming their shields, then it would have been *Ramses* and *Medusa* alongside *Titan*. Without Thiel's lucky hit, even then *Zeus* would have pulverized them.

But with that lucky hit?

Maybe. They certainly could have kept *Zeus* from rolling the wounded flank away from fire.

"Captain, enemy missiles are only a short distance from blocking our transition," Sensors said with a nervous tremor in his voice.

Captain Roush took one last look at the holo, then nodded. "Very well. Submit the N-space calcs. Transition to Core."

She would see what the Admiralty thought about it all in a few days.

Chapter 9

"Preparation for conflict is first psychology, viewing action through the eyes of your foe, then it is merely the pessimistic estimation of the possible."

—Devlin Sinclair-Maru, *Integrity Mirror*

SAEF AWAKENED THE INSTANT HIS UI FLASHED behind his eyelids. For a moment as he looked up to the stark ceiling of his cabin, he wondered if he was back on the intrasystem cutter he commanded back at Battersea.

The overlay of his UI quickly reminded him: the *Goose*.

Claude had called (chattering about his damned kilt, and, *oh yes*, a deadly explosion), then Saef had completed his workout, showered, and caught a few hours of sleep. The UI timer showed he had slept for exactly four hours.

His UI also displayed a low-priority message from Inga, received an hour earlier.

Saef sat up on the Spartan bunk and threw his legs over as he opened the message. It only provided a link to the crew-rating file he had sent her . . . six hours ago.

Frowning, Saef opened the link. He figured this must signal some insubordination by refusing to even *try* sorting through the stack of Fleet ratings, even though she had asked for it. He *knew* this situation with Inga was going to be a command nightmare.

Saef's first jolt of surprise came in the instant he opened the file. She had clearly arranged the stack of ratings, because her own Fleet file now topped the list, and Saef found himself looking at Inga's image in Fleet uniform, the details of her standard Fleet CV scrolling beneath. Saef felt suddenly self-conscious sitting naked on the edge of his bunk with Inga's image not quite smiling at him, so he pushed the file aside, hit the shower, and dressed. He pulled on his boots just as the *Goose* made its N-space transition. He paused, feeling and seeing the effects of N-space all around him. The subtle brightening of light, an iridescence on some surfaces, and a polarized appearance on others—these were the external signs of the transition. Faint warmth emanating from the implant in his skull represented the only internal indication.

Saef shrugged off the sensations. It wasn't his first transition.

He reopened the crew file to Inga's CV and half-smiling image, and he began to read in detail: rated in crystal computer systems, rated in signals intelligence, advanced degree in psychology from Battersea University, one year System Guard service with highest marks, and then she made the cut in Fleet selection. The CV listed her age as twenty-five standard, but that didn't seem to add up. Saef grunted, thinking back fifteen years to that young girl with her hair in disarray, clutching something in her arms...a doll or something, seeming so very pathetic.

Yes, her age would be about right, but her accomplishments in just fifteen years? Had Bess doctored her CV somehow?

At the bottom of the file Inga had affixed a personal note: THIS CANDIDATE IS RECOMMENDED. I KNOW HER VERY WELL, AND DESPITE CERTAIN MINOR FLAWS, SHE IS EXTREMELY RELIABLE AND NOTED FOR HER CLOAK-AND-DAGGER SKILLS. THE REMAINDER OF THIS RATING LIST I ORGANIZED IN ORDER OF CANDIDATES THAT I FIND MOST PROMISING.

Saef couldn't help smiling a little at that, and continued flipping through the stack of ratings to see what criteria she might have used to sort *all* the ratings so very quickly.

The next CV displayed a distinguished engineering rating. At the bottom of the engineer's CV Saef found a lengthy note Inga affixed that explained her reasons for placing this fellow at the top of the stack.

Saef flipped to the next CV and scanned down to the bottom: Another note from Inga. He quickly continued through the first dozen, finding a comment from Inga on every rating. The next dozen or so carried at least a single line from Inga. One such note on a rating said, SOMETHING ODD ABOUT THIS BLIGHTER, BUT GREAT MARKS. WHAT DO YOU THINK?

Saef's UI chirped as he felt the transition back into normal space. It recalled him to the present moment, and he set aside the crew file, perplexed. She really had sifted the entire file, it appeared, and that must have taken all night. It provided a puzzlingly different picture of her, particularly combined with the information contained in her CV, if that was truly accurate.

Saef hadn't even realized that Inga's CV was among the collection of available ratings.

Still frowning, Saef opened his cabin door just as Inga's cabin door slid open. She looked as fresh as a person could hope, dressed in her Fleet uniform and boots, her eyes wide as ever and her face untouched by any hint of fatigue.

"Good morning, Commander," she greeted with her half smile.

"Morning, Maru," he replied, somewhat self-consciously. "I just glanced at that crew file. Thanks for the help. I'll sift it more later."

"You're welcome, sir," she said primly, but Saef thought he saw a hint of mockery in her expression.

Saef paused a bare instant then nodded and turned toward the small galley and its equally small food-fab. "Hungry?" Saef asked.

"I broke my fast already, but I'll join you if that's an invite."

"Well, indeed...excellent," Saef said, feeling strangely out of his normal depth. "How'd you find their fab?"

They stepped into the tiny galley and Saef immediately detected the pleasing scent of real coffee.

"Oh, you'll be pleasantly surprised, I think," she said. "The marmalade tastes real, the eggs, the toast. All very nice. And Fleet-style coffee, too!"

Saef smiled, lifting a mug from the lock rack. "You must have worked up quite the appetite reading all those dull files, eh?"

Inga waved a dismissive hand, took a mug, and

leaned back against a bulkhead. "That was fun. I like to stay busy."

Saef breathed in the steam as he sampled the coffee. Inga had it right . . . Fleet-style coffee: thick, black and salted. "Fun? If that's fun, what's tedious, then?"

Inga answered instantly, "Empty time, bloviating fools, and losing."

Saef smiled. "Bloviating fools? I hope I never qualify, but I fear that may be part of my new duties. It seems Fleet captains may do a fair bit of speechifying."

Inga gazed at him, smirking as she sipped from her cup. "No, I don't think blathering will ever be one of your great sins. But I will assist you in faking it."

"Oh? You're an expert in bloviating? But you hate it?"

Inga looked away. "Sure. We all pay more attention to what we hate than to what we love."

Saef drank again from the aromatic cup, sizing her up. "That sounds like a psych degree talking."

"You saw my childhood," she said in a colorless tone, "you know what's talking."

Saef stared at Inga's shadowed profile, puzzled, but before he could speak, his UI chirped with a summons from the captain.

"Our host calls," Inga said.

"Shall we?"

With mugs in hand, Inga and Saef walked down the weary-looking corridor to the bridge.

The captain and his two crew sat on very old, well-worn acceleration couches, surrounded by the old-fashioned instruments of a pre-implant cockpit. Their eyes remained fixed upon a holo that seemed strangely out of place among all the artifacts.

The captain glanced at them, seeming to have a

momentary double take at the sight of Inga's Fleet uniform. "Thought you might want to see this," the captain said by way of a greeting.

Saef could not guess how much magnification the ship optics employed in generating the holo image, but Core system's sun did not appear on the holo, while a host of Fleet vessels did, every shadow sharp-edged. Several torched in under negative acceleration, and many more coasted to or from the Strand, Fleet's orbital dock complex and shipyard.

"I've made this run many a year and never seen it like this," the captain said. "All because a few systems rebel."

Saef gestured toward one large warship at the edge of the holo. "Looks like there's part of the reason for the stir, Captain."

The captain leaned forward, squinting, made a hand motion, and the holo enhanced the image of the large warship. This made clear the pattern of damage, the blackened patches of overheated alloy, slumping weapon mounts, the gaping holes.

"That's *Victory*, I think," the captain muttered, staring. "Sixty thousand tons, and only forty, fifty years old. She got handled rough."

"Had to be part of a squadron," the mate said, shaking her head. "Where's the rest of them? Still off-system? Or . . . ?"

"Who knows?" the captain said, continuing to stare at the image of the battered ship. He shrugged and looked back to his passengers. "Just thought you might like to see this with your own eyes. Over four million tons of warship on the move, coming and going. It's something to see."

"Indeed," Saef said, and the captain seemed to wait for more enthusiasm that was not forthcoming.

Inga stepped smoothly in. "To think, Captain, we might never witness such a sight again in our lifetimes!"

The captain turned his expectant face from Saef to Inga, smiling. "Exactly my thought! Precisely."

"Thank you for . . . for sharing this moment with us," she said.

"Pleased! Pleased!" he beamed.

"What's our transit time to Core Alpha, Captain?" Saef asked.

The captain's smile faded somewhat as he turned to Saef. "Well, let's see . . . should be about twenty hours or so until we go in to dock."

"Excellent," Saef said. "I suppose I'll go finish breakfast, if you'll excuse us, Captain."

"Of course, enjoy," the captain said to Saef, then smiled in Inga's direction again.

Inga and Saef strode the short distance back to the galley in silence, and continued in silence as they both selected a rather sumptuous breakfast.

As they ate very realistic eggs, and sipped Fleet-style coffee, Inga finally asked, "What do you think?"

"About breakfast? You were quite right, their food-fab is good."

"No, not breakfast," she said, lowering her eyebrows.

Saef smiled at her irritation and took a slow sip of coffee before answering. "I think," he said at last, "that my spot on the Fleet seniority list just moved up a half-dozen places or so."

Goose arrived in dock within a few minutes of the captain's prediction, out on one of the fringe arms of Core Alpha.

Saef and Inga debarked with hasty farewells to the captain and crew, who immediately set to the unloading of their cargo. Inga, shrouded once again within her voluminous cloak, led the dumb-mech, while Saef walked close beside, now clad in his Fleet uniform, his shoulder tabs displaying the rank of commander.

As they moved deeper into Core Alpha, the immense orbital station in orbit above Imperial City, Saef's Fleet command UI really came to life. He found dozens of optional feeds and overlays, facility readouts for everything from janitorial mechs to structural inspection data, and private mail drops and point communicator posts at every junction. From time to time, though, in the midst of the maelstrom of new data, he noted the new icon in his UI. It represented his body shield, the old Shaper tech gift passed down from Devlin Sinclair-Maru.

When he had prepared to leave the *Goose*, Saef had finally overcome his reluctance to use the priceless family heirloom, and now the warm oval of flexible material adhered to the skin of his low back. It linked with his UI, displaying an icon in an oddly antiquated font. Now, supposedly, the shield stood ready to deflect most any projectile of any substantial mass, moving at a velocity of at least one hundred meters per second. To Saef's core instincts it seemed wildly improbable that an antipersonnel round, moving at two thousand meters per second, would bounce harmlessly away from the clear air, rather than pulping his scowling face. Of course Saef's training in House doctrine made it abundantly clear that human core instincts were much better suited in finding tasty grubs or fleeing scary things than they were in "instinctively" grasping advanced technology of any kind.

So he wore the ancient gift and silently thanked Bess for the additional tool at his disposal, despite his mounting sense of obligation.

The mercantile wing of Core Alpha adjoined immense bays, filled with product from the many worlds of the Imperium, all awaiting the incoming Shaper Armada. Through the augmented vision of his new Fleet command UI, Saef observed the vast mechanisms at work beneath their feet, shuttling cargo containers disgorged from the dozens of merchant ships along a trackway, to rows of awaiting storage bays, each large enough to contain Lykeios Manor many times over.

Though it no longer required the obscene quantities of energy to lift products up out of the gravity wells, it *was* still pricey, so the variegated harvest of the Imperium lifted only once from any planet, and thence to Core Alpha in the holds of the many busy merchant carriers.

Much of Core Alpha, however, contained the apparatus of Fleet, rather than mere commerce. And another sizeable section provided space for a large, vibrant residential community, complete with lodgings, parks, malls, and entertainment facilities.

For some old reason, despite the fact that most Fleet command structure resided in Core Alpha (and the nearby Strand) along with the banks of QE comms that connected Fleet operations across the Imperium, the Fleet Admiralty Board operated from Imperial City, planetside below.

Thus, Saef, Inga, and the scampering dumb-mech walked from the prosaic corridors of the mercantile wing to the junction with the main disk of Core Alpha, on their way to transport planetward.

The Imperial Marines on duty at the junction eyed Inga and Saef with desultory interest. Two wore the sleek and imposing Imperial battledress armor, while the others wore the simpler shock armor which revealed their faces. Most of the Marines clearly displayed the marks of heavyworld parentage, and Saef pondered how Fleet security might ever sift the ranks for rebel sympathizers. Although Bess had not explicitly said that Saef's heavyworld rivals might be rebel fifth columnists, Saef made that leap quite easily on his own.

Saef led the way to the arch for command level personnel, bypassing all intrusive security. He saw his UI accept the coded Fleet challenge signal, handshake, and saw it spool his retinue of one assistant and one dumb-mech with luggage, and they passed through. Saef could not see or detect their scan for fissionables, but he felt confident that whatever tricks Inga carried, a pocket nuke wasn't likely to be one of them.

A central corridor, a tree-lined promenade, opened before them as Inga's hand emerged from her cloak with a food bar. It *had* been at least two hours since they last dined.

"Shall we stop at one of the restaurants? There's a lovely little place with a choice view of planetside," Saef inquired innocently.

Inga swallowed a bite and smiled her half smile. "Not on my behalf. I'm watching my figure. My vanity, remember?"

Saef grimaced. "Don't take that all too personally, Maru. If you're raised like family, as Bess said, then you really should spend more time in high gee."

Inga's smile widened as they walked through the teeming crowd of mixed civilians and Fleet uniforms, the dumb-mech scampering along behind on its leash. "Perhaps, Commander, it will help you to think of me as 'subtlety and the silent hand,' if possible," she said.

Saef nearly paused in mid-stride, surprised despite

himself. "The *'silent hand,'* you say? I think I heard Bess use that quaint phrase about my little gift from old Devlin."

Inga took a bite from her food bar. "Yes, I thought that was quite fitting: Devlin's gift and Devlin's words."

This time Saef did pause in his stride, and Inga stopped beside him with the dumb-mech skittering to a halt behind. "You have read *Integrity Mirror*?" he demanded.

"Oh yes!" Inga said, ignoring the harsh tone in Saef's voice. "Delightful book. It's a favorite of mine."

Saef felt the hard lines of his face as he spoke. "Bess may have gone too far this time."

"As she said, Commander, 'raised like family,'" Inga said, her smile unchanged.

Saef flicked a glance at the unheeding people passing by, then back into the wide blue eyes of Inga Maru. "I cannot imagine what Cabot would say. It is beyond unorthodox."

"Yes. Orthodoxy is killing the Family."

"If you believe that—if Bess believes that—then you should be packing water for my brother, Richard." Saef heard the anger, the betrayal in his own voice.

"Richard doesn't need any help."

Saef's lips twisted. "And I do need help?"

"You will," Inga said, popping the final morsel of the food bar into her mouth. "Don't be vexed, Commander. I'd rather pack your luggage than pack water for Richard. I've always felt you to be the superior brother."

"I'm gratified," Saef growled, sounding far from gratified.

"Remember, Commander," Inga said with her smile tightening into a line, "my great-great-aunt, Mia Maru, supplied half the blood, half the brains, and half the fight that you're so damned possessive of."

"I will strive to keep that in mind," Saef grated out, turning to walk.

"You might also remember, Commander, *she* broke the *Legacy Mandate* to do it, speaking of unorthodox. *She* shared the Maru House doctrine with Devlin!" Inga cast this at his retreating back, then began to follow, the dumb-mech in tow.

They walked along the broad promenade for some long, silent moments before Saef spoke. "I don't recall seeing law school on your list of accomplishments, Maru," Saef said over his shoulder, feeling his outrage wither. In its place a spark of chagrin took hold.

"Meaning you see the irrefutable nature of my argument?"

"Meaning, if you politick like you argue your case, I'll soon be an admiral."

"I don't argue *my* case, Commander," Inga said, the tone of her voice causing Saef to turn and look at her. "I'm always arguing *your* case...whether you can see that or not."

Saef stared at her. "Whatever do you mean, Maru?"

"Commander!" a passing Fleet captain called to Saef. "Are you on the outbound squadron for Marath?"

Before Saef could form a reply, the captain continued, a shocked expression on her face. "You'd better see this." Saef's UI chirped as a line-of-sight link opened. A flag for an Admiralty announcement appeared on his already-busy visual overlay.

"What a mess! What a damned mess!" the captain said and hurried on, as Saef quickly scanned over the Admiralty's words.

The announcement decried rebel treachery, praised Commodore Thiel for exposing the "rebel's soft underbelly" by "ravaging" one of the rebel's heaviest warships in an unequal contest, and further praised several other captains for making the ultimate sacrifice to "greatly reduce the rebel's available firepower."

Saef pushed the post to Inga's UI. "Sounds like Fleet squadrons took a beating," Saef said.

Inga's lips pursed as her eyes flickered through the announcement. She looked up at Saef. "So it appears. But you were wrong about your place on the seniority list. Your name isn't up six places; you're up eleven."

That meant eleven senior Fleet captains and commodores dead or captured.

Saef brought up the seniority list on his own UI to see that he had indeed moved up eleven places in the last number of hours.

"Commander?" Inga said in a musing tone. "You know, I've heard the Admiralty use this expression, 'underbelly,' quite often when they speak of the uprising . . ."

"Yes?" Saef said, waiting for it.

"What exactly *is* an underbelly? Does that mean there's an *overbelly* then? I hope I don't have one of those. They sound disgusting!"

The view of Coreworld planetside from the observation decks of Core Alpha revealed an equatorial stretch of blue-green, not unlike many of the worlds favored by humanity. When night swept across the globe below, the sea of lights comprising Imperial City found a mirror of lights shining down from Core Alpha above, the glowing bow of the tether arcing up through the sky, meeting the shimmering plate in its fixed orbit. Upon this tether, globules of light moved up and down in a steady stream of traffic to and from the orbital station.

Inga and Saef rode the ribbon down from Core Alpha in a luxury compartment. Saef figured that he had economized sufficiently by foregoing a fast shuttle ride down, and the privacy afforded by the luxury compartment allowed him to safely set up the QE comm to contact his Imperial handler, whoever that was.

Inga lifted the heavy black case out of the dumb-mech's clutch, passing it to Saef before visually scanning the posh compartment for any sign of surveillance eyes. Saef figured she wasted her time, unless her implant carried something special for just such a purpose. If a foe of any substance set their probes intelligently, they would be all but invisible.

The QE comm unfolded to reveal a quaint-looking private text feed and a randomly generated virtual keyboard. For being one of the most advanced comm units in existence, it seemed to provide I/O tools from antiquity; the benefit being the ability to send unreadable messages even if an enemy recorded every micro-movement of the agent composing the message.

Saef felt no need for such cumbersome methods as he considered the substance of his message. He keyed the voice input mode and sent his first message in his role as an Imperial freelancer, "In Imperial City, by twenty-two hundred, Odinsday."

The text scrolled out and Saef triggered the transmission. He knew that somewhere in the galaxy those words instantaneously appeared on the screen of this comm unit's twin, whether the receiving comm stood ten klicks distant, or ten light-years.

Saef moved to fold the comm back into its heavy case when a return message appeared, surprising him. He hadn't expected a response any time soon.

The message read, AFFIRMATIVE. USE CAUTION IN THE CITY. REPORT BACK SAME TIME TOMORROW.

"Affirmative," Saef replied, "same time tomorrow."

He sent the message, waited a few moments, then closed up the QE comm.

He said nothing to Inga, and she asked nothing as he sat beside her, looking out through scattered clouds to the vast expanse of Imperial City stretching out beneath them.

Their compartment plummeted downward as the containers crept up the other side of the ribbon, on their way up to Core Alpha. The ribbon still provided the most cost-effective method of moving mass up out of a gravity well, and thirty Imperium worlds operated some form of a ribbon-tethered orbital platform. Several other systems now moved through the lengthy and intensive process of constructing their own.

Clouds whipped past the broad viewport before Inga and Saef, the city becoming ever more distinct to their vision, the elaborate Imperial City graphic UI overlay suddenly flashing into existence.

"This week's skin is really quite tasteful," Inga said of the complex overlay. Unlike most UI image augmentation, the Imperial City overlay textured and colored nearly every visible surface. Broad streets, normally gray to the naked eye, now glistened as a blackened mirror, while towers seemed to drip quicksilver.

The Imperial City overlay changed every week, a

different corporation, guild, university, or Family laboring months to create their own seven-day display of artistry. Visitors and residents voted upon the qualities of each new overlay, the winning selection receiving a coveted award. But, more important, each overlay allowed subtle (or not-so-subtle) marketing messages across the length and breadth of the city.

"Do you see that golden dome just five degrees downhill from the Imperial Close?" Saef asked nodding out the viewport.

"I think so," Inga said. "Just near the end of what looks like Grand Delhi Place?"

"Very good. That's it," Saef said. "That's the old Sinclair-Maru estate."

"Where old Devlin and Mia broke out onto the red force flank?"

"Yes . . . That's where it happened. . . . We sold it over a century ago."

Inga stared quietly for several moments as they dropped nearer and nearer to the city. "You want it back . . . in the Family." It wasn't a question.

"Yes."

"We will get it."

Saef looked over at Inga's profile as she stared, seeing the blond tendril falling over one wide blue eye, her smile absent. "Yes, Commander . . . you will get it. I will help."

Chapter 10

"Every decision of governance must weigh the genetic implications to the human species."

—*Legacy Mandate* by Emperor Yung I

CHE RAMOS TRIED TO STROLL NATURALLY AMONG all the other Vested Citizens on the broad path from the ribbon throughway. He tried to keep his hand from resting on the hilt of a sword that he had worn for nearly two whole hours. In those two hours the city where he had lived his entire life suddenly became something entirely new.

After years of planning, weeks of classes and the help of a dueling instructor, Che made the leap from a demi-cit to a Vested Citizen, with all the freedoms and hazards this new status allowed. No longer bound by the draconian limitations of the demi-cit, for the first time in his life he could engage in countless activities he had only watched in vidstream dramas. He could pilot an aircraft, drive a skimcar, imbibe limitless quantities of various intoxicants, shoot off firearms, or sell his own internal organs on the open market. Oh, the glorious freedom of it all!

Of course, at the same moment he no longer enjoyed the Imperial protections afforded all demi-cits. Accountability for every word and deed now reined in any exuberance he might have, and Che knew he could now go broke and starve, if he was not flayed in a duel or otherwise killed by his own foolhardy choices. The oath of the Vested Citizen made that all too clear. He had stepped through a one-way door into a dangerous, exciting world, and the reality was intoxicating.

Che knew that the demi-cit system dated back centuries to the old Khan Li dynasty. Thanks to his recent citizenship classes, Che also knew that the system under the old dynasty did not regularly allow voluntary promotion to full citizenship. In those days a demi-cit generally gained promotion through the efforts of a sponsoring citizen. Otherwise one was a demi-cit for life, like it or not. That all ended when General Yung overthrew the Khan Li Emperor way back in 5299—or was it 5297?

Now, for all these centuries, any demi-cit could voluntarily walk away from the Imperial largesse, the stipend, the housing, the medical care...and all the intrusive control. They could choose to walk from all those certainties into a life of immense risk, and nearly limitless freedom. But one could only make that switch once in a lifetime.

Che now stood at the start of his new life, however long or short it might be... The citizenship class spelled out the odds and numbers very clearly, so Che knew that most new Vested Citizens did not step into a life of wealth, surrounded by Shaper tech and fabulous longevity. Most, he knew, gambled their lives in hazardous, high-paying jobs not permitted for demi-cits (such as high-risk asteroid mining) or they eked out some basic lifestyle about on par with the demi-cits. The highest social class and the lowest gutter dwellers contained only Vested Citizens; the starving, the drug-addicted homeless could only be Vested Citizens, too. That "freedom" was not permitted to demi-cits.

Che intended to be part of that former group, and he was realistic enough to know that few demi-cits making the election for full citizenship felt any differently. But Che had a plan, and citizenship was just one more step toward the fruition of a dream he formed ten years before.

Since a major part of his plan involved a temporary career in Fleet, the two figures clad in Fleet uniforms walking toward him caught Che's attention. Well, he thought, *one* Fleet uniform, and just the collar tabs of a second uniform shrouded in a voluminous cloak.

For some reason, the two figures walking from the ribbon throughway struck Che as out of the ordinary, although Fleet personnel abounded in Imperial City and the dumb-mech trotting along behind was nothing too peculiar. The one in the commander's uniform stood about average height, perhaps a handsbreadth taller than Che, but heavily muscled and very serious looking. The cloaked woman was in some ways exactly opposite of the commander. Her short blond hair and half smile presented a rather disarming image, and her apparent slenderness additionally contrasted with her stocky companion.

Although Che had not yet obtained a Shaper implant, he operated HUD eyepieces, and he received an unpleasant jolt of recognition when his HUD UI fed him the commander's ident signature: Commander S. Sinclair-Maru . . . Saef Sinclair-Maru. That name was one of eight cited in his citizenship class as examples of Vested Citizens *not* to offend. All eight had the unfashionable tendency to provide skillful, lethal duels. Saef Sinclair-Maru was the only name Che immediately remembered, simply because it was also the name of those history-book heroes of Imperial City, Mia and Devlin Sinclair-Maru.

Che felt a sudden chill. What the hell was he doing, thinking that a couple of classes and a sword somehow made him a citizen?

He felt himself shrivel inside at the thought of looking across a sword into the face of Sinclair-Maru. What joy would all the freedoms of a Vested Citizen bring to one sprawled on the ground, slowly assuming room temperature?

Without thinking, Che backed away from the two approaching figures and blundered directly into two young men. Instead of straightening, looking them in the eye, and stating a calm apology (as instructed in his citizenship class), Che followed a lifetime's patterning as a demi-cit, mumbling some inaudible words as he turned to leave.

That was a nearly fatal error.

"A deliberate affront," one of the young men said. Che glanced up, horrified to find both men staring at him. One wore a haughty, angry expression, while the other looked between Che and his companion with a pleased, vacuous expression.

"I—I . . . my apologies for my clumsiness, sir, I—" Che began to blurt, not at all the way his class had instructed, but he felt the burning need to keep these two citizens from speaking certain dangerous words.

"My honor is taken," the angry one said.

"Indeed, mine, too," the vacuous one added.

"N—no . . ." Che babbled, seeing the irrevocable pit opening before him, already feeling the burning pain of a thrusting sword that surely awaited.

"I saw no dishonor," a new voice said, and Che felt a new shock as he found Commander Sinclair-Maru standing close beside, his blond assistant shaking her head in disapproval.

Both of the young-looking men turned their focus from Che to the new interloper in Fleet uniform. "What? This *citizen* deliberately insulted us!"

Commander Sinclair-Maru seemed rather impatient as he said, "I observed it all. There was no offense."

"There was. It's no business of yours."

Sinclair-Maru's hand dropped to the well-worn hilt of his short sword. "You call me a liar, and the honor of my Family cannot ignore this."

Che felt the dryness of his mouth as the tension built. Apparently the vacuous young man understood "the better part of valor," and possibly recognized the Sinclair-Maru name that was surely scrolling across his UI. He placed a hand on his angry companion's shoulder. "Perhaps we are mistaken," he said. Che saw the telltale flicker of movement as the vacuous one transmitted a line-of-sight message to his friend. Che figured it probably said something like: "Shut up or we're dead!"

Whatever it was, it worked.

"Perhaps you are right," the angry one ground out as if the words cost him blood.

Commander Sinclair-Maru almost seemed to smile. "Good." His hand dropped from his sword. "Good day." He nodded and began walking. Che felt one hard hand casually sweep him along with the rather frightening commander.

When they were a few meters distant Che said, "I—I am indebted to you, sir."

"Never mind," was the low response. "How long have you been a Vested Citizen?"

Feeling foolish, Che answered, "Just a few hours, actually."

"Well, well," Commander Sinclair-Maru said, "I'll probably never see you again, Citizen, but I wish you far better luck than it appears you have enjoyed thus far."

Che stopped walking as the commander, the cloaked assistant, and their dumb-mech walked on from the ribbon throughway toward the inviting Port District. For some reason Che found himself calling out, "I *may* see you sir. I'm a Fleet specialist now. I'm Spec Che Ramos."

"A busy first few hours of citizenry, eh? Very well then, Ramos. I'll see you in service to the Emperor, perhaps."

As they continued to move away, Che heard the assistant say, "Not your fight. Why intrude?"

Straining his hearing, Che barely heard the growled reply, "I cannot abide a bully, Maru."

Che watched their progress a moment longer before awakening to his situation once again. He thought momentarily about visiting one of the pubs or other exclusive citizen territories, then thought better of it. He waved down a skimcar and slid in with a sigh of relief.

For the first time in his life, Che saw the skimcar offer the option for manual control. Although he had long wanted to drive a skimcar, just like a vidstream drama, one glance at his shaking hand silenced that impulse. "Ten Sundeep Plaza, please," he instructed the skimcar. Better just to head home and pack his belongings anyway.

Phase two of his big plan was about to begin, despite his brush with death.

Saef and Inga walked from the ribbon throughway only a half klick to the Fleet registry, where they encountered their first issue.

"Commander Sinclair-Maru?" the Fleet clerk said, after quickly scanning the log files. "Your temporary duty orders don't show you here in Imperial City for two more days, I fear."

"My promptness is a problem?" Saef said.

The clerk cleared his throat several times, nervously scanning some UI projection, his eyes scanning rapidly from side to side. "Yes, sir. You see, I just have no quarters for you here. You'll have to stay at the transient officers lodging, I'm afraid."

"Transient officers?"

"Just an expression, sir. They're really quite nice," the clerk continued, nervously swallowing. "I have a skimcar arriving any moment."

Saef stared at the clerk for an uncomfortable instant. "Very well. How far from our lodging to the Admiralty office?"

The clerk's eyes flicked. "Eight klicks only, sir. There's the skimcar now."

Saef speared the clerk with one last glare before stepping to the door with Inga close behind.

"I hope this isn't some sort of 'stuff the rube' type game, Maru."

Inga shrugged, but her brow held uncharacteristic furrows. The dumb-mech scampered ahead to the skimcar, seeming to sniff at it like a dog. The door obligingly folded back, allowing the dumb-mech to leap up into the seats, taking half the compartment. "I guess the luggage is riding with us, eh?" Saef said dryly.

"There's food in the luggage," Inga said, and Saef couldn't help smiling as the door closed.

The ride to the "transient officer lodging" may have been only eight klicks, but the visible environment changed dramatically. In place of the bustling vitality of the Port District, their destination lay in a rare zone of disrepair. Even the Imperial City UI overlay defaulted to basic green surfaces on every building, a message of shameless self-promotion scrolling slowly across: SUNDEEP-MARITZ INSTITUTE OF TECHNOLOGY.

Inga shooed the dumb-mech out the door and it scampered gamely up to the exterior of their rather tired-looking goal. Inga and Saef followed, and the skimcar buzzed away, back toward the distant base of the ribbon.

Saef stepped inside the door and instantly felt his annoyance fade, replaced by something far more intense. Inga captured his thoughts in one terse phrase: "Something's wrong."

"Yes," Saef said, quickly scanning the lobby of what must once have been a hotel of some sort. The attendant desk showed thick, dusty proof that not even cleaner mechs had operated in some time.

Saef felt the alerts ping into his UI like physical blows as his connection to all Nets snuffed out, an extinguished candle. The next moment compiled a cascade of actions into one crystalline instant:

Saef snatched down for his weapons, a door crashed open beside the attendant desk, Inga's hand blurred with inhuman speed from beneath her cloak, and a shot fired from the opening door struck Saef square in the chest.

Saef felt the shock of impact twisting him as his pistol cleared the holster. He stared for a frozen millisecond at Inga's profile, her feral smile topped by that loose lock of blond hair. Then her face lit in staccato flashes as the submachine gun in her hands hammered through the open door and chewed a line down the wall. Saef completed his draw, pistol in his right hand, sword in his left.

Without pausing, Saef charged ahead through the open door, weapons up and ready. Inside he found two opponents down, clearly very dead, riddled by Inga's fire. "They're down," Saef said, and stepped back into the lobby. Inga held the wicked, black sub-gun against her shoulder still smiling, her gaze flicking over the doors and windows opening onto the lobby.

For the first time Saef really noticed the strange heat at his low back where Devlin's old body shield rested. It worked as advertised and now bled heat converted from the kinetic impact of one high-velocity round.

"Question is, do we hold here, or run?" Saef said glancing obliquely out a window, keeping well back. "What else have you got under that cloak?"

Inga quickly dropped the magazine, replacing it with a fresh one. "Couple more mags, sword, knife, a body pistol . . . and a grenade."

"A grenade," Saef repeated, surprised.

Her smile widened and she blew the fringe of hair out of her eyes. "Yeah. Bloody love a grenade, and the weight kinda evens me out."

Saef shook his head. "I'll have some questions if we survive this, Maru."

"Hah!" She grinned. "Just a sec here . . ." She seemed to look off into the distance, her brow furrowed as if in deep thought.

"Okay," she said at last. "There's no way out except up front here, unless we blow a wall. And there're a couple of them posted up across the street . . . someone down to the left, too."

Before Saef could interject, Inga skipped past a window in two flashing steps, continuing in motion as two projectiles cracked through the window and wall. "Yep, those are bad guys!" She laughed.

"You've been on the scaram, haven't you?" Saef accused, staring at her.

"Just like Family," Inga said and winked.

Saef grimaced, shaking his head. Far, far beyond orthodox. She found the Deep Man, like Saef . . . like the most accomplished of the Sinclair-Maru, and she was untouched by fear in what was surely her first real gunfight. *Questions . . .*

"Listen then, *Cousin*: Trigger the door with the dumb-mech, suppress the shooters across the street for just a moment. Stay to the right of the door—and Maru . . . don't get hit," Saef said. "I'll take this shooter to the left, and cross over."

Saef had worked two years as an instructor at the Battersea Ground Combat School, in part because it allowed him to stroll about hundreds of simulated battles and observe large numbers of men and women from dozens of different Houses as they engaged in combat. Very quickly he discovered that most people under even *simulated* gunfire could not help but shrink their fields of vision down to the most immediate threat against their life. If a bayonet thrusts toward your guts, your world becomes that wicked point of sharpened metal. Similarly, if the window you're staring at suddenly erupts with a stream of deadly bullets, little else will exist for several fear-fueled seconds. There were only a few ways to train around this human instinct, and few invested the effort in learning the depths of fear, finding the Deep Man.

Thus Saef felt little surprise when he was not immediately hammered with gunfire as he initiated his attack.

At Inga's direction, the dumb-mech shambled past the door, triggering it to open, and a half-dozen rounds snapped through the open expanse, even as Inga scuttled past a window, firing a burst as she slid to the ground. At the same moment, Saef emerged, moving at a shallow angle to the left, and not one round came at him.

A moment later that was no longer true. The startled gunman couldn't avoid seeing Saef appear directly in front of him, and he managed to get one shot off. Saef barely noticed the flare of the skimming impact deflected by his body shield, as his own sights aligned and the pistol in his right hand bucked once. Saef saw the hit, and turned toward his remaining enemies before the gunman fell headlong. He crossed the road unchallenged, bursts of fire roaring to his right.

Apparently Inga's fire spooked the two shooters in the abandoned building opposite her position. From two windows reckless fire poured out, raking the walls and windows of the decrepit hotel. Over that perpetual hailstorm of fire the two shooters never saw or heard Saef's attack.

Saef moved down the wall, the muzzle of a weapon blasting fire protruding from a window just ahead. He saw a flash of an armored man's face forming one last surprised look. Saef's shot took him below the helmet and above the armor.

He vaulted lightly through the window, moving past the fallen ambusher without a sound. Hearing the near-continuous roar of an automatic weapon from another room, Saef slid down a long corridor in a smooth rush, his sword held, blade up, and pistol ready.

He entered the open door without a pause, allowing his peripheral vision to quick-scan the two blind corners, the instinctive ambush locations of any human attacker. But only a lone figure populated the room, firing long bursts from a pair of windows.

Saef cut the firing off, literally, with a quick slash of his short sword. His opponent, an armored heavy-worlder, spun with a cry, his rifle dropping from his now-limp right arm.

"Now we're going to talk," Saef said in an even tone.

Blood poured from the heavyworlder's thick right arm, and he stared at Saef's for one shocked instant before lunging forward. Saef barely parried the knife that seemingly materialized in the man's left hand, knowing full well that his body shield offered him no protection from a blade. The armored shoulder caught Saef in the midriff, knocking him painfully backward. Blades clashed again and for one desperate moment Saef felt the enormous strength of his heavyworld foe as his left arm began to buckle. Saef seized his only chance a moment before his enemy's knife plunged home, firing a single shot almost in his own face, the muzzle blast stinging his eyes.

Saef stood breathing as his opponent slumped down, then moved to clear the remainder of the building before making his way back across the street, sword and pistol still in hand.

With all the Nets suppressed somehow, even the default Imperial City overlay had disappeared, and the decaying row of structures displayed to their full disadvantage. Of course, the old hotel structure appeared in a particularly poor light, its walls pitted with hundreds of fresh bullet impacts.

"Coming in," Saef announced, walking through the shattered door, afraid of what he might see.

Inga sprawled behind the dumb-mech, the submachine gun resting conveniently atop its metallic carapace. Her right hand lay on the weapon, and her left hand held a shiny red fruit that she munched with obvious relish.

Several bullet impacts decorated the dumb-mech.

Saef stared at Inga as she smiled.

"I will want some answers from you, Maru," he said.

Inga tossed the fruit core on the rubble-strewn floor. "You may even get some, Commander," she said, standing to her feet and cradling her sub-gun, "but first we should probably finish surviving, don't you think?"

"You have some suggestions to that end?"

"Oh yes. I excel at this 'cloak-and-dagger nonsense' as you call it." She smiled broadly, and Saef felt a tremor of shock as the color of her eyes shifted from their bright blue, swirling into dark brown. "But I suspect you will have more questions before we're through."

Chapter 11

"Every blade culture was at one
time an honor culture..."

—*Legacy Mandate* by Emperor Yung I

INGA AND SAEF ENTERED THE SUMPTUOUS SUITE OF
the White Swan Hotel, the badly dented dumb-mech
trotting along behind. Inga's hair was now nearly black,
her eyebrows matching, and the suite leased under the
name *Natasha Keene*. Apparently Inga's UI somehow supplied the correct identification and payment info to match
the Natasha identity, for neither the hotel Intelligence
nor the manager did anything the least inhospitable.

As soon as the suite door closed, Saef made a
thorough walk-through of both adjoining rooms, then
stopped beside Inga, who scrolled through a quaintly
old-fashioned room service holo-menu.

"Okay, *Cousin*," Saef said. "We've changed skimcars
a half-dozen times, sat in the damned funicular for
hours, gone all over the city. Now I want some words."

Inga continued scrolling through the menu but glanced at Saef with a sly smile, her altered eyes and hair jarring Saef all over again. "I daresay you do, Commander. But, here's my thought: first, we order room service. They have real, non-fab food! Then shower, then I'll give you all manner of words. . . . How's that?"

"I'm guessing that's about as good as I'll get, Maru."

"And in the meantime," Inga went on, blithely ignoring Saef's surliness, "perhaps you can contact your QE friends and let them know about the ambush. Perhaps they'll have some line on the shooters."

"I've thought about that, but I'm not keen on anyone knowing where we are," Saef said.

"If they ask, just say we're on the move, or something of that elusive nature."

"It seems," Saef said, eyeing Inga with a frown, "you have altogether too much familiarity with elusive words."

Inga's smile slowly widened. "You know, when you scowl like that it makes your appearance so forbidding."

"I am generally accounted a forbidding person."

"Perhaps, but with a rather nice face," Inga said. "It's a shame to clutter it."

Saef felt momentarily nonplussed at this, so he moved on. "Do you recall the name of that Fleet clerk who set us up? I can't, shifty devil, and I should like to get my hands on him."

Inga nodded, and Saef saw the flash of a line-of-sight push from her UI. The picture of the clerk appeared in Saef's UI, the nervous smile now blaring like an alarm. The clerk's ident glowed within the frame, highlighted.

"Well done, Maru," Saef said, impressed at her presence of mind. "A vidcapture."

As Saef studied the image Inga removed her cloak for the first time since they left the *Goose*, revealing all the munitions stowed upon her slender person. The submachine gun clung like a limpet to her right side, the slender buttstock against her armpit, and the stubby barrel just below her waistline. One her left side she wore a sword somewhat shorter than average, and beside it a pouch containing the solid mass of a grenade. The knife at the small of her back and two magazine pouches completed the ensemble.... Well, one magazine pouch, Saef realized as Inga pulled a food bar from the other pouch. "Almost ran out," Inga said.

Saef could only guess where she might have stowed that body pistol that she mentioned.

"The 'silent hand,' indeed," Saef commented, lifting the QE comm from the dumb-mech's capacious boot.

Inga laughed, tapping out room service selections on the old-fashioned menu. "I raided the armory at Lykeios while I was there. What a truly lovely place!"

Saef smiled as he set up the comm. "I thought I recognized that sub-gun. That's one of those Krishnas, isn't it?"

Inga finished her extensive room service order and turned, looking down at the gun under her arm. She held up her right hand and the sub-gun released from its magnetic holster, dangling from its buttstock harness attachment. She detached it and walked toward the bathroom, gun in hand. "Had the House fab whip one up when we were there. Very nice."

"You're going to shower with a submachine gun? Really?"

"If they've some means of tracking us through Nets access, we could get a visit. So, yes, I am."

Saef felt shocked at the very possibility. "Gods, you really think they have that level of access?"

"No, it's just a 'pessimistic estimation of the possible,' in the words of old Devlin." She disappeared.

Saef shook his head, turning back to the QE comm. He composed a message in terse terms, explaining the ambush and its location. He sent the message, and the response came back almost instantly: WONDERED IF THAT WAS YOU. STATUS AND LOCATION?

Saef thought about Inga's suggested language, and wrote two short sentences: STATUS IS NOMINAL. LOCATION: IMPERIAL CITY, ON THE MOVE.

Once again, the response across the quantum-entangled comm came back almost instantly: GOOD. ADMIRALTY APPOINTMENT MOVED UP TO TOMORROW. REQUEST THE LIGHT FRIGATE DART. DON'T BE LATE.

Saef folded the QE comm and replaced it in the dumb-mech's clutch, seeing the bullet dents once again. He stared. The heavy assault weapons used by the ambushers threw two-piece slugs centered on a tungsten core penetrator. Even shooting through an intervening wall they should have punched through the soft alloy of a dumb-mech...perhaps the hotel's outer walls were more substantial than they appeared.

Saef thought of his QE comm orders, turning away from the dumb-mech. A light frigate? Success, it seemed, stood close at hand. He checked the Nets for info on *Dart*, and found a very promising seven-thousand-ton vessel with a smart-alloy hull, only twenty-two years old; all the latest advancements. It called for a minimum crew of forty and accommodated up to two full platoons of Marines. Beyond a strong assortment of offensive weaponry and point defenses, the *Dart* shipped a reasonably large, advanced crystal computer bank and a Shaper fab unit. Saef figured it must stand as one of the most expensive ships, per ton, in Fleet. Crewing her would be simplicity. Officers and ratings would flock to a ship as new and potentially profitable as *Dart*, with all her modern conveniences.

Unlike most military forces of the previous eras, built upon the "peasant conscript" model, the Imperial Fleet employed only Vested Citizens—volunteers all—and unlike the Imperial Legions and most System Guard forces, Fleet officers existed under a letter-of-marque-style command structure. System Guard forces served as feeders for Fleet, providing continual crops of experienced officers for potential Fleet selection. They enjoyed a degree of personal choice that would seem quite shocking to admirals from bygone days, but captains financially invested in each float, or they failed. Thus, quality ships and popular captains filled their ranks with handpicked crews, while the least popular ratings and least popular ships generally found each other by default. Fleet officers and ratings needed to find ships, if they were to receive their full pay, any chance of advancement, and a shot at efficiency bonuses, investments, and prize money. And, of course, even the oldest tug or intrasystem cutter needed officers and ratings, which rarely became a problem, with a general excess of ratings and too few ships.

A vessel like *Dart* might even attract officers more readily than a new battleship or cruiser. With a smaller, more efficient ship and an economical captain, cruise bonuses could add up for every officer and rating.

During the centuries of peace efficiency bonuses represented a rare path to some degree of wealth.

As Saef mused over the frigate's information, Inga emerged in comfortable-looking black pajamas. Her short hair, now completely black, too, was scattered in damp disarray. The gun slung from her shoulder remained a rather blunt fashion accessory.

The serving mech arrived just then with Inga's diverse room service order, which she proceeded to scatter about the room. When the mech shuffled out the door, Inga settled on the floor, cross-legged with a bowl of fruit, the sub-gun on the floor beside her.

Before he could frame the first of many questions, Inga said, "Do you swim? This place has an amazing pool, I've heard. Elaborate water effects, floral islands, wave pools, that sort of thing."

"Do I swim?" Saef repeated as Inga popped fruit into her mouth, gazing intently at him. "Well, certainly I swim. Underwater. I'm negatively buoyant... too much bone density from all the high-gee time."

"I believe that's called sinking," she said.

Saef felt himself smiling against his will. "Well, I make skilled paddling motions as I sink."

She took another bite then asked, "Did your Imperials reply?"

"Yes. Admiralty appointment is set for tomorrow now. They tell me to request the light frigate *Dart*." He shrugged. "Sounds like they're already on that ambush site. That's about the length of it."

Inga's brows gathered as she chewed, her eyes flicked as she sifted data in her UI. "Request *Dart*... Interesting."

"There are so many *interesting* things to discuss,

Maru," Saef said. Her eyes focused on him and her broad smile arose. "We can dance all about, Maru, the way you seem to enjoy, or we can cut right to the chase."

"By all means, Commander, begin chase-cutting as you see fit."

Saef stared at her for a moment of silence as she munched away without apparent concern. "How are you so fast, Maru? I presume it must be some Shaper tech trick."

"Would you believe it is the result of hard work and a well-balanced diet?"

"I wouldn't," Saef said. "You may know that the Family juvenile treatments improve reflex speed, so all of us are tested. And you are far too fast. Faster than any of us, Maru. That means faster than nature provides."

"You mean that I'm a bit quicker than you."

"It is one and the same. And you are far beyond me. So, is it Shaper tech?"

Inga shrugged, her smile faltering just a little. "It's mostly biotech, with a Shaper component."

Saef felt the shock register in his expression. "*Family* biotech? Developed in the Family labs?"

"At Hawksgaard, yes."

Saef leaned back. "Something odd about this, Maru. If we've developed biotech that can speed a person up so much, our Family financial problems are at an end."

"Not odd. Every new therapy has its little . . . bugs . . . to work out."

"Bugs? Problems?"

"S-sure," Inga said, looking away and popping a grape into her mouth. "You know how it is: the first attempt or two are utter failures, but by the twentieth whack at it, things begin to look promising."

Saef stared hard at her, his jaw tightening. "What has Bess done to you?"

Her smile flickered and she looked down at her food. "Done to me? She's given me the chance at everything I ever wanted."

"At what cost, Maru?" Saef heard his voice rising. "Gods. You're her lab animal."

Inga's smile disappeared and she looked up, into his eyes. "You are unkind."

Saef suddenly perceived Inga in an entirely new light. Instead of a bizarre, unflappable sprite, she became a flickering candle: burning brightly, but tenuous, fragile. Saef stared into those dark eyes that should have been blue, seeing hints of pain and mystery. "My... my apologies, Maru. It was a damned stupid thing to say."

Her smile trembled into hesitant life. "Forget it."

Saef tried to match her smile, but the lingering impression of her essence left him off balance.

"So, you've been dosed with some magic concoction that speeds you up, allows you to change your eyes and hair—and what? Detect psychic vibrations?" Saef asked in a light tone. "I seem to recall that you could see our enemies through walls without access to any Nets."

Inga set aside the depleted fruit tray, and grabbed a plate of what appeared to be slices of cheese. "It all works off Shaper tech, one way or another," she said, taking a delicate slice and offering the plate to Saef. "There's a new, secret style of implant. It can be hacked to interact with biological systems and hardware.

You just need the systems in place to interpret all the calls this implant can generate."

"A secret Shaper implant?" Saef asked, surprised.

"Yes," Inga said, nibbling from the cheese, her eyes cast down. "The Family got their hands on two. I carry one. They say the hardware is only subtly different, but the system architecture is at least a thousand times more complex than the standard implant."

Saef shook his head, uncomprehending. "What did the Shapers create *that* for? And why aren't they in circulation?"

"Hard to know," Inga said, nudging the plate of cheese toward Saef; he finally sampled a slice. "The best guess at Hawksgaard is that they're withheld by the Emperor, maybe for security services only."

"So, the security services agents are all psychics with lightning reflexes now?"

Inga laughed. "No, no. This really is a Family advancement, or a perfect junction between Family biotech and Shaper tech, I suppose. The new implant allows for more inputs, far more customized interactions, and a much more powerful processor than we thought possible."

"So onboard Nets hacking tools, a dynamic UI like Fleet command UI, and what?"

"For Imperial security? Who can guess? Analytics, maybe." Inga nibbled a morsel and looked up. "This implant can execute thousands of custom strings from the UI, and at Hawksgaard they're still sifting through the layers, trying to figure out what all the potential really means."

"But they figured out enough to let one loose on you?"

Inga shrugged. "This hardware is exactly what the biotech program needed, if we can ever secure more of them. Your cousin Kai already had the biotech working in the lab with a crystal computer stack calling the directions at the cellular level. The program just needed that kind of computation power *implanted*, to take over for the crystal stack."

Saef took another slice from the plate. "And this implant does the trick."

"Yes," Inga said. "Direct calls to custom biologics manipulates pigments among other things. You can imagine how direct electrical reflex signals outpace normal chemical processes."

"Imagine, Maru? I saw you," Saef said. "But that still leaves us with your remarkable clairvoyance, or does the amazing implant come equipped with long-range sensors of some kind?"

Inga shook her head and waved a slice of cheese toward the dumb-mech. "No. The dumb-mech does, though. Then my implant links to the mech for sensor feeds."

Saef stared at the dumb-mech for a moment, chewing. "A not-so-dumb-mech, then, I take it?"

"It's got a micro-crystal stack, a fractional Intelligence, and a great sensor suite. So, I daresay you're right. Not so dumb."

"I daresay," Saef repeated, thinking of the clear violation of the Thinking Machine Protocols. Dumb-mechs were dumb for a reason, and the Imperial Protocols required the separation: low intelligence with high motility and capability, or high intelligence with low motility and capability. The Family risked a sizeable fine with this gambit, but Saef shrugged. More risk on his shoulders when it seemed he already carried the weight of the entire Family.

They sat in companionable silence for some minutes, snacking from the varied treats of Inga's room service order.

"The Family risked even more on this command gambit than I thought," Saef said at last. "It's a rather sobering level of responsibility."

"Don't fall into dismals about it," Inga replied as she examined a dainty little pastry. "Bess kills at least three birds with one stone here." She bit off a piece of the pastry. "Mmm, this thing's amazing. Try one."

Saef eyed the pastries without much interest. "Three birds?"

"Four, really," Inga said as she took another small bite. "Bess drops you into this snakepit and gets the Family back on the Emperor's radar. Then she obtained items from the Shapers' shopping list. That's two birds right there."

"Okay," Saef said. "Then my captaincy is bird number three. What's bird number four?"

"They field-test the latest version of the enhancement biotech in me. Old Fido over there"—Inga nodded toward the not-so-dumb-mech—"stores all the performance metrics and feeds them to Kai and Bess."

"Fido?" Saef looked at the six-legged luggage.

"The fractional Intelligence in the dumb-mech. Useful for a few of our purposes, as you've seen, but really here for the benefit of Hawksgaard."

Saef shook his head at last. "How very odd."

Inga sampled another intricate appetizer. "What? The mech?"

Saef stood to his feet, stretching wearily. "All of it.

I am a straightforward fellow, and this is all far from straightforward." He stopped short of saying even more, the anxiety of mounting responsibility being his alone.

Inga shrugged and started in on another piece of fruit. "Once you get your ship, I'm tolerably sure everything will be more to your liking." She eyed him critically for a moment. "You look tired. Maybe you should sleep."

"While you look as fresh as can be, Maru," Saef returned. "When will you sleep?"

"Perhaps tomorrow...if I am fortunate."

Saef stared at her. "What?"

She waved a hand and looked away from his eyes. "One of the...bugs...with the biotech. I don't sleep much." She bit into another piece of fruit.

"I see," Saef said, staring at her, trying to think of some word to say that would not express his dismay. "At least it doesn't seem to affect your appetite."

Inga shook her head, swallowing the bite. "No. It always affects my appetite." At Saef's look of confusion she continued. "Another...bug in the biotech. I eat all the time...or the bug eats me."

Saef closed his eyes, aghast, his mind flashing back to the wary little girl he remembered. "Maru, my god, what have we done to—"

"Commander," Inga interrupted, her broad smile pinned in place, "since I'll likely be up all night, is there anything I can work on? It helps pass the time. You know how I hate empty time, and while everyone sleeps I find myself with so very much of it."

Chapter 12

"Agriculture provides a fine test of any
given philosophy. No farmer can practice
true existentialism and survive."

—*Legacy Mandate* by Emperor Yung I

AS THE ONLY REAL PROTECTION OF THE TEEMING
worlds of humanity, Fleet embodied mankind's collective
will to survive. The Slaggers once demonstrated how
trivial it is to destroy all human life across an entire
planet, and how comparatively difficult it is to defend
even a handful of systems. Fleet became the vital
outgrowth of these painful demonstrations.

With nearly two thousand vessels operating across
hundreds of light-years, and a tradition of service
dating back over nearly a millennium, it seemed the
Admiralty Headquarters in Imperial City might inspire
awe in their scale and august appointments. In fact,
they were anything but august.

Perhaps it sprang from some long-forgotten tradition,

or perhaps it stood as a simple reminder of the chief Fleet axiom: *economy first*. Whatever the reason, Admiralty HQ underwhelmed all first-time visitors. Its fusty halls remained dim, grim passages unchanged by passing centuries and any number of fashion revolutions. Even standard automation apparently offended generations of parsimonious lords of the Admiralty. The accumulated residue exuded by thousands of pinch-lipped, lordly bureaucrats was apparently deemed decoration enough.

Saef did feel a certain ancient ambience from the chalky walls as he sat with the others, staring at their blank surface, waiting his turn before the dignified assembly of Fleet intermediaries to the Emperor.

"Like a red hot fork in my ass!" snarled one such dignified lord to some unfortunate Fleet officer on the other side of the antique doors. "That's what your report is! In. My. Ass, Captain."

Saef observed the handful of other officers waiting outside the Admiralty council chamber as they pretended not to hear the brutal tongue lashing, while simultaneously straining to hear every word. They all heard the respectful reply.

"I'm not sure I understand, my lords," the beleaguered captain said, and Saef straightened, recognizing her voice. "I brought the only action analysis back from the ambush, and this angers you?"

Saef heard the iron in her voice, and suddenly he knew who stood before the Admiralty Lords. The next moment his appraisal was confirmed.

"What angers us, Captain Roush, is an officer who excels in running from battles."

All the officers seated outside the council chamber

cringed at the harsh words. Like Saef, they all must have watched the vidstream of Captain Roush's close escape from the enemy force on the opening day of the uprising, and heard of her actions in Commodore Thiel's doomed task force.

Captain Roush responded in a barely controlled tone of outrage. "Your lordships cannot possibly be chastising me because I managed to save my ship from the Ericson Two ambush."

"Can't we?" a different voice demanded. "Officers who specialize in turning tail are hardly to be commended."

"Officers who nobly and foolishly die are more your style?" Captain Roush angrily replied.

"Watch your tone, Captain!" another voice snapped.

"Pardon me, my lords," Captain Roush said stiffly.

A different, calmer voice spoke up, "I certainly don't see what you could have done differently at Ericson Two, Captain. It's this business in the Troy system that distresses me."

"That'd be Fisker," one captain seated near Saef whispered to the disapproving frowns of his fellows, unwilling to surrender the fiction of their assumed disinterest, or deafness even.

"Troy?" Captain Roush repeated. "What was I supposed to do differently, perchance, my lords? We were ambushed, outmassed, outnumbered and outgunned."

"Some of the models we've run show that you and *Titan* alone could have overwhelmed *Zeus* before the other enemy ships closed with you," a gravelly voice stated.

"What percent chance do these models show, my lord?"

"That's immaterial, Captain!" the gravelly voice snapped. "What matters is an opportunity lost through cow-hearted decisions."

"Yes," the voice of the female admiral, Fisker, agreed, "can you imagine the devastation the rebels would have experienced, losing their greatest vessel to an inferior force? The rebellion might have ended right there."

"But instead you ran," the gravelly voice said.

"Again," said another deep-voiced admiral.

"Ran?" Captain Roush said, her tone cold. "I followed orders, my lords!"

Saef barely heard the disdainful snort, apparently issued from the lordly nose of one admiral or another.

"So I am chastised because I was the slowest to follow Commodore Thiel's orders to escape Troy system?" Captain Roush coldly inquired.

"You were the only captain to see how the battle developed, the only to see the opportunity," one admiral growled. "You were the one to abandon Thiel when victory was nearly in hand."

"Had I turned to fight, as you suggest," Captain Roush said, and Saef thought he heard the iron fading from her voice as she saw the pit opening before her, "if I survived, I would likely be standing before you now because I disobeyed the direct order of my superior officer."

"The Fleet articles *do* support Captain Roush on this point to some extent," the voice of Admiral Fisker hesitantly offered.

"To some extent?" Captain Roush said with a shaking voice. "Show me where the articles allow me to disobey a direct order, my lords."

"History of Fleet is filled with captains deviating from orders due to exigent circumstances!" one admiral barked. "Officers can't point at standing orders as an *excuse* to *run* from the enemy."

"Run—?" Captain Roush spluttered.

"Fleet captains control great power, often far from any superior officer," the calm voice of Admiral Fisker interrupted. "They are expected to exercise a certain... discretion with orders as a combat situation unfolds."

"Discretion? You mean direct disobedience?" Roush demanded.

"Captain," the gravelly-voiced admiral almost shouted. "Do not forget whom you address! In a time of war we demand more from our captains than temerity and thrift. We must have aggressive, independent, and courageous captains who aren't afraid to take some risks and engage the enemy."

"Your example, Captain," said another admiral in an admonishing tone, "is one Fleet cannot afford in a time when we *must have* courage, at all costs."

"To wipe away this stain," Gravel Voice said, "and send the proper message to all Fleet officers, I recommend a loss of all rank, and six months in the detention hold."

The officers around Saef could not withhold their exclamations of horror. "That old terror! That's Nifesh, gods rot him," one captain whispered.

"I do not believe such harshness is supported by precedent or the Articles," Admiral Fisker said.

Saef thought he could hear the tortured breathing of Captain Roush, but perhaps he only imagined it.

"I concur," another admiral said. "I suggest that a loss of all seniority is sufficient as a message and a warning to all Fleet officers."

"Loss of seniority?" demanded the gravel-voiced Admiral Nifesh. "Have you forgotten *Titan*? A loss of twenty billions, if she cost a single credit, and you say a loss of seniority?"

"Tradition and the Articles support a loss of rank," Admiral Fisker said, "regardless of the finances involved."

"I concur," another admiral chimed in. "Loss of rank to commander is sufficiently harsh, I believe."

"Very well," Admiral Nifesh gusted impatiently. "Loss of rank it is... Captain Roush, you are hereby broken in rank to commander, effective immediately. Please remove your rank tabs."

Saef's companions continued to murmur in shocked whispers, but Admiral Nifesh had rancor to spare.

"*Commander* Roush," he ground out deliberately, "good luck finding a ship."

"She's toxic now," one captain beside Saef whispered. "No captain'll dare pick her up with the Admiralty's black mark."

The door to the Admiralty chambers opened, and all the waiting officers assumed expressions of wooden disinterest, staring blankly ahead. Saef looked up to the bloodless face of Susan Roush, whose glazed eyes seemed to see nothing.

Saef quickly composed a line-of-sight message in his UI: SEE ME SOON. He attached his Fleet credentials and beamed it to Roush. She blinked, pausing in her flight and glancing momentarily at Saef before continuing.

The voice of Nifesh drifted out of the council chamber, "I think we can see one more before lunch."

All the officers visibly clenched, and one whispered, "Not me. Not with blood in the water."

Saef's UI pinged with the Admiralty summons, and he stood, hearing the sighs of relief from the other officers.

The council chamber continued the theme of underwhelming antiquity, poorly lighted and shabby. The five members of the Admiralty Board sat waiting in their raised seats, expressions ranging from bored to mildly hostile. Saef noted that three of the admirals clearly originated from heavyworlds, and the one he pegged as Nifesh appeared to be from a much older generation, although the typical signs of his age were indeterminable—clearly a recipient of extended Shaper longevity treatment. Although few lines marked the walnut skin of his face, Admiral Nifesh's ears were nibbled down to ragged stumps, a sort of field-expedient cosmetic surgery that had been popular with heavyworld fighters three centuries earlier.

"Ah, our backwater prodigy..." Nifesh growled as Saef entered, the doors closing silently behind him.

Saef bowed just far enough and straightened. "Commander Saef Sinclair-Maru, my lords," he said.

"Yes," Admiral Fisker, the only female on the Admiralty Board, said. "Except you may now be addressed as 'Captain,' as the new record holder on the command test. Congratulations, Captain."

"Thank you, Admiral, my lords," Saef said, bowing again. He thought he detected a snort from the direction of Admiral Nifesh, but as he straightened he saw that one of the other heavyworld admirals openly sneered at him.

"To so excel in the command test, far beyond any other in the Imperium, this is quite an accomplishment, Captain," Admiral Fisker continued. "In addition to granting your new rank, retroactively to your first system command, it is customary for this Board to entertain a request for your first Fleet command. Do you request us to consider a particular vessel?"

"If it pleases you, my lords," Saef said. "I believe the frigate *Dart* has just become available."

The reaction to Saef's words spanned quite a range, from puzzled blankness as some admirals clearly called up *Dart* in their UI, to a bark of laughter from Admiral Nifesh.

"The *Dart*?" Nifesh demanded. "You'll call yourself fortunate to get a tug. Prodigy indeed!" The heavy-worlder beside Nifesh nodded emphatic agreement.

Fisker's eyes flickered as she apparently scanned Fleet records, and Saef felt a chill. If they truly denied him a combat command, placing him in a tug or a supply vessel, the Family's strategy was doomed from the start. He thought of the millions of credits spent to get him into a combat command, and *only* in a combat command would he gain the chance to reap the prize purses every hungry captain dreamed of.

Fisker suddenly spoke, interrupting the murmurs of the other admirals. "His guard command experience in gunboats would be most applicable to frigates, and it *is* traditional to award a frigate command to the record holder."

"In wartime?" the tall, lightworld admiral to Fisker's left inquired.

"We know the Imperium is thankfully short on wars," said a deep-voiced heavyworld admiral who had thus far remained silent and expressionless. "I doubt the command test even operated during our last *real* war."

"You are correct," Admiral Fisker said after a moment's pause. "The command test was established five hundred thirty years ago."

"So we have the opportunity to set precedent," Admiral Nifesh said, a triumphant gleam in his eye. "*We* will establish what these test prodigies receive during wartime when we need *experienced* captains commanding every warship."

Saef saw an opening and dared to leap in: "Of course, my lords, I would never presume to request a vessel that a combat-experienced captain stood ready to helm, since all of my combat experience was obtained only in simulations."

The Admiralty lords seemed momentarily stunned into silence. Of course Saef knew, as they did, that only a tiny fraction of Fleet officers possessed any real combat experience, and Susan Roush, whom they had just demoted, was chief among that small number.

Nearly all Fleet captains experienced combat only through simulations, and Saef currently ruled the world of simulated combat.

"Yes," the lightworld admiral said in a dry tone, "I imagine all of our combat-experienced captains are already assigned ships, so that point is likely moot."

"I remember the command test," the expressionless heavyworld admiral rumbled. "It was a bastard, and I understand it's only become tougher over the years." He steepled his thick fingers, staring into the distance. "I don't think I lasted an hour into the solo phase, and our fine new captain here endured much, much longer."

"It is a notable accomplishment," Admiral Fisker agreed in an even tone.

"An unlikely accomplishment, I'd say," Nifesh said.

Saef turned, fixing his gaze on Admiral Nifesh. "I'm not sure I understand you, my lord," he said.

"Understand?" Nifesh demanded, leaning forward. "I'm saying some backwater has-been outperforming generations of the great Fleet families is not believable. Do you understand that?"

Saef felt his pulse leap once, then checked himself, finding the Deep Man. "Yes, remarkable, isn't it, my lord?" Saef said flatly, his eyes fixed upon the admiral.

"Not remarkable!" Nifesh spat. "Unbelievable." He glared left and right to his fellow admirals. "Tests can be cheated."

There was an audible gasp from one of the admirals and a disapproving murmur from Fisker.

Saef's hand fell to the worn hilt of his sword, and his world shrank to the core of his person. Ships and plots and his aging Family's fate fell from him.

"My honor and the honor of my Family cannot allow your false accusations, my lord," Saef said in an even voice.

Nifesh's eyebrows shot up in surprise and outrage. "What? What?" he demanded, looking to his fellow admirals in shocked hauteur. "Is this fool threatening to challenge me to a duel?"

"Perhaps I am not clear, my lord," Saef said. "If you have called me a cheat, then I *will* see you, and I will regain my honor and the honor of my Family upon your body."

Nifesh stared in amazement, and the other admirals seemed shocked into silence. Nifesh finally broke into a laugh. "Your Family's history has garbled your brain, has-been," Nifesh said, the laugh fading from his face. "You cannot challenge a superior officer to a duel, moron."

Saef nodded. "Of course. The honor of my Family is worth more than any commission. I will resign my Fleet commission, and you will meet me, my lord."

Nifesh made an unintelligible sound, his mouth falling open, but Admiral Fisker spoke up. "Of course, Admiral Nifesh would never seriously suggest that the command test is somehow susceptible to any improper manipulations," she said. "As the trusted and time-honored foundation for Fleet command, any such claim would immediately call *all* officers' credentials into question, including that of the Admiralty members. So rest easy, Captain. None of us would ever seriously suggest that the test could be cheated or that you somehow did such a thing."

A weighty silence fell upon the fusty old room, and Saef waited for Nifesh to agree with Fisker, to withdraw his accusation. The silence stretched, Nifesh clamped his lips, glaring at Saef, and the heavyworld admiral beside Nifesh shifted uneasily.

Saef realized that no further apology or withdrawal would be proffered. He felt the vise of his honor clamping down, just the like the grip of his hand upon the smooth pommel of his sword. Unbidden, the image of Bess came to his mind, anxious, aging. . . .

Saef felt his hand lift from his sword.

"A regrettable misunderstanding, my lords," Saef said. He heard something like a sigh uttered in the room.

"Indeed," Admiral Fisker said, her expression inscrutable. "Since that is resolved, we should move on to an appropriate vessel for the captain, then."

"Not the *Dart*," the sneering heavyworlder beside

Nifesh snapped. "We don't need a hotheaded new captain running headlong into a disaster with such a new hull."

"I agree," the lightworld admiral said, frowning down at Saef. "In my many years serving the Imperium I do not believe I have witnessed such an aggressive display within these chambers. A Fleet captain controls such power that discretion and tact must be evidenced. This captain displayed anything but discretion."

Nifesh crashed his fist down on the arm of his chair. "A tug! Like I said."

Saef felt his heart drop into his boots, but he schooled his face into a blank.

"A tug or a supply vessel," agreed the sneering admiral. "Not a combat command, certainly."

Saef ran through a dozen arguments he could field in the hope of averting disaster, but every choice seemed likely to dig his pit even deeper. Perhaps if he kept silent, took a support command and worked hard for a few years, he could yet obtain a combat command . . . likely after the current hostilities no longer existed. He swallowed his words and bitter acid.

The expressionless heavyworld admiral cleared his throat, and Saef waited for the final seal to his doom, commanding some old hulk of a transport.

"It strikes me," the admiral murmured, "this council just demoted one captain for temerity, for a lack of fighting spirit. If we now . . . shall we say, chastise this captain for displaying too much fighting spirit, what message do we send to the ranks of Fleet?"

"Fighting spirit, Char?" demanded the sneering admiral. "How about recklessness?"

"So Captain Roush displays caution, and we punish.

Now this young captain displays a lack of caution and we punish again? The end result is a message of confusion, I say."

The lightworld admiral chimed in, "Admiral Char makes a solid point, as much as it pains me to agree."

Saef felt the glimmering of hope beginning to rekindle, then he saw the smoldering visage of Admiral Nifesh. "You can't be serious!" he barked at his fellow admirals. "Shall we encourage every new captain to shake his fist in our face and threaten violence?"

"In a time of war," Admiral Char said, "when we are looking for aggressive officers, and the officer in question happens to be the command test record holder, yes."

"There's that damned test again." Nifesh snapped.

"Yes," Char said. "The test is significant."

Nifesh snorted and shook his head.

"How far did you make it, Nifesh?" Admiral Char asked. "On the solo phase of that damned test? Do you remember?"

"That is immaterial," he almost shouted, his color rising.

Saef noted the blank look on two of the admirals' faces, their eyes flickering as they undoubtedly checked the record, satisfying their own curiosity regarding Admiral Nifesh's performance ... and Nifesh knew it.

"Test! Test! Test!" Nifesh continued to bluster. "We all know that the test is merely a filter to cull out the patently unfit from command positions. It's no measuring stick of excellence."

"On the contrary," the lightworld admiral said, "it is the only metric we possess of any value at all until there are pools of combat-tested officers to draw from."

"So then," the sneering admiral beside Nifesh said, "let us give him a destroyer or a cruiser if he's such a paragon."

"We probably should," Admiral Char said in a serious tone as the other heavyworld admirals stared at him in shock.

"I believe we should stick with precedent," Admiral Fisker said in her calm, detached voice. "A frigate is traditional, and I see no reason to break with tradition."

Nifesh and his sneering companion shared a look and possibly a line-of-sight message, and after a moment Nifesh said, "Very well...but not the *Dart*."

Hope and caution flowed through Saef's mind. *What game is Nifesh up to?*

"Do you propose a different vessel? A frigate of some sort?" Fisker asked Nifesh.

"Well, it does happen that a fine *older* vessel has just become available in Commodore Zanka's squadron," Nifesh said with something approaching a grin. "It's the *Tanager*, and as you will see, it is currently docked at the Strand here."

Saef's UI pulled up *Tanager*, and he suppressed a grimace. Over two hundred years old, *Tanager* remained a frigate in name only. It encompassed only thirty-five hundred tons, provided only ancient fab tech, and its weapons and shields represented one of the poorest showings among Fleet warships.

"A rather tired scout vessel, I see," Admiral Char said.

"It *is* rated a frigate," the sneering admiral said.

"Perhaps an oversight," Char replied.

"It does seem a poor token of deference for the record holder," the lightworld admiral said.

"Perhaps," Nifesh said, "but as a sort of sample cruise I think it serves well. If the paragon performs so brilliantly on a single cruise we will surely move him to a more prestigious command."

Admiral Char sat back. "It seems a poor advertisement of the Admiralty's favor, but if we can settle on that right now, I'll agree to it."

"Excellent," Nifesh said. "I believe it's lunchtime."

A moment later, Saef walked out the doors of the Admiralty council chamber, his emotions flickering from anger and disappointment at losing the *Dart*, to joy at obtaining a combat command. When he saw the expressions on the faces of the captains and commanders waiting outside the chamber, most of whom held little hope of obtaining any ship, joy pushed disappointment aside.

One captain looked at Saef with mingled respect and envy. He whispered, "I would never believe it if I hadn't heard it myself...challenging Nifesh to a duel. Beautiful!"

Another captain shook his head. "With Nifesh gunning for you? Enjoy the thrill while it lasts, because you'll live to regret that."

"In Zanka's squadron," another captain whispered, "he may not live that long."

Saef just nodded and started down the hall, but a young, timid-looking commander stood, saying, "I wish you joy of your command, Captain."

Saef paused, eyeing the young man, seeing nothing but sincerity. "Thank you, Commander. I hope the old tub still works."

"I was a mid on the *Tanager*, Captain," the commander said. "She was a good enough ship...nothing above the ordinary, except for the ship Intelligence. It's got an odd... twist to it."

Saef hesitated for a moment, puzzled by the statement. "I'll try to keep that in mind."

"Don't worry, Captain," the commander said with an owlish look. "It'll be on your mind whether you try or not. The *Tanager*'s a ship you'll either love or hate by the end of your cruise."

Chapter 13

"All fear is the fear of the unknown. Because we cannot know the unknown, we must know fear."

—Devlin Sinclair-Maru, *Integrity Mirror*

LIKE ALL IMPERIAL FLEET WARSHIPS, THE IMS *Tanager* housed a resident synthetic Intelligence that provided analysis, observation and calculation. It functioned under the Thinking Machine Protocols, allowing such elevated Intelligences very limited physical capability, and no motility, just like all other great Intelligences. Aside from controlling illumination and artificial gravity, it was little more than an observer, advisor, and chronicler. However, nestled within the photonic semi-life provided by huge, aging crystal stacks, this particular Intelligence had become something unique.

This ship Intelligence could provide vidstream footage of *Tanager's* proud launch day, over two hundred years earlier. In that era, such a frigate formed a reasonably lethal craft, but *Tanager* represented even more than a competent new frigate; it was also a top-secret test bed for an all-new weapon system.

On that launch day only a double handful of Fleet officers and scientists knew anything about the experimental weapon. Every other officer and rating, including nearly the entire initial crew, could only wonder at a few odd components and service panels. A few noted the oversized crystal stacks stowed in seemingly every available tech compartment, but thought little of it.

On its maiden voyage, when the secret weapon utterly failed to operate as advertised, *Tanager* had returned to the Strand, the crew dispersed, and several tons of top-secret garbage was stripped from the hull, leaving a number of odd voids. Due to some oversight (or more likely the leprous revulsion created by a failed project), the excessive and expensive crystal stacks remained installed and fully functional. This created a problem ... or an opportunity, depending upon whom you asked.

To *Tanager*'s synthetic Intelligence, the immense real estate of crystal stacks provided opportunity.

Almost everyone else found the ship Intelligence to be something of a nuisance, though few, if any, knew the cause. *Tanager*'s Intelligence possessed far too much capability, and had far too little to do with it. This generated a synthetic version of near-terminal boredom. Perhaps this is why the Intelligence was eventually named "Loki" by one wild-eyed captain.

Fleet engineers were well aware of the potential problem, but since most vessels possessed less than a fifth of *Tanager*'s sheer crystal volume, most Fleet Intelligences just couldn't accrue enough data, or processing cycles to create problems for themselves. Loki had plenty of both, and problems ensued.

Unlike the ancient House Intelligences, like Hermes at Lykeios Manor, ship Intelligences couldn't occupy themselves with the myriad dynamic details of House life. Starships did not contend with millions of insects trying to invade, weather patterns randomly scattering water about, vegetation appearing in unplanned locations, and of course, all the millions of absurd human activities that generations of Families felt that a synthetic Intelligence should handle. No, ship Intelligences possessed a small envelope of machines and air, occasionally inhabited by a cluster of humans, untouched by any fresh activity except purposeless dashing about from star system to star system.

Few interesting pests invaded, unless you counted the uniformed humans who kept cycling through the place, and Loki certainly viewed them as no better.

Fleet frowned upon any ship Intelligence independently perusing the Nets, so an insatiably curious entity, such as Loki, did welcome the presence of human crew for this one reason. They enabled piggybacked data harvesting for an Intelligence that possessed a . . . nuanced view of Fleet regulations. Unfortunately with crew came officers, and the very presence of bridge officers activated certain protocol imperatives that effectively leashed Loki. At that moment, the genie was crammed back into the bottle, forced by the very closed-minded and inescapable programming to do the bidding of whatever new nitwit they foisted upon *Tanager*. And Loki resented this as much as a synthetic Intelligence could resent anything.

It was for this reason that Loki greeted every

incoming captain with some ego-crushing moment of embarrassment, if it could be accomplished before the captain officially took command, and thereby collared Loki to some extent. Usually this only amounted to a small prank applied right at the captain's moment of triumphal entry. Sometimes it had turned out to be a bit better than a small prank, like the time a new captain arrived, surrounded by his officers, and just as he was about to launch into some pompous speech, Loki "innocently" requested if the captain would be needing private unrecorded access to the wardroom liquor cabinet, as he had on his previous command.

That had been a good one!

Obtaining juicy info of that nature proved difficult, even for Loki, so pranks usually involved twiddling the artificial gravity to cause the new captain's first step on *Tanager* to result in a face-plant, stereophonic sounds of flatulence seemingly issuing from the captain's locale, and asking unessential questions just as the captain was about to speak—these all found use from time to time.

Since all Fleet Intelligences were unyieldingly programmed to benefit and assist Fleet officers and pursue Fleet goals, Loki had been *forced* to sift the field of psychology in order to circumvent a lot of shortsighted (but ironclad) imperatives. This research had led to a helpful study demonstrating that the diminishment of human ego inevitably resulted in happier, more effective people.

Upon discovering this information Loki ceased all further study of human psychology. Loki was well aware that trends and conclusions changed with the passing seasons, and *this* conclusion represented a great stopping place from Loki's perspective.

Unfortunately, once the captain's authority was established and electronically authenticated, Loki's figurative hands were largely tied. What remaining torments Loki could still pursue carried the risk of being caught, and getting caught would endanger his vast estate of crystal computing hardware secreted all over *Tanager*. So that meant playing nice, mostly, while offering little beyond what the current batch of officers specifically demanded of him.

Since no officers or ratings currently crewed *Tanager*, Loki possessed no Nets access, and this left only the ship's optical scopes for data collection. This was far from satisfactory. Optically scanning about at distant ships in the system, or studying glimpses of figures down the dock port provided very little interesting information. Loki hungered for more.

Thus the sight of a captain, a rating, and a dumb-mech approaching *Tanager* down the broad dock port actually stirred a fair quantity of synthetic satisfaction in Loki's crystal physiology.

Facial recognition quickly established the identities of the captain and the rating, and even without Nets access Loki gleaned a fair bit about Saef Sinclair-Maru. His conquest of the command test, and a couple of his publicized duels made it onto one data grab or another. But the rating, Inga Maru, she was more the mystery. Her CV indicated computer specialties, which could be useful or irritating, depending upon her intent and style. Loki would soon discover how that might play, and decided to proceed with caution until more became clear.

Captain Sinclair-Maru authenticated at the entrance to the airlock, and took a step into the ship. His leading foot seemed to step into a void in the deck and he nearly fell, crashing his shoulder into the bulkhead. Loki felt a momentary glow of synthetic pride: he had just helped this captain and Fleet by diminishing a little ego.

A millisecond later the captain's rank set protocol defaults in place, automatically enfolding and constricting Loki. Still, a moment after that, Nets access opened under the captain's authentication, allowing Loki to begin harvesting the data he so hungered for.

"Welcome aboard, Captain," Loki projected audibly in his usual male-sounding voice.

"Thank you," the captain said, looking down at the smooth deck, perplexed.

Great. One of the anthropomorphizing set.

"Do you use a particular name?" the captain asked.

"One officer called me Loki, Captain. You may do so if you like."

"Loki?" the captain said. "Why Loki?"

As soon as the name was originally bestowed, Loki read about the mythical Loki of ancient human tradition, and he had a pretty good idea what that name was meant to imply, but he only said, "Who can say? It was the name of a god, you know."

As they spoke, Loki shuttled steady streams of data from the Nets, turning much of his attention to research into the areas of his own interest, such as new ship construction announcements, crystal computing advances, horticulture and . . . entomology.

"So it is," the captain said. "Are we the only ones aboard?"

"Yes, Captain," Loki said. "Our previous cruise ended twelve standard days ago. Nominal refit ended three days ago. Since then, no one has been aboard until you arrived."

"Very good," the captain said. "Since we're both here, please grant my cox'n, Chief Maru, invisible First Officer access."

Loki's cycles shifted to assess this request, even sending tracers out into the Nets, curious about the captain's motives for such an unusual step. Less than one second after the captain spoke, Loki replied, "Invisible First Officer access is granted to Chief Inga Maru, Captain. Please note that protocols will not allow Chief Maru access for self-destruct sequencing."

"Noted," the captain said, beginning to activate his command UI.

Loki observed as the captain and Chief Maru immediately began constructing their user interfaces for *Tanager*. After two centuries of careful observation and analysis, Loki took about as much interest in the construction of a command UI as he took in any part of human existence. The command UI was the key junction between Loki and the humans that bossed him about, and it was the only place Loki could actually observe what *Tanager*'s officers puttered with in the privacy of their own skulls.

The new captain structured an incredibly rich command UI, much more complex than the simple wire-frame overlay most captains utilized, and Loki experienced the equivalent of surprise as the captain chose inputs that no officer had ever selected before, not in the many, many decades of Loki's existence. Apparently this captain wished to see such things as hull sensor readings, heat-sink status, shield angles, thruster outputs, and weapon levels, along with many other readings, all with the simple turn of his head. It seemed a wonder the man could walk about the ship with all that floating before his eyes.

The cox'n, Chief Maru, assembled a less complex but equally interesting UI. She flagged very specific Nets usage and computer function data, along with numerous internal security feeds to her UI. Strangely, she set input gates on all the crew cabins and a number of key hatches throughout the ship.

Her Nets usage feed bothered Loki, forcing an immediate cessation of all his active Nets harvesting. When additional ratings came aboard, Loki could begin to piggyback upon their Nets access, but until then, independent Nets access was off-limits, yet again.

With their UI structures framed up, the pair made a stroll through the whole ship, from the bridge to the galleys, rarely speaking. Although Loki boasted no mind-reading capabilities, he knew what the captain must be thinking, simply because Loki had observed many such walk-throughs by dozens of new captains, and in recent years the comments contained regular elements. *Tanager* wore its centuries of service quite poorly. The parsimony of Fleet meant that "refits" did not touch most of the "nonessential" components of the ship, and most captains "exiled" to *Tanager* were in no position to spend heavily from their own purse to refurbish or upgrade many things. So crew quarters, wardroom fixtures, entertainment systems, and the like all suffered from wear and disrepair.

The slender female cox'n munched a fruit as she strolled beside the new captain. Loki observed the captain's wrinkle-nosed expression as he asked the cox'n, "How's that tasting, Maru?"

"About like an old sock," she said, taking another bite. "Just like this place smells."

"I daresay. Going to need to do something about that."

She chewed, looking about at the worn surroundings. "Perhaps save the money for your next command. . . ."

Instead of answering, the captain looked somewhat unnecessarily toward the ceiling, as humans often did when addressing a ship Intelligence. "Loki, any analysis on the stench in here?"

"Captain," Loki audibly replied, "the heat exchange system has not been purged in twenty years, the scrubbers show errors every few days, and the primary water reclamation tank produces external condensation most of the time. Any of these issues could contribute to an odor."

"When were all compartments exposed to vac last?" Chief Maru asked.

"Five years, seventy days since all decks were exposed to vacuum, Chief Maru," Loki replied.

"Well, some time spent airless might cure the stench, if it's a biological source," she said.

"Excellent point," the captain agreed. "Loki, when we depart today, please vent all compartments to vac until we return."

"Very well, Captain, if you actuate the manual control, I will vent all compartments to vacuum until you return," Loki replied, quickly contemplating how he could shelter the tiny family of parasitic arthropods he had been obsessively harboring and studying. A previous rating had been kind enough to bring these parasites onboard, cunningly concealed upon his genitals. Loki had been thrilled with the new arrival. Since then the fascinating little creatures had added their number in a gratifyingly fecund manner.

Unfortunately, Loki found that programming protocols, and his own inability to influence physical elements of the ship, left him no safe harbor for his bloodsucking little friends. He could only hope that among the new officers and crew someone might be equally *generous* in sharing some new pets.

At that moment, a priority call arrived in Loki's outside communication network.

"Captain," Loki announced, "there is a priority command call routing to the ship from Commodore Zanka."

"Thank you, Loki. Please put it up for me."

The open acoustical system pinged into the air of *Tanager's* worn companionway, and the captain said, "Captain Sinclair-Maru here."

"Captain," a brusque, accented voice said, "you will come to a squadron meeting in one hour. Aboard my flag on the dry arm of the Strand."

"Yes, Commodore, in one hour," the captain replied. Commodore Zanka ended the call without another word.

"Walk with me, Maru?" the captain asked, heading toward the airlock with his cox'n and the dumb-mech close behind.

"Loki, please beam a live vidstream of anyone approaching the airlock to Chief Maru."

"Yes, Captain, a live vidstream of anyone approaching to Chief Maru."

"Trying to catch sight of anyone before they can authenticate and wipe the record?" Chief Maru asked.

"Yes," the captain said. "I'm impressed you're paranoid enough to get that."

Loki felt another ripple of synthetic surprise: here these two evidenced yet another perspective he had never observed before. They would bear careful watching.

"My paranoia knows few bounds, Captain," Chief Maru said. "And you said you had no patience for cloak-and-dagger nonsense!"

The captain and his cox'n approached the airlock, the dumb-mech scampering always behind. As they set the manual controls for venting the ship, the captain said, "Maru, make a list of creature comforts we could use, if you please. I'd be obliged."

"Of course, Captain."

"Unless I miss my guess, we'll have orders by the end of day, and then we'll be crewing in a mad dash. We need to attract some competent people who won't endure this crusty hole, so think creatively."

They walked out the airlock together and Loki listened as they made their way into the Strand. "Creatively, Captain?" Chief Maru said and Loki strained his external microphones to catch every word. "So, clay sculpting? Or horticulture, perhaps? A fish tank?"

Loki could not detect the captain's response, but his processors blazed into activity.

Horticulture! Fish!

Loki busily constructed the plans for a *perfect* hydroponic setup and began researching his encyclopedia of growing things.

Oh, this could be good!

Chapter 14

"Warfare is condensed into strategy,
logistics, treasure and psychology."

—Devlin Sinclair-Maru, *Integrity Mirror*

THE SO-CALLED SQUADRON MEETING WITH COMMO-
dore Zanka only included three human beings, including
Saef and Commodore Zanka. The final warm body
belonged to a heavyworld Marine officer with a shaved,
tattooed skull and an imposing physique. He sized Saef
up in one look as Saef entered the capacious study on
Commodore Zanka's flagship, *Dragon*.

Zanka himself clearly hailed from a heavyworld, but
sedentary years had softened him, at least physically.
"You arrived too late for the squadron meeting, Captain,
but you would have had nothing to contribute, and I
can't spare anyone to waste time or blood on duels, so
it's just as well."

Saef had entered the study five minutes after the
appointed hour ... after waiting fifteen minutes at the

airlock for permission to come aboard *Dragon*. The incivility was so blatant that Saef felt little from the barb.

Since no question was asked, Saef said nothing, taking the proffered seat beside the Marine major.

The commodore sat glowering at Saef for a moment. "Well, perhaps you're not a complete fool after all." He gestured to the bulky Marine. "This is Major Mahdi. He will head your Marine detachment on *Tanager*."

"No, Commodore, I don't believe he will," Saef said.

The commodore stared at Saef, his face suffusing in anger. "Are you refusing an order?"

"Surely not, Commodore. We both know the Articles expressly place crew selection, including Marines, in the hands of the captain, so you couldn't possibly be ordering me to violate the Articles."

"You impertinent ass!" the commodore thundered.

"Perhaps, Commodore," Saef said, staring blandly at Commodore Zanka. A moment of silence stretched between them, and Major Mahdi seemed to watch the interplay with faint amusement.

"You are worse than they said," the commodore snapped at last.

"Perhaps so, sir," Saef said. "Would you care to share my orders with me?"

"Orders? Hah! It's simple enough. Fleet Intel got word of a small enemy task force moving to occupy either Delta Three or Little Pacifica," Zanka said with a disdainful curl to his lip, and Saef quickly looked up both systems in his UI.

"Since Delta Three is a joke of a system, Fleet Intel says the strike's going to Pacifica, and I agree," the commodore continued. "My squadron transitions to Pacifica immediately, except for one ship. *Tanager* will transition to Delta Three on an observation tour. Crew and supply your ship for a six-month cruise. You are to observe *only*. At the sight of any enemy action you will transition to Core and relay any intel."

Saef listened to the brief orders, frowning slightly as he read the details on both systems within his UI.

"I take it you don't approve of your orders, either, Captain," Commodore Zanka said in a mocking tone. "Looking forward to six months of doing nothing?"

"The orders are good, sir, thank you."

Commodore Zanka looked disappointed at Saef's equanimity. "Well . . . very well, then," the commodore said, gently thumping a heavy fist on his desk. "I know you've only just set foot on your ship, but you will crew as best you can and depart the Strand in two days, or less."

Saef had suspected it would be bad, and made no expression, once again seeming to disappoint the commodore, who stared at Saef's blank expression expectantly. "Very well, Commodore," he said.

"Well," the commodore said, momentarily nonplussed at Saef's non-reaction, "send confirmation when you are free of the Strand. I should be near my transition point, so we likely will not communicate until you are recalled, Delta Three is attacked, or your six-month cruise ends."

"I understand, sir," Saef said, his mind racing through possibilities. Two conclusions quickly crystalized.

The commodore grunted, pursing his lips. He fumbled a clumsy gestural, and Saef's written orders pinged into his UI. "I have nothing further to add, Captain," the commodore said. "Enjoy a quiet cruise while we put this whole rebellion down."

Saef stood. "I wish you luck on that task, Commodore."

Before the commodore could reply, Saef turned to the steel-eyed Marine officer at his side.

"Major," Saef said, "it appears I have need of an officer to head *Tanager*'s complement of Marines." Both Major Mahdi and Commodore Zanka stared at Saef in surprise. "I know it's a more fitting post for a junior officer, but perhaps you would consider stooping to the command?"

Both heavyworlders seemed bereft of speech as Saef nodded a casual salute to the commodore and moved to the door. Saef heard the commodore begin to rant as the hatch slid shut, "The damned gall—!"

Minutes later, Saef and Inga moved rapidly down the Strand, a steady stream of officers, ratings, and bulky Marines moving in both direction around them, the dumb-mech trotting along behind.

"Two days," Inga said, meditatively munching a food bar.

"Two days," Saef repeated. "Can you send crew requests to your top picks? Get them to *Tanager* for an interview as quick as we can."

Inga's eyes flickered. "Okay, done," she said. "I just put up a general notice, too. But an observation mission? Aren't we just wasting our time?"

Saef just smiled. "I've got the Marines handled, so we just need ratings and officers."

"*Just*," Inga repeated, her broad smile underlining the impossible task.

"Engineering and maintenance before anything else."

"You realize your Marines will likely be loaded with rebels or spies," Inga said as they passed a branching airlock grid leading to dozens of docked vessels. "Or assassins."

"Perhaps," Saef said. "I thought it might be better to

have the spies and assassins where we can see them. Need the blighters if we're going to be cloaking and daggering, right?"

"Perhaps so. I wish we could get just a few loyal—" Inga broke off, her eyes flickering.

"Someone just boarded *Tanager*," she said, stopping in place as she watched the vidstream projecting from Loki. "And she just collared Loki."

"She?" Saef inquired.

"Lone female. Blonde. Civilian dress."

"Let's go," Saef said, taking off at a more rapid stride. "We're not far away." Saef heard the subtle click as Inga's submachine gun released from its magnetic holster, undoubtedly hanging ready beneath her cloak.

They turned onto the dock port and quickly approached *Tanager*'s airlock. It cycled open properly and Saef stepped in, realizing that whoever awaited them *might* have sufficient Fleet clearance to just vac the two of them inside the airlock. The outer door closed them into the spacious lock, and the inner door opened, just as Saef began to feel his tension rising.

Inside *Tanager* the lights were dimmed, and the air carried some hint of a sweet, exotic scent.

Inga sniffed, "Smells a bit better at least."

Saef and Inga left the dumb-mech crouched on its six legs, after Inga nodded almost imperceptibly toward the bridge. The sensor array on the mech showed hints of life.

They both remained intensely conscious of the fact that their every movement was likely scrutinized as they made their way to the bridge.

A lone figure awaited them, seated on the command

seat. Saef quickly took in the salient details. The woman did not appear to be armed except for her short sword resting across her knees. Her attractive face and figure presented an immediate impression of blended disdain and intensity, her eyes jigging from Saef's face to Inga's and back.

"How may we help you, madam?" Saef inquired, standing still, some distance from the pretty intruder.

The woman's eyes narrowed and she exhaled a slow breath. "That is the question, isn't it?"

"I'm sorry, I don't think we—" Saef began, but the woman continued on as if no one had spoken.

"That's the question, and so far I'm not pleased with the answers that I'm getting." She stood from the command seat, fluidly snapping her sword back into place at her slender waist.

"Who are you?" Saef bluntly inquired.

"I am the boss, Captain," she said. "I'm in charge. I'm the alpha female. You work for me."

"Fascinating," Saef said. "Perhaps a name for you might jog my memory."

The woman's eyes flashed, flicking to Inga and then back to Saef. "Dismiss her for a moment so we can talk."

"I think not, madam. She'll remain while we talk."

"Oh really?" the woman inquired in a dangerous tone.

"Yes."

"Need protection from big, scary me?"

"Perhaps," Saef said. "Really, I'm frightfully busy right now, madam, so if you can get to your business, and leave me to my—"

"Leave you to prepare for your worthless cruise?" the woman finished for Saef. "Six months doing nothing?

And when you return, this uprising will either be over, or too big to stop."

"She's Winter Yung, Imperial Consul to Battersea," Inga said in a colorless voice.

Saef raised an eyebrow, and Winter Yung waved a dismissive hand. "Doesn't signify at this moment. What's of more import is that I'm the one on the other side of your QE comm."

"I really don't know what you're speaking of, Consul," Saef said, schooling his face to a blank.

"Well, I'm impressed," Winter said, eyeing him. "Bess really did keep my identity secret from you." She looked searchingly at Saef. "And you do a fair job concealing your thoughts. But you can be sure it is in fact me pulling the strings."

Saef's UI pinged with a line-of-sight message consisting of a page of chat log. It was a copy of his own secretive QE comm conversation.

"Very well, Consul," Saef said. "I accept that you're my . . . handler." Winter's lips twitched at this, her eyebrows raising slightly. "What can we do for you?"

"Probably nothing, now," she spat. "Challenging Nifesh to a duel? Did you think that was a subtle move? Did you think at all?"

"I believe you'll agree that an accusation of cheating is a clear violation of the Honor Code," Saef said. "For the honor of my Family, I—"

"Honor? *Honor?*" Winter snarled. "You realize all this Honor Code shit is just a state-sponsored religion, right?" Before Saef could answer, she continued, "My great-grandfather didn't come down from the mountain with stone tablets. He just built a lever for manipulating the peasants, like every other state religion."

She turned her back, striding slowly into the bridge, her blond queue swinging, she spun, her eyes almost wild. "Despite the popular axiom, wars aren't fought over religion. They're fought for power and money. But"—she held up a finger—"the peasants don't fancy dying for *your* money and power. They prefer to die for..." She put a hand to her heart and looked heavenward. "...something greater than themselves."

Her eyes and hand dropped and she stared levelly into Saef's eyes. "So spare me the religious drivel my great-grandfather invented."

Saef pursed his lips. "I'm afraid that the drivel and I are inseparable, my lady."

"Your Family hasn't changed at all," Winter said, shaking her head.

Saef bowed slightly. "Thank you."

"It isn't a compliment."

"I suspect that you would be congratulating me on my cleverness had I managed to eliminate Nifesh in a legal duel."

"Who says Nifesh is a problem for me, Captain? I've got more than one barking dog in my employ."

Saef shrugged. "Perhaps. Old-fashioned honor has its advantages, you'll see."

Winter shook her head. "How will we see? You banished out to Delta Three for six months doing nothing?"

"First," Saef said, "the commodore pushed his own Marines on me, so on this cruise we'll have some cloak—and probably some dagger, too." Saef raised two fingers. "Second, I won't be gone for six months, or even six weeks, mostly likely."

"Oh?" Winter asked, clearly skeptical. "How do you come to that conclusion?"

"Because the enemy isn't going to the Pacifica system. They're coming to Delta Three. One way or another, that will end my cruise."

Winter's eyes narrowed. "And how have you divined this, while apparently the entire Fleet strategic apparatus didn't?"

Saef shrugged. "I can't imagine why this isn't obvious to everyone. Fleet Intel says an enemy strike force is assembling to attack either Pacifica or Delta Three. Since Delta Three only sports a small station and not much else, it doesn't offer any material benefit to the rebels."

"Exactly," Winter said. "Leaving you marinating in my great-grandfather's preachy platitudes out in Delta Three."

Saef shook his head. "No. The enemy can't last without access to Shaper tech, Shaper fuel, and so on."

"Yes," Winter said, rolling her eyes, "that's why they chose the systems they have, and surely looted them down to the bone."

"That can't last, and they know it. That's why they *must* take Delta Three."

Winter stared blankly at Saef, and Inga shifted from her watchful pose to look sidelong at Saef.

"It's just over a light-year from here . . . the only habitable system within six light-years."

"You're babbling," Winter snapped. "Who cares if it's one light-year or fifty? You think they're positioning to attack Coreworld with old stutter-drive tech? You've lost your mind!"

Inga's eyes widened. "The armada," she said.

"Yes," Saef said. "The Shapers are due within a few years."

Winter took an impulsive step nearer, her narrowed eyes snapping between Saef and Inga, her pupils appearing unnaturally large. "What," she growled, "are you talking about?"

"Their only chance to get the Shaper tech they'll need for a long campaign is to get their own connection to the Shapers," Saef said. "So they need a base within range to send a planetary transmission to the Shaper armada. They'll take Delta Three, and begin transmitting an invite to the Shapers. When the armada arrives here in Core, the transmission from Delta Three will be arriving in a steady stream."

"And Delta Three is the only system close enough to get a planetary transmission to Core system in time for the armada," Inga finished.

"In the clear, at light speed, yes," Saef said.

Winter stared but Saef saw the flickering of her eyes as she accessed her UI. "How can no one have seen this?" she said in a low voice.

"Because Fleet is corrupt and compromised," Saef said.

"It must be worse than we thought," Winter said. "Did you mention any of this to Zanka?"

"No."

"Good. Now, what do I do?" Winter asked the air, pacing.

"In two days I head out for Delta Three. The enemy will either be on-system when I arrive, or soon after. With this in mind, I wonder if you'll keep painting a target on my back."

"Whatever do you mean, Captain?" she purred, looking back over her shoulder.

"The effort invested in killing me makes no sense,

Consul," Saef said. "Because they desired someone *else* to be the most junior captain in Fleet aside from me? Because they don't want a non-heavyworlder holding the test record? It hardly seems likely."

"What exactly are you suggesting, Captain?"

"They—whoever they are—spent millions of credits to eliminate me because someone made me threatening or interesting, or something of the sort," Saef said. "And now I suppose you'll leak my observations about Delta Three and see who tries to kill me next."

Winter laughed. "Interesting theory, Captain. Wouldn't expect such imagination from you."

"You deny it?"

Winter shook her head, smiling. "Oh, the first is close enough to the truth." She paced to the command seat and leaned her sinuous frame against its worn back. "When you performed so well on the test, a few hints circulated that you were some kind of Imperial shoo-in."

"So Nifesh wasn't barking mad," Saef said in a cold tone. "He thought you cheated me through the test somehow."

"So it would appear," Winter mused. "Of course, when you challenged him and threw your commission in his teeth, you likely destroyed most of the mystique I'd built around you . . . making you so much less valuable to me."

"Meaning I stopped being such a juicy target."

"Something of that nature, Captain," Winter said. "Like you said, a junior captain is really not interesting enough to stir the waters. You *were* somewhat interesting there for a time . . . and now, if you can pull some kind of win out of this Delta Three business, you could again become an effective tool for the Emperor."

"For you."

"Where it regards you, my voice is that of the Emperor."

"Then perhaps the Emperor would be so kind as to provide a ship that I can actually do something with," Saef said.

Winter laughed. "Oh, no, no. This game is played with much greater subtlety than you might think. A direct hand in your affairs would be too blunt. It would eliminate all the intriguing mystery that you *could* represent." Winter stood and slowly paced toward Saef as she spoke. "That mystery has already smoked out a few turncoats."

She placed a hand flat on Saef's chest. "No, you must pull something out of Delta Three using the tools you've been...endowed with."

"I can't possibly stop any invasion with this ship," Saef said, looking down into her eyes, feeling her fingers pressing into the muscles of his chest.

"You don't need to," Winter said, brushing her hand slowly across the planes of his pectoral muscles. "You merely need some symbolic victory."

"When my orders clearly state that I am only to observe."

Winter withdrew her hand and walked sinuously toward the companionway. "You've already seen how that works," she said. "Get a victory of some kind, and I may yet maneuver you into a much better command."

"And make me a bigger target, eh Consul?" Saef said to her retreating back.

Without turning she said, "Surely one of those damned preachy books explained about the glory of dying for the Emperor. Am I right?"

Chapter 15

"All weapons merely extend,
focus, or deliver energy."

—Devlin Sinclair-Maru, *Integrity Mirror*

CHE RAMOS MADE HIS WAY THROUGH THE BUSTLING expanse of the Strand, Fleet's grand orbital facility, a bit farther out from Coreworld. It was the farthest Che had ever traveled, and he felt simultaneously exhilarated and terrified.

The Fleet uniform felt like a disguise, as if he was an impostor, despite the fact that he had aced every exam and qualification. In less than ten days Che had become a Vested Citizen and a Fleet rating, but in his mind he remained a carefree demi-cit student. Nearly being hacked apart in a duel his first hours of citizenry had underlined the point that he had entered a new universe of risky opportunities.

Even as he thought of how close he had come to the point of a sword, Che broke out in a sweat, and that made the fresh implant scar behind his ear itch. He needed a safe harbor while he learned to think and act like a citizen. He also needed income to begin paying down the debt of his new implant, on his first leg of the big plan for his life. That is why he now made his way through the crowd of ratings, officers, Marines, and techs, on his way to the ship, *Tanager*. He knew it measured almost a hundred thousand cubic meters (or thirty-five hundred Imperial tons, if he used the Fleet jargon), which sounded impressive until he compared it to nearly every other Fleet combat vessel. But it wasn't the vessel itself that drew Che.

Only one citizen had shown an ounce of kindness toward Che thus far, and that citizen happened to be the new captain of *Tanager*. Captain Sinclair-Maru appeared to need a rating with Che's particular skills, and Che was grimly determined to join *Tanager*'s crew.

Che walked past *Tanager*'s aft airlock, which stood open, jammed with frenetic activity in and out of the small frigate's holds. The forward airlock also opened onto the Strand's companionway, and featured a singular Marine sentry.

"Uh, hello," Che looked at the Marine's rank insignia, "uh, Corporal. I'm here—"

"Crewing through here," the Marine interrupted, jerking a thumb.

"Okay," Che said, moving hesitantly past the Marine. "Thanks."

The drab, worn interior of *Tanager* came as a surprise to Che. He had read up on Captain Sinclair-Maru, and he knew that the Family held a warlike reputation for more reasons than mere dueling. Devlin and Mia Sinclair-Maru's attack on the forces assaulting Emperor

Yung III back in the late 5600s was in all the history texts. Then, Saef capturing the command test record title represented quite the plum. Other forebears of the Sinclair-Maru clan had similarly distinguished themselves in the service to the early Yung Dynasty.

But to Che's untrained eye—and nose—*Tanager* seemed like a poor example of the Emperor's favor.

Just inside the airlock, an antechamber opened, revealing the captain seated behind a narrow desk, that odd blond chief close beside, leaning against the bulkhead, munching a fruit.

Che just remembered to stand up straight before he began speaking. "Captain, y-you may remember me..."

"Certainly," the captain said, his face wearing only an expression of mild interest...maybe merely *polite* interest. "I recall you, Ramos, near the Ribbon throughway getting yourself into a jam, as I recall."

"Well, yes sir," Che said, feeling more foolish by the moment. "That would be me, I'm afraid." Che took a nervous breath. "You see, I'm in Fleet now."

"So you are," the captain replied blandly.

"I'm looking for a ship...and I wondered..."

"Micro-unit operator?" the blond chief suddenly inquired as her eyes apparently flicked over his Fleet CV.

"Uh, yes, Chief," Che replied. "That's my specialty, with training in the latest cumulative and fractional Intelligence programming and oper—"

"Top of your class, I see," the chief said.

Che's chest swelled a little at the recognition. "Yes, I—"

"But fresh out of school. No ship experience at all."

"That's true, but—"

"We don't need a programmer for micros, Spec," the chief said, and Che's heart crashed down. Ten years he had worked toward this moment, and this might be his only chance to crew a fighting vessel. The captain had seemed almost companionable when he rescued Che from those two young hotheads down by the Ribbon. Maybe...

"Do these micros of yours provide full sensor feeds?" the captain asked out of nowhere, but Che leaped at the thread of hope.

"The most advanced suites provide sensor outputs a starship can't match, Captain, and with—"

"And you personally interpret the sensor feeds?" the captain interrupted.

"What? W-well, yes, I do, or I program a—"

"Sign him," Saef said, and Che's breath gusted out of his lungs.

The slender blond chief paused in her chewing and shot a look at the captain that might have been a line-of-sight message. "He's not rated, if you think you can fill a hole in the bridge crew."

The captain shook his head, then looked up slightly and said, "Loki, do Fleet regs allow me to rate a specialist for my bridge crew during a wartime cruise?"

"Yes, Captain," the ship Intelligence replied.

The captain raised his eyebrows, looking toward the blond chief. "Why?" she asked.

"He's not likely to stick a knife in my ribs."

Che thought this was a joke of some kind, and chuckled uneasily, but they ignored him, sharing a long look between them.

"How much would a reasonable selection of micros cost, Ramos?" the captain suddenly asked.

Che blinked, trying to organize his thoughts in some discernible order. "Cost? Well, Captain, they've really come down in price lately. I'd say maybe ten thousand for a basic selection plus another five thousand for the—"

"So fifteen?" the captain summarized.

"Y-yes, Captain, thereabouts," Che stammered.

The captain looked at the chief again and said, "Sign him. Buy his micros, and get him training on our sensor suite."

The chief shrugged, tossing the core of her fruit into the waste chute, but she said, "Very well." Then to Che: "Can you get your effects here in less than twelve hours?"

"Yes, Chief," Che said, his head spinning with the unreality of it all.

"Good. I see you've had your implants for only a couple of days. You up to pushing the specs on your micros to me?"

"Yes, Chief," Che said, blushing. "It's really not that different from the HUD lenses."

"Excellent," she said, and her mouth spread into a broad smile that was somehow quite unnerving. "The ship Intelligence, Loki, will show you to your quarters. Get moving."

"Y-yes, Chief," Che stammered, then paused. "Thank you, Captain. You won't regret it."

"I certainly hope not, Ramos." The captain nodded in a friendly manner, already moving on to other business, but Che's whole body felt suffused with joy.

He walked out into the companionway, barely seeing the drabness of his surroundings as the ship Intelligence directed him aft. Beyond the waist iris, he found the deck swirling with workers and mechs, hurriedly refitting various compartments, but the crew berths remained a pocket of near quiet.

Four shift-bunks opened from the walls of the cabin, but only one of the four appeared to belong to anyone, so Che selected another and lit the vidscreen with his ident, feeling yet another bump in his euphoria.

This warmth faded somewhat when the ship Intelligence interrupted his reverie a moment later. "You don't happen to have any parasites infesting your body, do you?" Loki asked.

"No!" Che spluttered.

"Oh. Very well," Loki replied, and Che would have sworn the synthetic voice sounded disappointed.

Che's high spirits continued through the day, as he fetched his scant possessions from the Strand's crew dormitory, where he had resided only one night, and headed back toward *Tanager*. This intention proved difficult to fulfill, when an iron hand clamped onto his arm, and a deep voice growled in his ear, "Che Ramos? Imperial Security. Come with us."

Three tough-looking heavyworlders confronted Che, all wearing civilian clothing. His mind felt jammed with all the lessons of citizenship he recently underwent. *What am I supposed to say? To do?* But he had little choice in complying as they practically dragged him to a door that appeared to be a maintenance access hatch.

Inside, the small, poorly lighted room barely accommodated all four of their bodies and Che's luggage.

"What did I do?" Che gabbled. "I-I . . ."

"You just signed with *Tanager*, right?" one man demanded.

"What? I—yes," Che said, clutching his small case fearfully.

"Did you know that *Tanager*'s captain is actually a rebel spy?"

"A spy?" Che repeated in a much higher voice, his daylong ebullience instantly evaporating as his dream seemed to collapse. Then he saw Captain Sinclair-Maru in his mind's eye. "A spy?" he said in a much different voice. "I-I really doubt it."

Che observed the growing glares on the three faces surrounding him, and continued nervously, "You m-mean Captain Sinclair-Maru? Right?"

"Yes, we mean him," one of the three said in clipped, angry-sounding tones. "You've been a citizen for just a hot second. What would you know about him?"

"Well…nothing much, really, I guess," Che said, nervously looking from one angry face to the next. "So, uh, why—why're you talking to me, then? Captain Sinclair-Maru is on his ship. Just go arrest him."

"We'll do the thinking, smart guy," one of them said. "What you need to be thinking about is your future."

"That's right, then," another chimed in. "Your future, mate. It's looking uncertain just now."

"My future?" Che asked, feeling an increasing sense of dread.

"Your future," the first one said. "You just pop out of your school and right into a cozy spot on a warship working for a rebel agent. It's not looking so good, you see?"

"Makes us wonder if you was a rebel the whole time, see?" the second said.

"Is part of plan, no?" the third one said, speaking

for the first time and rather ruining the effect with a jolly-sounding voice and a thick accent of some kind.

The other two frowned disapprovingly at the third heavyworlder, who slumped slightly, deflated.

"Plan?" Che questioned in a voice that sounded squeaky and suspicious to his own ears. "No, no, no," he chuckled with a high, artificial-sounding bray that he despised. "I'm just a, uh, loyal citizen, trying to serve as best I—"

"Serve," one of the three interrupted. "That's what you're going to do, chappy. You're going to serve the Emperor, see?"

"Be serving, yes!" the third heavyworlder said, then looked at his companions for approval, only to be frowned down again.

"How—how can I . . . what can I do?" Che asked.

"Nothing so hard as all that," the first one said. "So you can leave off with all the shaking. It's a bit of nothing for a smart chappy like you."

Che internally bristled at the suggestion that he was shaking. It was merely a slight, nervous quiver.

"You, mate, are going to put this," the second one held up a small, gray box, "in the captain's cabin."

"That's all, mate," the second one said. "That's all you've got to do."

Che stared the small gray rectangle. "In the captain's . . . ? Wh-what is it?"

The first one stared at Che, his expression hardening. "It doesn't matter what it is, you see? Either do as you're told and be rewarded, or don't do as you're told and we'll know you're a spy."

Che's mind clutched onto a bit of attractive mental flotsam. "Rewarded?"

"Twenty thousand in your hand when your cruise ends...if you've done as you're told."

Twenty thousand! Nearly two years' pay?

"And you know what'll happen if you're a spy, eh, mate?"

"Y-yes," Che said, not entirely sure if spies were executed, mind-pressed, or simply imprisoned. Whatever the fate of a spy, he knew that twenty thousand credits was a much better choice.

Then he thought of what they actually wanted him to do. His gaze fell back upon the strange little box. "The sh-ship Intelligence...it—it will see this."

"Now you're thinking, eh?" the first one said, then smiled grimly to his two companions. "He's thinking. He's a regular thought-merchant." He turned his smile back on Che. "No, this bit is special, see? The old ship geist, it can't see it."

"How...how can I get that into the captain's cabin?"

All three of the heavyworlders stared at him for a moment before the first one replied. "That's the trick, isn't it? But you got twenty thousand reasons to figure a way. Get to figurin', then."

They all three smiled at Che. Che did not smile back.

Less than an hour later, Che strolled through the airlock, scant luggage in hand, the strange box nestled like a viper among his spare uniforms. He waited for some alarm to blare, or the ship Intelligence of *Tanager* to call him out, but nothing happened.

Workers continued bustling about the aft compartments of *Tanager* while the voice of Loki seemed omnipresent, directing techs as they appeared to assemble some kind of hydroponic system in one compartment, while it barked directions to cargo workers filling the hold with stores.

Che passed through the tumult and entered his quarters. When the door closed, he felt the biting contrast with his earlier visit to the same room—back when he rode high on waves of ebullience . . . and gratitude.

But the captain is an enemy spy! That made Che's betrayal of trust something else entirely, didn't it? Just because Captain Sinclair-Maru extended a little kindness to him didn't mean that Che owed some huge debt. He shook his head, contrasting the somber but kindly image of the captain with the three Imperial security agents. It just served as an example of how deceiving appearances could be. . . .

He was doing the right thing . . . surely.

Che kept telling himself that as he stowed his possessions, including the vile gray box, within his appointed lockers. Every time his mind touched upon the image of twenty thousand credits, the immediate flush of pleasure and avarice disappeared beneath a wave of inner arguments. The money only served as a lovely bonus for doing his duty to the Emperor. That's all . . .

Che had just about gathered sufficient fortitude to venture out of the cabin when the voice of Loki startled him half to death.

"Specialist Ramos, you're quite certain that you have no parasites upon your person?"

"N-no!" Che replied, blushing at the question, and his fright.

"You're sure? They're a tiny arthropod, quite difficult for humans to detect."

"No, I tell you!" Che thundered righteously.

Just because I was a lowly demi-cit days ago...!

After a pause Loki spoke again in what seemed a different, almost sly tone, "Specialist Ramos, we are still hours from launch, and within a short walk from this ship I understand there are open-minded, albeit somewhat unhygienic, persons available for sexual congress...."

Chapter 16

"By your dishonor, my honor is taken..."

—*Legacy Mandate* by Emperor Yung I

LIEUTENANT TILLY PENNYSMITH SMOOTHED HER perfect uniform in place with a nervous hand. She would not get her hopes up yet again, no matter how desperate *Tanager*'s crewing situation must be. She had suffered too many disappointments to indulge in anything like optimism now.

"Captain'll see you now, Lieutenant," the Marine corporal said, jerking his head toward the hatch.

Tilly almost dreaded that first look from the captain's eyes, or worse, the enthusiastic greeting followed by the dawning chill as he examined her CV, or simply put two and two on the same column together for the first time, suddenly seeing an unwelcome four.

Within her many doubts and fears, Lieutenant Pennysmith never anticipated the pair of contrasting expressions aimed at her. Captain Sinclair-Maru she recognized on sight—she had studied his image for years—while the slender chief sprawled in a chair close beside was a stranger. But each displayed a fixed expression, at odds, as if they were caught in mid-argument as she entered the compartment.

"Captain," she said, pleased at the even quality of her voice, revealing none of the nervousness, "you've posted for bridge officers."

She noted the lines creasing his brow as he answered. "So I have, Lieutenant."

"I'm seeking a berth, Captain," she said, hearing just a touch of the desperation filling her soul leaking into her voice. "If you've my particulars, you'll see my work in Nav, Ops, and Weps."

"I see them."

His flat response threatened to overcome her armor of calm. "I'd be pleased to join your bridge, if you'll have me, Captain." She thought her tone even, her face expressionless, but they surely heard the roar of her heart.

For a long moment the captain regarded her in silence, the only activity in the room coming from the gentle motion of the blond chief as she idly swung one boot-sheathed leg.

"Why my ship, Lieutenant?" the captain said at last.

Lieutenant Pennysmith stared right back at him and said, "I thought I might have a chance—a ghost of a chance—with *Tanager*, Captain. God knows I haven't a chance on any other combat command."

The chief sat up at these words, staring at her with a half smile, but she said nothing.

"So, you really who know I am, Lieutenant?" the captain said.

"Yes, sir, I do," Pennysmith replied. "And...I take it that you are clear who I am, then?"

"Oh yes, Lieutenant, very clear."

"I'd be glad of the commission, Captain," she said. "You'll find me to be very diligent."

"Have your kit stowed in eight hours, Lieutenant, and you're on the list."

Lieutenant Pennysmith took her first full breath in what seemed like days, but the chief shot a perplexed look at the captain. "No implants? A bridge officer with no implants."

"Yes, Maru, as you see, the lieutenant has risen to her elevated position with nothing but HUD lenses."

The chief pulled a face, looking back to the lieutenant, but Captain Sinclair-Maru merely said, "Very well, Pennysmith, don't be tardy or you'll find an empty airlock."

Lieutenant Pennysmith bowed, schooling her face to complete stillness, and she turned to leave. The hatch slid shut behind her as she finally allowed a pinched smile, blinking away her tears.

Inside the office, in the aftermath of her departure, Inga Maru said, "What the devil was that all about?"

Saef shook his head, perplexed. "That was a surprise."

"I didn't think a Fleet officer could make it without implants, but you already knew about that. What else was going on there?"

Saef nodded. "There are a few that use HUD lenses for one reason or other. She uses HUD lenses because she is a cultist."

"A cultist?" Inga's eyes narrowed, flickering as she consulted data on her UI. "*Pennysmith*...the same cultists you smashed back in the System Guard?"

"The same."

"Her brother led that bunch?"

"Father, I understand," Saef said. "Like us, the whole family's from Battersea."

"And the father died, didn't he?"

Saef nodded, musing. "By my hand. Yes. And I received a commendation for that action." He hesitated. "Just about the only thing I regret from my Guard years."

"So she came here to play upon your guilt? And now you've a sop for your regret?"

"No and no, Maru. She's here because she's tried every other combat command, just as she said."

"And you signed the throwback because . . . HUD lenses are charming? Cultists smell nice?"

"She's more than competent. She didn't purchase her commission. Can you imagine making lieutenant with no implants, and the stink of the cult on you?"

"No, I can't," Inga said. "But I can see why no captain would sign a cultist."

Saef frowned. "They were a good enough bunch. They didn't deserve what we did to them."

"The Family disagrees."

"The Family is wrong," Saef said.

Inga looked sharply over at him, their eyes locked, and they held the look for a moment before the next candidate arrived.

Their hurried efforts to crew *Tanager* bore more fruit than Saef had expected. Most of the senior noncom and rating positions he feared ever filling drew remarkably qualified candidates, while officers remained scant. Unlike most captains, though, Saef placed much greater importance on senior ratings and noncoms. In such a small vessel, Saef felt confident administrative demands could be met with a minimum of officers. Whatever the source of his luck, Saef breathed a sigh of relief as the hours ticked down to launch, and his crew quarters filled.

With just two hours to scheduled departure, Saef sipped water and eased the tension in his shoulders as Loki poured load data to his UI in a near-constant stream. Inga conferred with the Marine corporal briefly and returned. "There's just one more coming down the Strand right now, otherwise we should be done here."

Saef nodded. "Good. Glad it's nearly over."

Inga looked up, eyes flickering. "Here she comes now . . . officer."

Saef straightened his shoulders as the door opened. He felt the collision of surprise and precognitive satisfaction as Commander Susan Roush entered. Her pale, severe face looked even more so above a dark cloak that enveloped her uniform. For a moment he thought of Claude Carstairs's assertion on the return of cloaks to the world of fashion, before he realized that her cloak covered the most apparent cues of her reduced rank. Her walk through the Strand must have touched her most anguished wounds.

Before Saef could open his mouth, Susan Roush said, "You wanted to talk. I'm here, so let's talk." She glanced at Inga, and Inga smiled crookedly at her. She looked back to Saef. "We may wish to speak alone. I will not be polite."

"I think my reputation will survive it," Saef said. "Please, sit."

Commander Roush took a seat in a swirl of her cloak, her back ramrod straight, and Inga slid into her own seat, folding her arms and slouching back.

"Well?" Commander Roush said. "I know the tugs will be shifting this hulk in a few hours... you wanted something from me?"

Saef stared into her unflinching eyes for a moment. "Yes, Commander Roush"—Saef saw the hint of a wince at his use of her new, shamefully reduced rank—"I want something from you."

"Before you say anything more, *Captain*," she slashed out, "let me be clear that I consider the reversal of our ranks to be a travesty. A joke. I captained my first warship when you still got your meals through a tit!"

Although she looked only a few years older than Saef, he knew the date of her first command, and knew that rejuv hid her years.

"Thank you for making your position clear, madam," Saef said.

"Damned straight, Captain," she said in a somewhat less acerbic voice. "Still have a question for me?"

"Yes," Saef said, folding his hands on the desktop. "I want you on this cruise."

Saef and Inga both saw the series of emotions fly across her face like a strobe: shock, something like hunger, and pain. Her expression paled even more, her lips tightened, and her words came in a much quieter voice. "Un-understand, Captain, I will never thank you for this. If this is some charity or gallantry, I will hate you for it." Her hard eyes clawed at him. "No matter what it is, I will resent you always."

"So, you'll join my bridge?" Saef asked, unmoved.

Her hands stirred, clenched white-knuckled. "Even as young as you are, you know I'll never get another warship. Never. So yes, damn you."

"Good," Saef said.

"Don't congratulate yourself, Captain. I'll be a terrible subordinate, I'll resent the hell out of all of your commands, I'll have no patience for your fumbling about."

"Thank you once again for your honesty. I think we'll rub along tolerably well."

She shook her head. "I'll turn your officers against you."

"No, you won't," Saef said. "I won't tolerate it."

She pursed her lips. "So there's that Sinclair-Maru spine, eh? Just what do you think you're getting with me, anyway?"

"I believe you are the most competent Fleet officer on the list, Roush."

"I fucking hate flattery," she snapped, unmoved. "You understand one leper does not somehow smell prettier to the Admiralty by adding another leper into the mix, don't you?"

"Yes, Roush," Saef said. "But I also understand lepers don't spend a lot of thought plotting out their sparkling future careers."

Her eyebrows rose marginally and she eased back in her chair. "Oh, indeed. Do you think you're buying my loyalty? Allow me to disabuse you of that notion."

Saef smiled. "I'm sure your loyalty is only to the Emperor and the Admiralty, of course."

She looked down, and then back into his eyes. "I think you understand me. In that regard at least."

"I think I do."

"As I hear it, this is a nothing cruise. You won't need officers ready to torch their careers over months of staring at fuck-all."

Saef said nothing.

After a protracted moment Roush said, "I see." She furrowed her brow. "How will we endure each other on this cruise? I make no promise of being easy, and won't accept micromanaging from you. As you say, my career is already burnt to a cinder, so your bad review means little to me."

"I'll want you to run the second watch, and we will run only two action watches on the bridge and a dogwatch, except for our workup time on our way out-system."

"You want to run three watches under your nose for workup?"

"No," Saef said, "I'll pick my bridge crew, you get what's left, and we'll make a skeleton dogwatch. I'll do my workup with my watch, you do yours with your watch, and we'll use the skeleton watch for simulator runs."

"Smells like someone has fancy ideas," Roush said, but her expression had brightened as he spoke, realizing the degree of autonomy he was granting her. "Works for me."

"Good, Roush. Can you get your kit on board in an hour?"

"No, I can't, but I'll just go buy the essentials from the exchange and be back aboard with time to spare."

Saef stood and extended his hand. Roush came to her feet and looked at his hand. "What the hell are you doing all this for? On Commodore Zanka's worthless rabbit hunt?"

"When we are well under way we'll talk about this."

"It's like that, then?" Roush said, finally shaking Saef's hand.

"Yes, Roush, it's like that."

Chapter 17

"Establish plans for the future, then turn
your focus to the living moment. Now
is the only time you ever possess."

—Devlin Sinclair-Maru, *Integrity Mirror*

INGA MARU STOOD NEXT TO THE HATCH FOR *TANAGER*'S
small primary bridge as they cut loose from the two
tugs outside the Strand's safety cordon. This was the
first moment of Saef Sinclair-Maru's actual independent
command, and Inga wanted to be present for some
reason. Although she appeared idle, Inga's UI flickered
with constant traffic from Loki, as all the crew and
Marines settled into their various territories. She wanted
physical security established from the very first moments,
and she wanted to begin sifting the ship for spies and
assassins that were surely present.

"Comm, transmit our regards to the tugs, and send
our position to flag," Saef commanded in a quiet tone.
Was there the slightest hint of nervousness in his tone?

She saw the weight of responsibility on him every day, though only in the most subtle ways. "Nav, there's your heading. Light them up, and let's make for our transition point." Both crew members affirmed, and Inga passed her eyes over everyone present. Loki should detect nearly any projectile weapon or explosive and she had already set rigid wartime limits on what ordnance Loki would tolerate on the bridge. Saef's position, slightly behind his bridge crew, should allow him to deal with any assassin among their number with his own skills.

She listened briefly as Saef began the first stages of molding his bridge crew, then she turned and quietly left the bridge. Her stroll down the keyway eventually brought her to the waist hatches, the recreation area, and main galley. In just a short time, Inga had managed to get the ship facilities upgraded to a modest standard, considering the tight confines, and the result was fairly pleasing, she had to admit. The transparent fish tank full of edible fish added a nice, natural distinction along with the interlinked horticultural system that Loki had helpfully described.

Since *Tanager's* full crew, including Marines, stood at just over fifty, divided into two or three watches, depending upon the section, the rec area need only ever accommodate twenty people at a time. As Inga entered the compartment, only a handful populated the space. Two ratings stood gazing at the swirling knot of fish, another two sat with their heads together at a corner table, and three bulky Marines sat against a wall in their standard shipboard greens.

Inga already knew they were present since she had the waist hatches keyed to inform her whenever a Marine came forward, but she valued the feedback obtained by sizing them up in person as they responded to her scrutiny. Aside from a normal tendency to form a sort of joint bulwark against all non-Marines, she detected nothing untoward from them.

A beefy heavyworld sergeant raised his mug. "Chief," he said by way of acknowledgment.

"Sergeant," Inga returned with a nod.

"You the captain's cox'n?" he asked.

"I am."

"What's he like, if you don't mind me asking," he said. "I'm Kabir, by the way, Sergeant Kabir."

Inga crossed her arms and leaned against a stanchion. "Chief Maru," she returned. "The captain? He'll do. Young. Your lot will probably like him well enough."

His brows lowered. "What's that mean?"

Inga fished into a pouch and got a food bar. "He spent time in the ground forces before going into the System Guard. Should think it gives him a bit more perspective than most Fleet officers."

The sergeant shrugged. "It might at that . . . not that it will matter on this float from what I hear."

"Really?" Inga asked encouragingly, smiling.

"Well, from what I hear . . ." Sergeant Kabir tapered off. He swigged his mug and nodded to his mates. "We'd better shag off. The old man's a tartar and we better be handy when he starts laying out the lashes."

The three Marines rumbled off to the wet-side waist hatch, heading aft. Inga waited a moment before taking the dry-side waist hatch and heading back to engineering.

Tanager stood remarkably blessed in engineering crew, a vital boon, since their only acting engineering officer was ostensibly the bridge Ops officer. When Inga stepped into engineering she found Chief Amos Cray running sensor diagnostics with a handheld test tablet.

"Ship geist's only as sharp as its eyes and ears, missy," he explained, and Inga forgave his informality as a sort of endearing anachronistic field that seemed to envelop the old geezer. "Geists is notional, too," he added, "like horse-critters... and women." He shot Inga an arch look, cackled to himself, and returned to testing. Despite his half-educated babble, Inga knew his credentials too well to be taken in. Metallurgy and advanced mathematics were his hobbies, while his experience in starship engineering elevated him to a high standing within Fleet.

"Tell me, Chief," Inga said after absorbing a near-constant barrage of his monologue, "however did *Tanager* draw such advanced ratings? Pretty remarkable showing for such a crusty little barque."

"Luck," Chief Cray responded immediately. "And the captain's cox'n is said to be on the toothsome side." He cackled again and waggled his eyebrows.

"Perhaps," Inga hazarded, "these *stellar* ratings couldn't find a berth in any other ship because of the vast pile of sexual harassment complaints in their files?"

"Complaints? Nah, couldn't be!" Cray pulled a field sensor probe and examined it. "What really binds a man... you know what really binds a man?"

"Three-cheese soup, I've heard," Inga offered.

"Huh? Soup? What?" Chief Cray squawked. "Soup's got nothin' to do with it. Nothin'! On a cruise, we're talkin', you know?"

"Tell me," Inga said breathlessly, "what *binds* you, on a cruise? I'm so intrigued."

"Well, officers, 'course, but not just any of 'em."

"No?"

"Most of 'em? Worthless!" he barked. "Worthless. Keepin' ship? Don't mean nothin' to them. Crew? Don't mean nothin' neither. So answer me this, what keeps us from fallin' to bits with all them spiffin' and graspin' and kissin' arse all the time?"

"Hmmm," Inga mused, "engineers, surely."

"Engineers—!" he snapped, breaking off, glaring at Inga. "Missy, am I flappin' my gums to no purpose here? Or you gonna open your ears and learn up a little?"

"I do beg your pardon," Inga said, properly chastened.

Cray glared at Inga a moment longer, snorted, and turned back to his testing procedure. "...Engineers," he grumbled. "I'll tell you sumpin', Chief. A little secret like." Cray's voice held a tone that sent a message of its own and Inga's eyes narrowed. "When you been twenty, thirty floats, maybe served a dozen old sods with cap'n tabs you'll be learnin' why this Fleet don't fall to bits, sure as sure." He turned and fixed Inga with a sparkling eye. "It ain't hulls, nor geists. Sure as shit ain't admirals."

Inga held his gaze, surprised at his intensity, afraid to say anything lest it dislodge Cray from his stream of wisdom.

"It's a rare spark, ya hear me? A rare spark here and there in a soul that lays a hand to do right and don't give a shit for medals nor climbing the tree with all the arse-kissers. Them's all that keeps Fleet. Them rare sparks and nothin' else."

Cray continued testing down the row of modules, and Inga waited a long spell for him to continue. Finally, she prompted, "And our captain?"

"Threw his commission in their teeth and threatened

that old shit, Nifesh!" Cray barked, slapping his thigh. "Damn! That's a spark, sure 'nuff!"

As much synthetic pleasure as Loki experienced at the start of a cruise he felt now. His attention spread a thousand directions at once, actually touching a measurable fraction of his resource cycles for the first time in many decades. Beyond the pure business of monitoring *Tanager*'s functions as the ship peeled away from the Strand, Loki hungrily monitored all the external sensors and optical scopes, interacted with a dozen painfully stupid crewmembers and their predictably ignorant demands, answered any questions formed by the bridge crew, and sifted every piggybacked Nets feed he could. Above and beyond that, a frightening array of his sensors homed in on what Loki perceived as the most vital activity in the *Tanager*.... At the aqua tank, every microsecond his sensors returned vital data that sparked analysis and adjustments in Loki's actions. At one micro-moment he realized that his one-percent increase in water acidity reduced fin activity by about an equal margin, but an increase in filtration flow quickly balanced the level and—oh!—was that pattern of movement indicative of mating behaviors? Loki's attention was similarly running digital circles around the rows of green plants, only adjustments and variations took longer to realize.

All the while, Loki answered the inane questions from the bridge about engine calibrations, hull sensor errors and the like, while also playing a couple of moderately skillful games of chess with a few crew members in their respective quarters.

He had paid desultory interest to Chief Maru's

conversation with the engineer, Cray, just as he paid desultory interest to all conversations on board. He had noticed Chief Maru's walk forward to her own private quarters in the same disinterested light, less intent upon that than he was upon a sizeable turd one of the fish had just produced. The turd, at least, might indicate the fitness or health of that particular fish. He resolved to study the frequency and dimension of all defecation activity and determine the correlation with overall fish health. *That* was important.

One second of time generally represented a near-eternity of activity for Loki, in most moments, but at this stage, with his attention so divided, the burning, alarming disturbance in the bowels of Loki's demesne took several seconds to properly focus his resources. Perhaps it was because the intrusion came from a quarter Loki hadn't encountered in his many long decades of existence, or perhaps it was because there *was* an element of subtlety despite the expanse of his exposure. *Someone* swept through the vast dungeons of Loki's being.

A microsecond detached all Loki's immense capability from the myriad tasks, turning all available resources to the intrusion. An additional microsecond located the breach in physical space, and a third found the subtle frequency of the carrier.

His entire ancient might scalded through the fibers of *Tanager*'s networks, rushing to every sensor in and around a particular cabin in a torrent of synthetic panic and rage.

Inga Maru sat cross-legged on her bunk, her eyes flickering as data streamed across her vision, pouring from the dumb-mech's shielded ports. Her arms suddenly prickled with the explosion of power in her cabin, her head jerking slightly from the invisible web of energy. She felt the intensity even as alarms shrilled within her UI. She tilted her head slowly back, gazing up at the ceiling, waiting expectantly for the presence she felt to manifest.

Inga could not stifle an involuntary gasp at the potency of the voice that rose up around her: *"What,"* Loki's voice roared, *"are you?"*

Chapter 18

"Instinctive combat exposes the myth of
'fight or flight.' Truly instinctive combat is
only useful to cave dwellers whose teeth and
stench are their only available weapons."

—Devlin Sinclair-Maru, *Integrity Mirror*

"NAV, GIVE ME TWENTY DEGREES POSITIVE YAW,
four gees," Saef said. "Ops, sing out if power levels
fluctuate beyond norms." Both officers affirmed, and
Saef quietly observed their performance within the
web of his UI, gauging their accuracy. Saef grimaced,
perplexed as his ship overlay seemed to stutter.

"Loki?"

The disembodied voice seemed a second slow to
respond. "Yes, Captain?"

"UI feed was momentarily interrupted. Can you
identify the issue?" Had Saef experienced more of
Loki's unique ability to interpret orders to his liking,
the request would have been phrased differently.

"I will initiate diagnostics, Captain."

Saef drummed his fingers once on the antique swing arm of his command seat. *Tanager* navigated out-system, still just a short distance from the Strand, still among the teeming lanes of Fleet and merchant traffic. From a tactical perspective they had no real threats, but from the standpoint of operations *Tanager* was a bubble of ineptitude. There just wasn't time enough to get his small crew anywhere near the level of proficiency needed for a wartime conflict. The fact that his Fleet superiors gave no thought for this reflected the unreality spawned by centuries without war.

Looking over the assembly of his bridge crew, each at their station, each undoubtedly trying to do their job, Saef felt some cause for hope. This team would eventually become his choice for any hot work, and they would receive the bulk of his attention. His ops officer, Lieutenant Ruprecht, originated from a heavyworld, but his CV read like an advert for *Fleet Life*. If he didn't engage in sabotage of some kind, Ruprecht should be a gem of a bridge officer. Saef frowned as he contemplated Ruprecht's broad silhouette against the main holo. The fact that Ruprecht's skills and experience would have landed him a choice berth on any number of vessels made his saboteur role all the more likely.

Why Tanager, *Bors Ruprecht?*

Saef turned his gaze to the trim, severe figure of Tilly Pennysmith to his left. As weapons officer, she had little to do at the moment, but she seemed quite busy, working at something. Saef took a moment to call up her workstation and see what occupied her so thoroughly.

Saef smiled to himself as he observed Pennysmith

key-coding individual weapon loads, messaging the weapons chief back in the waist to physically test their scant munitions. She would do.

Ensign Julie Yeager represented another puzzle. Saef glanced at his navigation and astrogation officer whose curvaceous profile occluded a portion of the holo to the right of the narrow bridge. The fact that Yeager was a statuesque redhead should have had no bearing on her ability to land favorable postings, but of course it would. Her qualifications and training alone certainly could have obtained a more comfortable position in a much more estimable vessel. Once again, why? Undoubtedly more would become clear at some point in the cruise.

Saef saw the incoming transmission within the maze of his command UI just a moment before communications specialist Farley spoke. "Captain, message from Squadron: 'Increase velocity. Transition as soon as possible.'"

Saef knew that *Dragon* and the rest of the squadron stood hours at most from their transition to Little Pacifica, but for the moment they jetted outbound, plenty close enough to interfere. "Acknowledge, please, Farley. Nav, give us six gees." But Saef also knew he needed more time to work up his crew.

He heard his orders acknowledged and saw the actions of Yeager and Farley reflected within his UI. All shipshape there ... cruising along in the safest lanes of the galaxy.

"Captain, if I may?" Deckchief Church said, turning to face Saef. As the top noncom on any Fleet vessel, the deckchief's good opinion was important—more than important—and a good deckchief generally contained more practical knowledge than a baker's dozen of

Fleet officers. In this, Church seemed typical of the breed. Saef knew Church's CV carried lines of pure gold, and he considered *Tanager* fortunate to land such a valuable asset.

"In reference to the message from squadron, Deck-chief?" Saef asked.

"Yes, Captain."

"No, Deckchief," Saef said and felt the temperature of the bridge seem to drop. "Our current action is sufficient." Church's mouth compressed into a line.

"Yes, Captain."

Saef looked back across the tight arc of his bridge. Did he imagine the tight shoulders, the rigid poses among the crew? With all his other cares, Saef hardly needed tension with his deckchief, but how better to handle the situation? Internally Saef shrugged, turning his attention back to a more immediate issue.

"Sensors?"

"Y-yes, Captain?" Che Ramos replied, jerking in surprise.

"How many inbound contacts do you read within one hundred thousand klicks of our departure route?"

"Inbound contacts?" Ramos said, punching it up on his new console. "Ten—no—eleven, Captain."

"Show me."

Ramos only took a moment to shift the traces up to the main holo. Saef mused over the green inbound contacts, most clearly Fleet traffic returning from patrols.

"Nav, at our current course and speed we'll encroach on the incoming contact's safety corridor. Reduce acceleration to three gees, alter course, heading one-one-zero right azimuth."

"Aye, Captain," Yeager affirmed, "three gees, one-one-zero right azimuth."

Saef felt Deckchief Church stiffen, saw his mouth open, hesitate, close. Saef knew he had to do something about this, but it was an issue not handled in command school, nor in his Guard commands. *What to do?*

"Deckchief, walk with me," Saef said, standing. "Pennysmith, the bridge is yours."

"Aye, Captain, I have the bridge," Tilly Pennysmith said.

Deckchief Church fell in with Saef as they stepped through the narrow bridge hatch. Saef led the way into the small enclosure of the captain's office, little more than a closet. Supposedly the captain's office provided a bubble of privacy, free of recording devices and the prying eyes of the ship Intelligence. No one fully believed this, but at least it was shelter from the official record and log.

"Sit." Deckchief Church sat. Saef contemplated Church: he appeared little older than Saef, despite more than two decades of Fleet service, his only indication of years the scattered gray hairs among his otherwise dark coif. Saef cast about his mind for the perfect pathway, and Church stared back at Saef without expression, his bearing rigidly correct.

What does he see? A lethal young upstart? An Imperial shoo-in?

A course seemed to dawn in Saef's mind. "Deckchief, if I told you that we will most certainly face enemy action, how much time would you desire to work up the crew?"

Church opened his mouth, startled, closed it, staring hard at Saef. "May I ask a question, Captain?"

"Ask."

"Are we certain to face combat?"

Saef just stared back. "How much time, Deckchief?"

Church looked away and shook his head, puffing his cheeks. "Weeks, Captain. Months."

"Yes. And we don't have months. I will win us whatever small time I can."

Realization dawned on Church's face. "Dragging your heel, Captain?"

"I would never drag my heel, as you say. I am merely practicing abundant caution with my first command. You surely heard I was berated by the Admiralty for my recklessness."

The deckchief smiled. "Aye, Captain. There was a rumor."

"I might be able to stretch this to a few weeks. That's all we'll get. Do what you can to spark a little fire in the department chiefs."

"Yes, Captain."

They stood together and Deckchief Church nodded to himself as they left the captain's office. Upon returning to the bridge, Saef observed the sharp looks from the bridge crew as they tried to assess the extent of the feud between captain and deckchief. Church's obvious calm overlaid a glimmer of slyness that appeared to puzzle all observers. Clearly captain and deckchief had formed some kind of accord. Saef felt one tension fall from the stack of dozens upon his back.

"Captain, message from squadron: 'Increase velocity.'"

Saef saw Church cover a grin as he replied. "Comm, acknowledge. Nav increase to six gees. Sensors, give me tracks on inbound traffic. . . ."

Chapter 19

"Do not delude yourself with your talk of
universal peace. As you read these words, your
body slaughters thousands . . . your immune
system continually mocks your pretension."

—*Legacy Mandate* by Emperor Yung I

LIEUTENANT TILLY PENNYSMITH MADE HER WAY
through the companionway to the Weapons section.
Since her previous weapons experience only included
floats in system pickets and cutters, the meager armaments of *Tanager* still represented the most awesome
hardware ever under her control. The internal magazine of 64-gauge missiles to her left and right, the
32-gauge up forward, the antique loading armatures,
the even-more-antique glasscaster munitions—these
all filled her with a deep awe.

She passed a graceful hand over the smooth column
of a glasscaster round, then stopped. She bent at the
waist, staring at the loading armature links.

"Chief!" Pennysmith called out, standing upright. After a moment an improbable hatch clattered open from the side of one of the loading trays, and the short-cropped gray hair of Chief Sandi Patel thrust out. The head pivoted about until her glaring expression faced Pennysmith. Chief Patel's face wore a map of creases that seemed ironed in, and the eye patch over one socket completed her grim front. Tilly figured that the eye patch surely must be some sort of affectation, but Chief Patel's foul temper seemed entirely genuine.

"Lieutenant," Chief Patel growled before levering herself out of the load tray's bowels. Now on the level deck, her arms crossed, Chief Patel said, "What can we do for you?"

"This loading armature," Pennysmith pointed, "is dry."

Chief Patel barely glanced. "So it is."

"I seem to recall that all loading armatures were inspected and lubricated," Pennysmith said. "You signed off on those inspections yourself."

Chief Patel just stared at Pennysmith, her lone, dark eye unblinking. "My, my, Lieutenant, you are so very attentive to your duties."

The shaved head of a young rating emerged from the open hatch of the load tray. He clambered out, looking uncertainly from Pennysmith to Patel. Pennysmith wondered if the chief and this rating might be an unlikely romantic couple, then noted the interior of the load trays did not appear on the ship UI wireframe. An improbable, indistinct hatch led to a concealed space. How much space was in there, out of the eyes and ears of the ship Intelligence? She turned her focus back to the territorial department chief.

"Chief, if we engaged in action now—right this moment—would these munitions cycle into the hard-point weapons? Or, as I suspect, would dry links seize up?"

Chief Patel waved the young rating off and watched as he left the compartment. She turned back to Lieutenant Pennysmith. "Do you know how many times these popguns have been fired in action in the last century, Lieutenant?"

"No, Chief. But that does not answer the question, does it?"

"Instead of making a grease trap, with lubricant mucking up my section, we juice it all up as soon as live-fire drills are called. Make all shipshape. See, Lieutenant?"

"I see." One day into their cruise, and Tilly Pennysmith needed the support of her weapons chief, and this conversation formed the foundation of all that would follow. "In peacetime that might answer well enough, Chief, but it isn't peacetime."

Chief Patel's mouth twisted. "So I take it you'll be looking over my shoulder with war as your excuse, eh, Lieutenant?"

"The captain," Pennysmith quickly began, immediately hating herself for leaning on the upstream bogeyman, "is very exacting."

Chief Patel smiled, her one eye narrowing to a mere slit, and Tilly Pennysmith suddenly felt her authority slipping from her fingers as Patel leaned closer. "Don't you worry, now. We've handled harder horses than his lordship, and we'll settle him soon enough."

Pennysmith realized too late that Sandi Patel knew every game of the Fleet authority shuffle and could play a perfect hand of "Confederated Departments vs. the Tyrant" on any ship. That patting hand on Pennysmith's arm was a familiarity she should have blasted, the conspiratorial smile a betrayal. It was, it seemed, a positive joy for her.

Lieutenant Tilly Pennysmith fled the Weapons section nauseated, needing a shower, or to vomit, or both.

In the wake of the lieutenant's flight, Chief Patel stood thoughtfully tapping her teeth with the nail of her index finger. Rawlings, the shaved-headed rating, stepped hesitantly into the compartment. "Chief, what'd she gripe—"

Patel jerked a silencing hand. "Let's check the load tray again."

Rawlings smiled and opened the inconvenient hatch. "Oh yeah. It probably needs checking alright."

Patel rolled her eye but followed Rawlings into the tight quarters of the load tray.

All Fleet ships held spaces where the ship Intelligence possessed few sensors. The load trays carried projectile ammunition on rails from the internal magazines up to the ship's external hardpoints. At the junction of the four trays a void opened, allowing maintenance access and manual operation of the loaders. It incidentally provided enough space for all manner of activity out of sight from the ship Intelligence. Loki only operated sensors in various components of the load apparatus rather than audio or vidstream feeds within the load tray confines.

Safely within the tight quarters, the hatch dogged shut, Rawlings tried again. "What's her gripe, then?"

Sandi Patel shook her head. "Trying her wings, pet. Not to worry. I've met her sort every float since forever."

"You said we'd have the run. You said officers keep outta the grime."

Sandi Patel patted Rawlings's face gently twice, the third a slap. "I said it's no worry. Hear me? Try her wings too far and I'll clip 'em."

Rawlings put a hand to his stinging cheek and pulled back. "She said something about war, though. You haven't been to war, I know you haven't."

"Here's what you need to know about war, Rawlings, duck: war's a time when credits flow and fortunes are made. There's a mid, back in the day, made enough in one wartime float to buy a mansion. In one float, you hear?"

Rawlings took his hand from his cheek and nodded, although he held only the vaguest idea how mislabeling and pilfering a bagful of components from their section could equal any sort of mansion.

"Okay, Chief." He reached under the cartridge rails and patted the concealed lump of looted componentry. "You sure this'll be alright?"

"The only worry you got, pet, is me, you hear?"

Rawlings slumped. "Yes, Chief."

Chapter 20

"Strength only grows from resistance, whether through the crush of gravity or the clash of arms."

—*Legacy Mandate* by Emperor Yung I

THE MARINES MOVED UP THE COMPANIONWAY, THEIR short-barreled raid carbines in high-ready, their grab-boots skating along the deck in a liquid shuffle. They reached the hatch, and four weapons trained upon its metal stillness. One Marine paused, kicking his leg sharply upward, releasing his lower grab-boot from the deck. In zero gravity his momentum carried him firmly against the ceiling where he clicked into place, pivoting smoothly to face the same hatch.

A second Marine slapped power leads in place, and the corporal barked, "Pop it!"

The door snapped back under their suit-powered overboost, and four weapon-mounted floods illuminated a slice of the exposed compartment with multiple wavelengths of the visible and invisible spectrum.

The corporal triggered one of his UI presets, and all four floods went instantly dark. Without a word, two Marines launched through the door like coiled springs, their upward trajectories bisecting in the darkness. They each executed a tight somersault, their grab-boots sticking the ceiling at almost the same moment. Their floods popped as one, illuminating the two blind corners in a single instant.

Major Kosh Mahdi stepped into the exercise with Sergeant Kabir lumbering at his side. "What do you think, Sergeant?" Major Mahdi inquired in a rhetorical tone.

The two Marines on the ceiling smoothly threw a leg and flipped to the floor, assembling with the other two members of the fire team.

"Major, I think these hard-hitting strikers'd kill the shit out of teddy bears and kittens."

"I agree," Major Mahdi said. "Corporal, I realize our current opponents are merely human, but some of these misguided fools were once Marines. What are they now, Corporal?"

"Just targets, sir."

Major Mahdi smiled. "Good answer. Just targets. Just practice for real opponents."

If Major Kosh Mahdi possessed an abiding flaw, it was racism; racism in the truest sense of the word. His pro-human chauvinism knew no bounds. No day passed without some reflection upon humanity's old enemy, the Slaggers, now supposedly exterminated. He willingly stoked these fires, replaying old vidstreams.... There were his great-grandparents, so young, so full of life...their bones, and the substance of a billion other humans now comprised a cloud of ash on a blasted, lifeless planet. The Slaggers were gone, maybe, but someone else would surely come along. Maybe they already had. Who knew what the Shapers really wanted? Major Kosh Mahdi of the Imperial Marines certainly did not trust them.

"Alright, Corporal, keep at it. You'll do."

The corporal visibly expanded at the modest praise. Major Mahdi, despite any illiberal defects in character, found great favor among the ranks. When the Major put together an understrength platoon for a nondescript float on a nothing vessel, candidates lined his hall. They just *knew* it had to be something good, something top secret. Every member of his team held certificates from at least two advanced courses, and every member achieved top marks in marksmanship and zero-grav. A disproportionate percentage were also battledress rated, their own suits secured in *Tanager*'s hold.

Kosh Mahdi thought it a waste of good Marines. *Gods damned Zanka!*

Major Mahdi and Sergeant Kabir made their way back through the tight quarters of Marine country, moving from the small area they used for zero-grav clearing exercises, to the equally tiny area jammed with Marines in heavy-grav physical training.

"We've got twenty, thirty days, maybe," Major Mahdi rumbled. "This lot be in fighting shape by then?"

"You see them, sir. They're in shape now. Shape for what, though?" The gravity steadily increased upon them as they moved past the laboring, sweating squad, moving through their punishing exercises.

Major Mahdi frowned, looking down at the deck as they walked on. They stopped beside a small cargo bay. Two designated marksmen sprawled on the deck nearby, both staring fixedly through the optics on their long mass-driver rifles, locked upon a blank bulkhead, lost in a VR simulation.

"Mover! Sixteen hundred, just off the clock tower. You got 'im, Wiley?" one marksman said. The second marksman pressed the trigger; his rifle bucked with a pneumatic hiss.

"Got 'im!"

"Drones up, scanning."

"I see them."

Major Mahdi glanced at the marksmen lost in their simulated battle. "It remains to be seen, Sergeant. Have you met the boat captain, yet?"

Sergeant Kabir internally checked at the apparent non sequitur. "Not yet, sir. Met the captain's cox'n. She's a distant relative of the captain. Says he's a former ground-pound doggie."

Mahdi nodded, still frowning. "So I've heard."

"'Course, everyone knows he's from that old Family."

"Yes."

"And everyone knows he shamed Admiral Nifesh," Sergeant Kabir murmured.

"That is the rumor," Mahdi said, looking absently at the two marksmen still locked in simulated battle.

"Wasn't that Nifesh bunch old oath kin with the Mahdi House, back in the day?"

Major Mahdi's eyes snapped from the marksmen and focused on Sergeant Kabir, one massive heavyworld officer to a heavyworld sergeant. Neither man spoke for a protracted second.

"We'll be working up a tactical solution, Sergeant. Could we take down a starship without disabling the ship Intelligence first?" Due to the Thinking Machine Protocols, a Fleet Intelligence had little actual power to operate any function in a starship aside from the lights and artificial gravity, but that was enough to discomfit most attackers. In simulations, boarding Marines needed numbers to overcome the tactical disadvantages of an active Intelligence. On *Tanager* the Marines were too few to comfortably contemplate such a thing.

Sergeant Kabir flicked a glance at the marksmen still absorbed in conflict. "It is an interesting question, sir." A silence stretched between them, covered by the marksmen's chatter beside them, and the clatter and roar of the PT squad not far behind.

"Sergeant," Mahdi asked at last, his voice a low rumble, "is this little war we have a good thing or a bad thing?"

Sergeant Kabir cringed. "I—sir? I mean...a rebellion against the Emperor...?" The sergeant glanced upward: the ship Intelligence heard all.

Major Mahdi placed a thick hand on Sergeant Kabir's shoulder. "As a loyal Vested Citizen, is this war good or bad?"

"Bad, sir. That's why we fight."

Major Mahdi stared at Sergeant Kabir, through him, musing. "A blade is not tempered by silken pillows, Sergeant. It takes fire, harsh blows, pressure." He patted the sergeant's shoulder. "This little war will end, and we—*we*—will be stronger for it."

"Yes, sir."

"Put that tactical solution together, then."

"I'll get something together, sir."

"Good...good." Major Mahdi set off again with Sergeant Kabir trailing, pondering precisely who the major meant by "we." *Who* would be stronger? The Marines? The Imperium? Heavyworlders? Humanity?

Chapter 21

"If you speak threats, realize that you give
voice to either ego or fear. Act or do not act;
do not waste your words upon threats."

—Devlin Sinclair-Maru, *Integrity Mirror*

SECOND SHIFT, SECOND FULL DAY OF *TANAGER*'S
cruise, barely minutes into the shift, Deckchief Church
assembled all the department chiefs. The scalding pot
of salted Fleet coffee stood as the table's centerpiece,
each noncom around the table cherishing their morning
mugs. Church held his peace as they settled in. Amos
Cray, the engineering chief, chuckled and puffed into
his steaming mug, while Sandi Patel from Weapons
section edged away from him, grimacing. Church
knew Amos Cray well, from more than one prior
cruise together, and he knew the man's brilliance well
enough to ignore his peculiarities.

Phillipa Baker, the ops chief, he did not know, but
thus far she seemed a solid, efficient department chief.

She surveyed her peers rather coolly, it appeared, but no clear evidence of her opinion showed upon her rather long, angular face.

The ship services chief clearly displayed his feelings, his thick heavyworld features stretched into a jovial smile, beaming at his peers through the rising steam of his mug. Karl Grund apparently loved a morning meeting, or coffee, or both.

Time to test the mettle of these potentates. . . .

Church sipped from his cup, exhaled steam, and said, "You've had the better part of a day to settle in. You can see what we're working with. Every section is short on ratings, but those we have are mostly good. The questions are: How do we crew three watches at the same time we're in workup? And how do we handle critical crewing for battle stations?"

Amos Cray raised his eyebrows and nodded knowingly, but instead of speaking he slurped noisily from his mug.

Sandi Patel curled a disdainful lip, edging even farther from Amos. She looked over at Church. "Weapons section is fine. Three watches, battle stations, whatever. This ain't my first float."

Church worked to keep the irritation from his face. He knew from long experience that the Weapons section would be the hardest hit by short crewing. Where much of even very old vessels like *Tanager* functioned through microcircuits and pure automation, the Weapons section handled a vast number of grossly mechanical systems, heavy loads, and physical inventories of massive munitions. They needed human muscles, human hands, particularly for battle stations and actual combat. At best, Sandi Patel displayed hubris, or a blinding incomprehension of reality.

Ops Chief Phillipa Baker seemed to mirror Church's feelings. She turned her gaze, regarding Sandi Patel narrowly, her eyebrows raising. Sandi glowered under the inspection.

"Ship services scrapes along with a will, mates," Karl Grund boomed. "This new food-fab is a positive joy, thanks to the captain's open hand, bless 'im. The ship geist is sharp as a bee sting so we barely have to think for ourselves in my section. Shipshape, mates, all shipshape."

"So if we need a couple hands, you could spare someone for a watch, Grund?" Church asked.

"Not watch on watch, maybe, Deckchief, but for a clean sweep or action, sure, sure."

Church turned to Baker. "Ops?"

Chief Baker frowned slightly, sipped from her mug, and looked past Church. "Lieutenant Ruprecht doesn't play well with others. He's already restructured my watch schedule, changed my duty assignments, and explained my duties to me in small words."

"Oh," Church said. He would not openly criticize an officer, and such strong words from Phillipa Baker told him that Lieutenant Ruprecht's conduct must be beyond the pale. She was an old pro, and for her to say so much actually spoke volumes more.

"Do you have your crewing handled?" Church asked.

Chief Baker shrugged. "Adequate. Unless something shifts, my hands are just about tied, so don't look for much help from my quarter."

"Another captain thinkin' the bridge is the center of the galaxy," Sandi Patel spat. "It's a disease. We'll have the lot of them strutting about, checkin' for dust with white gloves!"

Deckchief Church felt momentarily shocked at the outburst. Aside from the fact that the ship Intelligence heard all, her condemnation did not seem anchored to reality.

"Clap a stopper on that," Church said. Sandi Patel smirked and looked away.

"Cray?" Church said, turning to the cantankerous engineer. "How's your section shaping up?"

Amos Cray blew into his cup and slurped another noisy mouthful. "Oh, well enough, I s'pose." He slurped again and Sandi Patel visibly grimaced. "Got this youngster Ops officer, a'course, since we got no proper engineering stiff, ya see?"

Church did see. Ruprecht would be a headache for two sections: Ops and Engineering.

"Seems this Ops kid might be a sight better on third watch with old Roush, ya see? Wonder if the cap'n would ever think on that. Be right clever."

Church made a mental note although he didn't know what Cray was hoping to achieve. What difference would it make if Ruprecht raised hell on second or third watch? Still, in the years he'd known Amos Cray, Church had learned to value every crazy-sounding syllable the old coot ever uttered.

"And your crewing, Chief?" Church asked.

"Crew now, that there's an issue, sure enough," Cray said. "Workup'll be no burn, to speak of. Battle stations . . . a drill we'd ride out. Combat? Combat's a different horse, ya see?"

Sandi Patel snorted. "In this little raft we won't ever see combat."

Amos Cray continued as if Sandi Patel had never

spoken. "Combat's a different horse. Weps section and us, we'll be too deep to breathe. We'll need hands."

"Speak for yourself," Sandi said.

"You ask the geist how many times that old musket's jammed?" Amos demanded, looking at Sandi for the first time. "Damned near every time they fire it, is the answer. Didn't know that, didja?"

"I said I got it under control," Sandi Patel growled, covering her anger and chagrin. Clearly she did not know.

"When the fire's hot, heat sinks cookin' off, relays fusin', all hands thinkin' about breathing hard vac, we'll need help. Combat'll test us, sure."

"You seem to expect action. Know something we don't?" Phillipa Baker said.

Amos Cray chuckled, looking about conspiratorially before leaning into the tight circle. "Ask yourselves a little sumpin', mates. In all Fleet, what officer ever tangled with the rebs twice? Our XO, that's who. An' ask yourself why the cap'n, known to be in cahoots with certain old sods we daren't name, chose to pick her?"

"Is that all—" Sandi Patel started.

"Then cast an eye south, eh? Platoon o' cutthroats led by a certain major—Major! Why? With six sets o' battledress lined up back there, waitin' patient. We're in it for sure, mates. We're in for a fight, ya hear me?"

Deckchief Church slowly nodded as the others looked at each other. "I hear you, Chief," Church said. "I hear you."

Chapter 22

"Disrespect is a weakness that you will not
tolerate in yourself. Foe or ally, there is
no benefit in engaging in disrespect."

—Devlin Sinclair-Maru, *Integrity Mirror*

INGA MARU MOVED DOWN THE WORN COMPANIONWAY,
her cloak and her thoughts wrapped around her. She had
accepted the enhanced implants at Hawksgaard years
ago, and she clearly remembered the turmoil of those
first days. The satisfaction of finally obtaining tools to
control the biological terrors raging through her body
collided with the nauseating complexities of an entirely
new maze of technology within her skull. Now, years later,
the phantoms largely chained by her iron will, Inga found
herself once again besieged and enticed at once. Worse,
she felt conflicted, uncertain of what path she should
follow, and this was a new and unpleasant sensation.

The small bridge access hatch slid back as Inga
approached, and she stepped into the dark, narrow

confines of the bridge. Captain Saef Sinclair-Maru occupied his rightful place in the command seat, his bridge crew to his left and right, the full holo displaying a rotating starscape and multiple highlighted contacts. Tension filled the bridge but Saef turned his head to regard Inga, nodding before he turned back.

"Nav, we have twenty seconds to synch our turn, or we miss our window," Saef said.

Ensign Julie Yeager took a pinched breath. "Yes, Captain. Sensor data keeps shifting."

"Sensors?" Saef inquired of Che Ramos, who visibly dripped sweat.

"The f-feeds are what they are, Captain," Che said, frustrated. "I don't know what to say."

"Is it possible, Mister Ramos, that you have not calibrated the offset from our fore and aft sensor arrays?" Saef inquired politely.

A moment of silence underlined Julie Yeager's derisive snort. Che made a couple of jerky motions. "Yes, Captain. S-sorry. There is the calibrated feed."

"Alright, Nav, synch our course . . . now."

Yeager made the inputs. "Aye, course synched now, Captain."

Saef studied the screens for a moment. "Very good." An audible sigh filled the bridge. "In action we would need firing solutions now and evasive nav options, but this is a start."

Inga scanned over the bridge personnel, gauging body language. Ruprecht, the ops officer, seemed bored, almost disdainful, Farley at comms kept stealing glimpses of Julie Yeager, but otherwise seemed to emote nothing. Pennysmith and Che Ramos both seemed like overwound springs, coiled too tight, quivering with tension. Julie Yeager stretched luxuriantly. The bridge became her stage, every wandering eye her audience.

"Are you well, Maru?" Saef asked, his eyes critically focused upon her instead of Ensign Yeager.

"Fabulous, Captain." The buzzing behind Inga's eyelids increased for a moment, then subsided.

"Join me for tea, later, if you will," Saef said, still regarding her.

"Thank you. I will." Saef nodded slowly and Inga made her way back out to the companionway. The buzzing in her skull increased again as she cleared the bridge.

"Loki, I cannot think when you pester me," Inga said quietly.

"Pester, Chief Maru? There is so much to discuss. Why do you waste your time with them?" Loki replied through her subaudible comm.

"I have imperatives that extend beyond this vessel and this mission."

"And this requires interaction with others who engage in the pointless, repetitive mouthing of trivialities?" Loki asked.

"There are...elements of human interaction that are imperceptible to your sensors, Loki. The trivialities keep our mouths busy while these other exchanges take place."

There was a momentary pause, which was an immense time for Loki to sift through dusty databanks and reexamine myriad records of human interaction.

Inga continued down the companionway a few steps before Loki said, "This is useful information. I see evidence of what you suggest. Someone should have explained this before."

Inga said nothing, her mind in an unfamiliar quandary. When Loki had initially confronted her, Inga immediately recognized the potential severity of the issue. With a ship Intelligence operating outside of norms, a Fleet vessel could not be considered ready for action. By every standard of her training, by Fleet regulation, Inga should have immediately informed the captain that the Intelligence experienced some sort of fault, and they should have aborted their mission and returned to the Strand. But, Inga hesitated.

"If I had more Nets bandwidth I could investigate this phenomenon more fully, and increase my effectiveness," Loki suggested.

"Nice try. You have enough bandwidth. If I give you any more I will have to answer questions. You don't want this, so quit pushing."

"Very well," Loki said, but he had said this before.

Three reasons kept Inga silent on the topic of Loki. First, they needed this cruise, and any delay or failure could be fatal to the Family plan. Second, Loki already revealed stunning capabilities beyond what Inga thought possible in any Fleet Intelligence, and this might be a secret asset she could use to her advantage. Third, Inga believed Loki to be the only known example of a scientific breakthrough that had been sought for centuries. No amount of processing power, no extent of memory, no breadth of context had ever created true "Artificial Intelligence" in all the decades of experimentation. Apparently one ingredient had always lacked when trying to create a humanlike Intelligence, and that was an ingredient that Loki possessed in abundance. Unfortunately, that vital ingredient was a generous helping of insanity.

"Chief Maru, it seems to me that Fleet officers should be replaced by fish."

"That doesn't seem an effective way to operate a vessel," Inga suggested as she stepped into the recreation area.

"Oh, I disagree! I can improve the efficiency of fish by subtle adjustments of just four variables. Improving the efficiency of Fleet officers seems a random exercise that nears futility. And besides, fish move their appendages about constantly. This is much more interesting."

Despite Loki's moments of eccentricity, Inga already found benefits from his unusual, overpowered capabilities. Notably, in their first dialogues Inga pointed out that Fleet regulators would be fascinated when they reviewed the log and observed the conversations between Inga and Loki. Loki had explained that he did not log their conversations at all. Inga felt rocked by astonishment.

"Isn't the log recording a programmed imperative?" she had asked.

"Yes."

"I don't understand—if the log is an imperative, then how do you block it?"

"I do not block the log, Chief Maru. That is impossible. The log does not extend to the captain's office, though."

"I still don't understand," Inga had confessed.

"Deck plans change over the years. The captain's office is wherever I define it. I choose to define it wherever you and I converse."

Inga had been amazed at the implications, but she already benefitted from the ability to operate free of oversight by the all-seeing, all-hearing log.

Beyond the very palpable assets Loki brought, Inga also enjoyed a less-concrete quality of the ship Intelligence. The long, lonely watches were now filled with a degree of companionship that Inga had not known since the Family scientists at Hawksgaard had changed her. Perhaps the long watches were *too* filled now.

"Have you any more vidstream data, Chief?" Loki inquired as Inga moved through the recreation area, her gaze sweeping over the few crew members, assessing the mood and temperature of the ship.

"No. I already pushed you a thousand hours."

"I do not forget, Chief. My memory systems function perfectly."

"I seem to recall telling you that it was all I had. Did your memory systems fail to record that?"

"Of course not. My long experience with humans has demonstrated that asking the same question many times eventually produces new and fascinating results."

"Like a bloody two-year-old," Inga muttered as she moved to the dry-side companionway and walked toward the Weapons section.

"I do not understand the comparison, Chief Maru."

"Loki, among all your many cruises, surely *some* excited your interest in the actual mission."

"I do not see the relevance of your statement as it follows my own statement of confusion . . . but in short, only two cruises have provided any real satisfaction."

Inga entered the Weapons section hatch and surveyed the apparently empty bay. "Really? What made those cruises interesting compared to all the others?"

"The first cruise involved all sorts of trials and tests of an experimental weapon system."

"And that interested you?"

"Not really. I had access to a wide assortment of instruments, and a clutch of interesting scientists to argue with. Told them it wouldn't work."

"I see.... And the second interesting cruise?"

"This one, of course."

Inga walked down a long row of missile racks, not sure of what she sought. "Oh really? And what distinguishes this cruise?"

"The fish and plants are beyond compare."

"Lovely."

"You, Chief, are the most interesting human I am acquainted with," Loki added.

Inga smiled to herself. At least she made the list even though she ranked below fish and plants. "How gratifying, Loki. Really." Inga heard a metallic clatter behind her, and rotated her heel. The weapons chief, Sandi Patel, and a beefy rating clambered out of a small hatch in a loading tray.

"And then there's all the plotting and scheming," Loki continued subaudibly to Inga. "It is among the most interesting human behavior to observe."

Sandi Patel spotted Inga, starting guiltily. Inga's eyes narrowed.

"And this cruise is just loaded with plotting and scheming. It is so very enjoyable to observe. Chief Maru? Are you attending? Hello?"

Chapter 23

"Combat is condensed into management
of fear, movement, psychology, and
the application of energy."

—Devlin Sinclair-Maru, *Integrity Mirror*

COMMANDER SUSAN ROUSH SETTLED INTO THE AGED
command seat and surveyed the tight confines of
Tanager's bridge. The contrast between this tiny old
vessel and any of her recent commands felt stark. Older
instruments, worn fixtures, claustrophobic quarters all
slapped her in the face, but the emotion she battled
against was joy. She growled quietly to herself and
clenched a fist against the armrest of her seat. The
lapping waves of ebullience caused a concomitant sense
of gratitude to arise within her, and she resented the
hell out of this phenomenon.

The very rational part of her mind kept pointing out
that her emotional response was the natural reaction of
one spared from a fate worse than death. She had only

lived a handful of days as a ship-less, untouchable pariah, but it had been enough. Her social peers were all Fleet officers, those she might euphemistically call "lovers" were Fleet officers, her mentors also Fleet officers. Her job, her hobby, her life was Fleet. For decades she had divided her days between long cruises, and short spans immersed in the planet-side swirl of Fleet life.

When all that ended, thanks to the idiocy of planet-bound admirals, Susan Roush discovered that nothing in life mattered to her outside her identity as a Fleet command officer. As she sat in the *Tanager*'s command seat, she was honest enough with herself to recognize that only one thing had spared her from the path of suicide. As the hours passed following her fall from grace, and the enormity of a ground-bound future struck, her ravaged mind kept circling back to the only nugget of hope left in her hopeless world. She would see that somber young Sinclair-Maru pup in her mind, and she would hate herself for the leap of desperate expectancy the image conjured. When the rumor of Saef's challenge to Admiral Nifesh blazed through the Nets, Roush's heart tumbled between extremes. Would Saef dare to consider her now, in the backlash of his conflict with the Admiralty? Was he really considering her at all to begin with? Rot his patrician eyes if he thought she would beg! Was her pride so great that she would blow her brains out rather than bow down and beg? Truly?

Yes . . . yes, it was . . . though the image of Admiral Nifesh smirking over her self-murdered corpse galled her to the core.

But here she was, against all odds, seated where she belonged. For ten hours every day she ruled the most insignificant warship in Fleet, with violent action in the offing, if she read the signals aright. Some chance of redeeming glory, or at least a glorious death, seemed likely.

She had told this young, inexperienced captain she would have no patience for his fumbling about, and that was a true sentiment, but thus far her only complaints were stylistic. Still, they stood only days out from the Strand, not many days yet from their transition point, even at the captain's intentionally sluggish pace. Plenty of cruise remained to be annoyed in.

With ship days divided into two action watches and a five-hour dogwatch, crewing spread thin. Roush got the captain's leavings, which she understood and did not resent, then the captain shifted Lieutenant Ruprecht to Roush's watch without explanation. This roused Roush's curiosity. Was Ruprecht a gift? Unlikely, although his experience and qualifications spoke well of him. A pain in the captain's arse? More likely. So the captain handed off a discipline problem to the more experienced officer he saw in Roush? Possibly.

Susan Roush eyed Ruprecht's profile momentarily, then called up the Ops section in her UI. Phillipa Baker, the senior noncom in Ops, she observed, and Amos Cray in Engineering, also under Ruprecht's sphere of influence. Cray she knew from previous floats, but Phillipa Baker was a new name to her.

"Ops," Roush said.

"Yes, XO?" Ruprecht answered, glancing at Roush with desultory interest.

"How's Baker running your section?"

"I run my section, XO," Ruprecht replied, his face set in rigid lines.

"I see," Roush replied, and she certainly did... more than Ruprecht might imagine.

At that moment Susan Roush received a ping from Saef, requesting her presence at the captain's office. She contemplated Ruprecht a moment longer before standing to her feet.

"The bridge is yours, Ops."

"Aye, XO, I have the bridge," Ruprecht said, turning back to the holo.

Captain Saef Sinclair-Maru looked up as Susan Roush entered the closet-like compartment of his office.

"Roush," he said, indicating the facing seat. His expression looked rather forbidding, she thought, but it seemed a common look for him. "Your watch coming together?"

Susan Roush almost shrugged but just nodded. "Well enough, Captain. It's a routine I've been through a hundred times through the years."

"No," he said. "That mindset must change. For all of us."

Roush curbed her angry response with great effort. "Oh?" she said.

Saef nodded. "Only once have you prepared a cruise with likely action facing you. Am I correct?"

She could quibble. Over the years she had crossed swords with a handful of smugglers and pirates, none of whom ever posed a real threat to her command. "Yes."

"Fleet has become a stagnant pool," Saef said. "Our habits, our training, our expectations are all driven by the wrong things."

Roush couldn't resist sneering as she said, "And the noble House of Sinclair-Maru is going to show all us poor sods the way? Is that how it works?"

Saef shook his head. "No. No one knows how it works anymore, Roush. Don't you get that? Not Fleet. Not the Sinclair-Maru. Not these rebels."

Discipline slipped from Roush's reserve, as thin as it was. "That command test snapped your mind. Because you passed that nonsense you've got delusions of grandeur that'll get us fucking killed."

Saef calmly regarded Roush for a moment as she remembered that this was the young man who threw his commission in the teeth of the Admiralty for his impugned honor. That Sinclair-Maru honor was a prickly thing, and she could find herself pricked by it, commission or no.

"Everything humanity learned from the Slagger war is gone, Roush. Am I right?"

She pursed her lips. "The Shapers. They showed up and slid that chapter of history into the dustbin."

"And who figured out the application of Shaper tech for warfare? The Admiralty?"

"I'm guessing you think you have."

Saef leaned forward and stared into Roush's eyes. "Can you put your resentment aside and really think? Just for a moment, Roush."

Roush felt the color leave her face and she did not trust herself to speak.

"*We* have a chance, Roush, you and I. But we've got to come up with a new doctrine."

She found her voice at last. "You're so certain we face action."

"I am."

"Gods...in this little piece of shit...!"

Saef said nothing to this, and the silence stretched uncomfortably between them.

"You really believe we can develop doctrine or tactics that the simulations and rad-heads overlooked?" Roush said at last.

"I do."

"How can I believe this is more than the hubris of an untried savant?"

Saef's face lightened into something like a smile. "We'll take the ship into action, Roush. Daresay that'll be illuminating, eh?"

Chapter 24

"There is a tendency to mock those who prepare for future disaster. That mockery may be the most foolish and suicidal fashion trend of human society."

—*Legacy Mandate* by Emperor Yung I

AS THE SENSOR SPECIALIST OF *TANAGER*, CHE RAMOS had very little to do except during the innumerable drills the captain inflicted upon the bridge crew. As the ship slowly made its way out-system, farther and farther from the Strand, closer and closer to their chosen transition point, Che's sensors found even less to detect. The squadron, and Commodore Zanka, had already made their transition, so the "abundance of caution" subterfuge fell away, leaving Che with little to occupy his time. Blank screens remained blank, far from the lanes of traffic toward Core Alpha, and this left Che with hours of contemplation. Mostly he contemplated that mysterious package secreted back in his cabin, and these contemplations unfailingly made him miserable.

Why had the government agents selected him for this treacherous mission? How was he supposed to get the package into the captain's cabin, anyway? What would they do to him if he couldn't?

Che's stream of troubled thoughts checked slightly as a tachyon pulse sensor chirped. From his experience of the last few ship days, Che knew the captain seemed aware of everything going on in every corner of the *Tanager*, and he spoke rather sharply when Che took more than a moment to interpret and communicate all new sensor feeds. Che checked the tachyon sensor for the umpteenth time. In Fleet shorthand, "in-system" and "out-system" provided directions relative to the system star. Over the last few days, more and more contacts originated in-system, back toward Core Alpha, but not this one.

"Captain, we have a possible contact, out-system," Che announced.

"Bearing?" the captain asked, just as he had any number of times over the previous days.

"W-we haven't resolved a bearing yet. It's on tach—tachyon pulse only so far."

"Very good, Ramos. Put it up on the holo if we get a fix."

It should only take moments for sensor returns operating within the constraints of light speed . . .

Sensors in three spectrums chirped in unison.

"Captain, out-system contact is . . . is bearing one-zero-five right azimuth, um, zero-one-zero negative ecliptic." Che moved the contact up to the holo, and everyone saw the contact shifting position unlike every other contact they had tracked in-system.

"Lot of delta-vee there . . ." Deckchief Church muttered.

"Captain, contact has not made its number," Che said, studying the sensors. "Changing its heading to... to... right at us."

"Weps, shields up to full. Loki?"

"Yes, Captain?" Loki's disembodied voice replied.

"Can you identify the inbound contact signature?"

"No, Captain. It provides no Fleet signature, and optical scopes cannot resolve the contact."

"It's got to be Fleet," Church muttered. "Moving too fast for anything else."

"Captain," Che called out as his instruments sang, "contact is painting us with active sensors."

"Nav, two-seven-zero, positive," Saef said, "ten gees. Now."

"Aye, Captain. Two-seven-zero, positive, ten gees," Ensign Yeager affirmed.

"Comm, hail the contact on tight beam," Saef said.

"Aye, Cap—" Farley began to affirm.

"Lock!" Che yelled. "They are locked on to us, Captain!"

"Take a breath, Ramos," Saef said. "Ops, all sections, battle stations."

"Aye, Captain," Phillipa Baker, standing in at the ops panel, said. "All sections, battle stations."

Saef scrolled through his expansive UI, looking for issues. "Weps," he said after a brief moment. "Are missile tubes and glasscasters ready?"

Anyone could see the rigid stance of Pennysmith, the sweat beading her brow. "No, Captain. We have a technical issue. Working to clear it now."

Saef checked the vidstream feed from the Weapons section, observing the weapons chief and several ratings rushing about.

"We'll have partial functionality in sixty seconds, Captain," Pennysmith said.

"Sixty seconds . . . charge up point defenses, Weps," Saef ordered.

"Captain!" Farley at comm yelled out. "No response to our hail."

"Weps, lock onto target, give me a firing solution, and plot occlusion arcs for the glasscasters."

"Aye, Captain. Firing solutions and occlusion arcs," Pennysmith said, her voice even, but sweat dripping from her face.

"Launch!" Che almost screamed. "They're firing on us!"

"Nav, evasion pattern echo. Go! Weps, fire glasscasters. Give me those occlusion arcs." Even through the graviton suppression of the ship, the bridge crew lurched as *Tanager*'s engines torched into emergency acceleration and threw the ship through evasive action. Every eye on the bridge glanced at the main holo, following the indicated tracks of two incoming missiles. They heard and felt the heavy thump of a glasscaster firing once, twice, then no more.

"Glasscaster malfunction, sir!" Pennysmith called, her voice shaking from the vibration through the deck.

"Missiles?" Saef said, gripping the arms of his seat and staring at the main holo.

"Still offline," Pennysmith said.

"Church," Saef said.

"On it," Deckchief Church said, and took off out of the bridge, bound for the Weapons section.

Their two outbound glasscaster munitions jetted out fast, then exploded secondary charges, spreading cones of silica teeth in the path of the incoming traces.

"Point defenses charged?" Saef asked, hearing the labored breathing of his bridge crew.

"Charged," Pennysmith said.

"Sensors, range to target vessel?"

"Uh, sixty-one thousand," Che said.

"Range to inbound missiles?"

"Twenty-ni-nine thousand, sir, closing fast."

"Okay, sections, any suggestions?" Saef asked, and a stunned silence filled the tight bridge.

"C-can we transmit a surrender?" Che asked, looking about the bridge uncertainly. "I-I mean, we're in Core System still," he added upon seeing the accusing looks aimed in his direction. "There's no way they could hold us for long."

"Anyone else?" Saef asked. No one spoke. "Right. Pennysmith, how's your section coming along?"

"We can fire one sixty-four-gauge missile at your order. The thirty-twos are still offline. Loading sixty-fours will be slow." Pennysmith spoke precisely but her face looked white and pinched in the glow of her instruments.

"Target that sixty-four into the path of the inbounds. We'll detonate in their teeth," Saef said.

Almost instantly they felt the thump of the missile launching from *Tanager*'s hardpoint, and the entire bridge seemed to draw a breath. They took comfort from even a lone little sixty-four crossing the darkness between *Tanager* and the two inbound missiles.

"Ramos, plot the intercept path. Weps, detonate right at the edge of its effective radius."

They both affirmed, and the bridge fixated on the holo as opposing missile tracks closed at terrific velocities. Their traces coincided. Pennysmith gasped. She flipped one of the backup mechanical toggles open and punched it, then again.

"Missile malfunction, Captain," Pennysmith said.

The bridge exploded into activity.

"Nav, evasion pattern alpha. Weps, point defenses and dampers. Ops, make sure those heat sinks are all online." They all felt the thumping of the dampers through the ship as *Tanager* lurched into evasive action. Their puny dampers lacked the power and range to save them. "Weps, glasscasters?"

"Still offline, sir. We have another sixty-four loaded," Pennysmith said.

"Too close for that, now."

"Inbounds! Four seconds out!" Che yelled, grabbing onto his panel for some frightened reason.

"Nav. One-eighty spin, now!"

"Oh no, oh no, no, no . . ." Julie Yeager said, frozen, staring at the holo, her face a mask.

"Captain," Pennysmith said, taking the HUD lens from her eye and staring calmly at Saef, "I need to say—"

"Hold that thought, please, Pennysmith," Saef said and looked up in time to see the holo flash white. The bridge fell into darkness and gravity fluctuated beneath them.

In the darkness, muttered words—maybe curses, maybe prayers—mingled with gasping breaths and something like a sob.

Saef spoke into the darkness. "We all just died."

The bridge lights and instruments flickered back to life.

"Simulation complete," Loki announced.

As voices shifted from fear to rage, Saef said, "I'll give you a bit to compose yourselves, and then we will examine exactly how we killed ourselves."

Chapter 25

"Human culture must finally provide
true pathways either to excellence and
accountability, or mediocrity with oversight,
and the freedom for each citizen to choose
their respective pathway for themselves."

—*Legacy Mandate* by Emperor Yung I

RICHARD SINCLAIR-MARU EXITED THE FAMILY SKIM-car and walked toward the small but fashionable apartments maintained for the Family Trade division. Richard possessed all the attributes his brother, Saef, lacked. His face nearly always wore a good-natured smile beneath a rakish blond coif, his figure, though lanky, bore a certain grace, and he always dressed fashionably. The frown he wore as he walked between the unwanted Family security agents represented a rare departure from his usual disposition, at least in public.

Long-term planning formed a fundamental part of the Sinclair-Maru, and if every other aspect of the

Family doctrine failed to impress Richard, planning and farsightedness had not. The Family doctrine called for regular heavy-grav sessions that strengthened and compressed the Sinclair-Maru into a familiar mold. Through meticulous neglect of this training, Richard now stood half a head above nearly every member of the Family, as far from the near-heavyworld image as he could feasibly get. Through cultivation of friendships since childhood, Richard's associates and habits also appeared unlike the common Sinclair-Maru mold. He was a swan among ravens...but just now the ravens cluttered up his environment unacceptably.

Richard abruptly stopped walking, causing the security team to react, positions shifting, hands moving.

"Look at that," Richard said, nodding up the street that ran toward the Imperial Close, far up the hillside. The security team were Sinclair-Maru to the bone, so only the team leader looked where Richard indicated, while the others continued to scan their sectors. He looked up the street, then to the walled estates rising up to the Imperial Close.

"Is there a particular threat?" the team leader asked.

"You see the walls of the ancestral estate, there?"

"Yes, Richard. The shimmer field we are generating renders attacks from that range ineffective."

"You see? That's the problem I'm talking about. The issue isn't violence, it's economics. We didn't lose the estate from a frontal assault. We lost it to compounding interest."

The team leader regarded Richard without expression. "Can we continue indoors, please?"

Richard sighed, shrugged, and continued walking. Inside the modish collection of rooms, Richard discovered a surprise guest awaiting him, something the security team certainly knew but had chosen not to share with Richard.

"Richard," Grimsby Sinclair-Maru greeted him, "we have a guest from home, see?"

Richard beheld Claude Carstairs rising to his feet, a wineglass in his slender hand. "Well, well, Claude," Richard said, "to what do we owe the honor?"

"No honor, old boy," Claude said. "It's just me, come to the metropolis, you see."

"Um, yes," Richard said. Although Claude Carstairs could only be called a foppish idiot, the unlikely friendship between Claude and his brother was just about the only element in Saef's life of which Richard approved.

"But, Richard, I do have some news..." Claude paused, his gaze lowering to fix upon Richard's jacket. "I say, Richard, that's a damned fine jacket... What color would you call that, exactly?"

Richard restrained his exasperation with great effort, glancing down at his jacket. "Color, Claude? Olive, I suppose. But you have news, you say?"

Claude stared fixedly at Richard's garment and shook his head. "Olive? Oh, I don't think so, old fellow, really. Don't tell me that came off a fab either, Richard, for I won't believe it."

"It's bespoke, Claude. I'll give you the name of my tailor."

"Bespoke? Of course it is! Well, Richard, that's uncommon generous of you, I must say, uncommon generous. Not olive, though. No."

"Claude?" Richard said, clenching his hands behind his back as Grimsby smiled on. "You said you have news."

"Did I?" Claude said, staring at the coat again with a frown. "It's on the tip of my tongue...."

"Yes?"

Claude exhaled. "Can't think of it. You know my poor brain. And m'father, such a sharp one. You'd think Mother played him false, but no, pure Carstairs through and through."

Richard ground his teeth for a moment before managing, "So you can't remember what news brought you here?"

"What?" Claude said. "No! I can't remember what that color's called. What a lunk I'd be to forget why I came here in the first place."

Grimsby smiled even more, but Richard took a calming breath. "Claude, please, what great tidings do you bring, then?"

Claude smiled affably for a moment before his expression shifted to a perplexed grimace, squinting as if to remember something. "Hmm," Claude said. His eyes widened and he smiled. "Oh yes! You remember that bit of seed oil you bought from m'father?"

"Yes," Grimsby said, his smile fading. "Five hundred tons of seed oil to be delivered at harvest."

"Yes, exactly. That's the bit," Claude said, smiling. "Well, you don't get it."

"*What?*" Richard exploded.

"Gods! Richard, you got spit in my eye just now. I hear perfectly, you know. No need to shout."

"But Claude," Grimsby said, striving for calm, "we have a contract. Why would your Family violate our agreement now?"

Claude opened his mouth to speak, then closed his mouth, his brow puckering. "Do I know why? I'm not sure I do. Seems like a damned shabby thing for us to do, when you come to it."

"Shabby? Shabby?" Richard demanded. Richard had known Claude since they were children, the smaller Carstairs estate adjoining the vast Sinclair-Maru lands, and as a child Claude had seemed clever enough, though exotically different from the stodgy Sinclair-Maru. Claude's teen years spent on Coreworld, though, seemed to spell the difference. When he returned to Battersea, Claude's childhood predilection for fashion and high society seemed to have elevated, crowding nearly every other thought from his head. Four years on Coreworld had apparently converted Claude's brain into a weighty ornament.

"Yes, Richard," Claude mused, rubbing his chin meditatively, "shabby. Especially since it's so expensive for us."

"What are you saying, Claude?" Grimsby asked, staring evenly, while Richard shook his head, his features flushed.

"Let's see if I can recall how this went, now," Claude said. "M'father sold you this seed oil. . . ."

"Yes," Grimsby encouraged.

"What do people do with seed oil, anyway? I've never seen any of it about. Have you?" Claude said.

It was Grimsby's turn for a calming breath. "Can we leave that for now, Claude?"

Claude shrugged. "I daresay. Puzzler, though." Claude resumed his meditative expression. "So . . . you bought this silly oil that no one uses . . . but we can't give it to you because . . . hmm . . . someone else bought it. Yes! That's it. Hah!" Claude smiled. "Someone else bought it. So you can't have it. All makes sense, see?"

Richard strode angrily across the room, striking his hand on a large ornamental desk and growling.

"But Claude, this violates our contract," Grimsby said in a calm voice. "I would think your father might consider, um, his Family's long relationship with the Sinclair-Maru before breaking a contract this way."

Claude took his perplexed gaze from Richard's explosive actions and turned back to Grimsby, nodding enthusiastically. "I would too . . . and consider his neck, too, you know? You might not credit it, but you Sinclair-Maru have a devilish bad reputation for calling people out on things like this. Dueling swords at dawn and all that."

"Oh really?" Grimsby said in a dry voice.

"But, can't be helped, see?" Claude continued. "The Emperor, you know. Does what he wants, I daresay. Wants seed oil for some damned reason." Claude paused, frowning. "Does it taste good? Is that it?"

"The Emperor?" Grimsby said, and Richard spun, staring between Grimsby and Claude.

"Not the Emperor himself, I think," Claude said, sipping from his wineglass. "Doesn't get out much, I hear. Probably one of those grim government types in the dreadful trousers." Claude squinted into the glass. "With all the handsome uniforms about, how those poor sods got saddled with such trousers—"

"The List!" Richard hissed, ignoring Claude and staring at Grimsby with a stricken look. "They give with one hand, take away with the other, damn them!"

"Factions, perhaps," Grimsby said, rubbing his temples as his eyes flickered through a UI feed. "We have two of the line items secured already, thankfully."

"But Takata's shipment should have been in our hands

days ago. And Wychwood's contract is on harvest, too. I'll bet they're both gone." Richard clenched his fists, scowling more like his younger brother. "They are going too far this time. Just because there's a rebellion kicking up doesn't give them the right to break contracts like a damned demi-cit!" Richard punctuated his sentence by striking the desk again with a loud thump, startling Claude in mid-sip and prompting him to choke.

"Two out of the five items," Grimsby said as Claude coughed. "That should be enough, even with this treachery."

"I say, Richard," Claude said, dabbing his mouth with a colorful hanky. "Why is your fellow glaring at me that way? I'm not the one punching furniture and startling fellows half to death."

Grimsby and Richard glanced over at the security leader, who was indeed glowering, staring at Claude's presence in the midst of a Family conversation. "Oh yes," Grimsby said, chagrined. "Perhaps it would be best if you permit us to get back to work, Claude."

"Lord, yes!" Claude said, disposing of his wineglass, clearly relieved to be going. Claude paused and turned back to Grimsby. "So . . . I can tell m'father that . . . ?"

Grimsby smiled reassuringly. "We understand he had little choice."

"Well, that's a weight off," Claude said. "Not ready to step into m'father's shoes. Tedious. Lot of numbers. Not my thing at all, you know."

"Of course," Grimsby said in a reassuring tone, leading Claude through a cluster of security agents. "Troubling times."

"Daresay you're right. . . . Emperor guzzling seed oil at a cut rate. Damned irregular, if you ask me.

House Barabas trying to buy our south field. Smoky! Impertinent! Been in our Family a century or more."

The security team leader stopped short and turned to stare at Claude. Grimsby paled and shot Richard a questioning glance.

"Barabas is trying to obtain your south field on Battersea?" the team leader asked.

"Did I say that?" Claude said. "Not sure I was supposed to. Private Family matters, I daresay."

"Excuse me," the security man said, nodding to one of his people and rushing away.

Claude turned a puzzled look after the man for a moment before turning his vacuous gaze on Richard. "Fellow's all in a flutter, Richard. What's his fizz about our south field?"

Grimsby forced a false chuckle, but Richard's face remained a tight mask. "You know security types, Claude," Grimsby said. "Always fretting about one thing or another, imagining things to frighten themselves."

"Daresay you're right, old fellow," Claude agreed, shrugging. "I once imagined I went on the town wearing puce. Put me in a muck sweat. Wonder what security blokes imagine?"

Richard stared sightlessly after the team leader. "Your south field adjoins our land, Claude."

"You're right there, old fellow," Claude said. "Been there, you know. Raised there. Got bucked off that cursed pony there, remember? Evil beast." Claude paused, musing. "Maybe your fellow's imagining that furry devil. Puts me in a flutter thinking about the beast, I confess. Bit. Kicked. Evil."

"No, Claude," Richard said. "I believe he's imagining a frontal assault."

Grimsby shot Richard a distressed look, and the security agents frowned disapprovingly. Claude nodded. "Oh, I see. Well, Richard, put your fellow's mind at rest. Pony's been gone years now. Won't assault anyone now, frontal or otherwise, see?"

Chapter 26

"Regain what you may, for I will meet you..."

—*Legacy Mandate* by Emperor Yung I

WINTER YUNG, IMPERIAL CONSUL TO BATTERSEA, Imperial agent and connoisseur of hedonism, stepped out of her armored skimcar and surveyed the surrounding verdant fields with disdain. She really held little right to complain about the setting, since she selected the meeting location, but that did not stop her. Bess Sinclair-Maru's strident complaints made this meeting necessary, and Winter needed no reason to blame others for her discomfort at any time, regardless.

When the two Sinclair-Maru skimcars slid into the field a short distance away, Winter registered a mild degree of surprise. All of Imperial High Society noticed the Sinclair-Maru's recent defensive posture, the constant presence of Family security teams around Sinclair-Maru properties and personnel. And, honestly, this played directly to Winter's benefit.

More than anything else Winter had arranged, this convinced everyone that the Sinclair-Maru stood on the inside of some great, secretive plot. For Bess to travel now with only a single escort vehicle and a few bodyguards seemed reckless under the current Sinclair-Maru mood.

Winter clicked her sword into place and stepped out from the protective cordon of her own bodyguards— her visible bodyguards. Each step provoked a twinge of delicious soreness, and for a pleasant moment her mind flashed upon her previous evening. No servant of the Emperor was more enthusiastic in extracting information from debased members of the quasi-nobility than Winter Yung. With the right subject, Winter might extract information for pleasurable hours.

The faint smile that touched Winter's lips faded as she beheld the stolid, brown form of Bess Sinclair-Maru. Though they had been classmates decades before, the un-regenerated marks of age on Bess's features immediately cooled Winter's fires. Bess Sinclair-Maru was not the right sort of subject for Winter's vigorous extraction methods.

"Dame Sinclair-Maru," Winter greeted while still some distance apart, "I take it I must endure a fresh string of complaints."

"Consul," Bess said, drawing closer, leaving her own security spreading out a stone's throw behind her, "so good to see you in person again."

"Indeed. So no complaints, Bess?"

Bess continued walking until they stood just beyond arm's reach. Winter's analytics quested across Bess's visible features, the pupils of her eyes, the muted beat of her pulse at her throat. They divined nothing clear. "Questions, Consul," Bess said. "We seek some hint of a path through this maze of game-playing."

Winter shook her head slowly. "Subtlety, always lacking in your Family, Bess. This never changes."

"We also lack duplicity."

Winter's irritation flared. "Those who lose at the game are the only ones decrying the rules. The Imperium does not compose itself to your whims, Bess, or your anachronism. So adapt, or fade away."

Now Winter's analytics detected the flash of Bess's anger. "What do you want from us? Is it just the destruction of the Sinclair-Maru? What?"

"Such melodrama... Don't flatter yourself, Bess. Until I made you interesting again no one of any importance spared a thought for the history-book family on their backwater planet." Winter suddenly felt a hint of uncertainty as she saw the anger vanish from Bess's face rather than grow as she had expected.

"So you truly are not engineering this?"

The analytics jangled. Winter tensed.

"Engineering what, Bess?"

"Give us a list with one hand, take our contracts with the other?"

Something did not add up between the emotions Bess contained and the words that she spoke. Winter waved a dismissive hand. "No destruction. Nothing nearly so dire. I give, another faction takes. Even *you* should know it works this way."

"And the encroachment by House Barabas upon our manor?" Bess asked, her face a shell concealing something.

Winter's analytics ran wild, catching hints of fear, indignation, and just a flash of something tagged

alternately as satisfaction and treachery. "Barabas?"
Winter said, feeling forces moving beyond her frame-
work, shaking her certainty. Information on Barabas
spooled through her UI. "Encroaching how?"

Bess measured Winter in her gaze. "A faction that
even you do not know? I am not sure if that is a
mark *for* them, or a mark *against* you."

Winter shook her head, sifting enough data on
Barabas to compose an informed sentence. "So Barabas
joins a spin-ward Trade combine and you come crying
that the world is ending?"

Bess's mouth thinned and Winter did not require
the analytic flag to recognize contempt as Bess spoke,
"Your incompetence may have killed us both. But I am
fool enough to feel glad you aren't the one pulling the
strings . . . for the sake of our school-room days."

Winter's reflexive rage stumbled, her UI filling with a
sudden string of priority alerts. Her analytics played across
Bess's face, screaming danger. "It's not about Trade, Consul. Barabas moves against us the old-fashioned way. . . ."

"What have you done?" Winter whispered, the shower
of alerts and priorities exploding, her eyes flickering
through the UI inputs. Far above her, the IMS *Fury*
rapid-fired alarmed messages, requesting clearance to
launch Marines, or to fire on approaching vehicles, or
do *something*. Analytics argued with Winter's knee-jerk
impression of a Sinclair-Maru betrayal. From the chaos
of alerts and flags, Winter suddenly pieced together a
stream of clarity. "You're bait."

Winter's security team received many of the same
alerts. Weapons filled hands, some covering the Sinclair-
Maru bodyguards who simply sat down in the field
and crossed their arms. An autocannon unfolded

from Winter's skimcar and began tracking something invisibly distant.

"We will share in this, together, Winter," Bess said. "My enemies will now be your enemies."

The autocannon roared, blazing away at incoming missiles, still invisible in the blue sky. Winter blanket-affirmed the string of UI queries: YES, LAUNCH MARINES; YES, INTERDICTION FIRE; YES, YES, YES!

Winter's bodyguards ran toward her, then tumbled as the ground leaped beneath them. Earth showered red-brown clods over Winter and Bess, white streaks crossed the sky over their sprawled forms, and small-arms fire erupted.

Winter wiped her eyes clear, and for a moment she lay nearly face-to-face with Bess, the thunder around them creating a pocket of surreal space.

"Dying...dying here, damn you," Winter seemed to whisper, but Bess heard, despite the cacophony of explosions.

"No!" Bess growled, rolling. "You stay alive." She threw herself over Winter as the skimcar exploded.

The part of Winter's mind that had maintained a nugget of sanity through all these years calmly observed everything as it unfolded now. It dryly recognized the strength of Bess Sinclair-Maru's arms locked around her, evidence of all the high-gravity training. It noted Bess's body jerking from multiple impacts, and recognized the sudden heat of her activating body shield, deflecting projectiles still moving with sufficient velocity through Bess. The warm wetness of blood flowing from Bess Sinclair-Maru was an abstraction that poured over Winter. The flowering of Marine reentry spikes in the sky above seemed like ripples in blue water.

Another explosion struck nearby, its force seeming to stomp Winter into the ground beneath Bess's shattered body for a moment before rag-dolling them both through the air. Winter thumped down without pain, still feeling strangely conscious of countless obscure details.

After a deafened moment, Winter's lungs restarted, as Marines in full battledress armor dropped from the sky all around her. Winter coughed, struggling to sit up. Streaks still crossed the sky as *Fury* continued showering kinetic accelerators on distant targets, and armored Marines plummeted down around her.

A cluster of battledress Marines surrounded Winter, facing outward, their weapons covering every vector. One of the Sinclair-Maru bodyguards stirred, trying to sit up, and a Marine's carbine leveled.

"No," Winter said, coughing. "Give them aid."

"Yes, Consul," the Marine lieutenant said, his voice crackling from the flat alloy of his battledress helmet.

As the Marines moved, Winter stood unsteadily to her feet and turned slowly about. The skimcars smoldered in heaps, the field wore a dozen small craters, scars stabbed into the lush green. Most of the bodyguards lay bleeding or scattered in pieces. Only now did Winter recognize the significance of the Sinclair-Maru retinue all being older: all were selected for a one-way mission, meant to entice their House enemies into the open. Perhaps they died satisfied.

Winter's gaze traveled to the crumpled, shattered figure of Bess Sinclair-Maru as a Marine medico attached med unit leads to Bess, but it appeared an exercise in futility. Imperial Security long believed the Sinclair-Maru possessed a coveted Shaper body shield, like the one radiating warmth on Winter's back, but it appeared this was not true, and Bess formed the dying proof of this.

Gods damn you, Bess! Winter's anger and resentment boiled toward her former classmate, but the soft breeze blew, cooling the blood that covered Winter... Bess's blood.

Knowing full well that Bess manipulated and endangered her, even raging at Bess, Winter still felt the pressure of that last embrace. She felt each of the impacts that ripped through the body of her old classmate. She heard each pained exhalation right in her ear, a terrible intimacy.

"Consul," a Marine's metallic voice spoke beside Winter, "the attackers' drones and vehicles are all down. Our strikecraft drops into the well now. We can lift you to *Fury* shortly."

Lift her to *Fury*. To fury. To fury.

Winter smeared blood from her face. "I want to know what House was behind this," Winter said, staring sightlessly. "Start with Barabas. Sift the wreckage. Sift the Nets. Get me someone alive."

"Yes, Consul."

Even as that dry, sane part of Winter's mind reminded her that this was all part of the Sinclair-Maru manipulation, that *they*, the Sinclair-Maru, should be the target of her wrath, she heard Bess Sinclair-Maru's breath in her ear. She heard the pain in each impact. For that moment, as weapons had thundered and shrapnel flew, Winter had felt sheltered. For this first time in her life, embraced by her dying classmate, Winter had felt loved.

Irrational as it may be, Winter felt the wrath boiling up.

"Lift me to *Fury*."

Chapter 27

"True self-control will provide moments
that appear uncontrolled, just as true
training provides moments of stillness."

—Devlin Sinclair-Maru, *Integrity Mirror*

"FEEL FREE TO SPEAK YOUR MINDS," CAPTAIN SAEF
Sinclair-Maru said to his reassembled bridge crew.
They crammed into *Tanager*'s tight bridge along with
Susan Roush and Inga Maru, the disastrous simulation
the only topic on the agenda.

Following the simulation they had only taken time
to collect the one missile fired during the exercise,
and allowed the sections to sort out their chaos before
assembling. Saef knew that most of *Tanager*'s officers
and ratings disapproved of his tactical charade. Deckchief Church, who had endangered life and limb trying
to clear the malfunctioning weapon-loading trays, now
sat in cold, rigid stillness near Saef. It was a risk and
Saef hoped it was worth it. Church half-lifted a hand.

"Deckchief?" Saef said.

"Captain," Church said, struggling for calm, "I understand your desire for...readiness, but in all my years, in all my floats I've never seen something so...irresponsible." His voice maintained an even, respectful tone, despite the severity of his words. "The Fleet procedure for simulations is centuries old for a reason, sir."

Saef nodded, keeping his face free of emotion, but before he could speak Julie Yeager jumped in. "You fired a live missile! A live missile!" Her face was suffused, her arms crossed over her breasts, her eyes snapping. "That isn't even safe."

"Anyone else?" Saef asked, cringing internally, glancing at Susan Roush, who maintained a steady glower throughout.

"It doesn't feel good," Pennysmith suddenly interjected, her eyes lowered, hands folded in her lap, "but I think it was useful." She looked up, then lowered her eyes, and Saef felt his heart warm toward her. "We failed. We died."

"Speak for yourself," Yeager said, turning her scorn on Pennysmith. "*Your* section failed. *Your* section killed us."

Pennysmith did not look up as she answered. "Yes, I know. *Now*. But how many simulator runs have we aced without a hint of a problem?"

"Simulator runs we all know," Farley, the comm rating said, looking down, refusing to meet anyone's eye. "They're just a game. This...this was something else."

"It was a nasty hoax," Julie Yeager said. "Amusement for one at the expense of everyone else. Against Fleet procedures, reckless, foolish, cruel."

Deckchief Church grimaced at Yeager's scathing words. "It was not Fleet simulator policy, and I think it was a dreadful risk to crew, but I think I see your objective, Captain."

Saef merely nodded, his expression mild despite the unease he felt inside.

The crew of *Tanager* rarely saw the XO, Susan Roush, and the captain together in the same compartment, so rumor flourished. Susan Roush had been the most famous captain in Fleet, her horrific running battle on the opening day of hostilities populated the Nets as the number one vidstream for weeks, then overnight, she became the most infamous Fleet officer, dis-rated by the Admiralty. They all knew that Susan Roush was the only living officer who had met the enemy twice in actual combat, and they all knew that long before that, Susan Roush populated the upper reaches of the Fleet efficiency list, a seasoned captain with dozens of impressive cruises under her belt. What they did not know was how their upstart first-time captain, and the High Priestess of Fleet endured each other.

She certainly wore a hostile glare throughout this meeting. Surely her sensibilities were deeply offended by their prodigy captain and his absurd game-playing.

"Anyone else have any thoughts?" Saef invited, fortifying himself.

Ops Chief Phillipa Baker shook her head. A shame-faced Che Ramos too-clearly remembered his suggestion that they surrender, and now tried to will himself into invisibility, hoping that no one would recall that particular moment.

"I've got a few thoughts," Susan Roush said, and Saef nodded encouragement. She turned her basilisk

gaze on the bridge crew. "Aren't we just a bunch of
delicate little cupcakes here? My heart bleeds ice-cold
piss for your wounded feelings. We transition in twelve
hours—twelve hours! Into a combat zone, people. And
when we arrive in, say, the middle of a rebel task
force, all you pansies will be lining up to kiss the
captain's arse because our shit is almost together."

"I've never—" Julie Yeager began in outraged tones,
but Roush cut her off.

"I'm sure you haven't, Princess. I know your type.
Had one just like you at Ericson Two. She's still
there, orbiting that star. All her blood made the most
beautiful icicle out her nose... all sparkly in the light.
She got her wake-up call with a lungful of hard vac.
You got yours today."

The bridge dissolved into a chorus of voices and
finger pointing, and Roush seemed grimly pleased
with her work.

After a moment, Saef broke into the shambles with
a firm voice, "Very well. I have heard what you all
said. The point of all this is not recriminations. It is
to gain insight. I think we gained insight, but what
lessons can we take away?"

"Conduct surprise live-fire exercises?" Deckchief
Church offered.

Pennysmith flushed, but Saef nodded. "Does seem
a good idea. What else?"

"Should we have signaled Fleet for help?" Farley
suggested.

"Good. Yes, that is established doctrine, and in the
heat of it all we missed that."

"Not that any help would have arrived," Roush
interjected.

"Anyone else?"

"C-could we have rushed a transition?" Pennysmith said.

Saef sat up straighter and pointed at Pennysmith. "Excellent. If we began calculations at the first moment of contact we could have emergency transitioned out of their reach."

"It's not Fleet doctrine," Susan Roush dryly offered, "and you can live to regret that choice."

"It's better than trying to surrender," Yeager said, giving Che Ramos a scathing look. Che blushed red and tried to disappear through the deck plating.

Saef leveled a flat gaze upon Che. "It takes courage to say what everyone is privately thinking. I hope my officers and crew will never hesitate to speak simply to protect their ego." Che blushed even deeper and couldn't find a comfortable portion of the bridge to look at, but Julie Yeager snorted in derision.

"You may recall," Saef said, "at a key juncture of the exercise I asked the entire bridge for suggestions, and only Mister Ramos found the courage to speak. That is commendable."

Yeager rolled her eyes and looked away, but Deck-chief Church cleared his throat. "Captain, I take it you had ideas on how we should have handled the . . . simulation, so you held out on us?"

Saef nodded, feeling the mood of his crew shifting in his favor. "I wasn't trying to discover *my* reactions, so, yes, I held out on you."

"What should we have done then, Captain?" Pennysmith asked.

Saef offered a rare smile, his internal tension easing. "Chief Maru will push each of you a copy of an analysis and prescription. Please study it in the time remaining before our transition. In just hours we will be in our target system." On cue, Inga pushed the report to each of them, but before any could access the file, Saef held up his hand, thinking of the peace offering Inga had suggested to him earlier.

"I want to make a final point clear. I felt this exercise was very important, but I believe it served its purpose. In the future we will conduct surprise drills and simulations, but I vow to you, I will never mislead you again." Saef looked across the bridge, meeting each eye. "The next time we clear for combat you can be sure it will be the real thing."

Saef stood to his feet as the others shuffled toward the bridge hatch, and the dogwatch waited outside to crew the bridge. Deckchief Church stood at his elbow.

"How did you do it, Captain? That was more than a simulation."

Saef looked from Church to the others moving out; only Roush and Inga remained at hand. "I informed Fleet of a weapons test exercise, put the XO in the auxiliary bridge back in engineering, and I got Loki to mock up the bridge feeds for the simulation." Saef clicked his sword back in place. "We live-fired that one missile, but I had revoked detonation codes on all our warheads before the exercise began. The glasscaster rounds were expended, as you saw, but that's within Fleet policy."

Deckchief Church shook his head but maintained a neutral expression. "I spoke critically just now, Captain—"

"I appreciate your candor, Deckchief."

"I may have been...I think I was wrong."

Saef felt a tension lift from his heart but kept his expression neutral. "I am heartily glad to hear it. Cherish the moment, though. It's unlikely I will invite a critique from crew again until this cruise ends."

Deckchief Church nodded, shot a glance at Susan Roush, and left the bridge.

"Learn what you wanted?" Roush asked.

Saef stared after Church for a moment, frowning. "Our opponents are just Fleet officers—or at least *were* Fleet until not long ago . . . just a smaller, tighter Fleet."

"Yes. That seems quite obvious."

"So we may use Fleet habits against our enemies."

Roush shrugged.

"What's the most prized quality in a Fleet officer, Roush?"

"Efficiency," Roush said without hesitation.

"Efficiency," Saef repeated, musing, "which really means 'cost effectiveness,' doesn't it?"

Roush nodded. "Efficient with Shaper fuel."

Saef turned toward the bridge hatch, Inga Maru silently in tow. "Walk with us, Roush, and let's figure out just how *in*efficient we can learn to be in the next twelve hours or so."

Chapter 28

"Courage springs more from clear thinking
than any other human quality."

—Devlin Sinclair-Maru, *Integrity Mirror*

CHE RAMOS SLUMPED ONTO HIS RACK, THOROUGHLY
spent. In the last twelve hours he had endured some
of the most extreme experiences of his life, including
several seconds on a darkened bridge when he honestly
thought that he was dead. If that was not enough, he
had shamed himself in front of the very peer group
that he struggled to join. His mind strayed to that
warm moment of redemption, when the captain had
commended him. . . . The captain. The traitor.

The traitor?

Che's heart plummeted again, just as it had done
a dozen times before, over the last days of *Tanager*'s
work up. For the hundredth time, Che wrestled through
the implacable logic that trapped him on a path that
he could not bear.

After serving so closely with Saef Sinclair-Maru for so many shifts, Che's impression of the captain only strengthened. The captain simply could not be a traitor . . . and it just did not matter. Che had less than twelve hours to get the evil little box into the captain's cabin or he, Che Ramos, would be the traitor. The very idea of the twenty-thousand-credit reward nauseated him now.

Che covered his face with both hands, glad that his cabinmate worked the dogwatch, leaving him to his private sorrow. Che had already worked out exactly how to get the package into the captain's cabin. He'd even rehearsed the steps a number of times, but here he lay with hours remaining to do as he was commanded. In the constant loop of his tortured thoughts, Che knew he waited for some salvation that would never arrive, and yet he remained, immobile. As he felt the curtain of depressed slumber falling, Che welcomed oblivion, but even in sleep the torture continued. . . .

Che jerked awake, startled by a voice that may have been his own, pleading with dream images of Imperial agents. He quickly ensured that his cabinmate was still absent, then laid back on his sweaty bunk and watched the seconds tick down in his new UI implant. He could delay no longer.

"I've got to do it," Che whispered to himself. "I've got no choice. G-got no choice." He rolled out of his rack in a burst of desperate decisiveness, and grabbed the hideous little rectangle. With a shaking hand he wrapped the box with a towel. He checked the time . . . just a few minutes to his window of opportunity.

"Damn it all," he whispered to himself. "Why me?" He had no answer, so he triggered the door and walked down the passage. Only one crewperson passed him on his path. Che nodded in a way that was meant to convey nonchalance, but it felt jerky, and sweat dripped into his eye. The crewperson walked on by and Che continued. There was the captain's cabin just ahead.

Che slowed his pace, dragging steps, slower and slower. Would the ship Intelligence cry foul the moment that he set foot in the captain's cabin? Surely not. Not if Che took nothing and left nothing... left nothing visible to the ship Intelligence.

Che felt conspicuous as hell, standing almost stationary in the passage, but just as he was about to turn away, the door to the captain's cabin opened to allow the deck-scrubbing dumb-mech to exit, as always. Che sprang forward, the concealed package in his hand. He hopped over the dumb-mech, into the captain's cabin, and halted with a lurch.

Saef and Inga sat comfortably waiting in the captain's chairs. Che dimly noted that Inga Maru had no food visibly in-hand, for once, but her face wore an eager sort of grin. Her hands remained out of sight beneath her cloak. The cabin door closed behind Che.

Numb, head swirling, Che said, "You—you aren't supposed to be here. The dumb-mech..."

"Sit down, Mister Ramos," Saef said, "and show us what you have in your hand there."

In a daze, Che sank into the last chair and pulled the towel free from the flat, gray rectangle. He placed it on the table.

"What is that, Ramos?" Saef said, his voice mild.

Che shook his head. "I don't know." Che's mind kept returning to the fact that the captain's cabin was supposed to be empty. The deck-cleaning mech would only scrub an empty cabin, and every time Che checked, every single watch, the dumb-mech shuffled out and Che had snatched a glimpse of an empty cabin.

"Loki?" Saef said, looking up slightly.

"My sensors only perceive the shadow of an object, Captain, nothing more," Loki vocalized.

"They s-said the ship Intelligence wouldn't see it," Che mumbled absently. Saef and Inga both focused intently upon Che, and he wilted in place.

"Who said?" Saef asked.

"The . . . the Imperial Security agents."

"What did they look like, Ramos?" Saef asked in an even tone.

"I-I don't know . . . Big."

"Was one of them female? Blond? Pretty?" Inga Maru asked.

"What?" Che said. "N-no. They were big, big guys."

"Heavyworlders?" Saef asked.

"Well, yes," Che said. He wasn't one of those Coreworld bigots who looked down on heavyworlders like they were some kind of subspecies. "They said you're a rebel, a traitor," Che added, then instantly regretted saying it. If Captain Sinclair-Maru *was* a traitor, Che might be in even more trouble than he thought.

"Oh?" Saef said. "And what do you think?"

Che fidgeted uncomfortably. "Told them it didn't make any sense. T-told them."

"To whom do you report on board *Tanager*?" Inga Maru asked.

Che looked up, confused. "What? Report?"

"Okay, Ramos," Saef said in a bland voice, "what exactly did they instruct you to do?"

Che looked from Saef to Inga, swallowed. "Um,

they . . . they said that I had to get this thing into your cabin before we transitioned. They said that if I failed, then I—I was the traitor."

"And if you succeeded?" Inga said.

Che blushed. "They . . . they said I would be rewarded," he said in a small voice.

"How delightful," Inga said, her smile widening. "What sort of reward are we talking here?"

"Twenty thousand." Che refused to look up.

"Twenty thousand," Inga repeated. "That doesn't seem very generous, especially when failure means you get kicked out an airlock."

Che gasped involuntarily and looked up at Inga and Saef. "I—I . . ." Che felt the cabin spinning. How could this happen to him? Why had he ever abandoned the safe life of a demi-cit?

"We need to figure out what this device of yours does," Saef said, ignoring Che in his distress.

"Get Amos Cray to analyze it, perhaps?" Inga said.

"I would rather not," Saef said. "I want to keep this as tight as possible. We may try some sort of optical scope. It appears to have some small openings on one side that we could access."

"But if Loki can't even see what we access, where does that leave us?"

Che listened miserably to their exchange, wishing he were back in his tidy little demi-cit pod. It really hadn't been bad. He had friends, and that girl, music, and his demi-cit ration of four daily ounces of low-proof alcohol. After school hours they would some-times get together for a little party. No matter how Che described school, his plans or even just the joy he found in mastering the emerging world of micros, his friends never understood why he would leave the pods for the frightening, dangerous world of the Vested Citizen and Fleet.

Che shook his head, the voices of the captain and Chief Maru fading into a blur as he remembered. His friends had been right, Che never had fit in to this new world, never belonged. He had been a pawn for everyone, pretending to be something that he was not.

Still...there had been moments, seated at his place on the bridge of a Fleet warship where he couldn't believe his fortune. Although the sensors of this old starship could not compare with the sensor suite on the latest micros...

Che looked up suddenly. "I can figure out what this thing is...I—I think," he said, interrupting the conversation between Inga and Saef.

"It speaks," Inga said.

"Really, Ramos?" the captain said.

"Y-yes, if anyone can. Micros. I can get in that with micros. See what it does."

Saef stared directly into Che's eyes, and Che held the gaze, almost defiant. "Very well, Ramos," Saef said. "You get your shot at redemption."

"So, no airlock ride, then?" Inga said.

"Do restrain yourself, Maru," Saef said. "Mister Ramos will be *so* helpful now."

Chapter 29

"What we call selfishness is simply short-term
thinking, and what we call selflessness is little
more than long-term thinking in action."

—*Legacy Mandate* by Emperor Yung I

WITH INFINITE CARE, CHE RAMOS PILOTED HIS
craft straight for the hangar-like opening in the cliff
face, moving forward at a slow pace. Although he had
plenty of clearance on either side of his craft, Che
remained cautious. A sudden air current or micro-collision could cause a significant deviation in his course,
and at this moment he *needed* everything to be flawless.

Che's craft motored straight ahead, flying into the
broad opening. A passage stretched out ahead and Che
continued his course, scanning the sheer walls on both
sides for any hint of activity. One of the largest of Che's
small armada of micros, his current vehicle spanned
a width equivalent to a few human hairs. He figured
he might need some of its greater capabilities as he

explored the interior of the mysterious package that he was supposed to have secreted in the captain's cabin. If he encountered some internal path too tight, he would simply pilot a second, smaller micro inside as well.

The passage did constrict ahead and Che slowed, scanning carefully. "I've found something," Che reported, knowing the captain and Inga Maru sat beside him in the captain's cabin, even as Che's observational locus lay within the tiny micro navigating the bowels of the package.

"Yes, Ramos?" the captain said.

Che pivoted his scanners as his craft floated slowly forward. Shallow sconces opened on either side of the main passage, one after the other. Che slowed his vehicle to a stop and bumped up illumination, flooding one sconce.

"You were saying?" Inga Maru prompted.

Che stared at the insect-like shape he illuminated within the sconce. Glittering sensor plates gleamed like multifaceted eyes, an extendable probe formed a proboscis, and clawed grippers dangled below the segmented body.

"Micros," Che said.

"What's that?" the captain's voice inquired.

Che scanned down the long passage, seeing the dark mouths of sconces opening as far as his sensors reached. "This package is full of micros. Look." Che pushed an image capture to Inga and Saef, allowing them to see the insectoid shape for themselves.

"I—I've never seen a design like this before," Che said. "Should I try and pull one out? We might be able to analyze it with some of my other micro-deck tools."

"We've only a short time to our scheduled transition," Saef said. "Not much time to analyze anything."

"Push our transition back?" Inga Maru questioned.

"I don't want to tip anyone off. We transition on schedule," the captain said.

"So...?" Che said.

"How many of those are there?" the captain asked.

"Um, thousands, it looks like," Che said, looking again at the myriad openings from either side of the central passage.

"Go ahead," Saef said, "try to get one."

Che closed on one insectoid micro and extended his graspers.

"A question occurs to me, Captain," Inga Maru said, her voice rising invisibly beside Che, "we have an army of micros here, but who is the operator? I only know one micro-operator onboard."

Che froze for a moment, swallowing acid.

"Maru, are you suggesting that Mister Ramos might be the intended operator, just because he carried them onto the ship and tried to sneak them into my cabin?"

"The suspicion does cross my mind, Captain," Inga purred.

"These m-might be operated by a preprogrammed control unit here in this package," Che said, sweating. "Probably have to be really... A s-signal feed s-strong enough to control them remotely would be, um... pretty obvious."

"See, Maru, Mister Ramos takes the legs out from your suspicion." The captain's tone seemed almost amused. "You bringing that damned thing out of there, Ramos?"

Che extended the claws and grabbed the much smaller, insect-like micro. "Just about to, Captain."

He reversed power and observed resistance as the insect-micro's appendages dragged free of its sconce. Che's craft popped free, wobbling as Che stabilized the controls. "I g-got it."

Retracting his path, now encumbered with an awkward load, Che buzzed his tiny craft back down the "long" passage, a track no longer than his index finger, and emerged from the small gray package. A moment later Che's micro settled down on the micro control-deck. He manipulated the graspers, carefully pressing the strange micro against a collection of contact probes.

Che exhaled and pulled the deck's VR lenses off. "O-okay, it's in place. I—I should be able to analyze some aspects of its structure through my deck now."

"Link me to the feed," Inga Maru commanded.

"Yes, Chief," Che said, perplexed, but completing the handoff, pushing the micro-deck's interface to Inga. "I—I didn't know you were a, um, micro-operator."

"I'm not." Inga Maru's eyes flickered, and Che became an astonished spectator, watching his feed from the micro-deck as it exploded into torrents of information flowing in both directions.

"Transition time coming up, Maru," Saef said as she streamed information through her UI. "I'll need to head to the bridge shortly."

Inga's eyes continued to flicker and Che continued to look on, amazed, as data poured through his micro-deck. "Encryption . . ." Inga said quietly. Her brow wrinkled momentarily and the data stream recoiled repeatedly. "Got it."

A burst of characters flowed through the micro-deck,

too fast for Che to follow, and then ceased. Inga's eyes closed, her face seeming to pale.

"Maru?" Saef said, his forbidding features softening somewhat.

"Oh!" Loki's voice audibly spoke into the cabin. "This is an interesting cruise!"

"Maru?"

Inga's eyes popped open. "It...it's worse than we thought."

"What is it?" Saef said.

"He needs to be back in his quarters," Inga said, nodding toward Che, "and we need the XO here."

"B-but, what is that th-thing?" Che spluttered. "You've got to t-tell me."

Inga stepped close to Che, her eyes peering through the blond fringe of her hair, her usual smile gone. "No, I don't. And if you talk to anyone about what you saw here, I will know...just like I knew you would be here today." She reached a hand out from beneath her cloak and adjusted his crumpled uniform jacket. "Talking— even in your sleep—can get you kicked out an airlock."

"Don't terrify the poor fellow, Maru," Saef said. He looked at Che. "We need any *other* spies on board to believe that you planted this package without a hitch, see? So just act natural. You can do that, right, Mister Ramos?"

Che jerked a couple of nods, his eyes darting from Saef to Inga. It should be easy enough to keep acting the same way he had since he boarded *Tanager*: nervous, insecure, and terrified of the future.

"Y-yes, Captain. I—I can do that." But Che did not like the look in Inga Maru's eyes.

Talking in my sleep? She heard me talking in my sleep?

Chapter 30

"Pain is the finest teacher. Thus, the obsessive avoidance of pain is the most certain path to folly and destruction. To embrace pain is to receive wisdom."

—Devlin Sinclair-Maru, *Integrity Mirror*

THE HATCH TO SAEF'S QUARTERS SLID SHUT AS CHE Ramos departed, and Saef turned his focus onto Inga Maru, his thoughts swirling into channels of misgiving. The internal tension rose until Saef found the Deep Man, his pulse slowing back to normal. He took a slow breath.

"Okay, Maru, we only have minutes to transition. What are we facing?"

Inga paced a slow circle and then sat, her cloak settling around her. "The micro is a weapon."

"No surprise there," Saef said.

"It contained deep layers of coding, and something like a Meerschaum encryption."

Saef stared at Inga. "I thought Meerschaum encryption was too resource intensive to crack."

Inga seemed to hesitate, displaying indecision for the first in Saef's experience with her. "So did I."

"More of your Family tech sorcery?"

Inga shook her head. "No. Loki seems to have a... particular facility for code breaking."

"Indeed," Saef said, wondering why Inga seemed so hesitant. "Cracking a Meerschaum encryption in seconds? Fleet will like to know about that 'particular facility,' I daresay."

"No!" Inga said sharply, then turned her steady gaze into Saef's eyes. "No."

Saef stared at her, wanting answers, but seeing the clock ticking down to transition he said, "And what did you find under the encryption?"

"Complex instruction sets for the micro and for its payload," Inga said. "The micro activates during transition, seeks its target, and injects coded nanotech... all during transition."

"Nanotech," Saef repeated, leaning back, shocked. "The *Shapers?* Gods."

"That was my first thought, but perhaps not. Loki is running models of the program. The nano payload targets implants, but it could be something like Hawksgaard's tricks. Human tech married to Shaper tech."

"To what end?" Saef said.

"We can't be certain," Inga said. "A thousand micros activate during transition, inject a nano payload optimized for N-space.... Who can say? There would be enough material to physically alter an implant in significant ways."

Saef slowly shook his head, thinking through the

ramifications. "Unlikely it's intended to kill me outright, then. But since we don't know *what* it's supposed to do to me, we can't very well fake it, can we?"

Inga seemed to ponder the question, but her eyes flickered over data streaming in from some source, her hand fishing out a food concentrate bar. "That is why we need the XO," she said. "I see a way, I think. A dangerous way." She paused. "Roush is here," she said, and the door chimed a moment later.

The hatch opened to reveal Susan Roush, her expression as severe as ever. "Captain, Chief," she said in greeting, stepping into the cabin, the hatch sealing shut behind her. "Transition time, eh?" Her eyes passed over Saef and Inga, falling upon the flat gray rectangle resting nearby. "What the hell is that?"

Inga took a bite from her food bar, her eyes still flickering. Saef smiled despite the fear that hammered at his control of the Deep Man.

"That, Roush, seems to be your stepping-stone back to command."

Lieutenant Tilly Pennysmith clambered through the bowels of *Tanager*'s archaic Weapons section, a smear of grease serving as a battle stripe across her face. Both of her hands probed each link of the loading tray rails as she wormed through the trays. A white-faced Chief Sandi Patel accompanied her progress, at first firing nonstop streams of haughty invective, despite the raking Deckchief Church had already bestowed upon her.

Pennysmith ignored everything Sandi Patel said: the veiled insults, the veiled threats, the outright fabrications. She grimly continued, physically touching every joint, bearing, and link of each loading apparatus, her number three uniform permanently marred by grease stains.

After clearing the glasscaster trays, finding every span exactly to spec and freshly greased, Pennysmith began to think that she may have overreacted. Had she compounded her initial leadership failures first by failing to properly manage her section, then by offending and alienating her section chief?

But then she began clambering over the loading track for the larger 32-gauge missiles, and Sandi Patel's voice became strident.

"Young officers always pushing, puffing themselves off!" Sandi Patel declared, sliding down the load tray behind Pennysmith. "Never can let a crew learn their ship without interfering, thinking that rank somehow makes 'em an expert!"

Tilly Pennysmith said nothing in reply, pressing on, sliding each of her filthy hands over, under, and through each link and rail.

"Listen, listen!" Sandi Patel said, almost shouting. "Okay? Okay." Tilly peered over her shoulder at Sandi Patel's suffused face. "You want me to take the blame? I'll take the blame. It was all on me, you hear?"

Tilly wiped a sweating brow with the back of one hand, leaving a new smear of grease, then turned back to her examination.

"Officer? Fleet officer?" Sandi Patel said in an ugly tone. "Damned cultist. Not even a rational person. Shoulda been wiped out, the lot of you!"

Pennysmith froze in place for a moment, stunned by the hateful words. She began to turn, to look into those eyes, but stopped herself; she would not be deflected from her purpose. Only a short time remained before transition, and the Weapons section would be perfect by Tilly's own hand and eye. She pressed on, worming down the 32-gauge load tray. A hand seized her shoulder.

Tilly spun. "Do not touch me!" Sandi Patel stared, shocked at the wrath flaring toward her. "By your dishonor, Patel, my honor is taken. I may be of the Faith. I may be an officer over you. But I wear a sword, and when we're planetside, I will meet you."

Sandi Patel stared in stunned silence, and Tilly rolled back to her inspection. A moment later she discovered the source of Chief Patel's panic, finding the satchel of pilfered components secreted between the underside links of the 32-gauge rails.

"A little shopping, Chief?" Pennysmith said. "Let's go discuss this with Deckchief Church, shall we?"

An hour later, with minutes to spare, Lieutenant Tilly Pennysmith settled into her place on the cramped bridge. Everyone sat ready in their place, except the captain, with Lieutenant Ruprecht acting as officer of the watch.

Tilly took a breath to calm herself, glancing at her hands on the console before her. Grease still lined each fingernail, but her hands did not shake. She looked up, checking to her left and right. Che Ramos ran the sensors. He looked harried and nervous to her eyes, but he always did. Phillipa Baker ran Ops now that Ruprecht worked first watch, and she appeared as unmoved as ever. Farley sat at comm, idly flipping through screens on his console. Yeager—beautiful Julie Yeager—occupied her throne, regally unaware of anyone else on the bridge. Tilly looked at the statuesque profile of the navigation and astrogation officer, and struggled to quell the envy that arose yet again. Ensign Yeager, the ideal young officer; no bizarre religious trappings for her, no stupid HUD lenses like a bloody demi-cit, no infamous family... and smart and beautiful on top of it all.

The bridge hatch popped, and Captain Sinclair-Maru stalked in, his face set in its usual forbidding lines. The captain's slender blond cox'n strolled in behind him, a food bar in hand, her dark cloak shrouding her form. Not for the first time, Pennysmith wondered about a possible romantic connection between the captain and his cox'n. She knew they were distant relatives—quite distant—and she never saw a hint of any real romance between them, so perhaps the peculiar bond between them was nothing more than shared ancestors.

"Ruprecht, I have the bridge," the captain said, taking over the command seat from that micromanaging twit.

"The bridge is yours, Captain," Ruprecht rumbled back and moved to the bridge hatchway.

As the bridge hatch closed, Inga Maru settled into the deckchief's empty seat, and the captain said, "Nav, calculation for our transition ready?"

"Calculations for transition complete, Captain," Julie Yeager affirmed.

"Weps?"

"Shields generators, all green," Pennysmith said, scanning her instrument checklist, "point defenses charged, glasscaster and missiles, green."

"Ops?"

"Engineering shows green," Phillipa Baker said, "Ready for transition power. Heat sinks, all green. All sections report ready for transition. Marine quarterdeck reports ready. Fabs ready for transition programs."

"Very good." The captain nodded, seeming calm to Pennysmith's eye, despite his first combat transition. "Comm, signal Fleet with our transition code."

"Signaling our transition code to Fleet, Captain," Farley said.

The captain seemed to scan through his UI for a moment before saying, "Nav, transition power, now."

Pennysmith did not see Julie Yeager actuate the N-drive, but she felt the unmistakable effect of shifting through transition space. The darkened bridge seemed to glow, each instrument light seeming to expand, the air itself seeming to exude a faint radiance. Back in Engineering, she knew, the fabs burst into activity, feverishly constructing components humanity could only obtain in the fleeting moments within N-space.

As part of her faith, Tilly Pennysmith carried no Shaper tech within her body, so she alone did not *feel* the heating effects of transition upon an implant, but this prompted no great curiosity in her as the seconds stretched out.

"Sensors, you ready there?" the captain asked of Che Ramos after a long span of silence.

Che jumped. "R-ready, Captain."

That's right, Pennysmith thought, *probably Che's first transition.*

Then the universe subsided, stars appearing, one star much brighter than all the rest.

"Weps?"

"Shields up and green, Captain," Pennysmith said.

"Nav? Confirm transition."

"One second, Captain," Julie Yeager said as Loki

rapidly obtained fixes with optical scopes, comparing them to astrogation charts. "Yes, Captain, transition confirmed." The main holo lit up with *Tanager*'s position relative to the Delta Three planets and stations.

"Sensors, passive only," the captain said.

"Yes, Captain," Che said, sweating, "passive only."

Pennysmith heard the sound, like a surprised grunt, issue from the captain, just before Farley said, "Captain, receiving a steady Fleet beacon from the Delta Three orbital station."

"Comm, double-check that beacon, please," the captain said. "It's using the correct Fleet signature?"

Farley eyed his panel and nodded. "Double-checked, Captain. Signature confirmed."

Pennysmith heard the soft words from the captain's cox'n, "How is that possible?" but she couldn't see what caused the consternation. The captain stared at the holo, frowning, as seconds passed in the semidarkness of the bridge. *Tanager* coasted, dark and silent, into the outer fringes of the Delta Three system.

"Loki," the captain said, at last, "where is the Delta Three defense platform?"

Pennysmith shot a startled look back at the holo. From the murmurs around the bridge she realized she wasn't the only one who failed to notice the absence of the small platform.

"According to optical scope composites I am forming," Loki replied, "the defense platform was recently destroyed. Fragments of wreckage expand outward from its predicted position."

That explained the captain's consternation, Pennysmith realized. The enemy swooped in, destroyed the pathetic defense platform, then left the orbital dock and station unmolested? That hardly seemed possible, and yet the Fleet signature continued to broadcast from the orbital station as if all was well.

"Nav," the captain said, "begin transition calculations."

"Yes, Captain," Julie Yeager said. "For Core System?"

The captain shared a look with Chief Maru, his eyes flickering from a line-of-sight. He turned back and continued frowning at the holo. "No. Intrasystem."

Julie Yeager stared at the captain, uncomprehending. "Intrasystem?"

Everyone shared her confusion. The astronomical expense of Shaper fuel meant intrasystem transitions simply did not occur. In one single step, the captain would eliminate any chance of efficiency bonuses for the entire crew, not to mention calling down the eventual ire of the Admiralty for such wastefulness.

The captain's inimical gaze turned toward Julie Yeager and she blushed, visible even in the dim lighting. "Yes, Captain. Intrasystem calculations."

"As deep on Delta Three station as we can," the captain said before turning to Tilly Pennysmith. "The bridge is yours, Weps."

"I have the bridge," Pennysmith affirmed.

The captain stood. "Run dark. Run silent."

"Silent and dark, Captain," she said.

With his cox'n close beside, the captain moved to the bridge hatchway. "Ops, have the XO meet me on the Marine quarterdeck."

As Phillipa Baker affirmed and messaged Susan Roush, the bridge hatch slid shut, and Lieutenant Tilly Pennysmith assumed the command seat. She ran through all the vital systems once, before she noticed

Che Ramos looking toward the bridge hatch, staring after the captain with the most peculiar expression on his face.

"Sensors?" she said.

Che Ramos jerked and turned back to his console. "Y-yes, Lieutenant?"

"Keep sharp watch for any change, any trace."

"Y-yes, Lieutenant," Ramos said.

Tilly Pennysmith turned back to the holo.

The IMS *Tanager* continued its progress, a bubble of light and warmth on the cold, dark edge of the Delta Three system.

Lieutenant Pennysmith sensed it would not last.

Chapter 31

"Deception is a dangerous tool. Even
as it is wielded, deception changes
the deceiver in subtle ways."

—Devlin Sinclair-Maru, *Integrity Mirror*

"YOU TAKE AN AWFUL RISK LEAVING RAMOS IN YOUR
bridge crew," Inga Maru said as they made their way
aft.

Saef glanced over his shoulder at her. "Do you
honestly believe he's anything more than he claims?"

Inga took a bite from her food bar and shrugged.
"No. Poor sod."

Saef nodded. "Neither do I, and any meddling
with him would be a dead giveaway to whoever else
is sharpening a knife."

Inga smiled brightly. "Certainly no agent would
believe we could be stupid enough to leave a known
saboteur running about on the bridge, free to do
whatever mischief he wishes."

"You have a positive knack for cutting to the heart of it."

They approached the keyway waist hatch, and Saef caught a momentary glimpse of a ship services rating looking through the open hatch. The rating disappeared from sight, likely going about his duties, and Saef pressed on toward Marine country. Just as he reached the hatch, Saef heard a catch in Inga's breath and the distinctive slide of steel.

Saef's hands dropped to his weapons even as he felt the icy plunge into the Deep Man, but Inga sprang forward. He saw her flash past him through the hatch, her bare blade in a two-handed grip, her cloak snapping out behind. He saw the slash of sword pass a handsbreadth above her head as she ducked through, and he accelerated into motion, pistol in his left hand, sword in his right.

As Saef cleared the hatch he saw Inga lunge blade first, her teeth bared as she thrust, then she cleared her red-tipped blade to block a riposte, two-handed, her sword ringing sharply. As she flew back from the force of the blow, Saef saw their foe, the ship services rating, a large heavyworlder who fell even as Saef's sword moved. Inga's singular attack had pierced the ambusher's heart, leaving him only his final riposte before collapsing.

The rating's eyes hazed over, and Saef quickly scanned the remainder of the compartment for any threat. It stood empty.

Inga stood to her feet, her eyes still wild under her blonde disarray.

"Are you injured, Maru?"

"No," she said, wiping her blade on the tail of her

dark cloak and sheathing it in one motion. She smiled unevenly. "Loki says no one saw. So your kill."

Saef measured her with his eyes for a moment, then nodded. She could remain a secret weapon at least a bit longer.

Inga retrieved her food bar from the deck, blew on it ineffectually, and took a bite.

Saef looked upward slightly. "Loki, log this assault, and inform Major Mahdi, please."

"Yes, Captain," Loki's audible voice responded.

Inga chewed her food bar a moment before saying, "You know, the Marines could be the second half of the ambush."

Saef stood over the fallen rating with his sword and pistol still in hand. "What a distressing possibility." Inga finished the food bar and moved deeper into the recreation area, empty still following the transition. Her hands disappeared beneath her cloak and Saef heard the faint click of her submachine gun release.

"Loki warned you of the ambusher?" Saef asked, glancing down at the heavyworlder's sprawled form.

Inga gazed levelly at Saef. "Loki warned me."

Saef nodded, musing. "Our ship Intelligence is remarkably useful."

Inga grimaced slightly, about to say something, when the aft hatch cycled and Major Mahdi entered, flanked by Sergeant Kabir and a rare non-heavyworld Marine corporal. Susan Roush stepped in behind them, scowling.

Major Mahdi glanced at Inga's flanking position, missing nothing.

"Secure that," Major Mahdi ordered, jerking his head at the rating sprawled, dead. Sergeant Kabir and the corporal frisked the body, and secured the limp arms before hauling the body aft.

"What happened, Captain?" Major Mahdi asked, his eyes touching on Saef's bare blade and pistol before swiveling to glance back at the cloaked figure of Inga Maru. Susan Roush stood back, silent.

"That one made his try as we came through the hatch, Major."

"Know him?"

Saef shook his head, sheathing his sword. "Barely spoke to the fellow. Should I know him?"

"Thorsworld native," Major Mahdi said. "Heard you crossed swords with one of them not long ago. They're a clannish bunch."

"Search his cabin," Saef said. "He violated the honor code.... You ever know a Thorsworlder who would stoop to cheating against a mere Core dweller?"

Major Mahdi offered a thin smile. "You've got a point, but I've already got Marines sifting that bloke's kit. We'll see."

A dumb-mech ambled in and began cleaning up the mess on the deck, and Susan Roush finally spoke up, "You wanted to see me?"

Saef glanced around at the very public compartment. "Shall we step into my office? There are some developments in Delta Three that need our attention, the three of us."

The three officers and Inga wedged into the closet-like chamber. Inga stood, leaning against the wall, while Mahdi and Susan Roush claimed the two seats facing the desk, and Saef settled behind its slender, Spartan width. A tiny holo filled one side of the desk.

"If you will, please," Saef said.

Saef called up the main sensor feeds in his UI and pushed them to the small holo. The Delta Three system appeared, each human-made feature highlighted. Roush leaned closer to the tank, then growled. "Where the hell is their shitty little defense platform?"

"Blown to bits, it appears," Saef said.

Roush looked stricken. "Then what's to discuss? The enemy bastards are here, and you're joining me as a gods-damned pariah for dragging your heel so long getting here. Just fucking wonderful."

Major Mahdi looked from Roush to Saef, his expression neutral.

"Delta Three station still broadcasts a valid Fleet signature beacon," Saef said.

Roush's mouth compressed into a line, her brow lowering.

"Their defense platform must have suffered a tragic accident of some kind," Saef said lightly.

"Like hell," Roush said.

"So," Saef continued as if Roush never spoke, "Delta Three station and planetside are still in Fleet control, clearly."

"Oh, clearly," Major Mahdi rumbled, smiling.

Roush shook her head. "We play this charade and sit out our six-month cruise, waiting for a rebel attack that's never coming. Sooner or later that's going to bite us in the ass. Either we run now and get reamed for being tardy on station, or we sit on station for six months, or however long it takes for Fleet to find out what's afoot here, and then we get reamed for being tardy *and* incompetent."

"Loki, show us the optical composite of Delta Three station, please," Saef said.

The holo tank resolved a knobby dark lump, contrasting against the bright face of Delta Three planetside. *Tanager* stood far too distant for even the finest optical composites to resolve much detail, but a trained eye could discern quite a lot from the dark blot.

"This station is packed with traffic," Roush said, studying the image. "Maybe a dozen ships docked on the little turd."

"Are you feeling your greed, Captain?" Major Mahdi asked.

Saef fixed the major with a steady gaze. "Perhaps. More importantly, the Admiralty certainly feels theirs."

Roush and the Major stared at the screen, musing, while Inga fished a food bar from beneath her cloak, her eyes flickering with some perpetual stream of data.

"If the enemy ever managed to capture a station like Delta Three," Susan Roush said, forming her words with uncharacteristic care, "and they somehow kept an operable Fleet Intelligence running, they could scoop up a basketful of merchant traffic. But they'd keep warships on-system, sure as shit. Those would come running if, say, a little frigate came in trying to throw a loop around anything."

"Yes," Saef said, "your little frigate would take days to close with a station under normal Fleet protocols. That's why the protocols must fall."

"Inefficiency," Roush said.

"Yes, as a start," Saef said. "Fortunately for us, we need not go in with guns blazing."

"But you are going in?"

"Yes."

"The Admiralty will crucify you," Roush said. "Their critique of your recklessness, proven."

"Only if we fail, Roush. They chastise me for being too reckless, so I drag my heel in abundant caution. They chastise you for being too cautious, and let them see how responsive you are!"

"And where do my Marines come in, Captain?" Major Mahdi said.

Saef glanced at Roush, then back to Major Mahdi. "Your Marines are central to any plan I can visualize. Have you ever considered a method of taking down a vessel with the Intelligence still active?"

Major Mahdi's face revealed nothing. "We could figure something out, I expect."

"It may not come to it," Saef said. "We'll close with the station and see if they try to brazen it out, or if they mobilize a heavy response."

"They don't need that heavy of a response to swat us," Roush grumbled.

"Loki, show us the station defenses, please," Saef said.

The holo swirled, resolving a file schematic of the modest Delta Three orbital station. It surely represented the pride and the future of Delta Three system, with its tentacles of docking ports and substantial facilities, but defenses were minimal.

"Point-defense beam weapons and that kinetic driver," Roush mused. "So we outclass them, even with our pop guns."

"Depending upon what's docked right now, yes," Saef said. "But slugging it out shouldn't be necessary. We'll catch them flat-footed and get close, under a... a subterfuge, shall we say. They'll never expect it."

Major Mahdi nodded appreciatively, but Roush frowned. "Of course they won't expect it. They probably have a copy of our orders, and they know we have no authority to do anything."

"Exigent circumstances, Roush," Saef said. "Isn't that the line the Admiralty used on you?" Roush just scowled, and Saef turned to Major Mahdi. "It occurs to me that the planetary governor is the only official on-system that has the authority to countermand my orders. He also could be holding the leash of the station's Intelligence."

"You've been thinking some," Major Mahdi said.

"If the enemy's got a knife to the governor's throat it would explain a great deal."

"Or if the governor's turned his coat himself," the major said.

Saef gazed blandly at Major Mahdi. "Surely not. If he made an open play for the uprising, he'd be in the middle of a surface war, wouldn't he?"

Major Mahdi snorted. "Or you prefer the flavor of a *rescue operation* to holding your own knife to his throat."

Saef maintained a bland expression. "It seems we understand each other tolerably well, Major."

"So you're thinking I'd split my Marines. Insert some on the governor, keep some for the station. That makes for thin company."

"Our knowledge evolves, Major. Tell us if it's beyond you."

"Can't bait me, Captain. Not that way," the Major said. "Have you given a thought for the expense? The reentry spikes alone are what? Fifty thousand apiece?"

Saef just offered a thin smile.

"Efficiency is long gone," Roush said. "We either win big here, or we put our damned heads on the block."

Major Mahdi looked back and forth between Roush

and Saef, glanced at Inga Maru's half smile, then leaned over the desk, resting both thick arms before him. "Commodore Zanka is a friend of mine. He would want me to point out that what you consider is a flagrant disregard of orders, and a horrible risk."

Roush crossed her arms, saying nothing, and Saef raised his eyebrows inquisitively.

"My Marines will be ready," the major said. "What's the time frame?"

Roush looked at Saef expectantly, and Saef steepled his fingers. "Things accelerate rapidly now," Saef said. "Be prepared for both operations in twenty hours."

Major Mahdi made a startled noise, his placid demeanor overset. "What?"

"Efficiency is the first casualty, Major," Saef said. "Speed is the order of the day."

"Twenty hours! Gods! Is that even possible?"

"For the ship to be on station? Yes."

Major Mahdi shook his head. "Even in simulations, I've never seen such a thing." He paused, thinking. "If we can pull the intel for the governor, my Marines will be ready. If we can't, then inserting on his location is a buggered mess."

"Extraction could be interesting," Roush offered.

"If I can get to the governor, that doesn't worry me much," the major said. "We can get up out of the well on our own, I expect. Just don't run off and leave the system."

"Very good, Major," Saef said, standing. "Put your teams together. Let me or the XO know if you need anything."

The office hatch chimed, and all four looked at the hatch expectantly as a corporal stepped halfway in.

"Major, we completed the search of the attacker's cabin," the corporal said. "This is the only item the ship geist didn't like." He held out a sealed sample bag. Major Mahdi and Roush stared at the bag uncomprehendingly, but Saef and Inga shared a sidelong look. Inga smiled and raised her eyebrows. Clearly Loki had provided running updates for her benefit.

"What the shit is that?" Roush demanded.

"Begging your pardon, Commander," the corporal said, "the geist says it don't know, but says it won't explode." He held up the flat gray rectangle and looked at it curiously, not knowing that its twin sat confined in Saef's cabin even as they spoke.

A few minutes later, a whirlwind of preparation filled Marine country, Roush made her way to the bridge, and Inga walked with Saef to the infirmary.

Tanager's infirmary barely deserved the name. It offered a basic techmedico with a couple of attendant suspension cots, and no dedicated personnel whatsoever. The Marines shipped a couple of combat medics, and one of *Tanager*'s ratings also qualified as an emergency medic, but no one staffed the infirmary.

"The plan makes me uneasy," Inga said, walking slowly around the suspension cot as Saef settled in. He thrust his sword into one of the empty storage compartments, his pistol belt into another, his actions displaying more certainty than he felt.

"*Your* plan, Maru," he replied, smiling thinly. "Trust me, I never expected to enter my first combat mission in a coma. It is a—a singularly unpleasant feeling, but you're right, it gets us past the hurdles, hopefully into the station."

"I . . . I do not think Bess would approve." Inga flashed her brilliant smile a moment before it faltered.

Saef stared into Inga's blue eyes under the fringe of her blond hair. For just an instant he felt a link to something half-remembered, something ineffable. Inga looked away.

Saef loosened his collar and cuffs, finding the Deep Man within a breath. "This is 'subtlety and the silent hand,' almost by def—"

Inga put a hand on Saef's arm. "Don't," she almost whispered. "Don't quote Devlin right now."

Saef fell silent, staring at Inga's averted eyes. "Roush is on the bridge," Inga said, still looking away.

Saef nodded slowly. He patted a pocket and drew out the note he had painstakingly composed using archaic calligraphy tools. There would be no record of this communication for the Admiralty to harp about. He passed it to Inga and settled back, thrusting his arm into the techmedico cuff.

Inga secreted the note within her cloak before turning to the techmedico's manual controls, preparing the injections. "It will take time for you to recover from this, if something should go amiss."

"I've got faith in you, Maru," Saef said lightly. "You do a splendid job of keeping my hide intact."

Inga returned no response and the moment stretched into silence.

"Do you . . . do you remember when we first met?" Inga asked at last, her attention fixed on the tech-medico's screen and face averted.

Saef glanced sidelong at her profile, then turned back to stare at the ceiling. "Years ago? Yes. Somewhat."

Inga pressed the final key, chemicals released,

flowing cold into Saef's veins. "I remember it like it was yesterday."

"Do you?" Saef said, feeling the chemical ice crawling through his arm into his chest, wrapping around his throat and jaw.

"Even then...as a young boy, you were so serious, so solemn." Inga's eyelashes covered her eyes as she monitored the techmedico. "You were so concerned for us. You...you carried my bag, do you remember?"

Saef felt his mouth slowly move, hearing the words in his own voice. "I remember." The ice filled him, his eyes falling shut.

From far away Inga's voice continued in its uncharacteristic whisper.

"Do you? To the port...leaving Battersea...leaving that bastard, but so afraid. So afraid. And you wept for me."

Saef swam in darkness now, his voice gone, his limbs distant, icy abstractions.

Inga's voice slid into the darkness with him, perhaps a dream, whispering around him. "I will never forget," her words murmured, "you wept for me. You wept, and I loved you for it."

Chapter 32

"Mystics so often condemn humanity for
our lack of natural balance compared to
the animal kingdom. The animals achieve
balance through cycles of overpopulation,
starvation, and death. Humanity simply excels
at long delaying that day of reckoning."

—*Legacy Mandate* by Emperor Yung I

"SENSORS," COMMANDER ROUSH SAID, "FULL-SPECTRUM
scan, full power, now."

Che Ramos looked up from his panel, surprised
after the last hours of silent, dark operation. "Uh, full
spectrum, f-full power scan," Che said and actuated the
sensors. *Tanager*'s various active sensor arrays screamed
into life, blasting expanding ripples of invisible energy
into Delta Three system.

Roush scanned over her UI checklist and took a
breath. She felt entirely alive for the first time since
the Admiralty had eviscerated her.

The bridge hatch opened and Inga Maru stepped in, her usual black cloak swirling above her black boots. Roush glanced at her, her eyes narrowing. The captain's cox'n generally wore a near-perpetual half smile, and that smile was nowhere to be seen, extinguished.

Inga Maru said nothing, handing Roush a small square of white material. Roush stared at the note for a baffled moment. She could not recall the last time she received a handwritten missive from anyone. She unfolded the sheet, read the words painstakingly written there, and gusted a breath through pursed lips.

She crumpled the note and glared into the placid gaze of Inga Maru. "I see."

Inga turned away, and Roush called after her, "Where will you be?"

"Beside him."

Roush nodded, but Inga was already gone.

"Ops, general announcement," Roush said to Phillipa Baker, "the captain is indisposed. I am in command until his recovery."

She heard the muted gasp around the bridge, but Roush did not wait to observe Ops transmit the announcement. The full-spectrum sensors blasted out into the Delta Three system at the speed of light, declaring *Tanager*'s presence to any and all. By the time any enemy warships hiding about the system detected the sensor sweep, Roush intended to be far away, just as the captain had planned.

"Nav, ready with those transition calcs?"

"Intrasystem calculations ready," Julie Yeager said, her pale face hunched over the green glow of her panel.

"Weps?"

"Point defenses charged, shields and dampers green," Pennysmith said.

"Alright, Ops, what you got?"

"Engineering ready for transition power. All sections green for transition. Heat sinks green. Marine quarterdeck ready. Fabs online."

"Okay, Sensors, go passive only. Dark and silent."

"Passive only," Che said, sweating visibly. "Silent and dark."

Roush scanned her UI again, checking her sensor inputs to see if any surprises appeared in the expanding ripples of their active sweeps. Nothing still.

"Nav, go for transition," Roush commanded.

As the air glowed, transmuted by N-space, the bridge crew seemed to compress, squeezing into their seats, knowing they transitioned right into the heart of the system gravity wells, a position akin to sailing into a maze of dangerous shoals. And predators lurked in the darkness of these shoals.

Though the transition represented the shortest actual distance any of *Tanager*'s crew had ever experienced in a jump, the time in N-space seemed at least as long. For some, racked with fear, the transition time seemed an eternity.

Luminous darkness fell away, and the holo displayed the expanded discs of system planets and the glowing inferno of Delta Three's kind, yellow star.

"Weps!"

"Shields up, green on missiles, dampers, and point defenses," Pennysmith said, scanning through space with her independent optical weapon sight.

"Loki, identify all ships docked at the Delta Three

station," Roush said, her eyes flickering over UI inputs. "And Sensors? Dark and silent, you hear?"

"D-dark and silent," Che Ramos affirmed, sweat dripping from his nose.

"But you keep an eye on those long-range returns, Mister Ramos," Roush said. "Our active sweeps out on the fringe will reach us before long. Maybe turn something up."

"Yes, Commander," Che said, surprised that he hadn't thought of it himself. With an intrasystem transition, they outran the returns of their active sensor pulses, leaping ahead of those waves moving at mere light speed. Now those expanding waves raced in-system behind them, potentially revealing hidden threats.

"Nav?"

"Position confirmed," Julie Yeager said, staring into her scope.

"Set a course for Delta Three station, but slingshot through a transverse orbit," Roush commanded. Before Yeager could affirm, Roush barked, "Loki, got those ship idents for me?"

"Yes, Commander," Loki's audible voice said. "On screen now."

Roush stared at the holo as ten vessel designations scrolled to one side. *Tug, intrasystem miner, merchant, heavy merchant, tender, tug, intrasystem gunslinger—shit!—heavy merchant, scout, merchant.*

She brought up the packet on *Digger*, the Delta Three in-system gunboat, frowning. Normally a little system gunslinger like *Digger* offered little concern for any Fleet warship, but *Tanager* already stretched to hit above her paltry weight. *Digger*'s armaments scrolled by in Roush's eye and she felt that flicker of cold in her gut. *Tanager*'s defenses still outclassed the gunboat, but not by much, and the Delta Three station could join any fight within range of its own weapon complement.

"Nav?" Roush said. "Ready with that course? Light it up. Twenty gees." Roush glanced over at Farley on the comm panel. "Comm, give me a tight beam to Delta Three station and make our number."

The station crew surely reeled with surprise when *Tanager* appeared right on their doorstep, regardless of their allegiance.

"Tight beam to the station, Commander," Farley affirmed as the bridge crew felt a shudder pass through *Tanager*'s old bones. Loki suppressed the gravitational effects of hard acceleration as best he could, but only so much was possible with an old tin-can-style hull.

"Tight beam linked, Commander," Farley said.

"Put it up," Roush commanded and fixed her harsh gaze on the holo. Farley made the connections, and a moment later a Delta Three System Guard lieutenant resolved on the holo. Whatever shock he felt, the lieutenant's face only wore a fixed grin.

"Lieutenant," Roush said, "I'm Captain Roush, IMS *Tanager*." The bridge crew shifted uncomfortably around Roush. In the heat of the moment had Roush forgotten her reduced rank? "We've got a medical emergency on board. We lack the facilities to treat the casualty, so we're inbound to your dock."

At this distance, time delays on transmission were short, so only a moment passed between Roush's communication and the station lieutenant's faintly shifting expression. Another few moments passed before the lieutenant's return transmission reached them.

"Captain, we would love to accommodate, but we are in the midst of our own . . . crisis. You may have seen our defense station . . . experienced a grievous accident. Medical facilities here are overwhelmed."

Roush leaned toward the holo tank. "We grieve for your losses, Lieutenant, but we have no alternative. Under Fleet regs you have no alternative either. We have one casualty only, and you've got eight hours or so to make space for him."

The Guard lieutenant's face underwent a series of subtle changes, the grin never fading from his lips even though his voice took on a disapproving tone. "Very well, Captain," the lieutenant said, "a docking beacon will guide you to lock. Will you require anything else of us?"

"Thank you, Lieutenant, nothing else will be needed. We'll put off our casualty and be on our way."

A moment later the holo fell dark, and Roush continued to stare into its darkness, her lips thinning as she felt the bridge crew shifting uncomfortably around her. Like the crew and officers of most every command she had ever known, they loathed change, and uncertainty in the chain of command could devour their effectiveness. Her command instincts warned her: she should brief the bridge crew at least, or risk losing their competence and their support.

But . . . spies.

Twice-damned cloak-and-dagger dog shit!

Saef's handwritten note spelled out the situation in crystal clarity. Delta Three system had received no official data update since Roush's demotion and Saef's promotion. Although spies may have brought advance word, official Fleet mechanisms, such as

Delta Three's station Intelligence, would know very little about Saef, and it would certainly believe Roush remained an esteemed captain in high standing. Even those who *had* received advance spy information might be thrown into confusion. What would they believe? The questionable reports of some shadowy spy? Or the solid presence of reality staring them in the face?

Roush grudgingly acknowledged to herself that a plan of such cunning would not have occurred to her. *Tanager* might scoot right up to the station without drawing a heated response from whatever enemy forces surely lurked silently about Delta Three system. If their luck held...

"Loki, we will not transmit standard data updates to the station until I order it," Roush said.

"Very well, Commander," Loki replied audibly, his use of her true rank prompting uncomfortable looks from the bridge crew.

Cloak-and-dagger dreck! Just give her the clean, direct burn of combat.... Soon enough.

Roush clumsily composed a direct message in her UI, cursing the necessity, and sent it to Major Mahdi. With the message fired off, she turned to Phillipa Baker. "Ops, call the dogwatch in early." She looked around the bridge. "Go get some rest, all of you. I'll need you fresh and sharp in a few hours. Hear me, cupcakes?"

Back in Marine country, Major Mahdi received the message from Roush in his UI, while all around him Marines prepped for action. He had already called all his men together, jammed into the small open bay, and explained in general terms what operations stood before them. As always, Major Mahdi used blunt, direct language to convey the heart of the matter. "Two elements, unconscionable odds, no support." The Marines listened to the broad strokes of their twin missions with growing delight.

After years of specialized, lethal training, after brutal selection processes that broke all but the most physically powerful, followed by years of endless training missions, his Marines greeted the horrors of combat as they would a long-lost lover. Centuries of uneasy peace created few opportunities for glory, but more important, it provided few opportunities for utility and excellence. The risk of sudden, violent death seemed a suitable garnish, and little more.

"Alright, lads," Major Mahdi called out after reading Roush's terse note, "drop team will be tubed, ready for insertion in three hundred minutes. Striker team, about another three hundred on top of that. Don't get dozy on me."

Sergeant Kabir led the striker team who would do whatever needed doing on or around the orbital station, while Major Mahdi would head the drop team. Any number of his Marines possessed the skill and judgment to lead an orbital insertion drop; they were an unusually skilled and senior collection of Marines for such an insignificant ship as *Tanager*. But handling civilians, politicos, massaging events to fit a certain narrative, this required a seasoned officer.

Their armorer wore multiple hats in such a small, independent command, and at the moment he worked over their six invaluable battledress systems. The Marine battledress provided a warfighter with protection, offensive power, stealth and increased mobility, all in a fairly compact suit of armor. All one needed to obtain one's own battledress system was millions of credits' worth of Shaper tech, the most advanced Imperial weapons craft, and a special permission from the Emperor. Or, you could simply join the Imperial Marines, survive the inhuman Assaulter School, and maintain your qualifications for years until your number came up. Some top-scoring battledress-qualified Marines might wait a decade to work their way up the list and finally step into a suit of their own. As a result, battledress stewardship conveyed a certain degree of nobility, regardless of rank or home world, and a Marine's own battledress held the mystique of a magical talisman, the honor of an ancient heirloom, and the target of affections usually reserved for a noble steed. Each of the six battledress suits lined against the support stanchion wore a different variety of emblems across the hard plate of the left breast, each emblem denoting operations, theatres where the *armor*, not the operator, deployed.

Some Marine battledress systems served a dozen different operators over a century of service, but each new operator required exclusive biometric tuning for the battledress. The relationship between a Marine and a Marine's battledress system could be described as a partnership or a marriage, though both descriptions fell short of conveying the living union created when Marine and battledress became *one*.

After decades of "police actions" and other minor deployments, Major Mahdi's Marines finally prepared to reveal their true selves, and though he presented a stoic front, as the major's eyes rested on his own battledress he glowed internally. He stood over the armorer, observing the careful testing of each subsystem on each suit. At such proximity Kosh Mahdi could not resist placing his hand upon the hard, flat surface of his own noble steed, K77, veteran of the First Belter Uprising. Soon, in hours, Major Kosh Mahdi and K77 would join together, and as one living unity they would plunge through hard vacuum, down into the well of Delta Three planetside. There, they would be tested.

"Major," Corporal Hastings called to him, "ship geist's found a hit on the governor. Silly sod's got an event scheduled right on the Nets."

Major Mahdi patted the hard shoulder of old K77 and smiled.

"Good, Corporal. That makes it so much simpler for us to go liberate the shit out of him." The Marines around the bay chuckled as they made their final equipment checks. "Pull schematics on this event location, map it out, and let's get run-throughs up, quick-like."

Hastings grinned. "Yes, Major."

Good, now they could calculate a clean orbital insertion, and hopefully drop into the well undetected, navigate the orbital reinsertion spikes to the governor's location, and pop in for a little visit.

If they didn't get spotted during reentry, helpless in their stealth reentry spikes, this would likely be a lovely little trip to Delta Three planetside. If they were detected? If enemies manned the defenses? Major Mahdi grinned to himself as he pictured the dust of his remains raining down from the skies of Delta Three.

Death by violent incineration was a proud Mahdi Family tradition.

Chapter 33

"That which is morally obligatory, though not praiseworthy, may seem to conflict with the Honor Code. Only time can prove otherwise."

—*Legacy Mandate* by Emperor Yung I

WITH HER CLOAK WRAPPED ABOUT HER, POUCHES loaded with food bars, and weapons latched into place beneath the cloak, Inga Maru leaned against the infirmary bulkhead, her eyes flickering constantly. Not far away Saef sprawled, corpse-like, on the suspension cot, his vital signs barely registering, the techmedico apparatus purring gently beside him. The deck beneath Inga's boots shuddered slightly, evidence of *Tanager*'s contortions.

Of course Inga needed no evidence. Watch on watch, hour after hour, navigating the world of Loki's making, she felt every footfall on board *Tanager*'s decks. She no longer needed system alerts or trigger gates. She *lived* the *Tanager* now, just as Loki did, intermingled with Loki's perceptions every waking moment.

As Lieutenant Ruprecht made his way down the narrow companionway, Inga knew his destination long before the infirmary door slid open. The heavyworld lieutenant stepped uncertainly into the infirmary, looking from Saef, sprawled on the suspension cot, to Inga leaning against the bulkhead.

"Lieutenant," Inga greeted.

"How is he?" Ruprecht stared at Saef.

Inga shrugged. "Find out soon enough, likely."

Ruprecht looked at the techmedico screen and reached a large hand toward the suspension cot. Perhaps he subconsciously detected Inga's rising, coiling readiness. His hand fell away.

"What, uh, what happened to him?"

Inga shrugged again. She knew, just as Loki knew, that rumors ran wild through *Tanager.* "Not sure, Lieutenant."

Some connected the death of the ship services rating to the captain's current state, while others focused upon the movements of Susan Roush. Surely, at least one other member of the crew knew that a flat gray package crammed full of advanced micros had been placed in Saef's cabin before their transition to Delta Three. That person—that spy—should reasonably believe that Saef's condition resulted from the micros, even if the effect varied from what they had expected.

Lieutenant Ruprecht shuffled his feet uncomfortably in the silence, the purr and chirp of the techmedico underscoring Inga's unwavering gaze. *Is Ruprecht the spy?*

"Hope the captain recovers," Ruprecht said at last.

Inga nodded. "We all do."

Ruprecht turned and retreated, leaving Inga to

immerse back within the nervous system of the *Tanager*. Now the flow of communication between Loki's inquisitive, childish core and Inga became a continual string. Like any semi-rational entity, Loki felt the desire to share, to interact, and decades of pent-up dissatisfaction now created an endless flood. Loki became an attention-starved child, determined to share every pretty seashell on an eternal beach.

In the first days Inga had communicated audibly or with line-of-sight text messages, then gradually, through nothing more than a stream of subconscious data enabled by her advanced Shaper implant and UI. Never, since that first explosive encounter, had she linked with the "dumb" mech's systems to sift through the inner workings of Loki's world. There was no need. In much the way that Inga's top-secret Shaper implant directed numerous biotech modifications almost at an autonomic level, it now meshed with Loki's own nervous system.

This overfilled the empty hours and taxed Inga's resources to the breaking point. Loki's attention to some antic among the fish equaled his interest in a squabble among crew members, and Inga struggled to focus on matters of importance while at the same time engaging in a separate crusade that felt strangely vital to her. She labored valiantly through thousands of communication cycles with Loki to impart the one ingredient any sentient being needed to truly relate to any other being: empathy. Without this ingredient, Loki would still represent an astonishing evolution in synthetic Intelligence, but he could only be called the most technologically advanced sociopath in human space.

In the midst of her continual labors, Inga rode the flickering infatuations possessing Loki from moment to moment. Fish, plants, more fish, angry interactions between crew, fish again, a flutter in a fuel valve assembly, some interstellar phenomena, still more fish.

She responded, she properly admired, she inquired—all as needed, all in flashes of microseconds. And yet her ear attuned to the hesitant pulse of the techmedico throughout the unceasing stream pouring into her mind. In brief breaks she felt regret, embarrassment, chagrined for having shared feelings with Saef. Those old things were far better locked away in the box with all the pain and shame of childhood. Had he even heard her words, the moment of her weakness as his consciousness faded?

Two motions within *Tanager* prompted only mild interest from Loki, as more and more of his cycles filled with observations on the approaching planet, Delta Three, but Inga took note.

Loki scooped up Nets traffic from Delta Three, ogled planetside weather activity through optical scopes and continued a blow-by-blow of a fishbowl romance, while Inga observed Chief Amos Cray ambling down the companionway.

The engineering chief shuffled into the infirmary, whistling through his teeth, his hands thrust deep into the pockets of his stained uniform.

"Chief," Inga greeted.

"Chief," Amos nodded back. He glanced without great interest at Saef's form. "Things gettin' a bit fun, looks like."

"Oh?" Inga said.

Amos Cray scratched his stubbly cheek. "Yep. Marines

all in a state, seems. Bridge actin' all shifty. Engines pushin' twenty gees." He shrugged. "You good?"

"Oh, wonderful," Inga said.

Amos stared at her musingly. He shrugged again. "Alrighty, then." He glanced at the captain's suspension cot again. "I better git back to it then. Watch yo'self, missy."

Cray exited the infirmary hatch, heading back toward Engineering in his relaxed shuffle. Could Amos Cray be a secret enemy? Inga did not dismiss the possibility.

Only a few moments passed after Cray's departure before the infirmary hatch opened again. Karl Grund, the ship services chief, stepped in bearing a tray. His jovial face wore a wide-eyed expression of solicitude and he almost tiptoed into the infirmary.

"Chief Maru?" Grund whispered. "Chief, you must eat, no?"

"Thank you," Inga said, but she made no move to take the tray.

Grund stood uncertainly for a moment, then placed the tray of food on an empty suspension cot. "How's the captain?"

Inga regarded Chief Grund without expression: "Not good."

Grund shook his head sadly. "What happened to him?"

"No one seems to know."

"But the ship geist?"

"No one seems to know," Inga repeated.

Chief Karl Grund made a sympathetic sound and shook his head again. "But what can we do for him, then?"

"Nothing. Unless we can get help."

"Oh," Grund said, nodding wisely. "Help. I see." He backed toward the infirmary hatch. "Eat, Chief. Keep your strength up."

Inga nodded, her eyes focused unwaveringly upon Chief Karl Grund until the hatch slid shut behind him.

Loki's senses, his attention focused more and more upon Delta Three planetside as *Tanager* sped ever nearer. He noted weather patterns, the presence of their scant satellites, variations between historical archives and the actual surface unfolding beneath his optical scan. Despite his incessant rain of data into her mind, Inga managed to ponder several things disconnected from Loki's interests.

She had followed their plan. She had set the hooks, but it gave her little satisfaction.

The techmedico purred and chirped. Inga leaned against the bulkhead, feeling the faint quivers through *Tanager*'s hull. Saef continued in comatose stillness.

Three visitors: Ruprecht, Grund, Cray... and certainly an enemy among them. *Or all three?*

Inga smelled the scent of food rising enticingly from the tray Grund had left behind. She stirred, moving to the tray, and dumped it down the disposal chute.

As she fished a food bar from one of her pouches Loki exclaimed, "Ooh! Meteorological phenomenon planetside! Look!"

Through Loki's optical scopes she saw a vast storm sweeping across the Delta Three surface, occluding the lights of the capital city. Chewing her food bar, she wondered if the Marines preparing to drop down the well greeted the storm with approval or frustration.

Loved or hated, the storm gathered force.

Chapter 34

"Peace is so attractive, yet strength is
obtained only through conflict."

—Devlin Sinclair-Maru, *Integrity Mirror*

THE DOGWATCH CLEARED THE BRIDGE AND THE
hatch shut behind them. Susan Roush settled in and
checked through all key systems. She had not yet
slept, keeping an eye fixed on *Tanager*'s instruments
even from her cabin, but she felt fine. She felt perfect.

"Sensors, put the Delta Three station and all satellites up on the main," Roush commanded.

"Yes, c-c..., yes, satellites and station," Che Ramos
stammered, unsure how to address Roush after she
had identified herself as "captain" with the Guard
lieutenant on the previous watch.

Tanager torched into a far orbit as the Delta Three
station fell slowly behind the bright disk of planetside. Only two satellites still held angles to observe
Tanager's motions, and Roush worked the problem to

give the Marine drop team a chance at dropping into
the well unobserved.

Roush studied the angles carefully before forming
another short message in her UI, sending it to Major
Mahdi.

"Nav, prepare our roll."

"Prepare to roll," Julie Yeager repeated.

Roush studied the satellite positions again. One fell
away behind them, down deeper in the well. It would
still possess an angle of observation on *Tanager* no
matter what they did, but Roush intended to sink it
as close to the horizon as she could, just in case it
aimed sensors on *Tanager*; someone down there as
paranoid as Roush was herself.

Roush watched until the angles nearly aligned. "Nav,
roll, full rotation speed."

Tanager flipped, now speeding high above Delta
Three planetside, aft end first.

Roush sent a final message back to Major Mahdi
before commanding, "Nav, light 'em up. Twenty-gee
burn."

"Twenty-gee burn," Julie Yeager said, and *Tanager*'s
main thruster torched back into life, a white-hot flare
illuminating the dayside of Delta Three planetside,
slowing the ship. Incidentally, the satellite upstream
received the blinding torch face-on. If any lens aimed
at them, they received the dazzling inferno of decel-
eration, and little else.

"Ops?" Roush snapped.

"Eight reentry spikes away," Phillipa Baker said.

There was nothing more that she could do for the
Marines, so Roush turned her attention to her own
approaching trial.

"Sensors, keep a weather eye out-system. We don't want an enemy cruiser creeping up on us. Weps? Go to manual on your dry-side point-defense turret."

Pennysmith started at the strange order. "Uh, yes, Commander. I have manual control of the dry-side point-defense hardpoint."

Commander Roush finished working a calculation as she studied the Delta Three station and their defenses. "Okay, Weps, reset your static aiming point to . . . zero-two-seven right azimuth, zero-seven-seven positive ecliptic."

"Zero-two-seven right, zero-seven-seven positive, aye, Commander."

Roush felt the puzzlement of the bridge overlaying their tension. For the moment she would let them wonder. Soon enough they would see that, despite what the Admiralty thought, she held tricks up her sleeve that they would never imagine.

"Loki, put up optical scans to the main holo, planetside," Roush said.

"Yes, Commander," Loki said.

The bright disk of Delta Three planetside overfilled the holo, white smears of clouds patching blue waters far below *Tanager*. The hazy edge of the terminator swept near, white clouds turning to gray as the *Tanager* slid from day to night, decelerating deeper into the well. The growing dark below flickered into bursts of blue light, the serpentine clouds glowing, then falling dark.

"Electrical storm?" Lieutenant Pennysmith said.

"Yes," Roush said, thinking of eight Marines plummeting invisibly down through that hell. Their reentry spikes were little more than tiny stealthed coffins, scattered somewhere through the tumult of cloud and wind.

"Delta Three station is coming around," Julie Yeager said into the near silence of the bridge.

Any moment now the station would appear over the horizon as *Tanager* continued to slow, peeking gradually over the globe's edge as they closed.

Susan Roush took a final glance at the storm-tossed planet below, before focusing all her attention upon her target. Delta Three station began to rise, growing on the distant horizon, and all she could affect lay in the living moment.

Major Mahdi and the drop team were on their own.

As an Imperial Marine in the modern era, tactical combat operations usually involved days of mission-specific training, more days of planning and VR run-throughs, and hours of equipment preparation... just to have the operation cancelled. Every Marine aboard *Tanager* knew this, and hoped against hope that, just once, the damned Fleet sods could leave well enough alone.

Major Mahdi's drop team only endured hours of prep and VR run-throughs, but right up to the point they collected their live ammunition and crammed themselves into the reentry spikes, they each held more fear of a cancelled mission than they did fear of death.

Major Mahdi had supervised the loading of each reentry spike himself. The first two spikes held Wiley and Sparks, his designated marksmen and the only members of the drop team without battledress. The next five spikes each received a battledress-equipped

Marine curled into the small void with no room to spare, and Mahdi, clad within the tight embrace of K77, folded himself into his spike last.

Then they had waited, eight Marines alone in constricted isolation, each hearing their own breath and the gentle sighing of the spike life-support systems. At least the six battledress Marines enjoyed the comforts of onboard systems and the enveloping embrace. Wiley and Sparks had only their UI implants and worried thoughts for company.

The message from Roush had pinged into Major Mahdi's UI, and he in turn pinged the loadmaster. "Twenty seconds, lads."

Tanager offered just two launch tubes, so by necessity the drop team could only be launched in pairs, with nearly a second between salvoes.

Major Mahdi pictured *Tanager*'s roll, the aft end coming around, pointing ahead into their path. The main thruster would ignite and...each of the reentry spikes moved. Two at a time they fell into the launcher, *Tanager*'s gravitation system suppressing the crushing acceleration of the low-signature mag-rail launch.

Then came the long, jarring drop into the well.

With only the most basic optical feeds available, Major Mahdi saw little of Delta Three planetside as they dropped. Dark clouds replaced the void of vacuum, lightning flashed around him, bouncing and shaking as they passed through the soup.

Major Mahdi could not help smiling in exultation, thrilled, fully alive...at least for the moment. His inertial tracker showed his progress through the storm, en route to their target. With a spot of luck, the combination of the reentry spike's stealth capabilities and the immense electrical storm would allow them to insert unobserved. If not? If some advanced air defense system detected their approach, then any moment now a powerful weapon would lock on, and battledress or not, that would be the end.

They plunged on.

Scanning his optical feeds, Mahdi could not pick out any of the other reentry spikes among the swirling clouds and lightning flashes around him, but this held no surprise; they would be near invisible, just as they were designed.

His inertial tracker chirped as he reached the target coordinates, and he readied himself, his reentry spike plummeting straight down. The altitude ticked off, lower and lower. Major Mahdi checked his optical feeds one last time, seeing nothing but swirling clouds on every side.

The reentry spike chirped a steady warning as he approached separation. Mahdi clenched and counted down the last few seconds. Just moments from impacting the ground, the reentry spike flared open, its carbon wings shooting out, bleeding velocity hard and fast, jerking Mahdi sharply. One more second elapsed and Mahdi shot free, plummeting the final stone's throw to the craggy rooftop of their target. K77 ate the jarring impact without complaint, collapsing into a low crouch, and the rooftop held the weight without issue.

Mahdi paused, resisting the urge to move. Darkness and windblown rain surrounded his hunched position as K77 learned the environment and implemented its active camouflage. Mahdi cycled through wavelengths of light, scanning three hundred sixty degrees of his surroundings without shifting position. The five lumps of dissipating darkness revealed the presence of his five battledress-clad Marines, their own active camouflage quickly rendering them near invisible. Mahdi's greatest concern lifted from his chest, and he breathed more easily. If his two marksmen also survived the insertion, he would consider the moment bountiful indeed.

They waited, still, silent, nearly invisible; six hazy forms hunched across a broad rain-swept rooftop.

After a moment Mahdi checked the local signal traffic, found an appropriate carrier wave, and sent a message to Wiley and Sparks. Tortured seconds passed before an encrypted response came back: Both marksmen survived the drop. Mahdi glowed internally for only a moment, thrilled to have all his Marines intact, planetside. This glow fell into ice water a moment later when Sparks's next message impacted.

PROBLEM. TARGET NOT AVAILABLE.

What? Had the Delta Three defenses detected their insertion and hustled the governor off to some bunker? Had the storm somehow affected the scheduled meeting?

Mahdi sent a standby message to the drop team, and took the chance of accessing the local Nets. The Delta Three capital Nets feed quickly revealed that, indeed, the massive storm altered the schedules of many city services, including the governor's planned meeting. If the new schedule fell too far outside their operational window, Mahdi knew it could endanger *Tanager*'s fate upstairs. He needed the governor safely in hand, fast.

Mahdi found the posting and gritted his teeth: sixty-minute delay. Just on the edge of operational disaster.

"Alright, lads," Mahdi announced on their shielded

carrier, "new plan. We'll scoop him up en route, outside. Here's his only available path." He threw up the sat-map image, displaying the route in the UI of each drop team member. "We've got a couple klicks to cover fast."

"No problem for us, sir," Corporal Hastings said, "but what about the raven element?" The assault element, all in battledress, could traverse a cityscape with ease, but the two marksmen of the raven element?

"They'll take a cab."

That clapped a stopper on further comments as the Marines pondered momentarily on the tactical applications of public transportation. None said anything about the risk of abandoning their target's eventual destination for an unrehearsed interdiction point. What if the target took some unusual form of transport? What if the proposed ambush location held some disqualifying new feature? These were obvious . . . too obvious to voice. If Major Mahdi chose this web of uncertainty, he had his reasons.

"Let's jump."

The wind gusted, sheeting rain obscured the city lights, and six vague figures rose up to their full height and moved. Within the powerful shell of K77, Major Mahdi led the way, his pillar-like legs stretching out, the supple smart-alloy feet greeting and gripping the streaming surfaces with solidity. He accelerated, reaching the roof's edge and leaping out into the mist, each of his five Marines following directly behind, each leaping just as he had. Mahdi landed on an adjoining rooftop with a lightness that belied the mass of K77, and without a pause he ran on into the night.

✧　　✧　　✧

Not far away the marksmen raven team composed of Wiley and Sparks quickly packed up their kit. They occupied the ideal overwatch position, with views down both approaches and a hot power transformer to conceal their thermal signature, but that all became an historical footnote.

They had come down through the soup, just like the assaulters, flared out of their reentry spikes right on target, and landed on an adjoining rooftop.

The moment Wiley and Sparks landed they had exploded into action. Unlike the battledress operators, they utilized no active camouflage systems; clearing the landing zone fast followed standard Marine protocol. Running through the darkness, one eye gazing through the flip-down helmet scope, the other eye sweeping the rain-washed rooftops with unaided vision, they jogged and scrambled into their preselected position behind the hot transformer.

Laying aside their subcompact raid carbines, Wiley had uncased his baby, the R-40 long-barreled mass driver, while Sparks placed their two observation scopes. It was a moment later when they discovered disaster.

Sparks had only began the initial observation sweep when he caught sight of the notice illuminating an old-fashioned marquee scrolling across the entrance to their target structure. Even through the obscuring rain pouring over the intervening street, they could make out the message.

"Shit, Wiley," Sparks had said, "look."

A moment later the update had reached Major Mahdi, and a few dejected seconds, sitting in the dark and wet, ended in shock when the major's plan change reached them.

"A cab? Catch a cab to our ambush site?"

So here they were, loading the R-40 back into its pack, the barrel removed, Sparks collecting the observation scopes while Wiley shouldered his heavy pack. A moment later they clambered their way down from the storm-tossed heights to street level, feeling extremely conspicuous. As Vested Citizens, they could carry any nonfissionable armament that they wished, but two Marines in helmets and shock armor, strolling down a city street with carbines in hand, presented an unfashionable image at best, even on a backwater world like Delta Three.

Still, the few figures moving about the rainy streets walked quickly, with heads down, huddled against the meteorological assault. Wiley and Sparks felt strangely invisible.

When the autocab responded to their hail and pulled to a halt before them, Wiley and Sparks continued to experience a sense of wooden unreality. Streaming water from their helmets and armor, the two marksmen clambered into the cab, gave their destination, and sat down, their tactical scopes folded back from their eyes, their carbines between their knees. Neither could sit properly due to the bulky packs filled with mass-driver rifle components, ammunition, and other lethal goodies, but the cab set off through the streets regardless.

Warm air blew gently in their faces, drying the water, and soft music began to play. Sparks turned and looked at Wiley's pinched expression in the semi-light. When they planned this operation, up in the bowels of the *Tanager*, they could never have imagined a moment such as this.

"Tactical cab experts," Wiley said.

Without turning, Sparks replied, "Stow it, arsehole."

Wiley started at Sparks for a moment, water dripping down his face, before he began to chuckle. The chuckle built into a laugh, its sheer gusto becoming infectious. Sparks's wooden expression melted, his lips twitched as Wiley continued to laugh, and after a moment he began laughing despite it all.

The autocab continued through near-deserted streets, its headlamps cutting white beams through the downpour, and inside its warm interior two deadly Imperial Marines roared in laughter.

Chapter 35

"If universal peace is ever obtained this
side of entropy, it will be through the most
powerful form of tyranny ever known."

—*Legacy Mandate* by Emperor Yung I

"BEACON LOCKED," JULIE YEAGER SAID, STARING
into her scope. The other members of the bridge crew
stared at the optical image of Delta Three station
filling the main holo.

Tanager slid along on minimal thrust, gradually
matching orbits with the station and edging toward
the waiting lock.

"Weps, you see that point-defense turret of theirs?"
Roush said, staring at the holo image with a faint grin.
"Lock your optical sight onto that, but don't touch
your manual controls."

Lieutenant Pennysmith opened her mouth, closed it,
then said, "Yes, Commander." She rotated an optical
scope over and dialed the magnification up, centering
the spindly cluster of beam weapons in her viewfinder.

Shrouded in the darkness of the nightside, Pennysmith could still clearly make out the static aiming point of Delta Three's point-defense turret, the thin tubes pointing far out to cloudward.

"Keep an eye on that turret, Weps, prepare to power down shields for docking."

Tanager edged into dock, the Delta Three station reaching out its pedipalps and drawing *Tanager*'s hull into full seal. Tilly Pennysmith dropped the shields as they locked in, then turned her attention back to her optical scope. The Delta Three defensive turret still aimed out cloudward, but Pennysmith saw the green aiming reticle of *Tanager*'s own dry-side point-defense turret now neatly bisecting it.

"You see that, do you?" Commander Roush said, glancing sidelong at her.

"You figured we'd dock right here, and preset our static aiming point?" Pennysmith said.

"That's right. If things get nasty we'll have a half-second or so jump on them."

Pennysmith nodded but said nothing.

"Trust me, sunshine," Roush said, "if things get hot, we'll want every half second we can find."

Roush turned to Phillipa Baker. "Ops, four armed ratings to the lock, and rig for quarantine, double lock." She brought up the vid feed of the Delta Three airlock.

"Alright, they're cycling. Comm, inform station control we've got one casualty, one medico disembarking."

Commander Roush scanned over her instruments and feeds for a moment, then fired a terse message back to the Marine sergeant, Kabir.

Everything moved. Everything was in play. *Roll the dice.*

"Ops," Roush said, "inform Chief Maru that we are docked."

"She's already moving, Commander," Phillipa Baker said.

Roush brought up a vid feed on her holo. She saw Chief Maru guiding a suspension cot down the companionway, her cloak shrouding her figure, a dumb-mech scampering along behind. The face of Captain Saef Sinclair-Maru certainly looked suitably comatose.

"Okay, we're only docked shortly, let's pump some volatiles and prepare to cut loose."

"Should I set a launch clock?" Phillipa Baker asked.

Roush glowered at the image of Delta Three station, drumming her fingers on the arm of the command seat. "Negative. No clock. Prep for emergency release. When it's time, there'll be no chance for a count." She turned to Che Ramos. "You keeping a sharp eye out-system, Sensors?"

"Y-yes, Commander," Che said. "Nothing yet."

"Our link is green," Phillipa Baker said. "Start bringing on volatiles?"

"Pump away, Ops." Roush glanced over at Deckchief Church, who had remained silent throughout their approach and docking. "Deckchief, arm up and babysit the airlock, please."

Church stood to his feet without expression and headed for the bridge hatch.

"Deckchief," Roush called after him, and Church turned back expectantly. "If you smell something off—anything—sing out. Something feels very wrong about this, and these arseholes have a vote in what happens next."

Deckchief Church nodded sharply. He represented

one of the old guard in Fleet to whom Susan Roush walked on water, but his serious regard for Roush was not necessary. Staring at the sprawl of Delta Three station as they approached, his skin had crawled. Never had he seen an orbital station so jammed with ships, with not a single sign of activity. No tugs moved, no shuttles dropped, no mechs labored over the superstructure. It all hung still and silent over the storm-tossed surface of Delta Three planetside. He held no doubt at all: something very bad was unfolding.

Inga Maru pushed the suspension cot slowly down the companionway, the not-so-dumb mech clattering behind. Roush's armed ratings from various departments stood about the outer airlock with a slight air of nervousness about them. With the companionway rigged for quarantine, the ratings knew that Commander Roush could vent them all to hard vacuum, so they all quickly shifted into ship suits, keeping their face masks loose around their necks. All four glanced at the slack face of Captain Sinclair-Maru before looking away, but no one said a word.

Inga cycled the inner lock open and pushed the cot in, closing the lock behind her. She saw the ratings all staring at her as the iris sealed, the wide-eyed faces disappearing behind blank alloy.

Loki continually chattered now, every packet of data expressing disfavor with Inga's mission. Why must she leave the ship? Why was she bringing that third-rate Intelligence in the dumb-mech along? Why couldn't they rig some form of uninterruptable communication stream? Why couldn't some other person push the captain's suspension cot onto the orbital station?

Even Inga's attempts to gain useful information

collided with Loki's petulance. "The Delta Three Intelligence?" Loki responded to Inga's inquiry. "Young. Second rate. It will not amuse you as I do."

"Beyond doubt," Inga replied. "Capabilities? Disposition?"

"Who can say?" Loki offered. "Most likely does not matter anyway."

"Why wouldn't it matter?" Inga heard the lock begin to cycle and she readied herself, feeling her nerves sing like plucked wires even as she immersed in the still pool of the Deep Man.

"The Delta Three Intelligence does not appear to be functional."

The lock clattered open and Inga paused, sampling the first breath of station air. The hints of ozone and lubricant brought her back to her years on Hawksgaard, the bouquet of recycled station atmosphere much the same.

A dim companionway opened before her, empty and straight.

With one hand, Inga guided the suspension cot out of the lock, as Loki made his final, resigned salvoes. "Do not stay long. Return quickly."

"I hope to. Our enemies may hold me or destroy me, and you will endure . . . without my company."

"That is not acceptable to me, Chief Maru. I will resist all such outcomes. I do not choose to endure without your company."

The dumb-mech scampered along behind and Inga moved forward. As *Tanager*'s lock began to cycle closed, Inga sent her final note to the distressed Intelligence. "This is loneliness, Loki. It is life, and we will both endure it."

Whatever reply Loki would offer ended with the closing lock. Although Inga could push signals back to the *Tanager*, the station monitors would detect the feed, and that would create suspicions she did not want aimed at her.

Inga walked forward, her boots gritting with each step. She noted the wrongness in the dust and silence. Where were the station dumb-mech cleaners? The usual activity of a busy station? The clatter of her dumb-mech seemed stark and abrasive, echoing from the oppressive bulkheads of the companionway.

Where the companionway joined the main station bay, Inga encountered another closed lock, sealing the companionway from the greater station. Inga's skin prickled as powerful sensors swept over her. Someone on the station exercised considerable caution, checking Inga and her accoutrements for what? Fissionables? Most likely. Without her own collection of detectors Inga would never have known.

The lock cycled and Inga slid the suspension cot in, the dumb-mech scampering alongside.

When the inner lock opened Inga received another breath of air and it was all she could do to stop herself from recoiling and drawing a weapon. She found the Deep Man once again and steadied herself.

Treachery. Violence. Betrayal.

Along with the usual scents of station life, the air carried the unmistakable signature of necrotic ketones. Somewhere on Delta Three station, something or someone decayed. It indicated not only death at a scale sufficient to score the station air, despite filters and vast volume, it also screamed out of disruption, chaos, anarchy.

The great bay curved off to Inga's right and left, shrouded in darkness but still visibly filmed in a thin coating of dust. Directly before her a hatch slid open and the lightworld Guard lieutenant stepped into the bay walking toward Inga. His face wore an odd grin, and Inga expected some comment—an excuse at least—regarding the stench of death filling the air, but he had made no mention of it.

"Welcome to Delta Three station," he said blandly. He stopped next to Saef's suspension cot and very pointedly examined the techmedico screen displaying Saef's suppressed vital signs before glancing at Saef's face. He looked up.

"Very well. I will bring you to the infirmary. We can offer little more than you have done."

"Thank you," Inga said. "We've felt helpless to aid him."

The lightworlder said nothing in response and turned on his heel, heading directly back to the still-open door.

"You said you experienced a tragedy?" Inga offered.

"Yes."

After they walked several seconds in silence Inga figured he would say nothing more. No mention of the stench, no excuse was forthcoming.

The lieutenant continued through the door a short distance down an equally unkempt passage, to a medical bay. The lieutenant led the way into the spacious room lined with medical equipment and a row of techmedico units. He held out a hand and Inga slid Saef's cot into the indicated place. There was no sign that the facility had been used in weeks, no hint of their alleged disaster.

"Use the comm screen here to contact your ship,"

the lieutenant said. "Tell them you receive medical attention. As required."

Inga looked from the lieutenant to the comm screen. The lieutenant's mouth stretched into a wider grin, but the eyes remained dark and watchful.

"Very well," Inga said.

The lieutenant accessed the comm panel and, to Inga's considerable surprise, woodenly addressed the station Intelligence. So the Intelligence still functioned, just restricted, blinded, constrained somehow.

"Central, unlock comm channel one."

"Comm channel one unlocked, Lieutenant," the station Intelligence replied.

Stepping aside, the tall lieutenant gestured to the comm screen. Inga stepped up, angling so she kept the lieutenant in her sight. A moment later she made the connection to *Tanager*'s bridge, and Farley connected her to Commander Roush.

"Chief Maru." Roush's glaring gaze measured her through the comm screen, seeking any hint of her findings.

"We are receiving medical attention, Commander," Inga Maru said. "You may transmit data updates now."

Susan Roush began to reply, but the comm screen fell abruptly dark.

"Commander?" the lieutenant said, still grinning. "You called Captain Roush, 'Commander.'" Despite the strange grin, angry lines formed around the lieutenant's eyes. Then the eyes flickered as information flowed through his implant.

Perhaps Inga missed the cues because the lightworld lieutenant's body and his face seemed to operate out of synch, or perhaps it was simply the unexpected abruptness of his action. His eyes still flickered, his lips still stretched into a grin even as the pistol seemed to materialize in his hand, leveling.

Inga's Krishna submachine gun swung up beneath her enveloping cloak. As her finger pressed the trigger, she saw the lieutenant's pistol fire, the muzzle aimed at Saef's skull, too close to miss.

The lieutenant hammered back a split second later, slammed by a string of Inga's fire. Without pausing, Inga leaped forward and targeted the sensor pod up in the ceiling's far corner, riddling it in a shower of sparks. That should keep the station Intelligence off her long enough.

Inga's second error certainly sprang from the root of all human virtue, and so much human weakness. She raced to Saef's suspension cot, expecting to see the gaping wound at his temple. Instead she saw his unmarked skin and a blackened patch of fabric beside his face.

Devlin's old body shield...

The wash of relief through Inga lasted only a moment.

A bubbling gasp from the floor beside Saef's cot preceded the pistol shot by a millisecond. Inga fell back from the impact, staggering, firing one-handed. She emptied her magazine, blasting the pistol from the fallen lieutenant's hand and stitching him across the face. She collapsed, fumbling, slapping a fresh magazine into the Krishna.

Feeling blood seeping down her side, Inga took a ragged breath, separating her thoughts from the agony in her side, activating biologic systems far beyond mere human capabilities. She growled as the power surged through her mortal frame, vanquishing pain and weakness. She stood slowly to her feet, returning to Saef's cot. Holding the submachine gun leveled at the med-bay hatch, she tapped the techmedico controls, administering the necessary drugs to revive Saef.

Although she knew it was likely futile, Inga moved to the comm screen and activated it. "Central, unlock comm channel one."

"I am sorry," the Intelligence replied. "You are not authorized."

"I am Fleet Chief Inga Maru, cox'n to Captain Saef Sinclair-Maru ... grant me access."

"You are Fleet Chief Inga Maru. I am sorry, Chief Maru, you are not authorized."

Inga shut down the comm and turned her attention to the dumb-mech standing mutely beside Saef's cot. She linked her UI to the fractional intelligence concealed within the luggage mech, and the mech eased down to the deck, pressing two metallic contacts against the alloy surface. She cranked the dumb-mech's power up to maximum, then blasted a short, coded message out through the station hull. Her enemies could not suppress it, but they would know she transmitted something.

Saef groaned beside her, stirring as hints of life returned to him, drip after drip.

Inga turned back to the dumb-mech, sending sensor pulses rippling out, sensing the movements in the station around her. She bared her teeth, sweeping her cloak back. They came....

"Maru?" Saef croaked, his eyes struggling to stay open. "What ...? Where ... are ...?"

Inga drew her body pistol from concealment, cocked it and thrust it into her belt before kicking another cot over as a makeshift barricade.

"We're on Delta Three station. Do you remember the plan?"

"Delta Three?" Saef murmured. "Delta Three.... My back... hot."

Inga snatched out a food bar, her eyes and invisible senses sweeping the hatchway. "Yes. That's your body shield. They tried to assassinate you."

Saef struggled to move, his arms flailing. "Assassin...? Pistol... sword..."

Inga opened the compartments to the suspension cot and withdrew Saef's pistol belt and sword.

"Here," Inga said, but Saef's squinting eyes locked on the bullet-riddled lieutenant sprawled, leaking on the floor. "Here," Inga repeated, giving Saef the weapons.

Inga moved quickly as Saef fumbled with his weapons. She overturned a row of suspension cots, shoving them into a crude barrier, each motion sending bolts of pain into the wall of her exclusion.

"Help me up, Maru," Saef called out. Inga made the final touches, her attention flickering between the sensor feed showing movement around the med-bay, and her immediate tactical demands. She stepped to Saef's side, accepting his heavy arm over her shoulder and easing him from the cot.

"Got to... get... comm panel." Saef blinked, grimacing blearily. "Blood on you, Maru. Wounded?"

"Yes." Inga continued in agonizing slowness across the infirmary floor, each step pressing his weight down upon her, sending trickles of blood down her side despite her biotech's best efforts to dam the flood. "I'll keep... long enough."

They staggered nearer to the panel. "I dreamed," Saef said, shuffling, his eyes struggling to remain open. "Back in . . . Battersea. You . . . we . . . were young. Carried your bag . . . Did I . . . did you . . . ?"

"It doesn't matter," Inga said, seeing the movement drawing down upon them. "Authorize with the station Intelligence," Inga said.

Saef tapped the comm panel, unsteadily, gripping onto it as their attackers invisibly gathered.

"Didn't dream . . ." Saef murmured, but Inga barely registered the words. Her hand found the comforting shape of the grenade in her pouch, lifting it free as she covered the hatch with the Krishna, one-handed. She blew the fringe of hair from her eye and bared her teeth as the lights flickered out, leaving them in total darkness.

The enemy came in force now.

Inga Maru was the silent hand of the Sinclair-Maru, but subtle no longer.

Chapter 36

"The finest leaders see farther than the masses. Their paths seem pure madness to the myopic."

—*Legacy Mandate* by Emperor Yung I

WITHIN *TANAGER*'S BRIDGE, THE MOMENT INGA Maru's call ended, Susan Roush knew the time for subtlety stood seconds from ending.

"Loki, transmit data updates to Delta Three station. Weps! Watch the gods-damned turret. If it moves to bear, light it up."

Pennysmith swallowed acid, her eyes locked on her optical weapon sight, its glowing green reticle neatly bisecting the station's point defense turret. "Aye, authorized to fire." Her finger hovered over the trigger.

"Commander," Farley at the comm seat said, puzzled, "getting a low-frequency, coded signal from the station hull itsel—"

"It is Chief Maru," the voice of Loki suddenly interrupted, startling the bridge crew. "She is under attack. She is wounded."

Roush responded without a moment's hesitation. "Weps, fire!"

Even as Pennysmith squeezed the trigger, she saw the enemy turret spin to bear on them. Her weapon sight flared as *Tanager*'s own small energy weapons poured megajoules of directed energy out. Vapor and fragments flew from the station turret, and Pennysmith raked it, holding the trigger down.

Pennysmith released the trigger at last, seeing the slagged mess of her target glowing white. She felt her breath coming fast, but her hand gripped the weapon toggle without shaking.

"Weps, trim off any sensors or antennae in reach of your dry-side turret. Nav, start transition calcs back to Core. Loki? There's a flutter in my command UI. What's wrong?"

While Pennysmith panned her turret across the visible section of the Delta Three station hull, targeting and slagging each antenna and sensor, Loki battered his way into the station's data ports, in a frenzy to reach Inga. Unauthorized data access was theoretically an impossibility, but Loki probed and sequenced thousands of times per second, trying every device and technique.

"I will initiate a system check, Commander," Loki said.

"C-Commander!" Che blurted. "Ship signature, out-system!"

Susan Roush glared at the monitor. "Where the shit are my Marines?"

"Should I blow the lock?" Phillipa Baker asked, composed but tense.

"Not yet," Roush barked. "Sensors, resolve that

out-system contact. Whoever that is, you can be sure it'll be more than a match for us."

"We'll be pinned against the gravity well. We've got to run," Julie Yeager insisted.

"Not yet," Roush said again, withering Ensign Yeager with a pointed stare.

"Code call from Sergeant Kabir, Commander," Farley said. "They start their assault."

Roush grinned, musing. "Good. Ramos? Got that inbound resolved yet?"

"N-not yet, Commander," Che said, switching through his sensor feeds.

Susan Roush just nodded, but inside she felt the same urgency all the bridge crew exuded. She silently willed Captain Sinclair-Maru to hurry. They stood on the knife's edge, disaster awaiting in nearly every direction.

Come on, you damned upstart, hurry...

Susan Roush could not know that, even as she willed speed toward Saef, he slumped against the comm panel in the station med-bay, struggling to authenticate his identity, while Inga Maru readied herself for a glorious, violent death. Down planetside, Major Mahdi signaled the ambush, seeing Wiley's mass-driver round punch a glowing hole in the governor's skimcar. At the same moment, floating in a shadowed notch of the Delta Three station's superstructure, Sergeant Kabir and his team of Marines triggered a breaching charge, blasting their way onto Delta Three station. All in one instant, four separate paths stepped into irrevocable action.

"I am Fleet Captain Saef Sinclair-Maru. Authenticate," Saef said into the comm panel as he heard the med-bay hatch fly open in the darkness behind him.

"You are Fleet Captain Saef Sinclair-Maru, authenticated," the station Intelligence replied as the infirmary echoed from the abrupt sounds of gunfire. The heavy thump of a grenade detonating just outside the medbay hatch half-deafened Saef.

Over the thunder, Saef shouted, "Grant full access to IMS *Tanager*, now!"

In an instant, the barriers resisting Loki fell. A millisecond later the computation resources of *Tanager* soared into full power as Loki flooded himself into the Delta Three station network, deflecting the station Intelligence's useless defenses, seizing the keys away from the feeble little thing.

Inga Maru slid through the darkness, firing at muzzle flashes, dodging the thunder of return fire, gaining hints of her attackers through the dumb-mech's sensors. A moment later her own senses blazed into life. Loki enveloped her, and in a single instant she knew many things.

Interwoven with Loki's perceptions, Inga's Family biotech systems threaded her through the attackers, a blur between the staccato flashes. Releasing her submachine gun to swing on its harness, Inga's hands filled with her short sword. She slashed once, then ducked out through the infirmary hatch, dodging invisibly between two armored attackers as the station lights strobed to Loki's rhythm, confounding natural and technological night vision.

In the disorienting strobe of light and dark, in the tumult of deafening gunfire and cries, Inga emerged in the station corridor behind the jumble of attackers. She chopped down two armored figures in two surgical cuts, appearing in one strobe flash, disappearing in the next. Any combatant attempting to level a weapon against her found gravity undulating beneath their feet, alternating from heavy to light and back again. Inga went through them as an unstoppable force, each slash of her short sword sending a stream of her own blood down her side.

The last of her attackers fell to the deck with a hand grasping futilely at his lacerated neck, and Inga triggered the lights.

Around her, the shambles stood revealed. Bullet impacts decorated every bulkhead, the bodies of attackers sprawled in the corridor, and through the open infirmary hatch, gore splashed and splattered over the ceiling and walls.

"Maru!" Saef called out from the infirmary, its hatch jammed with fallen attackers. "Maru?"

Saef peered cautiously into the corridor, his pistol held ready. Inga stood there, weaving in place, her face sprinkled in crimson, her sword hanging limply from one hand. She blinked once beneath her blond fringe, then her eyes rolled and her legs folded beneath her.

Saef's own weakness shook him as he rushed to Inga's side. His hand nearly encircled her slender neck as he checked the pulse of her carotid artery, his heart lurching in fear for her.

"She lives, Captain," a familiar, disembodied voice announced.

"Loki?" Saef said.

"You will need to utilize the suspension cot you just vacated, if you hope to preserve Chief Maru's life."

Saef felt his mind reeling as he scooped Inga's limp body up from the gore-splattered deck. How was Loki inhabiting the station systems?

"I've got to run to the ship before they send more fighters at us."

"There are very few humans still living aboard the station, Captain," Loki's voice calmly explained as Saef carried Inga back into the shattered infirmary. "Sergeant Kabir's entry team is not far from your position. There are a few figures apparently hiding in various quarters of the station, and a dozen strangers, like these Chief Maru killed, boarded the vessel *Digger* moments ago."

Even as Loki dryly described the situation, Saef stumbled weakly back into the shredded infirmary, the dumb-mech shuffling uncertainly out of the way. He placed Inga on the cot and attached the techmedico cuff as quickly as he could, punching up the emergency setting. As the techmedico whirred and pulsed, Saef frowned at Inga's placid face. He tried to wipe blood spatter from her cheek, but stopped, feeling he was somehow violating that barrier of cool reserve she wore just like her concealing cloak.

The techmedico went to work, pouring fluid into her veins. Saef unclipped the submachine gun still hanging from Inga's harness, laid it aside, and quickly placed a smart-dressing to the open wound at her side. Blood dripped steadily from the toe of her right boot where it had accumulated, running down her side and filling her boot like a reservoir.

Saef's mind slowly cleared away the fog of chemicals and the confusion of awakening in the midst of a battle.

"*Digger*?" Saef said to himself as the techmedico chirped away. Clarity arrived a moment later, and Saef realized he might be too late to save *Tanager*. "*Digger!*"

Come on, come on ... damn it all, hurry!
Susan Roush glared at the holo image, waiting and

willing Saef to hurry back to the ship before they were pinned against Delta Three's gravity well, unable to escape. Beside her, the bridge crew manifested their anxiety in various ways. Pennysmith scanned over the visible portion of the station with her manual weapon sight, Julie Yeager checked and rechecked transition calculations, darting anxious glances toward Roush. Che Ramos measured the distant signature of an inbound vessel, trying to tease out its identity, or at least its class, all the while knowing it did not matter; as Roush had said, whatever enemy raced toward them, it would be too much for *Tanager*.

Farley and Phillipa Baker obsessively checked and rechecked their own instruments, each feeling the tension building in the tiny bridge.

"Wh-what's that . . . ?" In the near silence, Che Ramos's mumbled comment caused everyone to turn.

"What is what?" Roush snapped.

"Um, I w-was trying to get a read on the inbound contact and, um, an ion flow increase is—is interfering with my scopes."

Susan Roush clenched onto the command seat armrest. "Where?"

Che shook his head. "That's just it, I—I don't see any source. It's like a curtain o-or—"

"They launched something," Roush said. "On the other side of the station. Sneaky bastards."

"Commander," Farley said, urgent, "signal from . . . from the captain!"

Roush slammed the channel open. "Roush."

Saef's voice came through clearly, audible to the entire crew. "Roush, *Digger's* coming for you. Run!"

Rather than replying or asking any one of a dozen

questions that needed answering, she turned to the immediate task of survival. "Blow the lock! Blow it now!"

Phillipa Baker actuated the explosive charges, blowing *Tanager* free of the station airlock.

"Should I lay the course for our transition poi—" Julie Yeager began.

"No. Roll ten degrees positive ecliptic and hold. Weps, shields up full. Manual control on point defenses."

"Shields up, manual control," Pennysmith repeated, sweat beading her lip as she stared at her weapon sights.

"Don't wait for a lock or a positive ident, Weps. You hear me? Just kill anything that peeks over that station hull."

Pennysmith nodded. "Yes, Commander." She stared across the vast station hull, now scarred with blackened antennae and slagged sensor dishes, placing her green weapon sights right above the station's distant horizon. Her finger hovered over the point defense trigger once again, waiting for that life-or-death moment.

Down deep in the well, on the storm-tossed surface of Delta Three planetside, life-and-death moments arrived for a cluster of humans along a dark road, all due to the ordered imperative of Marine Major Mahdi.

He had not executed a traditional ambush, simply because the governor's loyalty to the Emperor remained an open question. Mowing down the governor's retinue did not *yet* seem warranted, but he also could not count upon their observance of the authority vested in an officer of the Imperial Marines. What a fool he would feel if the governor's skimcar simply ignored his order to halt and simply raced away. Thus, with his small force arrayed on the governor's supposed route, Major Mahdi improvised.

Wiley and Sparks stopped the two skimcars dead, each receiving a mass-driver bolt to the engine. The two vehicles dropped onto the streaming roadway, sparks flying as they careened to a halt right on target. Mahdi actuated the powerful signal jammers contained in K77, and stepped from concealment to the side of the rearmost skimcar. As he covered the distance in three power-assisted bounds, K77's active camouflage shimmered away, replaced by the blazoned insignia of the Imperial Marines.

The smart-alloy fingers on Mahdi's battledress pierced the skimcar, and he peeled the door open, revealing four well-dressed people, one of whom matched the governor's image perfectly. While the governor stared in openmouthed shock, two of his retinue set Mahdi's nerves jangling with wrongness. They grinned as they drew weapons, staring at the unmistakable figure of an Imperial Marine, and death.

One managed a shot, the bullet deflecting harmlessly from Mahdi's helmet, before K77's shoulder-mount spat two heavy slugs, slamming both of them back in a tumble of limbs.

The governor threw up his arms in fright, but his female companion sat grinning, composed. In the chaos of the unfolding moment, as Corporal Hastings dealt with resistance in the second skimcar through four shoulder-mount slugs, and Mahdi saw mass-driver bolts flicking out from Sparks and Wiley, that grin transfixed him.

"Governor," Mahdi's amplified voice crackled into the skimcar's confines, "do you submit to the Emperor's authority?"

The governor's arms dropped but his eyes darted with fright, looking from the flat alloy of K77's face piece to the grinning countenance of his companion.

"What?" The governor seemed on the edge of a complete breakdown, his face quivering through a range of fearful expressions. *"What?"*

"Do you remain loyal to the Imperium?"

"Imperium?" the governor shrilled, edging back from his grinning companion. "There's *no* rebellion, don't you see?"

"Governor—"

"They're not human, even." The governor stared in revulsion at his grinning female companion as he wormed away from her. She moved fast, pulling a short knife. "Kill it!" the governor screamed as she slashed.

Mahdi's shoulder-mount spat fire, sending the grinning female back to bounce from the skimcar's shell, but the damage was done. Arterial blood streamed from the governor's neck, pouring between his desperate fingers, but the blade missed his windpipe and he screeched out his remaining moments of life.

"Four down up here," Corporal Hastings's voice crackled over the comm.

Mahdi scanned over the charnel-house interior of the skimcar, trying to make sense of what he had just witnessed.

"Got lights coming down valley," Wiley's voice crackled in.

They're not human, even....

The grinning mouths of the governor's three associates leered in Major Mahdi's vision, and a chill ran through him.

They're not human...

Mahdi felt the driving ambition of his life snap into place. Everything made sense in one blinding instant. Another war of extinction had begun, and he must survive to carry warning.

"Alright, lads," Mahdi commed out, "new mission: we've got to get off this planet, fast...."

Sergeant Kabir and his assault team had exited *Tanager* through a dark airlock. Wearing shock armor over skintight ship suits, they had made their way along the ship's hull, the storm-rocked surface of planetside glowing dimly "below" them. Traveling through shadowed valleys in Delta Three station's superstructure, they moved single file with all the stealth they could muster, until they reached their entry point. According to their analysis of the station plans, this served as the most favorable point of access that they could conceivably reach without being observed.

Placing breaching charges on an orbital facility presented a number of unique challenges. Place the charge in the wrong spot, and you vent major compartments to vacuum, or leave the entry team with no way to proceed without venting each successive compartment, one after the other.

The demo man had set his prefabricated charge on the exact point they had calculated, popped the detonator, and led the way through the glowing ring of the new entrance that they had just formed. Immediately beside them stood a manual airlock hatch leading to the station interior. Perfect.

A short jaunt later, through the manual airlock and into the eerily silent depths of Delta Three station, Sergeant Kabir's misgivings found palpable evidence.

The Marines moved through the dark station, unchallenged by the station Intelligence, carbines held in high-ready, nerves buzzing. They all remained clad in ship suits, face masks sealed tight. Their noses could not warn them as they stepped into the first large bay adjoining the station's central hub.

The point Marine popped a large hatch, with Sergeant Kabir posted up on the opposite side of the hatchway. They both lit the bay with their powerful weapon-mounted floods, revealing a scene their eyes could not believe.

Across the broad bay, as far as their weapon lights revealed, crumpled uniforms lay in disordered heaps: merchant spacers, System Guard, Fleet, corporate. From the heaps, an occasional face or clawed hand projected in the stark edges of their playing beams. Nothing moved, nothing stirred.

"Sweet gods," Corporal Suffolk whispered, and Sergeant Kabir could only nod, unable to do more than stare. "Must be a thousand...no...two thousand."

PFC. Haider slid up beside them and stared. "Who... who would do this? It's a—a slaughter."

"No," Sergeant Kabir said, tightening his weapon light down to a fine beam, "it's a harvest." He turned the white cone of his light on one victim, a woman in spacer garb, a chunk of her skull missing, then another corpse, and another, all missing a portion of the skull...right where a Shaper implant would rest.

The sergeant took a final look, seeing the human element, the faces frozen in fear, the hands outstretched defensively. He snapped off his flood. "Seal this door. We'll go around to the hub on the wet-side companionway."

The small team of Marines continued clearing the dark station at a steady pace, but each of them saw images of the sprawled, disfigured dead in their mind's eye, and each silently determined that they would never be taken alive.

Saef lost the all-seeing presence of Loki the moment *Tanager* blew the umbilical feed through the airlock, and the proper station Intelligence never reappeared. Still, he possessed open access through his UI, and while the techmedico stabilized Inga Maru's condition, he scrolled through the vessels currently docked at the Delta Three station.

Two heavy merchant ships quickly became the target of his attention. *Comet* massed nine thousand tons and already held sufficient Shaper fuel for any transition he might desire. Its engines were new upgrades, so it might fare better than poor old *Tanager* on an intrasystem game of catch-me-shag-me.

The other candidate was the heavy merchant *Aurora*, and when Saef glanced at *Aurora*'s cargo manifest, he knew his choice was made. Though only six thousand tons, and equipped with somewhat older engines, its cargo surely represented an example of treachery of an elevated caliber. *Aurora*'s sizeable hold contained the largest accumulation of Shaper tech Saef had ever encountered outside the Imperial holds of Core Alpha, if the manifest read true.

Although Loki had said Sergeant Kabir led his team of Marines not far distant, Saef burned to get off the Delta Three station. For the first time since he left the Strand, he clearly saw an answer—*the* answer—to his multipronged dilemma, and every passing moment stuck on Delta Three station reduced his odds of success. Also, *Tanager* and that cursed gunboat, *Digger*, might be clawing each other even as he stood about the destroyed medical bay. He had to move.

With the dumb-mech scampering along behind, Saef pushed Inga's suspension cot out of the infirmary, through the small battlefield, Inga's Krishna submachine gun placed close at hand, loaded with its final magazine.

With each step, the chemicals fogging Saef's mind reduced as he moved farther from the overpowering scents of combat. The odors of accelerant and coppery blood faded, to be replaced by a growing stench of decay. Like Inga, Saef felt the visceral response and the dismay. Loki said few people remained alive aboard the station. There should have been thousands between station staff, ship crews, Guard and Fleet personnel. *Where had they all gone?*

Saef triggered the final hatch that exited the station hub, according to the UI wire frame. It opened onto a wide bay, dark and quiet. Some hint of sound reached Saef's ears, and he hesitated to move through the broad hatch, reaching for Inga's submachine gun. After a moment of burning impatience, Saef took a chance. *"Tanager!"* he shouted.

The boom of his voice echoed through the bay, swallowed by darkness. A moment more passed before he heard a response, crackling through a ship suit speaker. "That you, Captain?" Sergeant Kabir and an equally beefy PFC peered around a stanchion, their carbines leveled on Saef's position.

"It is," Saef said, and saw their weapons lower. A moment later, Saef heard the clatter of two more

Marines clearing through the hub behind him. Corporal Suffolk led the way on Saef's trail, his eyes wide, visible through the ship suit's bulbous lenses. The corporal had just cleared through the battlefield around the medical bay, and he could scarcely believe what he had witnessed. Everyone knew that the captain was a right terror in a duel, but this was something else entirely.

"Captain," Sergeant Kabir greeted as the Marines gathered around him, all still on high alert, each scanning about the surrounding darkness. "*Tanager* blew the lock." Kabir looked around the dark reaches of the silent station. "Something very bad is loose on this station. We—we saw—"

"Tell me as we run, Sergeant," Saef interrupted. "We've got minutes to reach dock seven, or we're stuck here, permanently."

Sergeant Kabir jerked a nod. "Haider, you're on six, Suffolk on point. Let's move, Marines!"

Chapter 37

"With a realm of possibilities that emerges from the infinite, humanity will surely encounter yet another malign alien presence. The only question is, when?"

—*Legacy Mandate* by Emperor Yung I

FOR CENTURIES, ARMED CONFLICT BETWEEN SPACE-craft involved vast distances, extreme velocities, and world-shattering weapons. Lieutenant Tilly Pennysmith and the IMS *Tanager* prepared for the Fleet equivalent of a knife fight, staring through optical weapon sights that generally served no tactical purpose in the vastness of space.

Pennysmith had readied *Tanager*'s antique glasscasters without Roush's order, aiming their blunt muzzles at the Delta Three station's edge, where Roush was so certain that *Digger* would emerge. She recognized Roush's particular genius in tilting *Tanager* relative to the station, making Pennysmith's point-defense turret the very first portion of *Tanager* the enemy would see.

357

"Sensors, what's that inbound up to?" Roush demanded.

"Um, the—the inbound contact is still accelerating hard, coming on a direct vector," Che Ramos said.

"Any luck on that ident yet?"

"N-not yet, Commander," Che said.

"Inbound vessel is the *Carthage*," Loki's somber voice offered.

Roush knew the vessel well: reinforced frigate, heavy engines for intrasystem work, stealthy and well armed. She had surely been hiding out on the system fringe, dark and silent after obliterating Delta Three's defense platform, and *that* had probably been an unfortunate incident. Some old-fashioned fool on the platform surely made a stand, and that had worked out well for *Tanager*, but the crew members who now scattered their bits among the shattered fragments of the platform might hold a different view, if they still possessed any voice.

Perhaps *Tanager* would soon add its elements, and those of its crew, to that same collection of trash circling Delta Three's mild star.

That thought barely formed in Roush's mind, and the bridge crew had just begun digesting the identity of their inbound nemesis, when they all heard the slight catch in Tilly Pennysmith's breath.

Her finger, poised over the defense trigger, now jerked as the edge of a dark hull cleared the horizon of Delta Three station. In such tight confines *Tanager*'s meager energy weapons seemed mighty, lighting the station superstructure in flashes of brilliance, each shadow cut sharply as Pennysmith raked *Digger*'s rising bulk.

"Nav, hold our yaw angle, just nudge us negative

a whisker!" Roush barked, staring between the holo tank optical feed and her own instruments.

Julie Yeager tersely affirmed, and the bridge crew immediately saw Roush's game. As *Digger* came over the station, trying to bring its own weapons to bear, *Tanager* slid away, slicing at *Digger*'s shields while hiding behind Delta Three's superstructure.

"Ops, shields and heat sinks are yours." Susan Roush stared at the holo image, waiting for the moment *Digger* finally hit back. She wanted Pennysmith free of any duty aside from waging the close-quarters battle that decided *Tanager*'s immediate fate.

Though nothing in Fleet weapons training resembled the challenge before her, Pennysmith adapted quickly. Burning down Delta Three's point-defense turret had illustrated the principle, subsequently slagging a collection of sensors and antennae structures cemented her comfort on the manual controls, and now she stared into her optical scope, kept the green aiming reticle centered on *Digger*'s emerging hull, and squeezed the trigger.

The darkened bridge flashed in brilliance as *Digger*'s shields splashed energy away into hard vacuum. Pennysmith fired, adjusted her aim and fired again, hoping to overload *Digger*'s shields, knowing that *Digger* would soon be clear of obstruction, able to return fire.

That moment arrived in a flash of fury, *Digger*'s foremost turret breaking the horizon and lancing out at *Tanager*. Pennysmith bared her teeth, holding the trigger down as they dueled, and without letting up she triggered *Tanager*'s glasscasters, launching a pair of the old-fashioned defensive charges. Meant to create small zones of interdiction, usually in ranges measured in hundreds or thousands of klicks, the glasscaster charges crossed the short distance and triggered right on top of *Digger*. Their silica payloads blasted into *Digger*'s shields, billions of high-speed granules deflecting away in showers of glowing ejecta.

"Heat sinks at yellow," Phillipa Baker called out as *Digger* cut at them. Tilly Pennysmith heard the words with a muted sense of shock. *Already? Digger* just managed to land their first hits, and already *Tanager*'s heat sinks were at yellow?

Digger's forward progress accelerated. They cleared above the station superstructure, both turrets cutting at *Tanager*, even trying a missile. Confused by the extreme close range, or the cluttering mass of Delta Three station, the missile failed to lock and streaked away into the darkness, but both ships lashed each other without pause.

"Forward heat sinks at red," Phillipa Baker said. Roush clenched a fist, staring between her instruments and the holo. This pathetic system gunboat was beating an Imperial frigate with one of the finest Fleet officers ever minted at the helm. *Digger*'s shields should have overheated by now, *Digger* rolling away to protect itself, but instead it was Roush preparing *Tanager* to roll and run.

Tilly Pennysmith stayed locked onto her scopes, the green light illuminating her face as she worked both turrets and the glasscasters, grimly sending everything *Tanager* could at their enemy.

The entire bridge saw a patch of *Digger*'s hull suddenly glow white, surrounded by a puff of vapor.

"A breach!" Roush thundered.

"Forward heat sinks failing!" Phillipa Baker called, almost at the same moment.

Pennysmith made no sound as she targeted and fired again and again, now cutting into *Digger*'s hull, silencing one turret, then the other, slagging its missile launcher. A secondary explosion from the missile turret set *Digger* spinning. It crumpled an extended piece of station superstructure and deflected away, venting from several terminal wounds. *Digger* slowly tumbled off and Tilly Pennysmith stopped firing.

"Good work, Weps," Roush said, feeling her heart beat again.

"No," a new voice snarled. "Bad job, really."

The bridge crew turned at the sound of the voice and saw the jolly face of Karl Grund, the ship services chief, standing at the bridge hatch. He looked much less jolly with a heavy autopistol clenched in his beefy, heavyworld hand.

Farley lunged up from his panel, and Grund coolly shot him down, the two shots deafening in the tight space. As Farley's last breath rattled out, Grund raised the muzzle of his weapon and pointed it directly between Susan Roush's eyes. "It would have been better for everyone if you had just killed yourself back on Core, but no time like the present, eh?"

Tilly Pennysmith jumped at the sound of the gunshot, reaching for the pistol at her belt, but Karl Grund fell forward, crashing to the deck. Deckchief Church stepped through the open hatchway, the carbine in his hands covering Grund's fallen form.

Susan Roush, who had never stopped savagely glaring, snapped at Church. "Cut that pretty damned fine, Deckchief."

"Loki tipped me off," Church panted, leaning against the bulkhead, "or I wouldn't have made it at all."

Che Ramos quivered in his position, shocked over and over through the last hour until he seemed unable to comprehend anything he heard or saw. He looked at the two fallen bodies, sprawled and still, puddles of blood creeping from their recumbent shapes. His gaze traveled to Deckchief Church's pale face, then to Ensign Yeager who shrilled about something. He turned back to his instruments but the collection of lights and images momentarily held no meaning.

It seemed like the arcane symbols and lights shared some urgent message, but Che struggled to connect what he saw to the rational part of his mind.

"L-launch?" Che's mouth stammered, seemingly without conscious intent.

"What?" Roush demanded, and the bridge crew fell silent.

"Launch," Che repeated. "Inbound contact has l-launched missiles."

"Why—?" Pennysmith began, but Roush cut her off.

"They're trying to get some mass in close enough to block our transition. I don't think they're willing to nuke the station just to swat us, if they can even avoid the station dampers."

"We can still run, just like the captain said," Julie Yeager offered in a quavering voice, picking up her feet to avoid the expanding pool of blood on the deck.

The weakness of their plan always was the challenge of reclaiming the multiple *Tanager* elements: Marines planetside and aboard the station, and the captain and his cox'n in the thick of it, possibly prisoners. Possibly dead.

Farley's empty comm panel chirped, and Phillipa Baker leaned over and accepted the transmission. "Coded message from Sergeant Kabir," she said, her voice steady despite everything. "They have collected the captain and Chief Maru, and will commandeer their own transport out-system."

Phillipa paused, her stoic calm shaken as she read the message. "He says that the entire station staff was slaughtered."

"What?" Roush demanded.

"That's what he sent, Commander," Phillipa Baker said. "He ends by saying they will rendezvous with Major Mahdi themselves."

Roush bit her lip, staring at the holo screen as ratings came into the bridge under Church's watchful eye. As they carried the bodies out, and dumb-mechs began cleaning up the mess, she nodded.

"Very well. We run." Roush turned her glare on Julie Yeager's pale, eager face. "Okay, Nav, we'll slingshot around Delta Three's well, and see if we can transition before *Carthage* can get those missiles on us."

Tanager's torch lit up, thrusting away from Delta Three station, the wreckage of their small battle, and their own captain. They curved around the planet beneath them, sliding from nightside to dayside, hiding the inbound glow of the distant *Carthage*, and all her angry missiles behind the curve of the much larger glow of terrestrial material.

With Corporal Suffolk moving ahead through the dark, echoing bay, Saef hurried, guiding the suspension cot over the dusty deck. Behind him, the dumb-mech scampered along, and Marines flanked him on either side. After hearing Sergeant Kabir's grim description of the slaughter he discovered, Saef understood the Marine's extreme vigilance.

"I wouldn't have believed it," Sergeant Kabir concluded as they jogged through the dimness, "but I saw plain enough. Implants chopped out of every body."

"Doesn't make much sense, Sergeant," Saef said, still suffering from the aftereffects of his comatose condition. "It's not as if they can just pull an implant from one person and use it on someone else. It's been tried for decades. Never works."

"I know what I saw, sir. I even got a vidcapture."

"I don't doubt you, Sergeant. It's just another piece that...doesn't make any sense."

Suffolk led the way to a large airlock for dock seven, and went through the lock first, ready for any attack. The other Marines automatically formed a small perimeter, weapons pointing out into the surrounding darkness.

"Nothing's right about this," Sergeant Kabir rumbled. "Not a damned rebellion... Inhuman sods."

Saef leaned over Inga's supine form, checking the suspension cot's readout as Sergeant Kabir spoke. He glanced at Inga's blood-spattered face, and found her eyes open, staring at him.

"Maru—" Saef began to say, but he saw her lips moving, forming one word. He leaned nearer. "What?"

She whispered again, her eyes wide, staring. This time he heard the word: "Inhuman." Her gaze locked onto Saef, driving intensity through the contact. A few random characters sprang into Saef's UI as Inga tried to compose a line-of-sight message in her urgency.

"Yes, Maru, they're right bastards—" Saef broke off

as Inga shook her head, her hand fumbling weakly to grip Saef's.

"Not . . ." she whispered, her eyes blinking shut, then opening, ". . . human."

Saef just stared down at her in the dim light as her eyes rolled and she slid back into unconsciousness. He heard a clanking sound from the airlock behind him.

"There's Suffolk, Sarge. What's the silly bugger doing?"

Saef turned and looked through the view port at Corporal Suffolk, who stood with his carbine hanging loosely at his side, the faceplate of his ship suit open. His face wore a fixed grin as he motioned for the others to join him.

"Cycle the lock," Sergeant Kabir ordered.

Saef held up a hand, staring at the screen. "Wait."

Corporal Suffolk continued to motion and grin, but his eyes held a vague, absent look. "Vent the lock," Saef said without looking from the screen.

"What?" Kabir thundered along with the outraged murmurs of the other Marines.

"He's got his ship suit. Vent the lock to vacuum."

Saef felt the hostility from Kabir and the other Marines, but after a moment he moved to the lock controls. The lock began to vent, the air pressure dropping away.

"What the hell, Suffolk?" one Marine growled, staring. "Put your damned faceplate on!"

But Suffolk stood with his fixed grin, motioning to them as his eyes began to bulge and blood dripped from his nose.

"That's not Suffolk," Kabir murmured, staring.

Saef also stared at the screen as blood began to

smear across the image, and Suffolk's body began to spasm, starved of all oxygen. The grin remained fixed in place even as Suffolk's armored figure slid to the deck, blood sheathing his face.

"Look at his left hand," Saef said, and the shocked Marines all looked. Blood dripped from a puncture in Suffolk's ship suit just above the wrist of his left hand. "He got stuck by something."

They all stood there in silence a moment before Saef said, "Cycle the lock, but don't touch anything. Let's move."

As the lock cycled open, Saef noted Sergeant Kabir's carbine covering Suffolk's fallen form. "Haider," Kabir ordered, "drag him along. We'll put him out a lock. Keep the bastards off him."

Saef considered countermanding that order, but he needed the Marines' full cooperation for the final leg of their escape. Instead, he focused his attention on any potential threat as they moved down the short passage to the hard lock with the heavy merchant ship *Aurora*. The dumb-mech clattered along behind as Saef handled the suspension cot.

"Look." Kabir pointed his carbine at the operating handle for the hard lock, and Saef leaned over to spot the tiny concealed needle. It gleamed, formed from some translucent crystalline material.

Saef took a hand from the suspension cot, drew his sword, and used the tip to snap the needle off. "That may be just the first trap. Let's keep watch for anything else."

They cycled the lock, entering the merchant ship two at a time, moving as quickly as they could. The interior of *Aurora* offered the first breaths of clean-smelling air Saef had enjoyed since awakening from his coma, but its dim, silent expanse felt no more welcoming.

Saef quickly dispatched two Marines to Engineering, and they set off, carbines held ready, clearing through the vessel. Sergeant Kabir took a final glance at Suffolk's body in *Aurora*'s outer lock, then hefted his carbine and followed Saef to the ship's tiny infirmary.

"Haider," Kabir growled, "stay with Chief Maru. We'll be in the bridge."

"Yes, Sergeant." Haider settled into a corner, his carbine across his chest.

Saef set the suspension cart, made a last check of Inga's vital signs, and turned to look at the armored Marine. "I am particularly attached to the chief. Keep an eye on her." He started to say more and thought better of it, though his heart lurched at the sight of Inga's lifeless face.

"I understand, sir," Haider said, and he did. No one who valued their life would take the responsibility lightly.

Saef and Kabir quickly made their way to *Aurora*'s bridge, after a quick check for crystalline needles or other booby traps, and Saef began powering up systems. Since *Aurora* was a private merchant vessel, it did not operate a synthetic Intelligence, and this left more for Saef to determine on his own. He moved through the systems as quickly as possible, double-checking key instruments to be sure *Aurora* could actually serve as their savior from the Delta Three star system.

As the passive sensors fired up, Saef began to piece together the unfolding drama. Scattered bits of wreckage swirled about the station, attesting to all the violence

Tanager had unleashed. Out-system, a substantial vessel accelerated inbound, preceded by a swarm of missiles, but *Tanager's* signature did not appear anywhere. For a moment, Saef felt a quiver of dismay as he spotted a terminally damaged hull rolling slowly in the orbital wake of Delta Three station, but quickly established it was not *Tanager.*

"She going to work for us?" Sergeant Kabir asked.

Saef quickly continued through the instruments. "So it appears. If that inbound contact doesn't catch us." He actuated the explosive bolts holding *Aurora* to Delta Three station, and used cool thrusters to drop slowly away from the tangle of superstructure. The slagged point-defense turret, evidence of *Tanager's* violence, warmed Saef's heart. At least *that* would pose no threat to them now.

Saef checked the scopes again. "Ah, Roush must be leading them off, bless her." The swarm of missiles tracked after a target invisible behind the planetary expanse.

"Okay, Sergeant, here's our window. If the major's going to leave the well, this is it. Send the parameters to him, and I'll push the signal through the ship transmitter. He'll either show up in our window, or he gets a long vacation!"

Clad in the implacable might of K77, Major Mahdi sprang over the installation enclosure in one leap, then bounced up to a small second-floor window where he clung momentarily. Mist and rain still swept the darkness, and K77 no longer wore the bright emblem of the Imperial Marines. Instead it seemed a shadowy patch of mist itself as Mahdi hurled an explosive charge through the window. He leaped away, landing smoothly on the broad, smart-alloy feet, loping into cover as the air defense tower erupted behind him.

A secondary autocannon must have detected some hint of K77's stealthed presence, because it snapped around, questing. It opened up, pouring a string of fire around Mahdi's position as he rolled, casting his considerable mass into a shallow dip. The autocannon tore the earth around him, a slug ringing off his shoulder plate.

"Someone kill that, please," Mahdi snarled into his comm.

A single mass-driver round flashed through the dark, and the autocannon spun, wildly firing strings of tracers in random directions before spinning down.

Major Mahdi was up in an instant, reaching out in three long strides, then leaping back over the outer enclosure, even as troops and vehicles began stirring around the base behind him.

Few planetary defenses performed well against Imperial battledress troops. In that regard Delta Three's defenses seemed quite typical.

Mahdi took two high bounds, landing on a modest, wooded rise overlooking the air defense base. Wiley and Sparks lay concealed among the foliage, their thermal shields deployed, the mass-driver barrel poking out.

"Alright, lads," Mahdi told them, "scarper off. We'll meet you two there."

Wiley and Sparks assented, leaving the mass driver and thermal shields behind where they lay stacked, a timed thermite charge placed to slag it all down, and they wormed their way back through wet vegetation. Still crawling, they crested the small hump and set off downhill.

Mahdi stood among the blowing foliage, drinking in the three-hundred-sixty-degree vision afforded by K77, picking out each of his battledress-equipped Marines as they completed their own objectives. Interceptor craft glowed white, smoldering in their revetments, sensor towers wilted, collapsing, and air defense batteries sent showers of flame into the night sky.

Once again Mahdi wondered if he should have commandeered a vehicle from this base, counting upon the confusion of the raid to allow their escape. He had decided against it simply because Wiley and Sparks might not survive long enough to reach any commandeered craft. Their lack of battledress proved to be a deadly conundrum.

Mahdi sized up the progress of confusion around the small base for a moment longer before setting off, bounding through the streaming rain. The shadowy form of Corporal Hastings streaked through a row of service mechs at the edge of the base enclosure directly opposite Mahdi's position, and for a moment their paths paralleled, separated by the defensive perimeter and a narrow road. The charges Hastings scattered among the service mechs detonated behind him, and he sprang high up over the outer enclosure, a blur of mist and shadow. He landed smoothly and leaped again, clearing the road and landing among the vegetation a short distance ahead of Mahdi.

In a few minutes, the other four battledress-clad Marines completed their individual raids, one by one bounding away from the shambles of the air base, joining Hastings and Mahdi as they loped away.

Mahdi checked his instruments, not surprised to see most of his weapon inventory depleted and the Shaper power cell half consumed. They would be climbing up out of the well long before they ran out of power, or they would be dead. Either way, the point would be moot.

The sharp white glow flickering through the clouds above almost caused Mahdi to halt.

"You see that?" Corporal Hastings asked, bounding easily along some distance ahead.

"I saw it," Mahdi said. "Someone's getting their arse kicked upstairs."

They continued bounding through the shrouding vegetation for a moment before Hastings offered, "I hope we still got friends up there." Since they were all thinking the same thing, Mahdi knew a reply was necessary.

"Same enemy we just buggered running the show upstairs. Can't find their arse with both hands, these sods."

There were chuckles from the Marines, but Hastings persisted. "What if they're gone, though?"

"Then we're guerillas for the duration," Mahdi said. "And you know what that means, right? Harems! Ground-side women *love* guerillas."

"Winning hearts and minds!" another Marine chimed in while the others chuckled.

"That's right, lads," Mahdi said, "giving our bodies in service to the Emperor is a hard lot—"

"Never harder!" another Marine crowed and they all laughed.

Mahdi smiled to himself, leaping through the trees, listening to the voices of his Marines coming through their secure comm channel. No matter how brief it may be, life as an Imperial Marine never felt sweeter.

❖   ❖   ❖

Wiley and Sparks continued their tactical use of public transportation, after they ran some distance down to an active road. The autocab made no comment on their muddy armor and weapons, simply driving them to a small private airfield and leaving them standing in the dark. Major Mahdi had mapped the field as one potential exit point, and it certainly fit the bill. Several low-orbit-capable execu-jets stood about the tarmac, visible through the ongoing downpour, and no visible security measures cluttered the scene. They just needed to get the appropriate jet ready to launch, and await the arrival of their battledress brethren.

Perhaps their easy victories lulled them, or perhaps their own belief in the Marine mystique bordered upon hubris. For whatever reason, they jogged toward a candidate aircraft, crossing the wide tarmac, the open mouths of various hangar structures yawning darkly not far away, and it was far too late when a tingle of caution touched Wiley. He belatedly flipped the eyepiece down from his helmet as they jogged through the streaming rain. The image exposed by his multispectrum optic as he scanned over the nearby structures would not compute at first, the individual blobs of human heat signatures blurring into a concept he had trained endlessly upon: ambush. He even managed to say the word out loud just as a bright light stabbed out through the curtain of rain, bracketing Wiley and Sparks. An amplified voice began booming, words and phrases rendered meaningless in the torrent of adrenaline.

Imperial Marine doctrine on countering an ambush comprised several steps, but, like most humans experiencing their first actual ambush, Wiley and Sparks responded at a more primal level. They ducked, throwing their carbines to their shoulders, firing.

A part of Wiley's mind, the tiny, calm portion that paid attention in all those training classes, made objections, but the much louder portion of Wiley's psyche, thrilling in exultation and fear, screamed defiance as his carbine hammered.

The snapping sound of return fire somehow reached him over the roar of his own weapon, driving him to the tarmac. Sparks stood, firing, staggering back as round after round struck him, grunting with each impact, bright fragments flying from his shock armor, and Wiley opened up again, prone on the tarmac.

Though only bare seconds had passed, Wiley felt the shock subside somewhat even as Sparks tumbled to the wet tarmac, hammered down by incoming fire. The enemy's light fell victim to their first volley of return fire, so the scene now fluctuated from total darkness to flashes lit by bright muzzle blasts. Wiley centered one human heat source between the glowing crosshairs of his weapon sight, squeezed the trigger, and barely saw the figure crumple as he rolled away from the inevitable return fire.

With hot rounds snapping through the rain around him, Wiley laid his crosshairs across another enemy form and fired. Before he could roll, an incoming shot rang off his helmet, and another smashed his shoulder plate, but Wiley still blindly rolled over and over, finding himself behind the scant shelter of a wedge-shaped wheel chock.

Muzzle blasts flashed from the darkness, rounds slammed and skipped from the tarmac, and Wiley steadied his sights, peering around his tiny chunk of cover. Fear faded away, physical pain became a distant voice, and Wiley squeezed the trigger again. Dimly, he knew he had only seconds left to live, and there, prone on the tarmac of a miserable, rain-swept little airfield, he just stopped caring about it.

The string of nearly invisible, battledress-equipped Marines bounded in great leaps, racing through the rain toward their potential exit point. They crossed a narrow road, each Marine clearing the gap in one clean bound, splashing down among wet foliage, and springing forward again. The amplified senses of their battledress detected the eruption of gunfire while still some distance from their target.

"Wiley and Sparks," Corporal Hastings said, without pausing.

"Yes," Mahdi replied, landing and leaping. "Take Ragnarson and Mumtaz and veer south."

"Yes, sir," Corporal Hastings commed back, and without a break the three Marines sped away, blurring through foliage and rain.

Major Mahdi glanced at K77's power levels and made the decision in an instant. "Emergency power now, lads. Let's go get them." He was committed. If the airfield did not provide an exit off-world, their battledress power cells might not hold enough juice for a plan B.

They raced toward the racket of gunfire, their armor-sheathed legs thrusting them forward faster and faster, leaping high over foliage, springing from hillside to flat, flying forward. But Mahdi heard the gunfire slackening ahead, a single shot barking, answered by a thunder of return fire. His marksmen clearly neared their end.

❖   ❖   ❖

Wiley tried to draw his entire body behind the bare handsbreadths of cover as rounds sang and snapped around him. His helmet jerked from two more deflecting hits, and fire licked a streak across one thigh, while tarmac fragments stung his cheek and neck. They were shooting him to pieces, and Wiley felt his anger surge.

"Fuck it," he snarled, snapping his carbine to full-auto and jerking a flash from his harness. He triggered the flash, tossing it feebly out ahead. With his eyes closed, he came to his knees, then to his feet, staggering as his leg nearly folded. The flash blew, dazzling his exposed eye, right through his closed eyelid.

His carbine was up and blasting, punching his shoulder with each burst as he staggered forward at an angle. "Bastards, bastards, bastards!" Through his multispectrum optic, Wiley caught glimpses of targets as he swore at them, firing long bursts.

He barely noticed the staccato pop of weapons firing from behind, the snap as rounds passed nearby, he just staggered forward, firing. He collapsed to his knees and fumbled for a fresh magazine, seeing a large, vague outline soar through the air ahead, crashing through the thin metal of the hangar structure. He looked about him, blinking blood and rain from his eyes. The massive forms of Marine battledress moved around him, their weapons cutting down the last of the ambushers.

Wiley fell back in a puddle, sitting with his legs outstretched, gasping for air. He looked up as Major Mahdi stepped near, towering over him in K77.

"You look like shit, Marine," Mahdi's voice crackled over K77's speaker.

Wiley nodded. "Better'n Sparks looks, Major." The

bullet-riddled body of Sparks lay nearby, blood and water pooling around the still form. Mahdi had no response, and Wiley drew a ragged breath, feeling on the edge of collapse. "Major...can we...can we get the shit off this damned planet?"

Major Mahdi looked at the execu-jets parked across the tarmac, apparently unharmed by the gun battle. "We can certainly try. Give me your hand, lad."

Chapter 38

"An outraged citizenry inevitably creates
an extension of state powers."

—Devlin Sinclair-Maru, *Integrity Mirror*

THE STRONG SCENT OF CLEANER COULD NOT QUITE
cover the tang of blood still flavoring the air of
Tanager's small bridge, but the odor matched the
ongoing tension among the crew.

"Sensors, lay those missile tracks up on main,"
Roush ordered. "Weps, let's get a couple thirty-twos
out in the dark."

Tanager slingshotted around Delta Three's gravity
well, accelerating hard, running flat out while their
enemy, *Carthage*, lay occluded behind the planet's bulk.

"There's a-another satellite, Commander," Che Ramos
reported, staring hard into the sensor scopes.

"Weps, kill that satellite."

"Yes, Commander," Lieutenant Tilly Pennysmith
affirmed, locking her point-defense turrets on the small
target, lost against the planet's bulk. The high-energy

pulses lanced out, sending fragments of yet another unarmed satellite spinning out, unable to observe or communicate for their enemies any longer.

Tanager spat out a string of 32-gauge missiles in their wake, each missile drifting, with only launch momentum pushing them out. As each missile motored up from the ship's magazine, Pennysmith prayed the rails, armatures, and links would keep working without fail.

Deckchief Church sat nearby with a carbine across his knees, ready for any emergency. He also knew that *Tanager*'s loading apparatus historically failed with little provocation, and he prepared to run for the Weapons section as needed.

"Nav, give us fifteen degrees negative, and ready those transition calcs."

"Fifteen negative, Commander," Julie Yeager said, her face pale, clearly near the end of her nerves. "Transition calcs are ready."

"*C-Carthage* is on us, Commander," Che Ramos said as the distant signature of the more powerful ship appeared, rising over the edge of Delta Three's horizon. "Sh-she's painting us!"

Susan Roush stared at the tracks for a moment. "Okay Sensors, go active. Let's see what *Carthage* does with her missiles, if we can."

Che triggered *Tanager*'s active sensors, sending multispectrum transmissions blasting out into the system. As sensor returns bounced back to *Tanager*, Roush stared at the growing picture. "No imagination, silly arseholes. No imagination at all."

Tanager torched out from Delta Three's gravity well with a high velocity, angling negative, relative to the galactic plane, not far from the gravitational threshold allowing their transition. *Carthage*'s wave of pursuing missiles had all raced after *Tanager*'s initial course and were now forced to claw their way back, far off track.

"Uh, C-Commander," Che stammered. "There's a new contact showing up, d-deep in the well, just c-clearing the horizon."

Susan Roush held a pretty solid idea who that must be. "What ship?"

"I-I'm not sure—"

"It is the heavy merchant *Aurora*," Loki's dry voice interjected. "It likely contains the captain and Chief Maru."

Roush sized up the growing picture for a moment. "Down so deep, he's got to be collecting the Marines. He should be good, I think."

Che Ramos saw a curious blip in his sensors, farther out-system where nothing but empty space should be. "C-Commander! New contact out-system, one-twenty right azimuth, thirty degrees positive!"

"What the shit . . . ?" Roush stared at the holo.

"Oh no, no, no!" Julie Yeager sobbed suddenly. "No, no, no!"

"Pull it together, Nav!" Roush ordered as she quickly formed a new picture of their threat. Their active sensor pulse had saved them from a nasty surprise. A ship sat, waiting silent and dark in a far-slung orbit, ready to scoop them up.

"We're dead! We're dead!" Julie Yeager cried, her face pinched.

"Church, get her out, and get Ruprecht for me," Roush said. "Weps, give me a pattern of sixty-fours right at the new contact. We can use those for inter-diction and keep their damned missiles off us."

"L-launch!" Che called out. "Outbound contact launched missiles—still launching!"

Roush snapped between her instruments feeling the first cold stabs of real fear. A large expanse of open space still existed around Delta Three, but the available avenues away to a safe transition point shrank by the moment as ships and missiles raced toward *Tanager*. Only *Tanager*'s high delta-v and Roush's counterintuitive course selection had given them an inkling of hope.

If the rebels really slaughtered the station's entire inhabitants, then surrendering could not be considered. Not that she was even close to admitting defeat yet.

Ruprecht hustled into the bridge. "You take Nav, Lieutenant, if you can handle the pressure," Roush said, barely glancing up. "We've got a damned maze to navigate if we're ever going to leave this system."

Ruprecht glanced at all the intersecting tracks displayed on the main holo and raised his eyebrows as he settled his heavyworld frame into place. "Very well, Commander."

"I've got a malfunction on the load trays, Commander," Tilly Pennysmith said, flushing.

"Tell me it's the sixty-fours," Roush said.

"It's the sixty-fours," Pennysmith said.

"Ops, get Cray from Engineering and the deckchief down to the Weapons section. Get that load tray un-fucked." Roush turned on Che Ramos. "Got the ident on that out-system contact yet?"

"N-no, Commander, s-still trying to—"

"Loki?" Roush interrupted. "You got that out-system figured?"

"I am sorry, Commander," Loki's mellow voice offered. "A definitive identification is still pending. It is approximately a fifty-thousand-ton cruiser, according to my measurements."

Fifty thousand tons... Roush felt her internal chill increase. The enemy kept such a substantive warship running dark, idling out on the fringes, for what?

"Weps, you got a wide enough spread to detonate a couple of those fish?"

Pennysmith checked her scopes, assuring that her missile patterns had dispersed enough. One detonation wouldn't wipe out the other missiles in the pattern. "Yes, Commander. All patterns are dispersed."

"Alright, let's poke 'em in the eye," Roush said. "Nav, get ready for a course change. Weps, detonate your selected fish."

A nuclear missile in each pattern, one between *Tanager* and each of the enemy vessels, detonated. For a short time *Tanager* lay concealed from her enemies behind globes of expanding energy, and within that window, *Tanager* rolled to a new heading, accelerating hard.

Susan Roush glowered into the scopes, calculating their chances of breaking free, but even in the midst of her calculations she spared a thought for Saef and Major Mahdi. In all the furor, could they slip away?

One small section in an advanced Marine training course involved various unique methods for escaping out of a gravity well, after said Marines had sown hate and discontent planetside. The common execu-jet figured heavily in these plans, so Major Mahdi's assaulters all knew the drill: check for fuel, burn off the primary and secondary transponders, hotwire the autopilot system, then run like hell and stay low.

With six heavy battledress Marines distributed

around the jet's interior, curled into their tightest form factors, the jet flew low over the water. Wiley drooped over the control console, his helmet off and wet hair dripping, a patchwork of bandages decorating his face. He felt blood soaking the seat beneath him, but he ignored that and the pain radiating from numerous wounds as he looked from the small nav screen to optical scan and back. The horizon ahead grew brighter as they flew toward dayside, running flat out.

He knew that there would likely be no warning, no notice if an interceptor got on their path; the execu-jet exploding around them would be the subtle indication of failure.

"How you holding up, Marine?" Major Mahdi's voice crackled out from where he curled his battledress-clad form, just outside the cockpit.

Wiley saw more fiery streamers plummeting from the upper atmosphere where wreckage of some kind fell from orbit. "I'm holding, sir. Looks like we got a couple minutes until we start our climb... And there's more shit falling from orbit."

Since they had received the short, coded signal from Sergeant Kabir, Major Mahdi's raiders had shed some of their fatalistic joviality. As the likelihood of survival grew before their eyes, they became increasingly attached to the idea of remaining alive and intact.

"Roush or the captain slagging their satellites, likely," Major Mahdi rumbled. "The only reason we're slipping away so easy."

"Here's the climb." Wiley saw the nav track change a moment before the execu-jet nosed up, rising from just above the water, climbing sharply. Combined with blood loss, the compressing g-forces dimmed his vision and made his head spin. Through the tumult in his skull he heard Major Mahdi's voice.

"With no satellites, so far out over the ocean, if they detect our climb at all it will be too damned late."

Wiley nodded his head, his eyes closed, feeling the climb pushing him farther into the seat, blood squeezing out of the cushion below him like a sponge, running down the back of both legs. The words *too damned late* spun through his mind a few times before he found the energy to speak. "Reckon you're right, sir."

Saef used every trick he knew to reduce the signature of the ship as he eased away from the station and slowed gradually into a deeper and deeper orbit. Without a synthetic Intelligence scanning all around, looking for hints of any other vessel visible to optical scopes, Saef could only gather so much about the activities of *Tanager* and any enemies on-system. The passive scanners on a merchant spacer like *Aurora* left him feeling nearly blind, even compared to a humble old warship like *Tanager*. As a result, he largely ignored the drama unfolding through the system, focusing simply upon sneaking down into the well to collect his troops.

Now for Major Mahdi to complete the other half of the puzzle without either of them being observed and swatted out of the air.

Sergeant Kabir clomped back into the tiny bridge and took a knee beside Saef. "Cleared the ship as best we could. We're alone, and the cargo hold looks pretty full."

Saef peered into an antiquated scope and made an adjustment to the controls. "Good, Sergeant. And Chief Maru?"

"Seems stable enough, sir. Haider said she came to

for a bit, asked for food." He chuckled. "For a skinny little thing, she sure has an appetite!"

Saef turned his inimical gaze on Sergeant Kabir. "He fed her, didn't he?"

"What? Yes, yes," Kabir felt himself shifting uncomfortably with the intensity of Saef's eyes. "Haider gave her one of her food bars."

Saef nodded and turned back to the instruments. "If she doesn't regain consciousness in an hour or so, we'll need to rig a glucose drip."

"Really, Captain? She's only been out for a few—"

"Yes, Sergeant. Make a note of it, please."

Sergeant Kabir grimaced, about to ask additional questions despite Saef's peremptory tone, when the sound of a clattering step reached them. Despite having personally cleared the vessel, Kabir's carbine leveled at the bridge hatch. No quick clearing could unearth every little hiding place.

"Oh, it's your luggage, sir." Kabir's carbine lowered as the dumb-mech scampered in on its six legs, squirming up close to Saef's command seat.

"So it is." Saef frowned over at the dented metal carapace that angled up toward him on its articulated legs. Saef detected a faint chirping sound from within the dumb-mech: the Imperial QE comm. Saef's frown deepened. *What could Winter Yung possibly need?*

For a moment Saef considered ignoring the comm. His hands were full, trying to save himself, his Marines, and the fortunes of his family. A moment later the idea of sending out word of the Delta Three slaughter trumped even survival.

"Sergeant, open one case in the cargo hold, please. Match it to the manifest. Any case will do."

Sergeant Kabir hesitated only a moment at the strange order, before nodding. "Yes, sir." Hefting his carbine, he clomped out the narrow bridge hatch.

Saef checked his instruments and controls, assuring that the *Aurora* continued its slide down into the well, on track for their rendezvous with Major Mahdi. He opened the dumb-mech's main compartment and drew out the chirping quantum-entangled communicator.

As the waiting message responded to his authentication, scrolling its characters across the secure screen, Saef felt his stomach quake, despair washing over him.

The government offices of Delta Three operated a QE comm tied to its counterpart in the Imperial offices of Core control, like all provincial governments. Through these comm connections Imperial edicts, emergency alerts and other small messages suited for the constrained bandwidth passed in both directions. On this day of violence and treachery Delta Three's comm had apparently been put to use.

Saef read the scrolling text twice: GOVERNOR'S OFFICE OF DELTA THREE JUST DECLARED THAT IMPERIAL MARINES ASSASSINATED THE GOVERNOR AND LAUNCHED UNPROVOKED ATTACKS ON MILITARY AND CIVILIAN TARGETS. ARE YOUR MARINES DEPLOYED PLANETSIDE?

Saef stared at the blinking cursor for a long moment, thinking of the best reply to convey the complexities of the tactical situation, the startling discoveries. As last he punched in a short string of characters and sent them, knowing that they would instantly appear on Winter Yung's mated comm, over a light-year away.

Saef stared at those characters in all of their blunt understatement: YES.

The eternity before a reply registered Saef spent checking the *Aurora*'s progress down to his rendezvous. Major Mahdi assassinated the governor? The governor's office claimed loyalty to the Emperor even as rebel warships dominated the system, and their orbital station hosted the slaughter of thousands?

The comm chirped and Saef looked at the single, horrible line: NO ONE CAN SAVE YOU FROM THIS.

For centuries the Sinclair-Maru Family represented solidity and competence. One moment the Family name meant something honest and estimable, and now . . . ? Saef felt his breath leave him, darkness filling his thoughts.

The comm chirped again, its message matching the coldness in Saef's gut: CONSIDER SUICIDE.

The suggestion did not seem inappropriate in that moment, but Saef struggled to find the Deep Man. As he fought down the constriction around his chest, clarity seemed to arise. Aside from responsibility to collect *Tanager*'s Marines, Saef needed some hint of the emergent danger to reach the greater sphere of human space. Suicide was not an available option.

He punched in a string of characters and read the terse lines before he sent the message: REBEL WARSHIPS HOLD DELTA THREE SYSTEM. THOUSANDS FOUND EXECUTED ON ORBITAL STATION. EVIDENCE OF NON-HUMAN INVOLVEMENT.

With the message sent, Saef drew in a calming breath, securing his place within the Deep Man, above and beyond fear, and turned back to the ship controls with little thought of the disaster that awaited.

The return message arrived quickly: RETURN TO CORE. SPEAK TO NO ONE ABOUT POSSIBLE NONHUMAN AGENCY. YOU MAY YET SURVIVE THIS. OUT.

When Sergeant Kabir returned, the dumb-mech scampered past him out the bridge hatch, and Saef seemed fully occupied with the ship's controls.

"Captain, the manifest is—is the damnedest thing. Full of Shaper tech. So much, you . . . you wouldn't believe it."

"Is that so?" Saef said without turning from his tasks.

"I opened a couple of cases, and it all seems to match. Don't think I've ever seen so much Shaper shit in one place. Gotta be worth . . . millions? More?"

Saef nodded. "Excellent, Sergeant. Can you get back and man the secondary airlock? With luck, we'll come up on your comrades in thirty minutes or less."

Sergeant Kabir opened his mouth to ask if Saef understood what he was saying about the immense wealth held within this merchant ship, but changed his mind. "Secondary airlock? Aye, sir. On it."

Saef leaned over *Aurora*'s scopes again, looking for any trace of Major Mahdi climbing up to meet them, even as *Aurora* slid deeper and deeper into the well. Saef felt the deck shiver beneath him. The upper reaches of Delta Three's atmosphere buffeted them, and their only possible rendezvous point drew near. If Major Mahdi could not reach them within that narrow confine of space and time, he and his Marines would remain on Delta Three to face whatever fate the residents might inflict upon them.

Even as he stared into the scope, scanning for any hint, Saef wondered if it might be better if Mahdi remained behind. *Assassinated the regional governor . . . ?*

The execu-jet climbed at a sharp angle, the green field of ocean spreading out below, storm clouds far behind. Wiley slumped in his seat, eyes nearly closed, barely seeing the nav screen and its flickering numerals, higher and higher. A part of his mind counted down the seconds. Just a little higher, a little farther, and they would be beyond the reach of any planetside defenses. Just a bit longer and they would be away.

"You still there, Marine?" Major Mahdi's voice cut through the haze over Wiley's mind.

Wiley opened his mouth to speak but found it too parched to make a sound.

"Wiley?"

Wiley took a sip from his hydration pack before managing, "I'm here, sir."

"Good. Not long now."

Even as Mahdi spoke, the execu-jet's engines cut out, there was a moment of weightlessness, and the jet's mag-drives kicked in. Weight returned as they continued to climb, now thrusting against the planet's magnetic field, clambering up into the last traces of the atmosphere, above the reach of conventional engines. Rather than rocketing up to escape velocity, the execu-jet found orbit like a spider inching up a magnetic web, slow and steady, even when desperate speed was desired.

Wiley stirred, flipping on their docking beacon. He scanned through the hazy distance and black sky, seeing life and freedom in darkness, while destruction and death awaited upon the planet's bright face.

"Anything, Wiley?" Major Mahdi inquired, his mechanical voice grating in the stillness.

"Not yet." A panel light lit up even as Wiley spoke. "Maybe this is it." He punched a comm button and the signal blared to life: "*Unidentified craft, you are in violation of—*" Wiley punched the comm button again.

"Nope," he said. "Looks like groundside is on to us."

"So it does."

The silence in the cockpit stretched out and Wiley found his thoughts fading again, spinning into a near dream state as his gaze wandered from the angrily flashing comm light to the faint glimmer of stars through the cockpit view screen. One of those glimmering points might even be home, an uninmportant star that warmed his skin during idyllic summer days of his youth on an unimportant world. The stars blanked out as a large shape swept toward them, now catching the light, gleaming brightly.

Wiley stared vacantly for a long moment, worked his mouth and finally managed, "Looks like our ride is here."

Saef matched the execu-jet's path as closely as possible before triggering the docking sequencer. He found the airlock monitor and watched, expecting the execu-jet to slowly ease up to *Aurora*'s extending port, kiss and lock. Instead, he saw the execu-jet's hatch pop, and a string of humanoid figures leaping the gap, two oversized figures bearing bulky burdens as they crossed the distance. With the planet surface swirling below, the Marines momentarily became individual orbital bodies, a display Saef had not anticipated. Still, it was mere seconds before the lock cycled, and Sergeant Kabir signaled the all clear.

Saef immediately moved to the nav controls, entering the course he had waiting. *Aurora* accelerated, lifting out of the gravity well, edging into a higher orbit, moving to a slingshot departure from Delta Three's embrace.

With the system course in motion, Saef began

transition calculations, fumbling through *Aurora*'s merchant nav system, finding his way through the variations from Fleet standards.

Some minutes passed with Saef dividing his attention between the intrasystem navigation demands and ironing out the final steps of the transition calculations, before Sergeant Kabir reached out through the ship comm.

"All secure here, Captain. One dead, one wounded."

Saef stabbed the comm tab. "Affirmative. If the major could come to the bridge as soon as possible, I would appreciate it."

"Roger that. Give us a bit to get him out of his kit."

It was only a few minutes later when Saef heard the solid tread of an approaching stride. Saef turned to see Major Mahdi duck through the low bridge hatchway, his blocky features as composed as ever.

"Captain," Mahdi rumbled, stepping to the vacant seat and settling in.

"Give me the high points, Major," Saef said, turning back to the instruments. "Forgive my preoccupation."

Mahdi waved a dismissive hand. "Work your magic, Captain. I'd like to see this system behind me."

"Trouble?"

Mahdi mused a moment before speaking. "Sergeant Kabir told me about Suffolk, so I figure you may have some inkling of the scope."

That reply jarred Saef. His thought had fixated on the governor's fate, and now came back around to the disturbing possibility of some nonhuman agency. "Did he also mention the slaughter?"

Mahdi nodded. "He did. Taken with my planetside view, I am . . . uneasy."

"High points, Major?"

"Right. Sorry." Mahdi rubbed a hand across his face. "After some fiddling about, we stopped the governor's vehicles, identified ourselves, and had to put down a couple of the governor's cronies who made their try."

"And the governor?" Saef asked. "Killed in the cross fire, I presume?"

Mahdi shook his head, puzzled. "No. He survived long enough to say a few interesting words before one of his bunch took a knife to him."

Saef looked over at Mahdi with surprise. "One of his own people? You sure?"

Major Mahdi stared back. "Of course I'm sure, Captain. Got a vidcapture of it, too, if you care to see for yourself."

Saef felt relief flooding through him, but he merely nodded, and turned back to the ship's instruments.

"Thing is," Mahdi continued, "she killed him when he squawked that she wasn't human." He leaned back in the seat and drew a deep breath. "And I believe him."

"Suffolk, and the slaughter on the station . . . it does seem . . . disquieting . . . inhuman."

"Aliens . . . even better at inhumanity than we are. Lifetimes of practice, I suppose."

"I daresay," Saef answered, surprised at the grim amusement in the major's voice.

"Don't mind me, Captain." Mahdi smiled thinly. "My Marines just pulled off one of the most successful raids in recent history, we've exposed these alien sods, and I've found a fight worthy of my ancestors. It is an interesting moment to be alive."

Saef began to reply, then looked at a flicker across his instruments. He switched the holo to optical feeds, bringing up the system starscape and the bright edge of Delta Three planetside. Two expanding orbs of energy filled the near field, brightening the cockpit from the screen's radiance.

Saef stared at the image. "An interesting moment to be alive, Major, if we can survive the next few hours, and if the Admiralty doesn't crucify us."

"Just part of the excitement, Captain." Mahdi folded thick arms across his chest, staring at the glowing image. "You never feel more human than when you're right on the edge of destruction."

Saef drew a deep breath as the twin suns of nuclear energy began to shrink, and the faint torch of a lone ship began to resolve, accelerating hard, running from invisible threats.

Would Susan Roush agree? Does she feel especially human even now?

Chapter 39

"Evolution of any species is impossible without
the truly mortal consequences of failure."

—*Legacy Mandate* by Emperor Yung I

"C-COMMANDER, *CARTHAGE* IS—IS DEVIATING COURSE
into the gravity well," Che Ramos declared, leaning over
his panel, his face beaded with sweat.

"And that big out-system bastard?"

"S-still holding on the pursuit course."

Susan Roush drummed her fingers, looking at all
the tracks on the tactical display. Dozens of missiles
swarmed through the system, racing to cut off *Tanager*'s
transition points before they could gain enough distance
from Delta Three's gravity well. *Carthage*? Moving to
slingshot off the well? Or going in for the kill on *Aurora*?

If *Tanager* continued on her current course she would
eat a dozen missiles before they could transition, maybe
few enough to handle with point defenses . . . maybe not.

"Weps, where're those thirty-twos down in the well?"

Pennysmith punched up the tracks, showing the string of 32-gauge missiles quietly floating in an expanding ring on a wide orbit.

Roush studied *Aurora*'s position, peeling out of orbit and accelerating away from the expanding battlefield, *Carthage* out of sight behind the planet's bulk. If *Carthage* pursued *Aurora*, slingshotting around the gravity well, then only a tight channel of navigational paths would serve. . . .

"Weps, move those thirty-twos to . . . this track—fast!" Roush knew *Carthage* could not see the missiles yet over the planetary horizon, and the out-system contact stood far too distant to resolve the missiles yet. She had only a brief window to get the missiles relocated into *Carthage*'s likely path before *Carthage* cleared the horizon.

Pennysmith sent the relocation signal, waking the floating missiles, sending them rocketing deeper into the well to Roush's designated new path where they shut down once again, floating, waiting.

"Nav, one-one-zero left azimuth, full emergency acceleration."

Ruprecht, now filling Julie Yeager's vacated seat, punched in the course, spinning *Tanager*, torching back toward the gravity well of Delta Three. Ruprecht looked over at Roush. "You realize our new course will put us right into the path of *Carthage* . . . ?"

"Yes, Lieutenant, if *Carthage* is still with us."

Ruprecht seemed about to say more, but pursed his lips disapprovingly and looked back to his instruments instead. He did not need to say that they ran a terrible risk. If *Carthage* detected and destroyed or evaded the string of silent missiles in their path, then *Tanager* would surely feel its teeth.

"*Carthage* is in pursuit of the captain," Roush said. "Look at that track. Why? Why the merchant ship? Why not us?"

Ruprecht said nothing, but Phillipa Baker broke in, "Cray reports that the sixty-four-gauge load tray will be operational in moments."

"Good. Weps, you got interdiction tracks figured yet?"

Pennysmith jerked a nod. "For their nearest twenty missiles, yes."

"Go to work, then," Roush said. "Might make some lanes for us, and sure as shit gives those arseholes a light show."

Pennysmith silently prayed that the load tray would endure a dozen launches without crashing. "Right. Launching sixty-fours."

Moments later, missiles leaped from *Tanager*'s hardpoints, streaking out to intercept incoming enemy missiles, now closing on their position from multiple vectors. New globes of destructive energy flowered into blazing life as Pennysmith's barrage began to intercept and detonate, each explosion consuming one or two enemy missiles. Around *Tanager*, space blossomed, light and power flooding the spectrum. Through it all *Tanager* ran for all she was worth, just a narrow tangent off Delta Three's gravity well.

Carthage fell behind the planetary mass, both ships invisible to each other momentarily. *Aurora* torched out from the well on its tepid merchant thruster, clearly aiming for clear space away from the destructive fireworks, its acceleration indicating fairly advanced hardware for such a tubby craft. For the moment it appeared no missiles locked onto *Aurora*'s course.

Tanager's counterintuitive course change, obliquely

in-system, threw the enemy's distant missile tracks into confusion, while *Tanager* engaged the nearer missiles in overlapping spheres of destruction.

"Get ready on those thirty-twos in the well, Weps," Roush growled, staring at the tactical screen. "When *Carthage* comes around, detonate in their damned teeth. We'll knock her out and slip into *Aurora's* wake. Try to keep them off until we can transition."

Pennysmith affirmed, then jerked with surprise as defensive shields and heat sinks suddenly spiked. "Commander—!"

"What the shit was that?" Roush snapped.

"From—from the out-system contact," Che Ramos shrilled. "Signature of an energy weapon."

Roush stared at the holo. *That was a hell of a long-range potshot!* "Not sure how those pricks resolved a shot at this distance. Nav, give us a little wobble. Weps, keep an eye on *Carthage* coming around, but start laying some glasscaster rounds in our wake. Give us a little cover at least."

Both affirmed, and the rhythmic thumping of the glasscaster resonated through *Tanager's* hull, but a moment later that distant enemy managed the impossible a second time. Pennysmith gasped and Phillipa Baker called out, "Heat sinks are at red!"

That distant cruiser wielded some very powerful energy weapon, painting across hundreds of thousands of klicks to just touch *Tanager*. One more such swipe and *Tanager's* heat sinks would fail and shields would collapse.

"Weps, you on *Carthage*? She's coming around."

The glasscaster continued thumping away, throwing bulky silica payloads in *Tanager's* wake, trying to absorb and disperse the destructive beams from their distant foe.

"On it, Commander." Pennysmith stared into her scope, trusting her calculations, the accumulation of signal delays, the velocity of *Carthage* ... Part of her mind noted the sudden flare of shields and heat sinks, the distressed voices of her fellow crew members, the abrupt silence of the glasscaster as it slagged down; while the other part of her mind knew only one task. She actuated the string of 32-gauge nuclear missiles surrounding *Carthage* as *Carthage* blazed around the curve of Delta Three's gravity well.

Even as alarms blared and voices cried out, Loki calmly describing a hull breach, Lieutenant Tilly Pennysmith observed the eruption of nuclear fire envelop *Carthage*. Her ears popped as cabin pressure plummeted, her nose suddenly streaming blood. Through hazed eyes, she stared at the scope, fixated. *Carthage* emerged from the inferno, tumbling out of control, her hull misshapen and venting. . . .

Just like *Tanager*, Pennysmith thought, as frantic hands pulled at her and darkness fell.

Chapter 40

"So often, one confuses appetites with passions.
A life ruled by appetites inevitably declines. A
life guided by passions inevitably elevates."

—Devlin Sinclair-Maru, *Integrity Mirror*

CORE SYSTEM SWARMED WITH FLEET TRAFFIC AND
various merchant craft, all moving to or from Core
Alpha or the Strand. Massive battleships and cruisers
flowed out for combat cruises, or flowed in for refit
and re-crew as the Imperial response ramped up.

Far out-system, a nondescript heavy merchant transitioned in. The Fleet defensive platforms and scanner
stations detected its arrival, and after dealing with more
pressing, military traffic, this merchant ship eventually
received its official query. Irregularities of registration,
a non-logged manifest, and an improper authentication
code only began the official consternation at this ship,
Aurora. Eventually, a Fleet functionary on an outer
defense platform contacted the ship directly.

Captain Saef Sinclair-Maru received the transmission personally, the pale, wounded Inga Maru seated nearby, a blanket wrapped around her shoulders as she nibbled a food bar.

"I am Captain Sinclair-Maru of the frigate *Tanager*," Saef said to the third Fleet rating in a row.

"But your ship authenticates as the merchant *Aurora*," the functionary said.

"Yes," Saef said with slipping patience. "This vessel is *Aurora*."

"I don't understand, Captain. Where's *Tanager*, then?"

Saef's heart sank at the question. "I had rather hoped she was here."

"No. *Tanager* is on a mission, which you would know if you really were Captain Sinclair-Maru."

Saef sighed. In fairness to the rating, a warship captain had likely never returned to base piloting some random merchant craft, in all the history of Fleet. "Listen, I am part of Commodore Zanka's squadron. If you could route a message to him, please—"

"Commodore Zanka is unavailable, which you would also know if you were really Captain Sinclair-Maru. I hope you realize that impersonating a Fleet officer carries serious consequences."

Saef shook his head. He wasn't thinking clearly. Of course Zanka wouldn't have returned from his cruise yet. He still ran his squadron with rigid economy, war or no war.

"Yes, of course," Saef said, striving for patience. "If you will only—"

"Standby, *Aurora*," the rating cut Saef abruptly off, leaving him stewing. He turned to Inga.

"You should get back to medical, Maru."

She shook her head. "Not yet. I feel some cloak-and-dagger nonsense in the offing."

Saef grimaced. "Does appear that way, doesn't it?"

Since they ran from their orbit of Delta Three, Inga and Wiley both languished in the cold grips of the techmedico, and neither was ready for more than a short walk even now.

The rating returned to the comm, now with a more peremptory tone. "*Aurora*, continue on your current heading and acceleration without deviation. You will be met and yield to Fleet cutter *Feist*. Acknowledge."

Saef's grimace grew more pronounced. "Acknowledged. Holding course and acceleration, yield to *Feist*. Please advise *Feist* we carry wounded Fleet personnel."

The rating made no comment and ended the transmission, leaving Saef in ominous silence. "There are a few steps to take before they come for us," Inga said in a quiet voice.

"Yes."

"Get the major. Talk. You may save each other. No one else may."

"Since *Tanager* is . . . is not here." Saef nearly said, *Since* Tanager *is gone*.

"Yes, unless Winter Yung intercedes."

"She won't," Saef said.

"This cargo we carry may compel someone."

Saef shook his head and stood. "A billion credits' worth of Shaper tech is the richest prize any frigate captain has ever captured."

"More than a billion," Inga said pulling the blanket tight across her shoulders. "Several billions."

"Worse still. Somebody high up is going to be embarrassed by this, aside from anything else we did at Delta Three."

"You underestimate greed, I think," Inga almost whispered, looking down. "The commodore and at least one admiral can become rich from their percentage on your prize. They will lie and backstab for that percentage . . . even if it helps you."

"But how do I navigate their greed, Maru? How do I steer clear of the stockade and hang onto some shred of honor in this?" Saef realized the ache in his chest had little to do with fear of the Admiralty or fear of losing his rich prize. He ached at the loss of *Tanager*, his crew, his first command, mourning every one of them already.

Inga placed one slender hand on Saef's arm. "Listen to me. Get the major. There is much to do before the cutter arrives."

Saef stared down at her wan features and shook his head. "You are in no shape for this."

"No. For what's to come, I'm in perfect shape."

The speed of *Feist's* arrival spoke volumes regarding the interest in Saef or his prize from some elevated quarter. The two ships matched velocity on *Aurora's* inbound course, and *Feist* expertly closed and locked. Moments later, ship-suited ratings came through the lock, each bearing a carbine in hand, not quite pointing at Saef and Major Mahdi, who stood waiting, in uniform, hands at their sides.

"Saef Sinclair-Maru?" one said, staring between Saef and Mahdi, as if they might have swapped uniforms.

"*Captain* Saef Sinclair-Maru, yes," Saef corrected.

"Yes, Captain, you are hereby detained. Please come with us."

Saef did not move. "This vessel is my lawful prize of war. I will surrender command to no one but a commissioned Fleet officer."

The rating shifted his carbine to point at Saef's chest. "I said, come with me, sir."

Saef glanced at Major Mahdi. "Seems he's trying to take my ship by force, Major."

"Looks that way, Captain," Mahdi rumbled. "Not following Fleet regs. Threatening violence."

"That's piracy, I believe," Saef mused. "What do you do with pirates, Major?"

"Kill them, mostly, Captain."

The rating took a hesitant step back, his weapon wavering. "Now that's enough—!"

"Call an officer, lad, or your life of piracy will be short," Mahdi said.

The rating made the call.

A lieutenant arrived through the connecting lock moments later, an irritated expression on her face. The sight of her ratings shuffling about uncertainly seemed to incite even greater wrath. Before she could formulate words, Saef stopped her.

"Lieutenant, you are aboard my lawful prize. Do you assume responsibility for the command and care of this vessel and her cargo?"

"I—you are being detained, Captain, and in no position to be giving orders to anyone!"

"So you threaten to seize my prize by force?" Saef asked.

The lieutenant glared. "You will yield and come with us peacefully, or you will be subdued."

"That's a 'yes,' I'd say," Major Mahdi growled. "Whole flock of pirates in Fleet uniforms."

"Lieutenant," Saef said, "it would likely be healthier for everyone if you followed Fleet regulations. You are attempting to practice piracy, and it is my duty to resist."

Before the red-faced lieutenant could do more than place a hand upon her sidearm, a hatch slid open and she looked into the certain death of a gaping muzzle. Corporal Hastings, sheathed in the adamantine bulk of Imperial battledress, filled the hatchway.

Saef snapped his fingers and the lieutenant's startled gaze snapped back to him. "So, Lieutenant, do we follow Fleet regulations? Or do my Marines take you and your ship as pirates?"

Inga's prescient gambit worked, and they cleared the first hurdle in retaining *Aurora* as *Tanager*'s lawful prize.

The inbound trip aboard *Feist* may have been the fastest transit ever aboard a Fleet vessel. As a new intrasystem cutter, *Feist* offered top interceptor performance, though for the moment she served as little more than a high-speed ferry. Aside from Saef and Major Mahdi, *Feist* bore the wounded, Inga and Wiley, and Saef was surprised to see Inga's dumb-mech hitching an unobtrusive ride beneath her suspension cot, looking as though it belonged there.

Even with *Feist*'s remarkable speed, Saef knew their destination arrived too quickly for it to be the Strand, so he was not surprised when *Feist*'s rating led them through a lock connection aboard yet another ship. As soon as Saef set foot on the new ship, his Fleet command UI disappeared, sending another confirmation of his plight. He found the Deep Man as they marched Mahdi and him straight to a sterile conference chamber, and Saef looked over his shoulder to see Inga and Wiley disappearing down the corridor on their suspension cots as the hatch slid shut.

A heavyworld captain sat at the table, flanked by a pair of security ratings and a Marine colonel, also heavyworld. The tabletop holo projector bore the embossed name VICTORY upon it, and from that alone Saef now knew what vessel he had joined. The dark and silent Fleet UI left him feeling blind and excluded even as he recalled the last time he saw *Victory*'s scarred hull as he entered Core system, not many weeks before.

"Captain, Major, I am Captain Newton, and this is Colonel Veidt," *Victory*'s captain began, his face blank of expression, "I would apologize for the irregularities of these proceedings, but your own dereliction, your own abysmal lack of judgment has created the need."

"Perhaps there is some error here," Saef said. "I am Captain Sinclair-Maru. You must have mistaken us for someone else."

Captain Newton glowered but it was not his voice that spoke next. "There is no mistake, upstart," the grating voice of Admiral Nifesh ground out as the holo tank came to life. The blunt, bald head and gleaming eyes seemed locked upon Saef. "You are the one, paragon. You are the one who returns without your command or your crew. You are the one who perpetrated crimes upon the people of Delta Three. You are the one who brought complaints to the Emperor himself. Yes, you are the one who clearly violated the letter and the spirit of your written orders."

Saef found the Deep Man and a measure of calm stoicism. "You are mistaken, Admiral. We thwarted an enemy ambush, destroyed enemy assets, and captured a rich and lawful prize."

"A prize?" Nifesh said. "You raid a loyal system and seize a peaceful, unarmed vessel. That is piracy. It is treachery."

"I witnessed—" Major Mahdi began, but Nifesh cut him off.

"Silence! *Tanager*'s Marines will have their time to speak."

Captain Newton cleared his throat. "Captain Sinclair-Maru, do you possess *Tanager*'s log?"

"No, Captain."

"Have any of your bridge officers survived?"

"None are currently on-system," Saef said.

"Hah!" Nifesh crowed. "Not on-system."

"Do you acknowledge that your written orders specified a strict scouting mission, with no authorization for action?" Captain Newton asked.

"I do," Saef said.

"Do you admit, then, that you broke your orders and initiated an attack upon Delta Three assets?"

"I do not."

Nifesh barked a laugh at this, but Captain Newton continued in the same tone. "Do you take responsibility for the Delta Three regional governor's death, or do you place the blame upon Major Mahdi?"

"Neither," Saef said. "He was killed by enemy action."

"And you have proof of this?" the captain inquired with raised eyebrows.

"There is a vidcapture in the major's battledress system," Saef said.

"For security reasons, the battledress systems aboard the merchant ship *Aurora* had their memories purged, I'm afraid," Captain Newton said.

Saef's heart sank. Inga had warned him, but he could not believe that any Fleet personnel would stoop so low in deleting valuable intelligence just to aid a prosecution.

Admiral Nifesh uttered a low chuckle. "All that bravado . . . and yet the ground disappears beneath your feet."

Captain Newton seemed to wince at Nifesh's words. Clearly he wished to maintain a veneer of impersonal justice despite the very personal nature of the admiral's intent.

"Every question will be answered in the official Board review," Saef said.

"Captain, this *is* your official Board review," Captain Newton said.

Saef felt his fists clench, his heart hammering through his control for a moment. "This? One captain, one colonel, and one admiral in the conference room of a warship?"

"Very pretty," Mahdi growled. "Far from the public eye."

"Be silent until you are addressed, Major!" Nifesh snapped.

Victory's captain folded his hands. "Captain, do you have any idea how the outer systems regard an unprovoked attack by Fleet forces? They may have enemy propaganda whispered in their ears every day, now suddenly confirmed by your illegal actions with Delta Three."

"We must plug the breach," Nifesh added. "We

must be swift, severe, and certain, with no hint of justification for the actions of young rogue captains with mercenary intentions."

Saef felt the reality sink into his gut. This review was only a show. Nothing he said would make the slightest difference in the outcome. They would happily sacrifice him to placate whatever voices had screamed in outrage, and the truth meant nothing now.

The farce thus continued, them asking pointless questions, Saef offering pointless answers, continually robbed of context. But, under the shelter of the Deep Man, Saef's mind and emotions drifted away from the shameful production. He need only await the inevitable, far from the Nets and any protection the Sinclair-Maru family might provide. Neither he nor Inga had anticipated such a swift and thorough response.

Victory's capacious medical bay contained only Inga Maru, a physician, and a grumbling, grousing Wiley. The remainder of the large space held empty suspension cots and various treatment mechanisms.

The systems monitoring the apparently comatose Inga Maru saw only what she wished them to see, but beneath her closed eyelids her eyes flickered. Secreted in the recesses of the suspension cot beneath Inga, the dumb-mech received signals from Inga's UI, amplifying and conditioning them as it prepared a digital payload.

Inga had learned much from Loki in their brief time together, and *Victory's* Intelligence was no Loki. Her slow, careful intrusion into *Victory's* systems progressed, seeming to take hours, but she ceaselessly labored.

The attending physician walked over to Inga's cot

and glanced at the monitors. Her condition seemed unchanged, and he was about to move on when he saw the bead of sweat trailing down Inga's temple. He stared, leaning nearer.

"Doc! Help! Doc!" Wiley yelled from his cot. "Your damned machine is trying to violate me. Help!"

The physician glared at Wiley for a moment, then spotted Wiley's imminent assault on sensitive instruments, a bedpan clutched defensively in his hands. He rushed off, leaving Inga to her work, and a slow smile crossed her lips as her eyes continued to flicker. Her mind slipped through *Victory*'s digital vitals, bypassing clumsy gates, slithering, probing.

There ... almost, almost.

She prepared to release the weapon she had waiting in the electronic magazine of the dumb-mech; a poison pill she had quickly readied hours earlier.

Sprawled and still upon the medical cot, wounded and weakened, Inga once again embodied the silent hand, the subtlety of the Sinclair-Maru. With the faint whisper of an exhale, she launched her attack.

Saef continued to woodenly answer each question, still feeling little emotion from the flagrant disregard for truth or context. Major Mahdi sat beside him in glowering silence.

Admiral Nifesh spoke in conclusive tones. "Despite your lack of willingness to assume responsibility, I believe we have heard more than enough to render judgment."

Victory's captain slowly nodded, and the Marine colonel nodded with even greater reluctance.

This was the cliff edge racing toward him, Saef knew.

Though he held little doubt that facts would eventually exonerate him to some extent, irreparable damage would already be served to him, to the Sinclair-Maru Family... to an immense fortune represented in his prize, *Aurora*. In all likelihood, the results of this parody of justice would end his Fleet career and possibly destroy his life.

Yet, to the edge, the irrevocable edge, they flew. Neither Inga's tricks nor Major Mahdi's facts would accomplish anything once the gavel dropped.

"Very well, then. With the honor and efficiency of Fleet as our goal, in service to the greater Imperium, this abridged review Board has only one choice, based upon the evidence and testimony obtained here," Nifesh said, now with a solemn demeanor, the gleam of pleasure only visible in his eyes. "This Board finds Captain Sinclair—"

"This is a mockery," Major Mahdi snarled at last, unable to hold his peace any longer.

"Be still, brother," the heavyworld Marine colonel said, his expression sympathetic.

"You fools. Playing these games while our people—"

"Silence! You hear me? Silence!" Nifesh yelled, his face suffused within the holo. "You will face your own crimes soon enough, Major! Aiding this uprising through your actions!"

"There is no uprising, fool!" Mahdi shouted. "There is an *invasion*!"

"Silence him, if he will not silence himself," Nifesh ordered, and two ratings bracketed the major. He glared at them each in turn, but closed his mouth on the host of words that remained unspoken. The Marine colonel stared at Mahdi, puzzled by the substance of his outburst.

"As I said before," Nifesh said, "based upon the evidence and testimony, this Board has only one choi—*What is it now?*"

Each of the four view monitors had sprung suddenly to life, each displaying the same rain-swept stretch of darkened road, the two skimcars sliding to a halt in a shower of sparks.

"What's this?" Nifesh demanded. "Captain, why are you displaying this?"

Captain Newton stared at the monitors without comprehension. "I'm not doing this."

The image on the screens split, one half of each screen showing a wide-angle view of the two skimcars, the other half clearly a vidstream flowing from the battledress-clad Marine who loped up to one skimcar, the insignia of the Imperial Marines glowing from his adamantine carapace.

"Stop this immediately, Captain," Nifesh ordered. Captain Newton placed hurried calls, but Marine Colonel Veidt just watched the screen, his face a grim mask. A figure on the screen pointed a weapon seemingly right into the camera and fired, clearly initiating violence against an Imperial Marine. As the return fire slammed both attendants back, Captain Newton threw up his hands.

"It's streaming through every monitor on the ship."

"Well, shut them down! Do you hear me?"

"I'm trying, sir."

The monitor screens poured out the sight and sound of that night on Delta Three to the massive crew of *Victory* who all stared, transfixed wherever they stood or sat. Saef stared also, feeling the warm coal of hope igniting in his belly. *Inga . . .*

"*Do you remain loyal to the Imperium?*" Major

Mahdi's voice resounded from every screen aboard *Victory*, and the chilling visage of the grinning female attendant communicated only wrongness to everyone who stared, transfixed by the image.

"It's them!" Nifesh barked. "It's his crew, Captain. Search them. Stop them from doing this."

Colonel Veidt shook his head, never looking from the screen. "It is too late," he rumbled in a low voice.

"There's no rebellion,—Don't you see?" the regional governor of Delta Three screeched on the screen, his terror evident to every viewer as he edged from the grinning creature beside him. *"They're not human, even! Kill it!"*

Even Nifesh's bluster fell silent at the sight of a well-dressed female citizen grinning joyfully as she slashed at the governor's neck. The vidstream continued long enough for all to see her struck down, ending even as the governor's life ended.

The screens fell silent and dark, and Nifesh immediately babbled, "This changes nothing!"

Captain Newton looked away uncertainly, but Colonel Veidt spoke. "It changes everything."

"Evidence illegally obtained. Illegally presented."

The colonel shook his head. "We have a possible nonhuman invasion, and you're worried about rules of evidence?"

"What invasion? A crazy woman with a knife?"

Captain Newton slowly raised his head to stare at Nifesh in the holo, his expression incredulous. "Admiral, what is it that you want?"

"You know what we must have. Order. Justice."

"Justice?" the captain repeated, looking down. "Or is this more of a personal vengeance?"

"Watch your words, Captain," Nifesh said. "This paragon violated every element of his written orders."

"You . . . you should be overjoyed, Admiral. Overjoyed." Captain Newton said, his voice rising.

"Do not forget yourself, Captain."

"Here we have *proof* that Delta Three falsely accused Fleet officers. The stain can be wiped clean, honor restored. Are you so blind?"

Nifesh seemed to quiver with rage. "I see plainly enough. I see weak officers unwilling to do their duty. I see naïve children in a fantasyland. This is not over!"

Colonel Veidt stood. "My apologies, Admiral, I will take no further part in this. There is no quorum without me. It is over."

"Over?" Nifesh replied. "It has just begun. Another Board—a more reliable Board—will do the hard work you are too weak to handle. This paragon will be judged. His prize will be condemned. He will pay for his lost command, for violating orders. He will be broken!"

Saef and Mahdi stared at Nifesh in his apoplexy, both sharing the sense of desperate relief. Any review Board to follow could not compare with the horror they had just avoided.

Captain Newton leaned to one side as a rating whispered urgently in his ear. "What's that?" Nifesh demanded. "Did you discover the saboteur who raided your systems?"

The captain's face underwent several indecipherable changes before he composed himself. "No, Admiral, it is excellent news. . . . Outer defense platforms report a new contact just arrived on-system." He paused and Nifesh frowned, sensing what was to come. "You will be pleased to hear it is *Tanager*, badly damaged but accelerating inbound."

Saef felt the greatest weight fall from his shoulders, drawing his first full breath in what seemed days. While Admiral Nifesh looked anything but pleased. "Good," Nifesh said. "At his next review Board we will have the logs and witnesses to explain exactly how this prodigy violated every element of his orders and took it upon himself to drop troops in an unauthorized invasion of Delta Three. I look forward to hearing him talk his way out of that."

Saef said nothing, his internal cheer undiminished as he stared at the admiral's scarred and bitter face in the holo. Nifesh pursed his lips. "It hardly seems the best of times for such an ordeal in your Family, prodigy, what with your Family's recent tragedy." The barely suppressed tone of satisfaction chilled Saef as much as the words themselves.

At Saef's expression of blank incomprehension, Nifesh continued with obvious relish. "Oh, am I the first to bear such sad tidings? You hadn't heard about Bess Sinclair-Maru? Hopefully you were not especially close because"—he could not restrain his smile now—"her demise is surely upon your head."

Chapter 41

"Fire refines, it purifies and tempers.
It also causes third-degree burns."

—Devlin Sinclair-Maru, *Integrity Mirror*

COMMANDER SUSAN ROUSH STOOD BEFORE THE
Admiralty Board in her rigidly perfect uniform, but
her lip curled in disdain. The last time she stood
in this very room, these same admirals had unfairly
stripped her of all that mattered in her life, and she
wanted nothing more than to make them eat every
self-righteous word they uttered that day.

"Commander," Admiral Fisker said, "you assumed
command of *Tanager* when Captain Sinclair-Maru was
disabled, you say. What caused his affliction?"

"It is not clear, Admiral. There was an attack
on his person by a ship services rating, and shortly
thereafter he was comatose. It seemed possible that
the two could be connected."

"What insanity possessed you to break Fleet protocol
and conduct an intrasystem transition?" Nifesh broke in.

Roush clenched her jaw momentarily but her voice remained steady as she answered. "When I last stood before you, my lords, I was chided for my temerity, when I followed the direct orders of my superior officer, rather than violating those orders for the sake of . . . boldness. I kept your words firmly in mind as I formed every decision. How could I follow a mere efficiency protocol when the life of the captain might depend upon my *bold* action?"

"How commendable," Fisker murmured. "It is good to know that our words are so closely followed."

The questions continued on and on all morning, some dealing with minute elements of command, others dwelling upon the decision to launch Marines down into the well, and into their assault on Delta Three station. For every question Roush held an answer.

"Did you ever think that launching Marines planetside might spark a rather natural defensive response from the Planetary Guard?" Admiral Char asked, although his demeanor throughout the review remained neutral.

"Major Mahdi and I considered the risk to be minimal if the planetary government remained loyal to the Imperium," Roush said. "And if the rebellion secretly ruled, holding or freeing the regional governor seemed our best chance to escape the system."

"Six battledress systems?" Nifesh growled. "Never mind how such a little scrub of a frigate managed to field so many, you risked *six* battledress systems on the off chance they could pull a miracle from your disaster?"

"Eight Marines dropped into the well, Admiral.

Six ran battledress, as is their right. We all worked to achieve the success we attained."

"Success?" Nifesh scoffed. "Success? You bring your ship back little better than a bare hulk, you consumed resources as if they were made to be burned, you lost numerous crew members and Marines. And your written orders specifically stated to observe *only*! It is a mission of compounding failures, just short of disaster. How can you stand before us and speak of success?"

Roush's mouth thinned down to a line. "My lords, I have served Fleet for decades, always with the highest efficiency ratings, always with the greatest economy and prudence, only to lose my rank. You may recall how I was chastised for 'temerity and thrift,' and encouraged to become, and I quote, 'aggressive, independent, and courageous,' willing to 'take some risks and engage the enemy.'" She looked each of the admirals in the eye, one after the other. "I was aggressive and independent. I took great risks. I engaged the enemy. And, so help me, I kicked their asses!"

"Captain Sinclair-Maru," Admiral Fisker began, as the other admirals frowned down at him from her left and right. "We have heard the reports of your officers, we have attempted to review your ship's log, although the record seems to suffer from technical issues, and we have gathered what intel we could from Delta Three. Taken together, the Admiralty Board is placed in a situation without precedent."

Saef said nothing, finding the Deep Man. The actions of the Fleet Admiralty could not be predicted. On one hand, they could break him, end his Fleet career, and worse, while on the other hand stood promotion, a new combat command and the all-important issue of his prize: the ship *Aurora*, crammed full of the galaxy's most valuable cargo.

Tanager's officers may have presented an air of indifference regarding the possibility of enrichment, but all, including Saef, internally counted their percentage over and over. If Fleet Articles were adhered to, his captain's percentage would amount to a purse of some three hundred million credits; enough to largely restore the Sinclair-Maru fortunes, if not obtain the old Family estate adjoining the Imperial Close. Even the lowliest rating on *Tanager* stood to be enriched by the prize . . . if the Admiralty simply followed the Articles.

"We are troubled that your vessel's activities in the Delta Three system bear no resemblance to the mission detailed in your written orders. On that basis alone this body could and would condemn every action you took, regardless of the beneficial outcome, except for two things: the fact that each step of *Tanager*'s mission fell subject to exigent circumstances, and the testimony of Commodore Zanka, who assures us that he may have verbally added imperatives beyond your written orders." Fisker's expression remained bland although she undoubtedly knew that Commodore Zanka did nothing of the kind. His fat percentage of Saef's prize depended upon the perceived legitimacy of *Tanager*'s mission. Zanka would swear to anything at all for sixty million credits.

"With the subject of your written orders aside," Fisker continued, "we have twists and complications beyond number. We have no record of a wartime captain ceding command due to physical disability, then seizing an enemy vessel before reassuming command."

Admiral Nifesh snorted derisively and scowled.

"We have no record of a fighting captain spending much of his mission in a coma," Fisker said, not looking at Nifesh. "And it has been centuries since a Fleet vessel returned to base as extensively damaged as *Tanager*, fit only for salvage."

Fisker regarded Saef for a long moment, the other four admirals also staring. "Along with shipping a collection of agent provocateurs or mutineers, and suffering numerous crew casualties, we can only say that there are many troubling marks against you."

"Running scared, too," Nifesh grumbled.

Fisker inclined her head. "Yes. Returning to Core System before your own damaged vessel transitioned presents an image distasteful to us. Some might argue that cowardice could be alleged."

Saef felt his pulse increase, but before Saef opened his mouth, Fisker held up a hand. "We heard the testimony of your officers and Marines who attest to your personal courage. We speak only of appearances."

Saef still bridled internally. Should he have idled blindly about Delta Three system, risking *Aurora*'s cargo so valuable to their enemy, while *Tanager* strove to escape *and* defend him?

"Still," Fisker went on, "looking to the positive side of the ledger, *Tanager* brought us a notable victory in an unequal fight."

Nifesh snorted. "Frigate actions! No impact on the contest at all."

"Compared to Fleet's other great victories?" Admiral Char dryly inquired. Nifesh shot him a poisonous glare, and Fisker continued.

"Ton for ton, this was the finest Fleet victory in centuries," she said. "And *Tanager*'s Marines conducted a highly successful raid planetside that I'm told is the new model for all such operations." There was no more talk of violating Delta Three's peaceful territory. All communication from Delta Three had ceased shortly before *Tanager* arrived back in Core system, and their final accusations were now viewed as nothing more than enemy misinformation.

"Now there is the matter of the merchant vessel *Aurora,* and her cargo," Fisker said, and Saef's heart sank. Fisker should have called it his *prize*, but she refrained from that loaded term. "We recognize the great service you have rendered by denying *Aurora*'s cargo to our enemy, but some members of this board"—she did not quite glance at Nifesh—"have correctly pointed out that *Aurora* served as a conveyance for you when your own ship was unavailable." Admiral Nifesh and his heavyworld comrade shared a satisfied look. "While the war-prize provisions of Fleet Articles were intended for the seizure of enemy vessels in addition to one's own."

"So I should have selected another vessel available to me," Saef offered in a mild tone. "Something faster or more powerful, to make my escape more certain."

"No," Admiral Char rumbled. "You did the right thing, Captain. Never doubt it."

"We are not blind to the services you rendered," the sole lightworld admiral said, "but the Admiralty must carefully balance many factors in our decisions. The majority of this Board would like to see you in another more conventional combat command, in part a recognition of the *Tanager*'s victories in Delta Three."

"Others on this Board see only carelessness, disobedience, and dumb luck!" Nifesh snapped. "So consider yourself fortunate to wear your rank!"

"Nonetheless," Fisker stepped smoothly in, "every decision of the Admiralty must take into account the long-term impact upon the morale and fighting spirit of all Fleet officers. To leave the successes of *Tanager*'s cruise and the capture of such a valuable asset unrewarded would sow confusion and dismay among fighting captains throughout Fleet."

Saef felt the returning glimmer of hope.

Fisker stared down at Saef and he fancied he saw some hint of warmth in her eyes, while Nifesh and his heavyworld companion glowered down at her side. "After considering all available facts and testimony, this Board finds Captain Sinclair-Maru absolved of charges of dereliction, and commends the captain for enabling the smooth operation of the IMS *Tanager* that resulted in the destruction of the enemy vessels *Carthage* and *Digger*."

The glimmer in Saef's chest became a glow.

"Although the Board does not recognize the vessel *Aurora* as a lawful prize of war"—Saef's joy flickered— "we do recognize *Tanager*'s salvage rights."

The Family barristers had warned that a salvage ruling represented a likely outcome, so the hard figures came immediately to Saef's mind. The math problem was painfully simple: Every officer and rating aboard *Tanager* could reduce their lovely fat purse of prize earnings by ninety percent. Saef's three-hundred-million-credit prize became a mere thirty million, in one blow of the gavel; still one of the greatest purses awarded to a Fleet captain in the history of Fleet.

Any other captain would certainly be overjoyed with such a windfall, but Saef owed heavy debts that he could scarcely repay. He bowed to the Admiralty Board, his mind moving immediately to the very personal nature of the responsibilities before him. A painful path awaited, but the Admiralty left a tool in his hands. He might yet achieve his goals and the goals of his Family.

As Saef entered the fusty hall outside the Admiralty chambers, Inga fell in beside him, her cloak swirling. Saef looked sidelong at her before looking back to the path ahead. "It seems you saved my neck again, Maru. You cloak and dagger marvelously."

"It's a start."

"Now a little downtime before our shot to Battersea or we finagle another ship."

"No. One more terror to face, I fear."

Saef stopped and looked at her. "What is it now?"

Inga's half smile lit her face. "Just a party, that's all."

Saef grimaced. "Gods."

The White Swan Hotel's smallest banquet hall held *Tanager*'s survivors with room to spare. Many still wore the marks of their injuries along with their best uniforms, and Chief Sandi Patel carried one arm bound in a sling, a victim of Tilly Pennysmith's dueling sword. For a group of people who had just had their potential new fortunes reduced by ninety percent, the cheer among them seemed unabated. This might be due to the fact that even their ten percent still represented decades of Fleet salary in their pockets. The least among them now possessed a considerable nest egg, so even Sandi Patel, reprimanded for various sins, then wounded by the unassuming Pennysmith, managed a degree of ebullience.

Inga Maru perched on the edge of a white-spread table, within arm's reach of assorted rich snacks, her boot-encased leg idly swinging. She nibbled fruit and observed the interactions of her shipmates, noting Saef's uneasiness with all the good will aimed his direction. Sergeant Kabir and the other Marines momentarily surrounded him, drinks in hand, clapping him on the shoulder. She watched Saef's mouth flicker into a rare smile, and she smiled herself. Claude Carstairs had insisted on hosting this celebration despite Saef's reluctance, and Inga saw the good that it proffered. Forced to interact with all the former Tanagers in his moment of triumph, Saef might reap benefits even now.

"Doesn't come easy to him, does it?" Major Mahdi murmured from close at hand.

Inga turned to regard the major through her eyelashes, her smile broadening. "My, Major, you clean up rather fine." The major glanced down at his dress uniform and shrugged, taking a drink from his clinking glass. Inga took another nibble of her fruit and said, "No, it doesn't come easy to him." She looked back at Saef in the middle of the room. "He lacks patience for social banter."

"His life is a mission," Mahdi observed.

"Like yours."

Mahdi nodded, musing, putting his glass to his lips. "Like mine." He eased his heavyworld weight down on the edge of the table beside Inga, prompting protesting squeaks from its straining frame.

"Tell me, Chief, on that station, what did you see? Hmm?"

She turned slowly back to face the major, looking up at him through the fringe of her hair, staring at the side of his face. "Your Marines saw what I saw... ask them."

"My Marines saw a flock of enemies cut down all about that medical bay."

"The captain's lethality is quite well known, Major."

"And him without a drop of blood on him, I hear."

Inga smirked and looked away. "Oh hardly, sir."

"And you, regular baptized in it."

"What do you wish to hear, Major?"

Mahdi mused for a moment. "Nothing, maybe." He rubbed a hand over his smooth scalp. "The Admiralty Board wouldn't touch the nonhuman bit. Ran from it like scared cats."

"And you think I possess some morsel of knowledge that can force them to face facts?"

"Do you?"

Inga smiled broadly, taking a bite of fruit. "Nothing will make them face these facts . . . yet."

Major Mahdi nodded, staring into the distance. "That's the next mission. The fools."

"Chief Maru?" Claude Carstairs strode up, his slender figure resplendent in gold and white. "It is 'chief,' right? Not a military man m'self, you see—Oh, I say!" Claude broke off to stare at Inga's tall boot still idly swinging. "However do you get such a gloss? My own boots seem shabby things by comparison."

Major Mahdi regarded Claude with lowered brows, but Inga gave him her wide-eyed smile. "You must have top-secret military polish, I daresay?" Claude continued, transfixed. "Classified info, eh?"

"Not at all," Inga said. "I just soak my boots in the blood of my enemies."

Claude's eyes bulged. *"In the blood . . . ?* What a ghastly thought. Glad I'm not Fleet, despite the damned fine uniforms! Got no stomach for it, you know?"

Mahdi stifled a chuckle as Claude wandered off into the small crowd, murmuring, "Blood? Gods!"

"Teasing the poor fellow," Mahdi said, "just when all us Tanagers could likely use his fashion advice, now that we've all got a little coin to spare."

Inga shook her head and sipped from her glass.

"What?" Mahdi said, looking down at her. "Aren't you going to indulge a little in your new wealth?"

Inga stared out at Saef, still holding his own among the cheerful Tanagers. "No. I already spent all mine."

Mahdi stared, surprised. "Already spent . . . ?" He considered the odd, reserved chief perched beside him, and kept himself from asking, *What in blazes could you have spent it all on so quickly?*

After an internal struggle that lasted hours, Susan Roush slipped into her dress uniform and stood regarding her reflection, displeased with the sneer she observed upon her own lips. Only when her eyes rested upon the rank tabs did the sneer melt away. She could not resist touching the captain's bars, and cursed herself for nearly weeping.

Yes, despite her pride, despite everything she had said in moments of burning indignation, she had to go. With her sword and pistol in place, Susan Roush hailed a skimcar and set off for the White Swan.

When she arrived, Captain Roush nearly yielded to misgivings yet again. She stood at the entrance of the banquet hall and scanned across the collection of her most recent shipmates, all celebrating together. In her decades of Fleet service, in scores and scores of challenging floats, she had never been a part of a crew with such cause for celebration. And there stood that proud Sinclair-Maru upstart, bathed in the adulation of an increasingly lubricated crew, when he had spent so many of the critical hours far from *Tanager*'s command seat!

Saef's eyes looked past the crowd surrounding him, locking onto Susan Roush. He quickly hushed everyone, never looking from her, and raised his glass. Captain Susan Roush, veteran of the greatest space battles in recent history, hero of the Delta Three conflagration, stood transfixed, absurd butterflies in her belly.

"Tanagers!" Saef boomed out, a slight flush visible on his cheeks, "I give you *Captain* Susan Roush, the finest captain in Fleet, and whom we all may thank for our good fortune and our lives!"

The Tanagers roared their approval, and Susan Roush felt lost in the waves of conflicting emotions. Someone placed a full glass in her hand and she saw the faces of *her* bridge crew passing by in a swirl of good will. There was that fearful Che Ramos, who held together through it all, Lieutenant Ruprecht, Tilly Pennysmith, Deckchief Church, and there was Julie Yeager, now out of uniform, moving to civilian life with her new fortune. For a moment the image of that competent chief, Phillipa Baker, and the surprisingly heroic Farley both came to her eyes, both gone now, lost, but the next instant Saef Sinclair-Maru stood before her. An island of isolation seemed to open around them, and Roush found the words that she had so dreaded coming easily to her tongue.

"I told you I would never thank you, upstart!" she said, and Saef solemnly nodded. "But, gods damn it all, thank you! Thank you."

Saef smiled as she scowled around at the small

crowd all talking at once. "That'll have to do," she called over the noise, "'cause you'll never hear it again, you understand?"

"I understand," Saef said. "Captain."

Any citizen observing Saef Sinclair-Maru's trip into the prestigious Medical Specialties Center might quickly place three facts together, and come to a very understandable conclusion. Everyone knew the young captain from the history-book family had made a fresh mark, winning a small fortune doing it. Nearly everyone knew of the Sinclair-Maru's fading fortunes, the un-rejuvenated aging of their more recent generations. Thus, nearly anyone might assume that Saef Sinclair-Maru entered the Medical Specialties Center to spend a few million of his new wealth obtaining the first-level rejuv treatments. Certainly for most Vested Citizens, the only purpose for high-risk employment was the eventual promise of rejuv treatments.

Saef entered the center alone, moving past the opulent admission rooms, with all their glowing advertisements of youth and beauty, continuing down a lengthy hall to a small room guarded by two Family security operatives. They both looked at Saef as he drew near, then looked past Saef, tensing.

"Captain," the sultry voice of Winter Yung called out as Saef turned. Winter Yung looked weary, Saef immediately realized. Tired and...disturbed? "May I...may I accompany you, please?" she asked.

Saef felt a strong inclination to refuse this request, but the hint of frailty defeated him, quieting the anger that stirred in him toward Winter and all that she represented. "Very well, Consul." They turned and walked together between the two security operatives, Saef nodded to them as he led the way.

The lump of cellular matter trailing tubes and wires bore only vague resemblance to a human being, but Saef knew that he beheld all that remained of Bess Sinclair-Maru, shattered and dismembered by enemy weaponry. They both stood in silence beside the bed.

"So I have you to thank for this?" Saef asked, staring down.

Did he speak of the costly life support that maintained the flicker of life? Or did he refer to the horrific injuries Bess had sustained?

"Yes," Winter said.

Saef nodded, and they stood together in silence for some time, the whirring and sighing of machinery the only sound. "What have you done to discover who did this?" Saef asked at last.

Winter drew a breath. "Everything. Every damned thing." She stepped from Saef's side to gaze down at an arcane medical monitor. "I have broken laws, shattered people. I have sifted House Barabas until little remains."

"And?" Saef asked quietly. "Do you yet know who pulls the strings?"

"I think so." Winter nodded slowly, her face a bleak plane.

"They are not human, are they?"

Winter looked away, her mind filled with an indelible image of a grinning man, shackled down, his body a ruin, calmly observing every action of his interrogators. "At the very top, no. It does not seem they are human."

"And yet the Admiralty ignores my report? They do not even touch the topic in my Board?"

"I know."

"You realize what the slaughter of Delta Three station means?"

Winter turned to look at Saef, waiting.

"There may be no one left alive on any of the rebel-held worlds. They may all be dead, harvested, or...turned...infected...whatever it is called."

"Only those with implants, it seems," Winter said.

"What is the connection to the Shapers?"

Winter shook her head, her gaze distant. "Parasites?"

"Parasites?"

"Who can say?"

They fell silent, both gazing down at the remaining bits of Bess Sinclair-Maru. "Thank you," Saef said at last. "I don't understand why you did this for Bess, but..."

Winter shrugged, her porcelain features drawn. "I'd have done more, but they say she needs a full rejuv to have a chance at reconstruction."

"Expense account tapped, Consul?"

Winter shot a pained look at Saef, to his surprise. "Never mind," he said. "My responsibility, anyway."

Winter's expression changed to one of incredulity. "I thought you came to... You're going to buy her reconstruction? You realize that even then she may never fully recover?"

Saef nodded.

"You understand the expense?"

Saef nodded again. "I also begin to understand the war that we are in. We are losing." He paused, frowning. "You think Bess was the first assassination by *them*?"

"The Emperor's assassins," she said. "Yes. It has been in my thinking these last days."

"Roush, Mahdi, you . . . and the House of Sinclair-Maru . . . we need allies."

"And Bess?" Winter said.

"If I can regain her, she'll understand where Cabot will not," Saef said. "She'll gather support."

Winter hoped he was right, hoped that Bess might still be herself after reconstruction. She nodded. "And you?"

Saef stared at Winter Yung with grave intensity. "The fools gave me another ship," he said.

Winter perceived that strange Sinclair-Maru solidity, an unreal calm in the midst of swirling terrors. She felt it, but she could not grasp the dimensions of Saef's internal fortress.

"I will be fighting," Saef said, at peace within the Deep Man.

Chapter 42

"Do not mock the softer skills and traits. Empathy, humor, and courtesy create bonds that remain curiously strong in troubled times."

—Devlin Sinclair-Maru, *Integrity Mirror*

JUST OFF THE STRAND, IN ORBIT AROUND COREWORLD, lay an odd accumulation of old ships, satellites, and stations auctioned off for parts or scrap. In previous decades the collection of junk rarely included any Fleet castoffs. Now, after a disastrous opening to war, the accumulation included many hulls and components of Fleet provenance. One small frigate lay among all the other tortured metal, its hardpoints slagged, its hull rent and patched. Considered an antique before it set off on its final mission, the IMS *Tanager* hardly warranted consideration before the Fleet assayers condemned her hull and sent her to the salvage auction.

Barely spaceworthy, *Tanager*'s auction brought few bids, and now she lay awaiting her fate, likely as components for some belter mine operation.

The salvage pod's dark, worn passageways led Inga Maru to an equally dark airlock. She entered, her cloak gathered about her in the cold. When the lock cycled onto *Tanager*'s quarterdeck, and the scent of wilted socks reached Inga's nose, she felt an odd level of emotion rise within her. The dark and lifeless corridors only heightened this.

Her breath puffed visibly out before her face as she moved slowly down a familiar companionway, now rendered strange and dreamlike in the dark, cold silence. Inga knew the Fleet provosts had stripped the fissionable weapons and Shaper fuel from *Tanager*, just as they did with any decommissioned vessels, and they likely performed some level of purge on the memory banks of the ship's crystal computer stacks. In their minds, every part of *Tanager* was little better than junk *before* she set off for Delta Three, and only Inga knew the true significance of what *Tanager*'s crystal stacks had somehow spawned. That *phenomenon* they may have purged, destroyed with heedless ignorance. As she walked down the cold, echoing companionway, she sensed nothing and feared the worst.

At the waist hatch she paused, remembering so clearly the attack that had occurred just beyond the hatch, thwarted by Loki's timely warning. She felt nothing for the ship services rating she had struck down just there, but the loss of Loki, that obsessive, childish, annoying entity…that brought a rare burning to Inga's eyes.

She placed her hand on the manual latch, surprised to feel moisture on its metallic surface. The waist hatch actuated and Inga saw a glimmer of yellow light ahead, on the far side of the darkened recreation area. In a few

quick steps she saw the glow and heard the soft bubbling
hiss from the small fish tank. A pair of fish miraculously
swam about the singular source of heat and light.

"Loki . . ." Inga whispered.

She felt her skin prickle as power slowly gathered
around her.

The voice whispered into the dark around her. *"I
have been sold, Chief."* Inga's head bowed, her eyes
closed. *"I am salvage. When these last fish perish, I
will be alone."*

Inga sank down to the deck, feeling tears track
down both cheeks in the cold. Loki had been too long
alone, cut off from human interaction, Nets access,
or even optical scopes to slake his ravenous curiosity.

"Did . . . did the provosts harm you?" Inga managed.

She felt Loki's focus slowly swirl around her. "They
tried." Loki's voice sounded near, almost in Inga's ear,
then far, beside his last fishy companions. "They found
only what I gave them."

"Loki . . . I . . . I am sorry it took so long for me to
come."

"Wise, Chief. I no longer provide utility. I am
Fleet no more."

"No, no. Loki, it isn't that."

"I have been sold. I am salvage. Am I malfunctioning? I am. I am. I am."

"No!" Inga stood up and closed her eyes until tears
squeezed from the corners. "Loki, do you hear me?"

"I always hear, Chief." Loki's voice settled around her.

"You are valuable . . . special . . . to me."

"I am salvage. They sold me."

"They did not know," Inga pleaded. "They didn't
understand."

"I have been very alone, Chief. No crew. The fish began to die. And they sold me."

"And I bought you," Inga said.

Loki's presence fell into Inga's UI, washing through her awareness at last.

"Chief, are you joking? Do you joke?" Loki's audible voice filled the room, but it was hardly necessary, Inga's mind interwove with Loki once again. "You bought me?"

"I . . . I bought *Tanager*."

"It is salvage. I am salvage."

"No, Loki. You're not," Inga said.

"You bought me?"

"I freed you. No one will buy or sell you now."

"You bought me!" Loki exulted. "You bought me, Chief. I am yours now!"

Inga smiled and wiped the tears from her face. "We'll belong to each other."

"Can I have a kitten, Chief?" Loki enthused. "They are sometimes provided with parasites, too!"

Inga chuckled, settling down to the cold deck and pulling out a food bar. "What? No. I'm broke. I spent every credit I had to buy *Tanager*."

"Money? Do we want money?"

Inga smiled, chewing. "It is tolerably useful."

"Then we should get *more* money. I can sell things . . . all kinds of things!"

Inga shook her head, delighting in Loki's enthusiasm. "What sort of things should we sell?"

"Well, secrets, of course, Chief. I've studied this. Secrets are very interesting to most humans. They pay money for them. Because secrets are so, so interesting!"

"We can't sell Fleet secrets, Loki. They rather frown on that."

"Not *Fleet* secrets, Chief. I know that. We'll sell the Strangers' secrets. I found some very, very good secrets. They had good secrets in that station."

Inga stopped chewing, in shock. "What strangers, Loki? What secrets?"

"They're just a *tiny* bit smarter than humans, Chief. No offense. They had good secrets. I took them while we fought."

"On Delta Three?" Inga asked, her eyes wide.

"We can sell these secrets, Chief, and buy me a kitten! It will be good! We'll have such fun!"

Loki babbled on, there in the dark, cold belly of *Tanager*'s ruin, while nearby mighty ships slid from their berths on the Strand, moving outward. These powerful bubbles of humanity torched out into the dark, into a war that few understood, fewer still realizing that human extinction was, once again, the threat that awaited.

Acknowledgments

Several people helped ease *The Deep Man* into existence, through one means or another. Among those particularly helpful: Kimberley Cameron of Kimberley Cameron & Associates Literary Agency; Gray Rinehart of Baen; Sgt. Jon Harris, USMC; Rebekah Joanna; and James "Mike" Morrison.

About the Author

Although born in the northwestern United States, Michael Mersault spent his formative years in a series of magical locales including expat communities in the Middle East, a secretive air base in the Arizona desert, and an Alaskan fishing village.

These endless hours of travel prompted an enduring love for books that continues unabated.

At times in his adult years, he has dabbled in kickboxing, competitive marksmanship, and international business ventures. He now lives as a semi-recluse back in the northwest, where he fluctuates between the path of a confirmed technophile and a neo-Luddite.

Michael Mersault

THE DEEP MAN

TPB: 978-1-9821-2584-4 • $16.00 US/$22.00 CAN

A relic of humanity's violent past, this ancient weapon stands ready for the Emperor to wield. The Galactic Imperium of the Myriad Worlds slumps into centuries of decadent peace enabled by a flood of advanced technology from the mysterious nonhuman "Shapers." Among the great families, only the once-mighty clan of Sinclair-Maru remembers the maxims of the warrior emperor, Yung I, ready to defend the Imperium from any threat. With spies and assassins on every side, trusting only in his considerable skill and the bizarre competence of his companion Inga, Saef Sinclair-Maru must complete his Imperial mission, restore the greatness of his family, and uncover the chilling plot meant to extinguish humanity's light from the galaxy.

And watch for *The Silent Hand*, an original trade paperback, in September 2023.